I0679053

Praise for Nemesis

"Nemesis is a seat of your pants read that I would rate 4.5 stars if Amazon would let me! There's nothing soft about the book, and the only thing soft about the main character is her ability to love. She's tough as nails with a cynicism about the opposite sex that she learned the hard way. But when it comes down to it, she's all about loyalty."

~Leona Bushman, Author

"Nemesis, quite the girlfriend!... The female freedom is sexy. Gervasio does a good job of showing sexual freedom and personal vulnerability."

~L.S. Fayne, Author

"NL Gervasio has a knack for well placed humor and action. Oh heck who am I kidding? Sarcasm is the primary language Nemy speaks, much to my delight. This ain't your momma's romance novel... Nemesis takes matters into her own hands to make sure Prince Charming doesn't get too big of an ego. She is very much the modern woman needed to spice up the romance world."

~R.C. Murphy, Author

Books by N.L Gervasio

Kick-Ass Girls Club series

Nemesis

The Prophecy series

The Dracove
Gods & Vampyres

Anthologies

Into the Darkness
Undead Uncensored

N.L. Gervasio

Nemesis

a Kick-Ass Girls Club novel

Just Ink Press, LLC

A Just Ink Press novel

Just Ink Press, LLC
1016 S Roosevelt Street
Tempe, AZ 85281

Nemesis

ISBN-10: 0988272113
ISBN-13: 978-0-9882721-1-8
www.justinkpress.com

Edited by Sharon Gerlach

Cover design by N.L. Gervasio

2nd edition paperback print, Just Ink Press, LLC: March 2013

Printed in the U.S.A.

Dedication

To my mother Marilyn, for her undying support in everything I do, regardless of how insane it sounds, which includes zombies. I love you, Umi.

Acknowledgements

To my beta readers - Cher Dawn, who always catches the disembodied parts and character inconsistencies; Hugh Fegely, who keeps my timeline in check; Christel Grady, who points out plot inconsistencies; and my "adopted son" Josh Mattison, whom I've trained well because he catches the little things the rest of us miss. All but Cher read through multiple versions of this book and the monstrosity it became near the end. Thank you!

To CJ Redwine for discovering a huge plot hole during her synopsis workshop, and without whom Sean the scary leprechaun wouldn't exist.

To my wonderful friends who have kept me on my feet through tough times these past few years without a single selfish thought. Heather, Deni, Sharon, Cyn, Denise, Juliette, and others—your friendship means everything and I will not forget what you have done for me.

A special thank you to Lee Osbourne, who went above and beyond, and kept me afloat in low moments. You are truly an angel.

And to my awesome editor, Sharon Gerlach, who kept me on my toes when it came to detail and consistency, slapped me upside the head for repetition, and didn't let me get away with a damn thing.

Trademarks Acknowledgement

The author acknowledges the trademarked status and trademark owners of the following words mentioned or possibly mentioned in this work of fiction:

Armani
Bacardi
Bailey's Irish Cream
Beretta
BMW
Bud Light
Chevrolet
Christian Dior
Dickies
Doc Marten
Dos Gringos
Fossil
Glock
Google
Goldschlager
Gucci
Guinness
Hallmark
Jack Daniels
Jameson
Jell-O
Jim Beam
Johnnie Walker
Lucky Thirteen
Maker's Mark
Mastro Steakhouse
MGD
Neiman Marcus
Nordstrom's
RA
Saturn
Vanilla Stoli
Wal-Mart

Nemesis Playlist

Each chapter title is the title of a song which can be found in the Nemesis playlist on Grooveshark under Jinxie G.

1. The Creeps - Social Distortion
2. Little by Little - Robert Plant
3. Wake Me in the Morning - The Bollox
4. Nemesis - Shriekback
5. No Man's Woman - Sinead O'Connor
6. Devil's Dance Floor - Flogging Molly
7. Next Contestant - Nickelback
8. Lick - Joi
9. I Will Possess Your Heart - Death Cab for Cutie
10. Another Hole in the Head - Nickelback
11. 3 Libras - A Perfect Circle
12. How You Remind Me - Nickelback
13. Something I Can Never Have - Nine Inch Nails
14. Not in Rivers, But in Drops - ISIS
15. Baby Did a Bad Bad Thing - Chris Isaak
16. Let It Die - Foo Fighters
17. King of Fools - Social Distortion
18. Foxy, Foxy - Rob Zombie
19. Winter Solstice - The Tea Party
20. You Do Something to Me - Sinead O'Connor
21. Head Like a Hole - Nine Inch Nails
22. We're in This Together - Nine Inch Nails
23. Feelin' Love - Paula Cole
24. You Know I'm No Good - Amy Winehouse
25. Tura' Lu - The Bollox
26. You Know What You Are? - Nine Inch Nails
27. Just a Girl - No Doubt
28. Weak and Powerless - A Perfect Circle
29. No, You Don't - Nine Inch Nails
30. Hour of Darkness - Social Distortion
31. Headstrong - Trapt
32. Feel Alive - U.P.O.

Nemesis

The Creeps

Tall, dark, and damn scary walks into The Fox Den. I wish it were a joke. He steps right up to my bar and leans forward, resting his thick arms on the hard black laminate surface. I haven't wiped that down yet, so I hope it's sticky because he leers at me until I make my way down to him. There are plenty of nearly naked women around the central Phoenix gentleman's club, so just for the leer, I take my sweet time. This only makes him stare harder until I get there, his piercing eyes boring into me, which has my skin crawling. My natural stubbornness to demanding men takes a hit. Time to get him away from my bar as quickly as possible.

"What can I do for you?" I note the rugged lines of his face with a scar down the right side, the short dark crew cut riddled with grey, and the muscles that look like they're about to rip apart the seams of his short-sleeved shirt. Normally, these attributes wouldn't bother me—rougher-looking men have worked for my dear old dad. But there's something in his eyes that makes me want to take a step back, which of course, I don't.

"Is Clancy 'round?" His voice is damn near Barry White deep and scarier with the Irish brogue laced through it. Eyes check me out thoroughly, running up and down my arms as he takes in my tattoos, and of course, lingering on my chest for far too long.

"He left a bit ago," I reply as the hair on the back of my neck goes on alert. "Don't know when he'll be back, but I could get you a drink if you'd like to wait." With the way my body's reacting, I'm hoping he leaves because he's just plain creeping me out, and I don't scare easily. I guess that's one silver lining to having a mafia dad. Unfortunately, I have to play the customer service game and be nice, regardless of the alarms going off in my head. Damn it.

He shakes his head slowly and stands. "Nah, just tell 'im I came by." There's a date tattooed on the left side of his neck going back fifteen years and it sits just under the circle of a silhouetted Celtic cross, all in black ink. Not a professional tattoo, if you catch my drift. In other words, this boy has been to prison.

"And who should I say stopped by?"

"Ye don' need mah name, Bettie. Jus' tell 'im I'm lookin' for 'im."

I arch a brow. "That's not my name." Though I'm certain his calling me that has to do with my pageboy haircut and the fact that I look like something reminiscent of a Bettie Page poster.

He grins. "Like it matters, Lass." He taps the top of the bar twice, winks at me, and makes a gun gesture with his fingers. Then he turns around and leaves the club, running into a patron on the way without acknowledging what he'd done. Well, he's a real peach, isn't he?

A creepy feeling crawls across my flesh, and I shake it off and attend to my next customer at the other end of the bar while waiting for Clancy to return so I can inform him of his visitor. That takes about forever . . . or at least feels that way as I keep checking the clock.

About an hour ticks away before tall, dark, and downright lust-worthy walks into the club. That'd be my boss Clancy. He steps up to the bar, near the entrance to the club, and leans over, his long black hair falling forward in a rush of waves. As soon as I finish with a customer, I grab a bottle of water and place it directly in front of him.

"Thanks, Nemy-girl," he says with a wink as his long fingers wrap around the plastic. "Everything okay tonight?"

He's the only one who calls me Nemy-girl. I hate my real name—Anna. No one calls me that unless they feel like being punched. I nod, shift my weight from one foot to the other, and tap my fingernails on the bar.

"Something on your mind?" His vibrant emerald eyes flicker, and it's hell stopping my body from reacting to the way he always seems to look at me.

"Someone came in looking for you earlier," I say, narrowing my eyes on his. "Not a very nice-looking guy, and I'm not talking about how ugly he is."

He chuckles. "Did he leave a name?"

"No. Said I didn't need his name in a thick Irish accent and then called me Bettie."

Clancy's eyes widen for a split second before his brows knit together. "What else did he say?"

"Said to tell you he came by and he's looking for you, that's all." I shift my weight again. "Had a tattoo on the side of his neck." I fill him in on the finer details.

He nods slowly. "Okay, thanks." He looks down the bar. "You have a customer."

I look, and sure as shit, he's right. I hop a step and greet the newbie. I know I'm not imagining Clancy's unease at my telling him about scary, creepy guy, but it's not really my business, now is it? Yeah, tell that to the sick feeling settling in the pit of my stomach. I'll probably be on my guard for a few days because my gut is rarely wrong. Clancy doesn't normally tell me I have customers either, which means he ended our conversation deliberately without me realizing it. Sneaky bastard.

While I'm preoccupied, Clancy heads back to his office, and he's back there for a while, which isn't normal. I shrug it off and drop some ice into a glass. Clear liquid splashes over the ice as I pour the rum, then depress the cola button on my gun, and the two mix in a swirl. Of course, in this joint I don't mix much more than Jack or Bacardi with cola and flip the caps off bottles. Such a glamorous life.

Just an FYI, Clancy makes all men look bad on every level. Not quite perfect, but damn close. In my book, men like him shouldn't even exist. In fact, I frequently remind myself men like him don't exist outside of my imagination. I've had two serious relationships and a few short ones, and every man

I've ever dated or befriended has turned into a jackass. I haven't dated Clancy—God help me if I do—but he's tipping my *all-men-are-jackasses* theory completely over the edge of the scale. To add insult to injury, he looks like the damn cover of a romance novel. I hate those covers.

"Nemy-girl," Clancy shouts from the end of the bar later in the night.

I turn to look at him, and he flashes a big toothy grin and shakes the ice around in his glass. I know he wants another drink, but the man owns the damn place, so why he can't get up and walk behind the bar to get his own damn cola is beyond me. It's not like he drinks alcohol at work.

I stroll down to him, pick up his glass while staring at him, hold the glass out, making a huge display of how easy this process is, and take *two* measly steps back to grab the gun. Fizzy goodness dispels into the glass, and when I'm done, I place it in front of him and start to head back to my *paying* customers. Okay, so he pays me too. I've worked for him for a year now. Yeah, a year of staring into those pretty green eyes is just fucking torture.

Clancy just chuckles and picks up the glass for a drink.

"You're right, Clancy, she does have a nice ass," says Scott, the club's manager, as he leans into Clancy to peer down behind the bar right as I turn to walk away.

I turn back and raise my right brow, my hands on my hips. "The two of you are just *now* noticing this?"

Clancy howls with laughter and slaps his hand on the bar as I turn to walk away again. Then, from the corner of my eye, I see him push Scott back to his seat as I help a customer.

"Mine," I see his lips form, and I almost don't catch it because I'm distracted. I might have heard it if the music wasn't so loud.

His? Are you kidding me? He's out of his damn mind. I'm half tempted to moon them both, but then that would defeat the purpose of working behind the bar where I get to keep my clothes on. The look on Clancy's face tells me he must have seen my expression, knows my thoughts, and is disappointed I don't do it. My fingers slip into the ice bin as I walk by, and I quickly toss the piece over my shoulder. I hear a faint clink and a splash and Clancy laughs again, drowning out the crescendo of music that begins the next song.

"Damn," he says. "Was that just a one-time shot or what?"

I turn and lean against the bar, and then give him a nod upward, silently asking, "What of it?"

He smiles, and it weakens my knees. It's a good thing I'm leaning against the bar.

"Can you do it again? I bet you can't."

My lips curve into a devilish grin, and I push away from the bar with all the strength I can muster. "What's the bet?"

"If you miss, you strip for *me*," he says, that wicked grin of his stretching across his handsome face. This is always the first thing he offers in our bets. I never take it, but it's not like the man is serious. It's just a game we've played since the day I started working for him.

"I told you I only strip in the bedroom, Clancy," I say, just like I do every time he suggests me taking off my clothes. "Not gonna happen."

He shrugs. "Someday you're gonna say yes."

"Bet'cha I won't." His eyes have gone pure, delicious evil at this point, and damn it if that isn't a weakness for me because my legs are about to go Jell-O. "Well?" I say, trying to banish the visual of that man with his hands all over me.

He concedes and bows his head. "Okay, if you can hit my glass again, I'll give you a raise."

I let out a short laugh because by now I'm making twelve bucks an hour due to these lovely little bets of his. Most bartenders make much less. "How much?"

Those fine brows go up. "Another dollar?"

"And if I miss?"

He scans the bar, and then checks out the rest of the club. His eyes return to me and have taken on the evil glint once more. Oh, God help me. "Take charge of the girls."

"Fuck you, no bet," I say and toss another piece of ice at him, a small one, which hits him right in the center of his forehead.

He jumps from his seat. "Damn it, you could've hit me in the eye!"

I cross my arms over my chest and lean against the bar once more. "I hit right where I aimed."

Clancy stands at the opening that lets me back here, like he's gonna come after me, and the glare slides off his face in seconds, replaced by that sinister grin of his. I glance at the top of the bar to gauge the damage I may cause if I hop up and slide over. It's Wednesday night and we're actually busy. I might damage a few customers in the process. My gaze flicks back to Clancy, and he gets this little sparkle in his eye . . . and sits down. I stare at him for a while, which I'm sure is the exact effect he wanted to have, and finally, I go back to my duties. This is far from over, I can tell.

Jesus, why does he have to be my boss? He'd at least be a nice little one-nighter, maybe all-nighter. Just the mere thought of an all-nighter with him makes me giggle, and then I tell myself to shut the hell up and get back to work.

Working in a gentleman's club is a trip and a half. Oh, laugh all you want; a girl doesn't have to take off her clothes to make bank. I'm pretty sure Clancy makes bank too, but that kind of stuff doesn't matter to me. Not when it comes to men. I'm not a gold digger like some women I've met, grew up with, would like to seriously beat into oblivion for making the rest of us look bad. I look for more important things in a man; things like how he's going to treat me. Of course, my track record isn't the best. The neurotic strippers I work with crack me up, though, thinking they can find Prince Charming working at a place like this. I await the day Prince Charming walks up to me because I'm going to punch that fucker dead in the face. I figure if he sticks around after that, he's a keeper.

I can't stand the idea of such a fairy tale fantasy that little girls are raised to believe. If he seems too good to be true, he's getting punched.

Of course, I've had two supposed Prince Charmings already, neither of which I hit.

And no, I haven't punched Clancy . . . yet.

Cherry (her real name is Christine) comes over and sits at the bar in front of me during a break. I smile at her and place a glass of good wine in front of her. She's actually a bit too refined for this gig, but I guess shit happens, and you do what you can to make ends meet. Christine is probably the only one I can deal with because she's intelligent. Well, much more intelligent than some of the other girls. It probably has to do with her background. They say beauty is only skin deep, and I say that stupid goes all the way to the bone. You can fix ugly with a ton of plastic surgery. Downright stupid can't be fixed with even the best education. Some people are just born that way. However, nothing will fix ugly on the inside without the removal of the blackened heart. I try my damnedest not to be ugly in that arena.

"So, Clancy digs you, huh?" Cherry says in a soft tone, those full lips spreading into a wide grin. Did I say she was intelligent?

I *hmpf* at her and say, "Don't be ridiculous."

"Oh no, I saw the way he looked at you earlier, Nemy," she says and lifts the glass to her lips. She stops just short of reaching them and winks. "That man wants you bad."

"Right," I say and wipe the counter down in front of her. Although, I'll admit his playing has been turned up a notch or two this evening. It's gone a bit beyond the norm.

"Too bad you're such a bitch," she remarks, her light brown eyes sparkling.

"Well, if the men in my life didn't always offer lame-ass excuses for everything under the sun, I wouldn't have to be."

She giggles. "They pretend to still be involved while they try to find a way out, right?"

"Exactly," I say and slap my hand on the bar. She's heard this rant many times, and once I get going, it's hard to stop me. I think it amuses her, seeing me get all worked up. "They tell you that *you* need counseling. Ha! I know just how broken I am, thank you, and I'm fine with it."

"I'm sure you are," she says. "I don't think you're broken, honey."

I glance up and grin. "Then you're more broken than I am."

She laughs aloud and sips her merlot. "Well, I am a stripper, aren't I?"

I nod with a smile. "Hell, we're all broken. It doesn't matter what we do for a living. Seriously though, the last two men? One treated me like his own personal mental punching bag, and the other tossed me to the curb like a cigarette with a nice little flick of 'fuck you' thrown in before I hit. Four years with one, five with the other. That's just a hair less than a third of my lifetime, you know?"

Cherry lowers her glass to the counter in quiet contemplation before answering. "Yes, but you still have time left to find the right one, you damn dramatic Italian princess."

"Not much," I reply, ignoring the princess remark because it's true. With the last one—Jeremy, but I tend to call him *Asshole*—my instinct tried to warn me, but we women never listen to our gut when we're in love. Not fly-by-night love or new-relationship love. Four years of *unconditional* love with an engagement ring on my damn finger. So much for unconditional.

"Right, because you're such an old hag now," Cherry responds.

"Shut up and drink your wine," I say as I lift a bottle to wipe it down. It's sticky as hell too. I'm so kicking Chris's ass next time we work together. I clean as I work. He just doesn't clean.

Cherry giggles, finishes her wine, and then hops up to get back to work.

Clancy decides to close the club early because there are only a couple patrons in the bar now and a few girls left working tonight. Fine by me, I have homework to do tonight—it's a big project too.

Of course, my lack of hurrying gives Clancy the idea that I'm available to stay after my shift, as indicated by his fingers slipping around my arm when no one's looking. A wave of heat rushes over my body and if I were the fainting type, I'd be hitting the floor.

Instead, I jump.

"Sorry," he says and lets my arm go. "Can you help me with something?"

I raise my right brow. "Can it wait until tomorrow night? I really need to get this project done tonight."

"What project?" he asks and slides back onto his barstool, crossing his arms on top of the bar and smiling at me.

"I'm editing a short film."

"Oh, that's right, I forgot," he says. "So soon? I thought you didn't have to do that for another week or so."

I snort. "It's been a week or so, boss-man."

"Hmm, you're not keeping me on my toes, Nemy-girl." His eye twinkles.

I quickly find something to distract myself from the images going through my head, all involving him and me and the top of this bar—

I grab my coat from underneath the bar and pull it on. "Is that my job? I had no idea. I'm going to need a raise then."

He laughs and stands to walk me out. The club doesn't sit in the best of neighborhoods and it's his rule that one of the guys walks all the girls out, day or night.

"We'll have to work that out later," he replies as we head for the front door. He opens it and I step outside.

A chilled gust of wind smacks me in the face. "Why do I have the feeling this involves a bet?" I pull my coat closed against the cold.

"You do know me well."

The parking lot is dark as usual, save for the one floodlight on the corner of the building. I hit the button on my car remote to shed some more light with the automatic headlights. "Obviously not well enough if I have no idea who that guy was tonight."

His right eye twitches, and then a calm demeanor shadows his face. "No one in particular. I doubt you'll see him again."

That last sentence didn't sound like the end of the conversation, as though he wanted to add something to it, but I leave it alone. It's not my business, right? Clancy's not mine. Why should I care? He just signs my paycheck, and I can get a job anywhere, if needed.

Yeah, I'll keep telling myself that, but I know better. Who'd want to give up staring at his beautiful mug every night? Not. Me.

"I'll give you a call tomorrow afternoon," he says and pauses before heading for his vehicle. He leans forward like he's going to kiss me; I arch away, and he straightens. "Goodnight."

I say goodnight to him and climb into my car, watching him climb into his truck and thinking about that odd goodnight. I stare into the rearview mirror. "Were you actually trying to kiss me?"

It's hard to mistake a move like that. Perhaps we've stepped over the line with our flirting. I'll have to put a stop to it as soon as possible. I mean, I know I've fallen deeply in lust with the man, and maybe I'm bound to think some of my fantasies are real—like the way he looks at me with such longing it practically shouts happily ever after—but I can't have it actually *become* real. Reality and fairy tales don't co-exist. A guy like Clancy wouldn't want a girl like me for very long, and I'm so over men right now, regardless of what he does to me. He probably likes blondes anyway. Guys like him usually do.

I start my little sports car and leave the small parking lot with the strangest feeling that someone is watching us; it's not like I didn't grow up with that feeling, so I try to ignore it.

Sometimes, when your gut twists the right way, that feeling is damn hard to ignore. I'll be checking my nightstand drawer to make sure my Glock sits safely within its wooden confines before I fall asleep tonight.

2

Little by Little

The distinct rumble of a Chevy engine brings my head up. From my table on the café patio, I can see the intersection and the familiar old beater of a truck coming around the corner. Crap, that's Clancy. He's supposed to call me before work later today for help with whatever that was. What in the hell is he doing in Tempe? I yank my hat brim down so he can't see my face as I continue getting my laptop ready to finish up last night's homework. Of course, my tattoos are quite noticeable from across the street, I'm sure, but I'm so not ready to speak with Clancy yet. I need caffeine first to get my faculties about me, although I don't know why I bother because the man scrambles my brain every time I look at him.

"Here ya go, Nemy," Adriana says, and I jump at the sound of her voice as she places the large cup of cappuccino on the table next to my laptop. It's nice and hot as the steam rises above the froth, regardless of the day's temperature—a balmy sixty-five degrees in the early November afternoon. It's just warm enough for a short-sleeve shirt while I sit in the sun.

"Thanks, sweetie." I dig out a few crinkled ones and hand them to her.

She shoves the money in her apron pocket and pulls something else out. "Tonka truck, I've got something for you," she says as she waves the biscuit back and forth in front of my wolf look-a-like. He's actually a pure white Alaskan malamute, but I suppose that's close enough to wolf.

I giggle at the name she calls him as Tonk jumps to his feet and sits pretty in front of her, holding out a paw for a shake.

"What do you say, Tonk?" I ask, and he howls a few vowels at her, which is akin to talking. They're quite a vocal bunch.

"That's just too cute," she says and hands him the treat. He takes it gently from her and commences with chomping it to smithereens. "I'll be back with your change." She then crouches down and places a small bowl of water next to Tonk before heading for the doors of the café.

"Keep it." I run my fingers across the mouse pad and connect to the free Wi-Fi the café offers. Before long, I'm surfing the web, but I'm kind of on autopilot because I'm looking for Clancy from under the brim of my hat, scanning the entire intersection and wondering just where he went while Adriana distracted me. I'm pretty sure I saw him pull into the parking lot behind the bars that sit diagonally across the street from my favorite café.

It doesn't take long before I spot him walking up the sidewalk and heading into the piano bar on the corner. It's downstairs and a pretty cool place, but isn't it a bit early in the day for a drink? Well, it's morning for me because I'm a night owl. I shrug and go back to my email. Again, it's not like the man belongs to me or anything, so why should I care what he does?

I mindlessly scan the internet while daydreaming about Clancy and stumble upon a story that has me gasping because my dad's name is right there in big bold letters: **Michael Mussolini Up for Indictment**. That can't be right. Dad's been living a quiet life in California for some time now . . . last I knew. I skim the story to discover the Feds are pulling something from years ago out of their asses, and I roll my eyes. There's no way in hell they'll make that stick, even if it's within the statute of limitations. My attorney brother Joey is all over it, I'm sure. Maybe I should give dad a call. I ponder that prospect for about two seconds before deciding against it; dad and I haven't been on the best of terms since I divorced Garrett five or so years ago. Not to mention the fact that he thinks my not having children is some sort of protest.

Whatever. I just can't get pregnant. It happened once and I miscarried early on in the pregnancy. To this day, Garrett thinks I lost the baby on purpose. Yeah, he's a real winner. Some Prince Charming he turned out to be. Putz.

Prince Charming number two—Jeremy—came along shortly thereafter. I don't even want to think about him. He wasn't much better than the putz.

An hour goes by as I sit and work on a few things—blog, poem, homework—and I look up to see Clancy emerging from the depths of the piano bar. There's someone with him I don't recognize—a gray-haired man nearly as tall as Clancy. Good Lord, where do they make these men? I'm a tall girl and tall men are hard to find. Not that men that size like tall women—some weird belief to do with the hook-up creating mutant children. Men are idiots.

However, Clancy isn't an idiot, not by a long shot. He has the brains that totally contradict his looks. Pretty boys, in my experience, aren't generally smart, and boy is he pretty. Our intellectual conversations are a major turn-on.

Crap, I think he saw me.

I duck my head down so the brim hides my face better. I think he saw me, but if he did, he'd come over and talk to me, since he's supposed to call me soon.

I sneak another peek. He's walking toward the back parking lot, a cell phone to his ear. I watch him until he disappears around the corner of the building, and then look at my phone. Nothing. Yeah, he must not have seen me. Works for me; I'm not quite awake yet.

Before long, I get into a groove on my homework and don't even notice the time go by. Then I look up from my creation for a bit of people-watching. When Tonk and I hang out at the café, I write down anything I happen to observe while sitting there and surfing the web. Never know when something will spark an idea I can use.

Boy, do I observe a lot. Like the fanatical born-again Christians standing on the corner of Mill and Fifth Street passing out pamphlets about how we're all going to Hell. A great documentary in the making if I ever saw one.

A short stocky blond of the male persuasion walks past my table, inclines his head slightly to view me, and heads inside the café. I'm used to it. Okay, his shortness may be about my height, but that's what I consider short. If I can't wear five-inch heels with a man without having to look down, I'm not interested. I get back to work. I know I'm too picky, but I figure if I only like guys who are six-five and up, there has to be a man out there who's interested in a woman half a foot shorter than him.

Besides, I kind of like being tossed around in bed. Short guys can't accomplish that with me.

I bet Clancy could.

Not that I'm interested in men right now. That last one was a doozy. It'll take me a while before I'm ready for the dating scene again. That doesn't stop men from flirting with me, although half the time I don't even realize they're hitting on me unless they're obvious, like "I wanna take you out on a date. What's your number?" Aside from that, I'm oblivious most of the time. It makes for quite an entertaining evening for my girlfriends. *Let's see how many men can hit on Nemy, and how long it takes her to notice it.* Thanks, bitches.

I scan the sidewalk and something catches my attention near the café door.

Oh goodie, there's Shorty again, and he's checking me out from his table two over from mine. I do my best to ignore him so he doesn't imagine any "signals" coming from me, but it's not working; he shifts in his seat and tries to get my attention by clearing his throat a few times.

And in go my ear buds.

My phone vibrates in my pocket and I nearly jump out of my seat. I pull an ear bud out to answer it so I don't slam the ear bud deeper into my ear by way of phone-ectomy. "What's up, chica?" I say, because my friend Teagan's picture popped up on the screen, red-haired vixen that she is.

"Girls' night out," she states in that demanding tone of hers that says *you'd better listen because I'm only saying this once.* "Mandatory. We'll pick you up at nine."

"Okay. I guess I can call Chris and see if he wants to make up for when I worked for him on Sunday."

"Yeah, do that."

"I'll call him now and hit you back with a text."

"Okay." She hangs up on me with no goodbye. Teags doesn't like long drawn-out anything, which makes her awesome because she's blunt as hell even when you don't want to hear it.

I scroll through my contacts and hit Chris up. It doesn't take long for him to agree, and I text Teags to let her know we're good. All she sends back is "coolio," which also means, "see ya then" and "bitch, you'd better be ready" in Teagan-speak.

Well, that settles it; I need to head home to feed Tonk and myself so I can get ready. It's getting a bit chilly anyway now that the sun has moved across the sky. Sorry Mr. Short, it's not gonna happen today . . . or ever.

As I load up my backpack, I notice a man across the street in the shadows, staring at me. I hop on my bike, *what-the-fuck-creepy* chills rippling down my spine. Then Tonk and I are off into the stony red yonder that is the street of Mill Avenue in old town Tempe, and what-the-fuck-creepy disappears into the fog of my mind.

"Go, Tonk, go," I shout at my not-so-mute malamute, who's in the lead and pulling my beach cruiser along at a nice clip. I've trained him well, but still need to work on it a bit. What I don't need is that guy that's just about to walk in front of—I swerve around him in a blur of black iron with pink and white flames, and get back on track. Whoa, that was close. I wave my hand over my head. "Sorry!" because Tonk knocked him clean off his feet--hence the extra training needed. I can't slam on the brakes because I'd probably break Tonk's neck.

I send a quick glance back at him; he's pulling himself up from the brick sidewalk. If he'd been paying attention like everyone else on the damn sidewalk, it wouldn't have happened. Okay, I probably shouldn't be riding on the sidewalk. Whatever.

It takes me about fifteen minutes to get home, and once I'm inside, my damn phone vibrates again. Great, *now* Clancy decides to call me.

"Yes, boss-man?" I try to un-wrap Tonk's leash from my legs before he knocks me over. He twists around me and I fall toward the wall, just barely catching myself before impact.

"Can you come in early so you can help me with that thing?"

I quirk a brow, you know, like he can see that through the phone. "I'm not working tonight. Got a mandatory meeting with my girls. I already set it up with Chris."

He growls. "Okay, fine, tomorrow night then. You *are* working tomorrow night, aren't you?"

"Are you getting snippy?" I finally get Tonk's leash off him and hang the damn thing up.

"Women get snippy. I don't." There's an edge to his tone I rarely ever hear. Oh my, he's upset.

"Okay, boss-man. Whatever you say." Poking the bear is something I'm well-known for and I'll never learn my lesson.

"Well, someone's had a good day."

"And it sounds like someone else hasn't. What's the matter, did the bar run out of Jameson?"

His hearty laugh resonates in my ears, and damn, do I love that laugh. It sends a warm tingly feeling through me, commonly called lust. "I'm a Maker's Mark man, Nemy-girl, and something didn't go the way I planned today, if you must know."

"Ew, Maker's Mark. Isn't drinking that like sacrilege for you? I mean, you *are* Irish and all."

"It's not about heritage, it's about taste, and I prefer that particular bourbon," he replies.

"Whiskey," I correct.

"Same thing," he says and I can just hear that smirk on those lips that I want to lick . . . okay, I need to stop or my shower will involve cold water.

"Well, I'm sorry you've had a bad day. Look on the bright side, you're" —oh, I almost went there with the tall and gorgeous comment— "a very successful man with a host of great employees." Whoa—cheesy!

A chuckle this time. "Quite true, and you're the best bartender I've ever had, so your cute little ass better be in my club tomorrow night."

"Aye, aye, Captain." I give a salute even though he can't see it.

"Have fun tonight." He knows exactly what I'm doing tonight. It's a common occurrence.

"Will do," I reply and hang up when he says goodbye. I linger and stare at the picture of him on my phone for a second before pocketing it. Yep, cold shower it is.

I feed Tonk and head to my bedroom. Halfway down the hall, it hits me.

Wait, did he just tell me I have a cute ass?

Holy. Crap.

Wake Me in the Morning

"Nemy!" shouts Echo, bounding from her seat near the front of the limousine and wrapping her skinny-ass arms around my neck before I can even sit down.

On my knees and struggling for breath, I choke out, "You do realize breathing is necessary for living, right?" She giggles and lets me have some air. Once Echo's done molesting me as only Echo can do, I sit down next to the door. Teagan hands me a drink in a short glass.

"Here, you're gonna need this," she says, flipping her burgundy hair over one shoulder with a slender, scarred hand. Teagan enjoyed playing with fire when she was younger. The accidental disfigurement of her hand really hasn't deterred her from doing it since. She's just more careful now. She's not allowed to have matches or a lighter when she visits my house.

I sniff the contents and raise a brow to her. "What the hell for?" It's Johnnie Walker Black, no ice. Works for me; I could use a stiff drink. We won't discuss other things that may be stiff that I could use. But Jesus, I'm about to hear bad news.

The girls have rented the limo because it means we're getting annihilated. Another clue bad news is coming my way.

Teagan jerks her head to the right. "Jada caught James cheating."

My eyes flick from Teagan to Jada, and I say, "Get the fuck out!" I know there's more to the story here because it's not the first time the idiot man has ever done that, but I don't ask. Most likely, James hit her when she confronted him, but Jada will never admit it and the bruises aren't in plain sight.

Jada nods sheepishly, her long black curls barely springing with the motion. It kills me to see her like that. Her light blue eyes abruptly shift away from mine; yep, he hit her. These actions are a total opposite of the girl she used to be. She'd always been strong, could handle anything thrown at her. I want to beat James into oblivion for making her so damn weak. Physically, she reminds me of a porcelain doll, delicate and sweet because she's so tiny. I always feel like I'm going to break her when I give her a big hug.

"Fucking asshole," I mumble and throw the J. W. back. I ignore the burn when it hits my throat and look at Jada. "I'm sorry, sweetie." She nods again without making eye contact and takes her drink in one gulp. "Give her another." I'd ask her if she wants my dad to take care of him, but my girlfriends don't know about my dad. I keep that part of my life as private as possible. Hell, I'm trying to be an honest woman here by not getting into the family business, even though I've shown one hell of an aptitude for it. I'm daddy's little girl, after all.

"Shit, chica, we've been drinking the whole way here," Alanna claims, a twinkle in her deep brown eyes. A black curl over her left eye flutters when she blows it away and bounces back onto the red bandana she's wearing Rosie the Riveter style. Her many tattoos are on display since we're going out tonight.

"Well, shit, if you all didn't live in East Mesa, I'd have a good damn buzz right now," I say and toss back the next one Teagan pours for me. They all laugh. "Where are we going anyway?"

"Dos Gringos in Snottsdale," Lillian answers. I meet her smoky hazel eyes that men just melt over and I sneer because I hate going to that particular bar. It's nothing but a meat market. Well, *any* bar in Scottsdale is a meat market. She sticks her tongue out at me, which makes me laugh, and her light brown hair falls around her shoulders and frames her face. Lillian has a timeless look about her, one seen in classic films starring the likes of Greta Garbo or Bette Davis, but it's mostly in her eyes.

"Sweet," I say. "We can get you all laid tonight . . . except you, Echo." She's the only one aside from Jada who's not single. Echo is also the only blonde in the group, and simply because she's blonde, and her name is Echo, she gets all the blonde jokes thrown at her. She even joins in and makes fun of herself. With that name, we're thinking her parents are hippies.

"Oh, and not you, Nems?" Echo asks with a sly little grin.

"Fuck no, I'm done with men," I say while turning the glass in my hand and looking at Teagan with a raised brow. She pours me another. "Thanks, barkeep." She nods and pours the rest of the bottle into Jada's glass. It was probably Teagan's idea to bring the bottle. I catch the look Echo's giving me and it's one I usually only see on men. "Not done with men like *that*, girl."

She laughs and tosses back a shot.

I take stock of who's in the limo and frown. "Where's Kennadi?"

"She couldn't make it tonight," Teagan answers. "Work wouldn't let her have off." Kennadi works at one of the other strip clubs in town. Not as a stripper, but a bartender like me. Teags is also a bartender at a local Tempe bar. No strip clubs for her. Teags would probably kill the girls, which is my concern when it comes to Kennadi because the girl loves a good fight and enjoys playing with knives. In fact, I'm quite amazed we haven't had to bail Kennadi out of jail for assault yet.

"Too bad, I feel a fight coming on tonight."

Lillian glares at me for about half a second before her face returns to normal. She hates the fighting bullshit, but I just can't help it if people like to pick fights with me.

Alanna gets a mischievous grin across her almost-too-handsome-to-be-pretty face. "How's your boss—what's his name—Clancy?"

I look her dead in the eye and smirk. "I wouldn't know. I haven't had him yet."

"Yet?" Teagan asks, her mouth twisting into a smile as the lilt in that one little word goes up.

"You know what I mean."

Teagan shakes her head. "Uh uh, you said *yet*."

I glare at her. "You know I can't be responsible for the things I say."

I know my plans for the night didn't please Clancy when he finally called me, but hey, he said he'd call in the afternoon and didn't until like six. Sorry buddy, a girl's friends come first because they stick around through all the bad shit. Men tend to run and hide, in my experience. Maybe not *all* men, but I keep finding the bad apples. If you ask me, I think Adam bit into that apple first, and then blamed it on Eve.

Echo laughs. "Yeah, and you guys make fun of the blonde," she says, pointing at herself like we don't know the color of her hair. "Nemy should be the blonde."

All I can do is raise a brow and roll my eyes. Teagan, Lillian, and Alanna bust up laughing, but Jada just lets out a little chuckle while hiding herself in her hair. I'm going to kill that bastard. I don't like seeing my porcelain doll broken. She used to have this perfect nose, but I'm damn certain James broke it early on in their relationship. Jada told us that she tripped and fell. Ri*iii*ght, because *that* excuse has never been used before.

We reach downtown Scottsdale—aka Snottsdale or Snobsdale—and we pile out of the limo when the driver opens the door. Heads turn—and not just men's and not just in admiration. We may look like pin-up girls a la Page (with flaws, of course, although I think Teagan's scars have a beauty all their own and Alanna's Mexican-Irish ghetto booty is pretty sexy), but it's rare to see a bunch of girls covered in tattoos.

We grab the first table we see, and I take orders and catch a server's attention. Not an easy task in a busy place like this. Three guys walk up not long after we get there and begin conversation with the worst line I've ever heard. I can't believe they still use it.

"So, you gals come here often?" one asks.

Really? I glance at my girls, smirk, and turn back to the three morons.

"Nah," I say. "We're just popping in on the way to our film shoot." I just can't help myself.

"What are ya filming?" guy in the middle asks, a little gleam in his eye that tells me exactly what he's hoping to hear.

"Hot lesbian porn," I say with a straight face. Honestly, what is it with guys and lesbians? Actually, little miss blonde Echo is a lesbian. Her partner, Katy, also couldn't make it tonight due to work, which sucks because she's a riot. Katy is totally my wing-girl, which tends to shock the shit out of the guy she's winging for me at the end of the night. Hey, a girl has needs. I just don't want to deal with the bullshit of a relationship, although it's been a long damn while now.

"Really?" another asks.

Oh, for fuck's sake, these guys are too stupid to talk to me. "No, I'm just kidding." Their faces go blank. Give it a minute.

The first one who spoke laughs and hits his thigh, and he points a finger at me. "That was pretty good. You had me going there."

"That was the intent." For him to be going, that is.

His eyes scan my arms and shoulders. "Nice tats. That shit hurt?"

"Oh no, they're all drawn on."

He looks at me a minute, and then laughs again. "You almost got me."

"So I did."

Teagan leans over to whisper in my ear. "Would you stop fucking with them? They're cute."

I turn my head to the side and lean over to her. "He's too stupid to be cute." I pause a moment, and then lean back to her. "He's probably too stupid to be good in the sack too."

"Thanks for ruining it for me," she states with a little sneer.

I grin. "Well, let's ask him."

Her eyes go wide. "Don't you dare!"

I reach out and smack his arm because he's talking to his friend. "Hey buddy, you any good in bed?"

Teagan turns in a huff. "Oh my gawd!"

He smiles big and kicks his chin up once at me. "Why, you want some of this?"

It's hell keeping myself from snorting. "Oh no, not me, I'm in a man-hating phase right now," I say and he laughs. "Just curious if you know how to please a woman." My right brow goes up and I smile.

He steps forward and his eyebrows jump. "I could get you out of your man-hating phase."

"Oh, really?" His buddies are staring at me now, checking me out. "That's funny, because you don't know why I hate men." I lean forward, closing the gap between us. "It has nothing to do with sex."

He gets real close, and I can smell the beer he's drinking on his breath. "Bullshit. If your man took care of you, you wouldn't hate men."

Why do all men think this? "There's more to life than sex."

"True, but great fucking sex can cure a lot of shit," he replies with a smile.

"Not really."

He eyes me a moment, and says, "If I had a chick like you, you'd be a very happy girl."

Doubtful. I smirk. "Maybe I'm psychotic."

He shrugs. "We all got issues."

Fuck me, he might not be so stupid after all. He's playing my game. I lean back to Teagan and mouth, "Go for it." She rolls her eyes and gives me a quick shake of the head. Yep, the dumbass is now interested in me. My mouth gets me in so much trouble.

He takes a step back and raises his right hand for a shake. "I'm Killian."

"Nemy."

His brow arches. "That's a different name. What's it mean?"

"It's short for Nemesis. I got the name because I was born on Friday the thirteenth and because I'm a fighter." What I don't tell him is that I'm certain there was a full moon that night too, which would explain the need to shed my human skin and go full mega-bitch on people at times.

"Whoa, does that mean bad luck follows you everywhere?" he asks with a smirk.

"Only with men," I reply, and he laughs again.

Upon the server's return, I pass out shots—Red-headed Sluts—to the girls, and we toast and down them. Then I grab my beer.

"So, what do you do, Nemy?" Killian asks and raises his beer to his mouth.

"I'm a bartender at The Fox Den."

His brow goes up and he almost spits out his beer. I get that reaction a lot if the guy knows the strip clubs around town.

"Really? Wow. So you're . . ." He takes a swig of his beer quickly, stopping for whatever reason, and then continues. "That's cool. When do you work? Maybe we'll stop by sometime."

I flash a smile at him. "I'm working tomorrow and Saturday night."

He nods. "Sweet."

Then it dawns on me that he's Shorty from the café. Crap. Did the guy follow me home and here? That'd be creepy as hell. I calm down by telling myself it's just a coincidence, but now I've just invited the man to visit me at my place of employment. Brilliant.

Whenever I'm out on the town, it's about getting more customers. Clancy loves that I bring in so many men. Well, his wallet loves it. I'm not so sure about *him* loving it. He always gets this funny look when guys I've met walk in and crowd around the bar. It doesn't take me long to get the girls to distract them, though, and they have a good time. The most important factor is that they come back, and they always do. I'm not certain I want Killian coming at all, though. I need to be more careful with my invites.

As the night moves on, I notice Killian is entirely too interested in me when he's not texting someone. Inside my mind, I have a full visual going of him fucking me, and it just isn't up to par. Sadly disappointing, but I've learned from experience my visuals are spot on. When I ignore them, I do not enjoy myself in the least. I'm not even going to mention the visual I get of Clancy. Damn thing nearly throws me into an automatic orgasm every time.

Killian puts his phone away and his hand pulls my right shoulder forward to turn me around. "Let's see that back piece."

I'm wearing a backless shirt tonight. It's a rare occasion. "Sure," I say, turn and bend over a bit. My head cranes back and I smile. "It's called Fuck-me Art."

His brow lifts as he carefully asks, "Why is it called that?" He's not certain he heard me correctly.

I bend over more. "Because it looks best when you're fucking me." I hop up and turn around, and Killian has the biggest grin on his face I've seen so far. "Don't get any ideas; you're not fucking me tonight." Gotta stop that mule in his tracks before he gets too excited. Of course, my bending over and talking about fucking me doesn't help any situation, I know. Those shots of Walker are getting to me, and so are the several other miscellaneous shots we've had. I can't be taken anywhere, it seems.

"We'll see about that," he returns with a sly grin.

I roll my eyes for the umpteenth time this evening as he removes his phone from his jeans pocket once more. Seriously? I've never seen a man text so much.

"No, really, I'm not looking for *anything*," I say.

He shrugs and glances up from his phone. "Just makes you more of a challenge."

"Ah yes, and men love challenges, don't they?"

Killian nods. "Don't we ever!"

I eye him a moment, and finally say, "You're still not fucking me."

He laughs. "Let me buy you another drink."

"No thanks," I say. "I don't let strange men buy me drinks."

"Yeah, I understand," he says. "My sister was roofied once. I should know better than to suggest that. Sorry."

"It's cool, but thanks for the offer." Killian isn't hard on the eyes by any means. He stands about the same height as me, which is still too short in my book, and has striking blue eyes that are so vibrant one could see them across a room.

Sex? Home? Sex? Home? Sex at home? Hmm, I need to get myself out of this situation . . . fast. I think the hard-alcohol goggles are kicking in. I don't recall him being so attractive when he and his friends first walked up, and my brain is making a desperate attempt to remind me of this afternoon.

I lean over to my most sober friend—not Jada because she's damn close to annihilation—and ask Lillian, "Is he even cute?"

She moves her head back and forth in two rapid motions, which means it's imperative I understand this.

"Fugly?" I ask. She gives a shake of the head again and I look around the bar while trying to find a distraction that won't have me going home with this Irish boy. He just had to be Irish. That's my one weakness. As my eyes scan the crowd, they stop and track right back to a tall guy with short dark hair and a tattoo on the side of his neck. The real fucking thing with accent and all. Jesus. I gasp and turn around to face Lillian with wide eyes.

"What's wrong?"

"Four o'clock," I say, and she looks the opposite direction. "*My* four o'clock, you nitwit. Tall, dark and scary."

She looks again and shakes her head. "I don't see anyone fitting that description."

I turn my head slowly, only to discover he's gone, and I spin around looking for him. He's nowhere in sight. Crap.

Teagan walks up and her forehead creases. "What's got you spooked?"

"Remember that scary, creepy guy I told you about that came into the club last night?" I say, and Teags nods. "I think I just saw him."

"Ooh, creepy," she says, and then shrugs. "Maybe he's just out for a drink."

"At the same club as me?"

"Could be."

I blow out a breath. "I don't believe in coincidences."

"Do you know him outside of last night?" Teagan asks, and I shake my head. "Then what reason does he have to follow you around? Chill, Nems. You're gonna give yourself a heart attack."

"I don't know, Teags." I grab the shot the server just left on the table and throw it back, then exhale slowly to calm my nerves. "Maybe you're right. It might just be my imagination." My alcohol-fogged brain attempts to piece together some sort of explanation, adding Killian's appearance to the mix, but all I end up with is a jumbled confusing mess.

Once again, the feeling that someone is watching me washes over me, and I know it's not coming from the Irish boy I've been talking to all night. I scan the thick crowd carefully, but can't find him again. If that fucking creepy leprechaun is here for me, it'll ruin my whole night.

And I get a little pissy when my nights are ruined.

4

Nemesis

"What's going on?" Killian asks as he steps up to us. "You okay?"

I shake my head.

He touches my arm, and I flinch, so he pulls away. "Come on, let's go up to the bar. I'll buy you a shot, no roofies. Looks like you need it."

This makes me smile; I'm not about to turn down a free shot this time. "That's about the fucking truth of it." I look into his vibrant blue ocean eyes. They remind me of Echo's and even offer the same expression of compassion. I turn to the girls. "Meet you on the dance floor."

Killian nods toward the bar, and I follow him. As we're walking along, he leans toward me. "Does this have anything to do with your man-hating phase?"

"Yeah, you all suck." Which makes him laugh.

"Some more than others. I can't apologize on behalf of all men, though. They'd skin me alive or castrate me."

I chuckle and turn to the bartender. "Two shots of Jäger." The bartender nods and obliges us with said shots. Killian tells him to put it on his tab, we pick them up, and he stops me for a toast.

"To men who only suck when you tell them to," he says with a big grin.

I laugh. "And the rest can fall off a cliff," I reply and throw the shot back. I slam the shot glass on the bar and eye him. "You're still not fucking me, Killian."

He shrugs and sets his glass down. "It's cool. I don't think I could handle you anyway."

My brow goes up. "Wow, not a lot of men would admit that." I turn, placing my back against the bar so I can see the crowd. "I'm too old for you anyway."

"Bullshit. You're what, twenty-six, maybe twenty-seven?"

I wave a hand. "Now, now, flattery will get you nowhere, dear."

"Shut up. Seriously, how old are you?"

I jerk my thumb up twice.

"Twenty-nine?"

I repeat the thumb-jerk.

"Thirty?"

Again, repetition of said thumb-jerk.

His eyes keep growing wider. "Thirty-one?"

"Oh, for fuck's sake. Thirty-four."

"Shut the fuck up! You are not."

I slide my ID out of my back pocket, place my fingers over the address and my full name, and show him my birth date. "See?"

"Holy shit, you really are thirty-four. Wow!"

"Let's not create a whole fanfare about it or anything."

He stares at me a moment. "Well, you don't look it."

"Thanks," I reply and slip the ID back in my pocket. "Okay, I have to check on my girls." I pat him on the shoulder. "Thanks for the shot" and I leave him at the bar.

I find the girls dancing and having a grand old time. Well, I'm not sure one would call what they're doing dancing. They're stumbling at this point. Jada's the worst of them. She keeps running into Alanna, who doesn't like being bumped while she's dancing. My only guess as to why Alanna hasn't thumped her on the head is because of the whole James situation, otherwise, Jada would probably be on the floor crying because Alanna is a fighter. Actually, as drunk as Jada is, I'm quite surprised she's not a heaping sobbing mess by now.

Echo grabs my arm and pulls me into the little group, and I dance until I feel the warmth of my buzz return. The girls want to do more shots, so I find our server and order some Jäger, but only five shots because Jada just doesn't need any more to drink tonight. We drop the shots back, Alanna howls like the crazy woman she is, and four of them head back out to the dance floor. Echo stays behind and slides up next to me.

"So, what's got you all weird?" My apprehension must still be showing.

I bite my inner cheek. "I thought I saw someone I really didn't care to see. Creeped me out a bit and I can't shake it, no matter how many shots I do, unless I feel like blacking out tonight."

"Was it Jeremy? Let me guess, a fucking booty call, right?" she says, sarcasm laced through her tone.

"No, not him," I reply. "Some guy who came into the club last night. Something about him just sets me on edge."

"What's he look like?" She looks around.

"Never mind," I say and run a hand through my hair. "Let's just forget about it."

"You're frustrated, girl." I know exactly where she's going next. "Hey, you could always take home that guy you were fucking with to get the frustrations out."

Yep, that was the place. I turn to find Killian looking at me. He nods and I turn back to Echo. "Um, no."

Her grin spreads. "Katy will be up when I get home," she says and her eyebrows jump. She's damn cute when she does that.

"You're so not funny," I reply and blow out a breath because the Jäger is hitting me hard and I'm still hot from dancing.

"Yeah, you still like the sausage," she quips and throws a wink at me.

I lock my eyes on her. "Shut up, lesbo."

She laughs. "Oh, come on, Nemy, I know you fantasize about me." Yes, Echo loves to tease every one of us, but she's never serious.

I grin at her, but my response is cut short by the display of aggression before me. Alanna is in the midst of a heated discussion with a couple of girlie-girls. Alanna hates girlie-girls. Time for me to step in before disaster strikes.

"Told you I felt a fight coming on tonight." I move quickly and step up next to Alanna. "What's going on, chica?"

She sneers and points at the two girls. "These stupid blondies keep running into me."

"Oh, I'm sorry, I didn't know you owned the dance floor," blonde number one says and takes a step forward, puffing out her fake chest.

I stifle a laugh because she's obviously true to her hair color if she thinks she can take on Alanna, who doesn't look one bit girlie-girl feminine. "I suggest you walk away now, before you get your ass—and those implants—handed to you."

"Fuck you," a very brave blonde number two says and pushes me. It must be the alcohol. That shit forms a set of brass balls on any man or woman.

Without a second thought, my fist flies through the air and clocks her in the jaw. She stumbles back and hits the floor as her friend screams. That was so not supposed to happen. I need to have a talk with my appendages.

"Oh shit." Alanna laughs and grabs my arm, pulling me quickly through the crowd. She knocks over blonde number one in the process.

I glance back as she drags me along, and catch a glimpse of creepy leprechaun guy, who nods at me, a smile stretching the boundaries of his face. "Fuck."

We catch up with the other girls near the front of the bar, as per our usual instructions if one of us ever gets in a bar fight. Teagan's waving her hands in front of her face to cool down. Jada nearly falls over trying to stand straight. We all laugh as we help her.

"Well, I think the party's over," I say. "Jada is officially drunk as a fucking skunk."

"You're not too far off," Teagan suggests. "We need to leave anyway after that shit."

I look up at her, throwing Jada's arm over my shoulder. "Yeah, but I can still talk straight. She's just mumbling." I look down at my little porcelain doll. "What the fuck is she saying anyway?"

"Who knows? Let's go." Teagan pulls her phone out to call the limo. That makes me happy because it means she will be the last one dropped off and will be able to help Jada into her apartment.

"Did someone pay the tab?"

"I took care of it," Echo states when she steps up next to Jada. "After that last shot when you went over to Alanna."

"Lemme know how much I owe ya." Killian calls my name and I turn, which Jada doesn't like one bit and slurs a protest. I hand her off to Echo as the limo pulls up; I don't want her puking on me.

"So, you're working Saturday night, right?" Killian asks as he walks up.

"Yep," I reply with a smile. "Come by and I'll buy you a drink."

He studies me a moment before saying, "Are you fucking with me again?"

I laugh at him. "No, I promise, I'm not. But you're still not fucking me."

He laughs and nods. "Have a good night, Nemy."

"Night, Killian," I say and climb into the limo, giving him a nice view of my Fuck-me Art one last time. As the limo drives away, I see him pull his phone from his pocket once more, only this time, he makes a call.

I lean back into the seat and rest my head against the window. My hand hurts from punching that stupid girl, but whatever. It'll heal in time and it's not my main concern right now. I'm more concerned about that guy. Clancy was wrong about assuming I'd never see him again, and that doesn't bode well with me.

My defenses just kicked up several notches, and tonight my gun is going under the pillow where I can reach it faster, although since I've been drinking, that's probably not a good idea.

Yep, going to leave that alone until tomorrow.

5

No Man's Woman

A shout cuts through the music as half-naked women scatter, and my eyes dart to Mike the bouncer, who's pulling some guy out of his chair. Probably touched the girl dancing for him—big mistake. Clancy watches Mike handle the situation. He doesn't need to intervene; Mike's already pushing the guy toward the side door, expecting the break bar to spring the door open. Instead, Mike slams into him from behind, and I hear the guy's loud *ugh* over the music. I cringe because that must've hurt like a mother. Mike's a big guy, and I mean *really* big. He's got a good run on the last guy I dated, was engaged to, who left me, motherfucker.

I see Clancy has cringed too, and then he looks at me. I give him a half-smile with a brow arched in silent inquiry. He just shakes his head and rolls his eyes as Melody (her real name is Sally—yeah, try to use that in a strip joint) runs over to him. She grabs his arm and lingers a bit too close, telling him what happened, all the time fawning over him. It's so damn annoying. Those who've been here longest know better than to fawn over Clancy. He's not interested, which I find very strange for a gentleman's club owner.

I don't realize I'm squeezing the cup of water in my hand until water runs down my arm and splatters on the floor. "Fuck." I drop the cup and reach for a towel.

Clancy looks up at me, sees the mess I've made, and his sinister grin appears at full volume. Crap, how stupid can I be? He pushes Melody away and tells her to get back to work. I crouch down and pick up the cup, which gives him a nice view of my ample cleavage, not on purpose. It's the corset I'm wearing. Damn thing is tight as hell. He steps behind the bar and heads my way as I stand again.

"You okay?" he asks, the grin still bright and shiny.

"I'm fine," I snap, and toss the cup into the trash and the towel on the shelf beneath the bar.

"Good thing that wasn't glass." He takes my hand and runs his fingers over my palm. I barely control a shudder at his warm touch. "Then I'd have to take care of you."

That's not a good subject for me. I yank my hand out of his. "I can take care of myself, thank you."

Clancy chuckles softly and leans forward. "I bet you can. Done a good job of it so far, haven't you?"

I roll my eyes and look at all of my customers, who are preoccupied. I'm not sure if I should be happy about this or not. I lean over the bar to grab an empty glass and the sensation of flesh on flesh hits me like a sonic wave. I feel fingertips running against my skin between my corset and my jeans, sliding right around my hip. I jump damn near out of my skin, drop the glass, which does break, and run right into Clancy behind me, where I become entangled in his long arms as he catches me.

"Oh, for fuck's sake, Clancy!" I grumble and turn around in the circle of his arms. Big mistake.

He laughs, and I can feel it rumble through my body. The sensation makes me want to melt where I'm standing, and I won't even go into how he smells right now, but oh dear God . . . what's my name again? I didn't know a man could smell this delicious.

He leans over again, his breath floating across my skin when he says, "A bit jumpy, aren't we?"

I snap out of my daze and slap at his chest. "Fuck off!"

He laughs again, steps to the side, and grabs a towel to clean up the glass. "You're a touchy one, Nemy-girl," he says with the evil grin.

Oh. Shit. I might faint. I refocus my attention back to anger because it'll save me. The man knows better than to touch me. He did that touchy-feely thing on purpose. Why is he tormenting me like this?

Clancy picks up the bigger pieces with his fingers and wipes down the shelf to catch the smaller ones. Luckily, the ice bin wasn't beneath me when I dropped the glass, otherwise I'd have to clean it out and refill it with new ice. Wouldn't want a customer to get a piece of glass in his drink, unless he's being a real creep.

I'm kidding.

"I'm not the one touching people where they shouldn't be touching people," I finally spit out.

He stands abruptly, surprised. "I'm sorry for startling you. It won't happen again." He throws the towel in the discard pile I keep off to the side and walks away. "Be careful when you pick those up at the end of the night," he adds over his shoulder, and reclaims his seat.

I blow out a frustrated breath from the close call that had me wanting to attack him, tuck a lock of my loosened hair behind my ear, and get back to work.

Clancy leaves the club for a bit, and wouldn't you know it, that's when scary, creepy guy decides to show up. Amazing timing this idiot has, I swear.

"Le' meh guess, 'e's not 'round again, is 'e?" he says to my chest.

I'm not real thrilled with the fact that he's here after I saw him last night. I tap the bar, and when his eyes follow my fingers to my face, I say, "You want to talk to me or my chest?"

He grins, eyes flicking up to meet mine. "How 'bout both?"

I smirk at him as my brows go up. "Try the face. It might get you somewhere."

"Will it ge' me into your bed?"

"Aren't you the forward one?" I laugh. "I don't think so."

"Too bad. Ye look like ye could be a bit o' fun," he says and runs a hand over his hair. "So, when'll your boss be returnin'?"

"Don't know, I'm not his keeper," I reply. "You wanna try waiting this time, or shall I give him another message?" Being that I'm originally a New York gal, my sarcasm is loud and clear, along with that damn accent I'd thought I'd buried years ago.

He chuckles. "Mah, but ye're spir'ted. Are ye certain 'bout not wantin' to give me a try? Don' know wha'cher missin'." He winks.

I nod. "Pretty damn certain, I'd have to say."

"Tha' was a nice punch last night," he says with a grin.

"Yeah, let's not talk about that." I pick up a glass and turn it in display. "What'll you have?"

"Well, if I can' have you, I s'pose I'll have a shot o' yer best whiskey."

"Done," I say and pour the shot for him.

He tosses it back, sits perfectly still for a moment, as though savoring the whiskey, and finally, he smiles. "Aye, tha' was good. Haven' had one o' them in some time."

"Got anything to do with that date on your neck?" I'm a nosy girl.

His right brow arches and he nods. "Aye, it would, lass. Tha' date'd be the day mah dear brother died."

I frown at him. "Oh, I'm sorry."

He gives me a half smile and sits on the barstool. "How 'bout 'nother shot?"

"Sure thing," I reply and pour it for him. As I push the glass toward him, he reaches out and catches my wrist.

"Tha's a mighty big rock on yer finger, lass," he says while looking from under hooded eyes. "Who's the lucky man?"

A chill, not of the good variety, rushes down my spine. I look at the one-carat diamond on my ring finger. I still wear it out and to work, only for the fact that it keeps most men away from me. It's my excuse for getting out of dates when they see me dressed in a leather corset and low-rise jeans.

"That'd be none of your business." I yank my arm from his grasp right as Clancy walks into the club. He stops dead, his face turning red. "But there's the man you're looking for."

He turns his head, and the two stare at one another for a moment. Then Clancy continues forward. Christ, the tension is so thick I can barely breathe.

"Sean," Clancy says with a nod, his voice guarded. I can't read the emotion behind it.

Sean extends a hand. "Clancy."

Clancy takes his hand briefly and leans against the bar. "What brings you here?" Mr. Serious has taken over his body in a way I've never seen before. Not even the hint of a smile shows. This Sean guy must be real trouble.

Sean smiles at me. "You've a mighty fine bartender 'ere, Clancy. Think she'd go out with me?"

I roll my eyes and look at my boss, who laughs.

"She doesn't go out with anyone, Sean."

"Righ', she's engaged," Sean says as his eyes flick to my ring.

"That she is," Clancy replies.

"To you?" Sean asks.

Clancy laughs again. "No."

I want to know why that's amusing enough to make him laugh, but I keep my mouth clamped shut, since he's trying to help me out.

"Righ' then," Sean says and swings his barstool around to face Clancy. "Ye know why I'm 'ere."

Clancy nods. "I do."

"Then ye know as well tha' I'm puttin' it behind me."

Clancy stares at Sean a moment. "That's good to know."

A customer takes me away from their conversation and when I return, Clancy's sitting next to Sean at the bar. I don't know what all happened between them to create the tension, but now I'm a bit nervous that Clancy seems so relaxed, because Sean is still throwing off out-of-whack signals. My stomach is in knots.

I stop in front of Clancy. "Cola or water?"

He looks up and smiles. "Maker's Mark, please."

I reach for the bottle on the top shelf behind me. When I turn back around, both men are staring at me and grinning. I raise both hands, one holding the bottle of bourbon. "What?"

"Tha's fine," Sean says with a shake of his head and grins again.

Clancy chuckles. "Nothing, Nemy-girl, just pour." He winks at me, and I pour his bourbon into a short glass with ice and slide it forward. "Thank you."

Sean arches his right brow and looks at Clancy. "Wha' in the bloody 'ell is tha'?"

Clancy raises his glass and smiles. "Good shit, that's what."

Sean shakes his head. "Jaysus, man, tha's a disgrace to your lineage."

Laughter explodes and Clancy takes a drink of his whiskey . . . bourbon . . . whatever. "I thought the mark of an Irishman was to appreciate a good whiskey. Am I wrong?"

The grin spreads across Sean's face and he shrugs. "I s'pose 'tis." He stands and leans forward on the bar, staring right at me. "Nemy, I like tha' name. Where's it from?"

"It's short for Nemesis," I reply.

Sean grins and winks. "Beautiful, lass. Got anything to do with that punch of yers?"

"Yes, it would," I say and smile at him as I flex my hand a bit.

Clancy's eyes drop to my right hand. "That explains your hand. Get in a fight last night?"

"It was nothing," I say.

"Nothing, my arse," Sean says. "She punched a li'l blonde girl who was fuckin' with 'er friend."

Clancy stiffens and his emerald hard stare hits Sean. "You saw Nemy last night?"

"Aye, she's a spir'ted lass when she's drinkin'," Sean replies with a nod.

Clancy chuckles, but his eyes lock on mine and say all kinds of serious. "She's spirited when she's sober."

"I'm noticin' that." He grins again, looks at his watch, and then he turns to Clancy. "I'll have to be leavin' now. Be seein' ye 'round, Clancy." He throws a couple of bills on the bar. "Keep the change, lass." And he winks at me again.

"Have a good night, Sean," Clancy replies as he turns to shake hands.

Sean points at me over their linked hands. "Ye keep this one workin' 'ere and I'll be comin' 'round often enough."

Clancy doesn't smile, and Sean leaves. I get the evil-glint stare once again, picking up right where we left off from earlier in the night, but there's a different quality to the look in his eyes now.

Oh, boy. I'm not certain what that means for me. Those eyes have a territorial quality to them.

6

Devil's Dance Floor

Closing time hits around two in the morning, and I work on cleaning up and cashing out my drawer. Clancy sends Scott to check on the girls, and when Scott's out of sight, his gaze settles on me.

Oh man, am I in trouble.

Scott reappears a minute later and distracts Clancy while I finish my duties. Manny the DJ and the other girls have finally left, and Scott yells "Night" down to me as he heads for the front door. I wave back. Mike returns from escorting the girls to their cars. He stops at the bar by Clancy, who is going over the numbers.

"Nemy, you need me to walk you out?" Mike asks as he leans on the bar.

Clancy answers without looking up. "I'll walk her out, Mike."

Mike glances at me, and I motion that it's all right. "Okay," he says, a bit of a whine enhancing his tone. "Have a good night then."

Mike definitely has a thing for me, but I don't date bouncers, especially those I work with. Besides, the man's name is Michael; I absolutely don't ever date guys who have the unfortunate curse of bearing my father's name. It's a girl thing; we either look for someone like daddy dearest, or run like hell from him. I tend to run like hell.

"Night, Mike," I say and gather up the used towels. Clancy's eyes briefly leave his paperwork, and I notice the glint is back. I can't move fast enough, and a nice chunk of ice hits my cleavage and sinks down into the black lace corset I'm wearing.

Clancy's arms shoot up into the air as he shouts, "Goal!" along the lines of which someone in my family would do while watching a soccer game.

"Motherfucker!" I drop the towels. The ice sits right between my breasts; sunken down into a spot I can't reach with my fingers, the damn corset is so tight.

"Want help?" he asks with a sly grin.

"You've helped enough."

He laughs and shakes his head. "You should be more careful with the ice. I've been waiting two damn days for that shot."

I look up at him, twisting in ways he probably didn't think were possible in order to get the ice cube out. It still proves fruitless, which sucks because it's cold as hell against my skin. "Fine, next time I'll throw a glass at you."

His gaze shifts from my corset to my eyes. "Just remember, whatever you throw will come back at you."

My hand shoots out for the tray full of various fruits, which isn't there because I put it in the fridge.

He howls with laughter.

"Damn it." Finally, I grab the top of the corset between my breasts and the bottom at my navel, suck in a breath, and yank the whole thing forward. The ice hits the floor.

Clancy's head shakes. "Impressive. I'm going to have to find something that'll get you *out* of that. Obviously ice doesn't work."

"Don't think you'll be getting me out of anything, Mr. Dolan." I head into the back to put the towels in the laundry bin, leaving his laughter behind. As I turn to head back to the bar, the mess in the girls' dressing room distracts me—clothes and stripper shoes strewn everywhere. Is that a bra hanging over one of the mirrors? Make-up is scattered all over the vanities and some smattered *on* them. I don't even want to know what their houses look like. If Clancy saw this mess, he'd be pissed and they'd never hear the end of it. I'm kind of neurotic in my own right with needing things to be in order and clean. Once I'm done tidying up, he speaks behind me, voice soft and smooth. I can actually *hear* his smile.

"I've always wondered what takes you so long to dispose of towels."

The look in his eyes makes me melt. "Well, I certainly can't leave it a mess, can I?"

He chuckles. "No, I don't believe you could, as clean as you keep the bar."

I try to walk past him, but he gently takes my arm in hand and leans over. Clancy towers over me. I could wear those five-inch heels with the man and not quite meet his eyes, but now I have to look up—way up—because I'm wearing sneakers.

"Care to help me with that thing now?"

"What thing?" I ask, looking up into those gorgeous green eyes. If he didn't own a strip club where I worked, I'd be all over the man, and it wouldn't have taken a damn year, no matter how I feel about men right now—a girl has needs. But I'm not stepping on the toes that pay me. It's a damn dangerous flirtation as it is.

"You'll see." He lets me go and leads me back to the bar where he'd been doing paperwork. The paperwork is gone, and in its place are—

"Floor plans?" I ask, and he nods. "For what?"

"My new house," he replies.

"And why do you need my help?"

He tilts his head and smiles. "Well, I'd like your opinion on some things."

"Okay, why?" I place my arms on the bar, crossing one over the other.

His eyes flick to my tattoos and a smile flits across his lips. "You're always talking about houses, your dream house, where you'd like to live. I figured you might be able to help me decide on what I need."

I frown. "Yeah, but that's what *you* need, not what *I* want."

He leans forward. "Maybe I trust your opinion."

I stare into his eyes for a moment, and well, I just can't say no to the man. "Okay, show me."

"Excellent," he says and sits up. He takes one of the papers and places it in front of me. "This is the one I want." He points to the best elevation as he moves his barstool closer, and by best, I mean the most expensive. "What do you think?" I can smell his cologne and it's a dizzying scent of wild musk. I'm not quite sure how I'm going to make it through this without attacking him. I'm generally not this close to him when I'm working. Oh boy.

I crinkle my nose because, in all honesty, even if it's the most expensive elevation, it's also the blandest one. I look at the one below it and point. "This one's better, in my opinion. I like the rock face on the front. Gives it a bit of a villa feel."

Clancy chuckles and shakes his head. "You would think that."

"Hey, you asked for my opinion, and I gave it. Don't get it if you don't like it."

He throws his hands up in jest. "Whoa! Chill, Nemy-girl, I'm just teasin' ya." He runs his fingers down my bare arm.

Oh shit, we've now moved into the realm of more playfulness, which is the kind that's entirely too close to foreplay for my taste. I roll my eyes, and he laughs again. I'm starting to wonder if my eye rolls are just that damn amusing.

"What else did you want to show me?"

He pushes the floor plan in front of me. I study it for a minute or so, following an invisible path with my eyes from the front door—oh wait, there's a courtyard before it, which I absolutely love—through the house and into the Master Bedroom. Nice Master Bath too. Big, like I like them to be. Mine's so freakin' tiny.

"What's the square footage?"

"Four thousand one hundred sixty-seven," he replies.

I choke and then cough a little. "Do you really need a house that big?"

He smiles. "I want children someday."

"Getting married soon?" I quip.

"Not likely." The glint hits his eyes again. I swear they change color when that happens, just a bit. It must be the lighting. "I have to find the right woman first."

Oh, he *is* single. Seriously, how does that happen when you're the owner of a strip club? You'd think I would know this, but Clancy keeps his personal life very private.

"That'll be tough." Sometimes I just can't stop my mouth and its opinions.

He frowns. "Why do you say that?"

I widen my eyes and lift my hands, gesturing to the room around me. "Hello? What woman in her right mind wants to marry the owner of a strip joint, or even let him work in one?"

He bites his lower lip. Damn, now I want to bite it too. "That'd be a turn-off for you, huh?"

"Absolutely."

"I don't fuck or date strippers," he insists, as though that's his only option.

"If you want to marry a good woman, it doesn't matter. The temptation is still there."

He chuckles. "Oh, Nemy-girl, you're a funny one." He slips his hand over mine. "I see tits and ass every fucking day. It's not what turns me on."

Oh shit, I think my heart just lodged itself in my throat. *Breathe*. I climb off the stool, pulling my hand from underneath his. "I need to get home," I say, probably a little too quickly. "Can you walk me out now?"

He hides his laughter, but I can see it in his eyes. "I'd be honored."

I reach around the bar to grab my purse and jacket while he waits for me.

"So, should I buy the house or not?" he asks as we head for the front door.

"Honestly, I'd have to see it in person before making a decision, if it were *me* buying it," I reply, and instantly want to kick myself.

"It's a date, then," he says and opens the door for me.

Kick. Kick. Kick. Crap.

He walks me to my shiny black Saturn—the sporty two-seater—I'd bought after the last man left me. Sort of a present to myself, like the giant rock my aunt bought herself as a divorce present—a blue topaz that's got to be like four carats or something.

Suddenly, Clancy stiffens. The man Mike slammed into the side door approaches in a drunken mess. He's got a gun. Clancy grabs my arm and slingshots me behind him so fast I'm dazed for a nanosecond. From over Clancy's shoulder I see the guy point the gun at Clancy's head. Not cool. I do not want Clancy's brains all over me, thank you very much. Hands, yes; brains, no, but the hands are in an entirely different setting from this fucked up scene.

Another nanosecond skips by, and I find myself looking at the trigger of the Glock 22. The guy's finger isn't on it, which means he's not as drunk as he'd like us to think. Ooh, clever little shit.

"Gimme the money," he slurs in regard to the bank deposit, which Clancy doesn't carry out at night . . . ever. It's in the bolted-to-the-concrete floor super-industrial safe that has a timer on it and won't open until like ten in the morning when Scott arrives, seven hours from now. The would-be thief is *not* happy about this and wags the gun in Clancy's face. I seem to not exist in this realm of theft because Clancy won't let me step around him; he holds me firmly with one hand on my arm. I'm afraid to try to free myself and get Clancy's head blown off. At the moment, I'm really wishing I had a damn video camera.

"Dude," I say and lean around Clancy. His gun aims at me, which is what I want because I know what Clancy will—*I hope*—do next. Clancy pushes me to the side with his right hand, away from the car and out of the gun's aim. I fall to the asphalt on my ass. He grabs the guy's wrist with his left hand so he won't aim at him again. I call 9-1-1, carefully watching the aim of the gun while they struggle. Finally, Clancy stomps on the guy's foot, knees him in the stomach, and introduces his face to his knee—Clancy's knee, guy's face. Blood spurts from the guy's nose and he screams, dropping the gun. Clancy kicks it underneath my car. As I tell the 9-1-1 operator what's happened, Clancy practically ties the guy into a pretzel. Damn, I didn't know he was that strong. That's kind of a turn-on.

"Jesus, Clancy, chill," I say, holding the phone away.

He punches the guy in the side of the head, knocking him out (I hope not killing him). He looks at me. "*Motherfucker* could've hurt you." Oh man, is he pissed. I've never seen him so angry.

"The guy's out cold now," I say to the operator, who tells me the police are coming soon. I say, "Cool," and hang up with her after giving my information.

Clancy steps up and kneels in front of me after making sure the guy's not going anywhere. "Are you hurt?"

"I'm fine."

His eyes narrow on me. "Don't you ever pull a stunt like that again! He could have shot you."

"But he didn't," I say and raise a hand for help up.

"What if he had an itchy trigger finger? Then what, Nemy? You'd be dead."

"Oh, stop being so dramatic and help me up."

He reaches down and grabs my hand. "You sure you're okay?"

"My ass is a little sore from landing on it, but I'll be fine."

He grins and pulls me to my feet. "Oh, I can make that better for you, if you'd like."

"I think you're the reason it hurts," I say and just want to staple my mouth shut because that grin grows about ten times as big. "Never mind."

He laughs . . . hard; his hand slips around the back of my neck and he pulls me forward. His lips hover above mine, and he whispers, "Nemy-girl, you saved my life. I didn't think you cared." His hooded eyes sparkle as he stares at me, waiting.

I lick my lips. "You sign my paycheck," I reply, and he chuckles once more before kissing me.

Damn it. Damn it. Damn it.

His lips move against mine, and I've fallen so deep in lust with the man I can't help but return the kiss. It's stellar anyway. Who's gonna turn that down? His hands slide down and round my ass, and he lifts me up. What else can I do but wrap my legs around him?

And take them right back down when the squad car pulls into the parking lot. I want to say Thank God, but I'm really thinking Damn it again. I so need to get laid.

Home? Sex? Home? Sex? Fuck. He's my boss! I do have some sort of moral code, albeit small. Looks like B.O.B. will be coming out tonight. Ever since I started working for Clancy, I've needed that damn thing just to keep me sane at work.

We give our statements, they arrest the guy, who now has a broken nose, and they gather the gun for evidence. It takes a good hour for all of this to take place, and during the entire process, I'm looking at my watch because I *really* want to get home now. It's four in the morning.

The officers still need to talk to Clancy, so I get my keys ready. Clancy tells them to wait a minute and moves toward me as I unlock my car and open the door. He stops the door with his hand. I throw my purse inside and stand just inside the open door. I don't want to look up at him for fear of attacking him right here in the parking lot in front of several of Phoenix's finest. He seems to figure it out.

"I'll call you tomorrow afternoon," he says.

My eyes drift upward to his face. "That's what you said the other night."

He chuckles and leans forward. "Goodnight, Nemy-girl." And he places a quick kiss on my left temple.

"Night," I say quickly and slide down into my seat. The top of the car nearly takes the 10-gauge earring out of my ear, and not through the hole. I wince in pain and my hand flies to my ear to check it. "Oh, that's gonna be sore tomorrow."

"So's your ass," he replies.

I laugh, and he closes the door. As I drive away, I look in my mirror and see Clancy just turning around to walk to the officers. His Beamer is the only thing left in the parking lot, aside from squad cars. He drives a 750 Li, black with grey interior, the one I want. Funny, I've only ever noticed it in the parking lot once before. He usually drives that old beater of a truck because of the shady neighborhood. I still watch him in the mirror and finally, I huff out a breath, look both ways, and drive away.

I reach for my iPod and plug it in one-handed while driving. The screen lights up and I hold it in front of me while steering and browsing the music. Flogging Molly's *Devil's Dance Floor* starts to play . . . extremely loud. A smile flits across my face.

I got to kiss Clancy Dolan, that beautiful fucking man. I'm a very happy girl.

Shit, what have I done?

7

Next Contestant

Ten o'clock on Saturday night finds me shooting a maraschino cherry from mid-bar like a pro-basketball star. When it hits Clancy's drink, I throw my hands in the air and jump up and down in a circle. The men at the bar, of course, *love* that. They're waiting for my breasts to fall out of the corset. That's not gonna happen because this sucker is so tight it's a wonder I can breathe. There are hordes of nearly naked women surrounding them, but I guess men want what they can't have. An evil smile drifts across my face at that thought.

Speaking of evil . . . Clancy eyes me, the sin-filled glint appearing with his delectable smile. Yeah, that cherry's coming back to me. He takes it from his soda, holds it high, his tongue wrapping around the shiny red fruit, plucking it from its stem. I step back and almost trip on the mat. My body reacts in ways I don't want it to when I'm in public, and I barely manage to control the tremor buzzing through me. When I look at him again, he grins like he knows exactly what he does to me. Tease. I have about four more hours of this.

"Nemy-girl," Clancy says when I near his end of the bar. "Did you get your project finished the other night?" he asks after I make a note in my phone, which I often do for projects.

I refill his glass and say, "Yep. Turned it in yesterday."

"What's it about?" His fingers graze mine when he takes the glass. I jump a little and grin as I pull my hand away from his glass, lowering my hand to my side and sliding my thumb into my back pocket.

"Strip club owners who turn into snakes."

"Oh, you're telling me we're not wolves?" he replies with a smirk and growls.

I laugh at him and mix a drink for some business guy who should probably be home with his wife instead of ogling

Cherry, who is dancing in front of him. But hey, I'm not here to judge him; I'm just here for his big-ass tip.

"When are you going to show me some of your stuff?"

I pause and turn to him, surprised. "You want to see my work?"

"Yeah. Why, is it bad? Should I not want to see it?"

"No, it's not bad!" I reply, a bit insulted because I'm paying big bucks for this damn degree I should have completed many years ago. I finish making the drink and walk it to the center of the bar, placing it in front of business guy.

"Eight bucks," I say, and he throws a twenty at me. I cash him out and bring his change—one five dollar bill, and seven ones so he can tip. He picks up ten, leaving me two, and I'm happy because I know he's going to pay Cherry for a dance and she'll tip me out at the end of the night. I love this job.

I check on my other two customers at the bar, and then scout out the cocktail servers to see what they're doing. Not much going on there, so I head back to Clancy. "What kind of stuff do you like?"

He shrugs. "Doesn't matter. I'll read or watch or look at whatever."

Okay, that's really helpful. "Well, my stuff's all over the internet."

He shakes his head. "Can you just bring it into me, please?"

"That's why I asked what you like, boss-man." I give him a smartass look—eyebrows up and eyes wide.

Clancy laughs. "Bring me anything. I don't care." He throws the same look back at me.

I growl softly, roll my eyes, and turn to face the man who just walked up to the bar. "What're ya drinkin'?" The man opens his mouth to say something, but Clancy's voice stops him.

"Did you just growl at me?"

I smirk. "Just returning it. Well?" I say to the new customer.

"Jack and Coke," he says. I make the drink while Clancy pursues our conversation.

"Watch out. I like the growling thing." His eyebrows jump once and I roll my eyes again.

"Six," I say to Jack-and-Coke, and he hands me a credit card. Really? He must not be married. "Starting a tab?" I ask, and he nods. I enter what I need into the register, place the card next to it, and walk back to Clancy *again*. "That doesn't surprise me in the least."

He laughs. "I doubt much would surprise you."

"Don't bet on that." I lean on the edge of the bar in front of him.

"So, is it boring documentaries on light pollution or the o-zone, or maybe something . . . Oh!" I jump up. "Wait, I could show you my idea for a magazine."

His brow goes up. "What kind of magazine?"

"Pin-up girl rockabilly type stuff," I reply with a huge grin. "I bet you'd like it. I thought I'd get my girlfriends to do some shots for me and publish them in the magazine. I also have a few friends who are great artists and photographers."

He eyes me. "Any burlesque shit in there?"

"Maybe you'd like full nude, then?" I ask, being completely facetious within my sarcasm.

He grins. "If you insist, bring it on." He holds up a hand. "But I want to know if you're posing in it."

Son of a bitch. "Um, no."

"Doing the photography?" he asks with an arched brow.

I shake my head. "Not for this. I have a photographer."

"That's too bad," he says with a shake of his head. His grin spreads from his cheeks to his eyes, and I can see exactly where he's going with this. "I wouldn't mind a little insight on your fantasies."

"Ha!" I shout over the music, and Jack-and-Coke turns to look at me. I ignore him, my focus staying on Clancy, just as he wants, the miserable bastard. "Wouldn't you like to know?" Stupid! Stupid!

"That's what I just said, Nemy-girl." His eyes show the delicious evil glint again.

I mumble something along the lines of questioning his parentage, and he laughs as I walk away to check on my customers at the other end, since Chris seems to have disappeared. That happens a lot.

"What was that? I didn't quite catch that one."

I flip him off over my shoulder and smile at business guy. "Ready for another?" I catch a glimpse of Cherry's dance for him and roll my eyes at the smile on his face. Inside, I'm laughing because that look says he wants to fuck the ever-living shit out of her, which I know won't happen. But hell, Cherry's hot. I'd do her, and I'm straight.

Fifteen minutes pass. I open the cooler to discover I'm low on beer, so I close it and tap Clancy on the shoulder. "I'm heading back to get more beer." Chris has returned from his little escapade of God only knows what and where, but he's super busy right now.

"I'll do it," he says. "I need you to stay behind the bar." He hops off the stool and holds up his pinky and ring finger on his right hand in question. I nod and off he goes. He doesn't need to ask which beer it is because he saw me open the cooler and he knows where everything is in this place, but seriously, why does Chris get to take a long-ass break and I can't even go get beer stock? When he returns, he's carrying two cases of Bud Light. I try to help him, but he turns to the side, bends over, and places them on the floor. Then he pushes me away in a gentle motion, which tickles. I jump back with a laugh, and he looks up and tilts his head toward the bar. "You have new customers."

I turn around to find Killian grinning at me. "Killian! What's up, man?" He's got like nine guys with him, holy crap. I lean over the bar. "Dude, I'm only buying *you* a drink."

His eyes flick to Clancy, who's filling the cooler. "Bar back, huh?" He apparently saw that little display.

I shake my head. "Try owner." I give him a look that says if he intends to start anything, his ass will be leaving my bar.

Don't piss off the bartender. She has the power to eighty-six you; that is, get you thrown out via a very large bouncer who may or may not rip your arms off in the process . . . or slam you into a door. Killian seems to understand and nods. "What'll you have for your first drink?"

"Beer?"

I give him the Spock eyebrow. "Seriously? I'm buying you a drink and you want a beer?"

He shrugs. "Make me a killer shot, then."

"You got it," I say and grab a short glass, even though what I'm making calls for a shot glass. Killian smiles when I grab the Goldschlager from the shelf behind me as well as the Blue Curacao, and I pour—a two count on the Curacao (a little extra) and a six, maybe seven, count on the Goldschlager. I don't need the jigger because I've mastered this shit. Besides, I want the man to be happy, since I invited him. This drink is called a Screaming Blue Messiah, and from the look on Killian's face, he's never had it before. I set the drink in front of him and grin. "Bottoms up."

He takes the shooter and tosses it back into his mouth, and then sets the glass on the bar. His grin reappears and he nods. "Nice."

"Glad ya liked it," I say. "Now, what can I get you and your many friends?"

"MGD bottles all around," he says and looks back, starting to count. "Ten."

"You got it," I say and take a step back. When I turn to reach for the cooler as Killian turns around to talk to his friends, I run into Clancy and jump. "Would you get out of the way? I'm trying to work here."

He slaps my ass and reaches into the cooler. "So am I." Four MGD bottles come out and he hands them to me. I take them, set them on the bar, and reach for my bottle opener and flip the caps off. I turn again and he's waiting with four more. Repeat and turn. Two more bottles, and hey, we work well together. Clancy leans over my left shoulder, his hand on my right hip, which surprisingly doesn't make me jump. "Give them a discount." Ooh, I just feel all shuddery and tingly from that touch. Fuck.

I cock a brow at him, but I nod. Bottled beer is, at any regular bar, around seven bucks. At the club, we charge five, because we get more money from the girls. Entertainment, you know. I'm dropping the price to four. It's still a nice profit. "Forty bucks, Killian."

"Seriously?" he asks. "That's fucking cheap."

I nod my head to the left. "Courtesy of the owner."

Killian looks at Clancy and raises his beer in thanks. Clancy nods and goes back to looking at an outline for my magazine that I'd left in my bag. I'm so damn nervous about it too, that he's looking at one of my creations.

I pick up the tip Killian leaves me—ten bucks, not bad—and Chris looks around his end of the bar and turns to walk over to me.

"That's a big crew," he says, motioning to Killian and friends, who are now seating themselves in front of the stage. "Where'd you find them?"

"Thursday night during girls' night out." I lean back against the cooler.

He smiles big. "Networking," he says. "Good job!" Chris is surfer-boy cute with dark blond hair in a messy not quite long, but not quite short cut. He's also built like a brick shithouse—stacked to the gills. Lucky for me, I don't desire men who look like him. Unfortunate for me, I desire men who look like Clancy. Damn him and his long black hair. Chris has a customer, so he leaves me sitting against the cooler. I glance over to Clancy, who's still engrossed in my outline.

About fifteen minutes goes by and Killian and crew are having a great time and on their second order, which means they're drinking hard and fast tonight. This could be good or bad, depending. I try not to think about it too much and walk over to Clancy, who has just flipped my outline over—it's essentially a mock-up of the magazine, so it looks like a rough draft. It holds all of my ideas, plus a few drawings.

"So, what'd you think?" I ask and lean against the bar next to him.

His green eyes flick up to me and he smiles. "I like it," he says. "Did you do the drawings yourself?"

I nod.

"Impressive. I had no idea you were so talented."

"Well, slinging drinks isn't my only specialty, you know."

He grins. "I'd like to know more about some of your *other* specialties."

I slap him near the shoulder. "Shut up!"

Barking laughter erupts from him and I swing a glance down the bar, where I catch Killian looking back at me from his seat in front of the stage. Okay, that's creepy. At least Sean isn't here to add to the creep factor. Clancy hands me the outline, and I reach under the bar and stuff it in my big-ass Gucci tote that my mother gave me for Christmas last year. I hate the name-brand shit, but she keeps trying. Name brands for me consist of shit like Lucky Thirteen and Dickies.

Clancy brushes his fingers against my arm when I lean on the bar again, softly stroking my skin, which has my body going crazy and heating up. I don't look because I can see he's not looking at me. This flirtation game has moved up several notches now, and I'm not sure what to do about it, since I'm not certain if I want to get involved with anyone again, especially my boss. But damn, he's a good kisser. I kind of want to taste those lips again. I let out a soft growl and stand.

Petite Kristi walks up to the server station and I get to her before Chris does. The boys want more MGD. This is the third call. I don't think any one of them is the designated driver, so I'm a bit concerned.

"Do they have a DD?" I ask Kristi, who shrugs until I give her a look that says to ask them. She goes back to their table. I grab their drinks and set them on the bar for her instead of on her tray because she'd just rearrange it anyway.

Kristi returns and says, "They have a party bus."

I flip the cap off the last bottle. Cool. Now I don't have to worry about me or the club getting into trouble if one of them kills someone in a drunken fiery car crash. The only thing that sucks about Kristi serving them is I have to split the tip with her too, instead of just Chris. However, the party bus is a good thing, because it means they won't be here all night. With the look Killian gave me a bit ago, I'm all down for that.

After they finish the last round, I notice the group getting up to leave, and I let out a sigh relief. Killian waves me to the end of the bar where Clancy sits, so I walk down to him and see Clancy's eyes tracking his movement. Clancy doesn't like it when people walk behind him. He's always on guard. Can't blame the man for that; I do the same thing.

"Nemy!" Killian says, not the slightest bit slurred. He embraces me in a huge bear hug, nearly taking away my ability to breathe. "Thanks for the drinks! We'll definitely come back."

"Good to know," I say and slap a hand against his back. "Be safe."

He pulls back, still holding me. "Wanna fuck?" Of course, he says this loud enough for Clancy to hear, and Clancy shifts on the barstool.

"I'm good, but thanks for the offer," I say and push him back.

Killian laughs and covers his mouth like a little boy. Wow, he *is* drunk. "What about that stripper—Cherry?"

"I think she's dating someone," I reply with a smile. It's a flat out lie, but I know Cherry wouldn't be interested in him, and she's too good for him anyway.

He nods. "How about your red-headed friend?"

Oh wow, did he just say that? "Not too sure about that one, buddy. She's probably more than you could handle." I look at my end of the bar. "Gotta get back to work. Have a good night, Killian."

"Night," he says and turns to Clancy. He puts his hand out. "Thanks for the discount, man. Fucking awesome."

Clancy takes his hand. "No problem. Stay safe."

Killian grins and I can see veins surfacing in his arm as he shakes Clancy's hand. A will of testosterone takes place before me, and I'm curious what it's about. Clancy holds fast, staring into Killian's eyes without flinching. After a moment, I move away to make a drink for the guy in front of me. They break—*finally*—and Killian leaves. Once he's gone, I see Clancy flex his hand and pick up his phone. He flips it open and sends a text message to someone. I have a feeling he told Scott or Mike to make sure they leave.

I serve the drink and make change, and go back to Clancy. "What was that all about?"

His eyes flick up to meet mine. "You." He grabs me by the belt loops on each hip and yanks me forward until my face is very close to his. "Be more careful when you do girls' night, please. I don't like stray dogs in my club."

"Sorry. I didn't know it was going to go there."

He nods and pushes me back. I stare at him, biting my lower lip. "Don't pout, you're not in trouble."

"I'm not pouting. I was just thinking."

His right brow goes up. "About what?"

"Nothing," I say and turn back to the bar.

Clancy chuckles as I walk away. "Uh huh." I glance back over my shoulder and stick my tongue out at him. There are several phrases he could have used, but he doesn't say a word.

The next time I'm near him, I grab his glass, refill it with cola, and then place it in front of him completely out of habit, all the while thinking of my magazine project. "So, you like the magazine idea?"

Clancy nods. "Yes, I do."

"Jeremy thought it was stupid."

"Jeremy is an idiot," Clancy replies. "I think you'll do quite well with it, to be honest."

"Thanks," I reply with a smile. "I just need to stop finding men who get jealous of the time I work on stuff like that because it takes away from them."

"Inconsiderate bastards." That makes me laugh and keeps a smile on my face the rest of the night.

8

Lick

Closing hits. I'm cleaning up near Clancy while the last girls finish up their dances. The others are already dressed to go home. Cherry sips her wine at the bar's center, sporting a wide grin because she's noticed Clancy staring at me as I wipe down a bottle.

I look to the side. "Take a fucking picture."

He laughs. "You don't like being stared at."

"Who the hell does?" I wipe the counter down, and as I turn, a goddamn cherry hits my cleavage and sinks into the small opening between my breasts. Stripper Cherry about chokes on her wine and covers her face to keep it from coming out of her mouth and nose. I put a hand on my hip, looking down at my chest, and then up at him. "How long were you holding onto that? It's warm."

"A while," he says while laughing. "Perfect shot, though, don't you think?"

I have to agree, and it's a rare shot, at that. That's two in a row for him. "You should have tried out for the NBA."

"Nah. Wasn't interested."

I look down again and try to stick two fingers in to pluck the cherry out. It doesn't work and I only end up pushing the cherry down further. This corset has a zipper in front, but I'm not unzipping it in front of him and everybody else. "Honestly, must you keep aiming for my cleavage? I just hit your drinks."

He chuckles and goes back to his paperwork. I finish my chores with a damn cherry stuck under my corset.

As usual, everyone leaves and it's just Clancy and me in the club. I still have a cherry in my corset. This is happening too often—him and me alone together. He closes the folder and pushes a piece of paper to the edge of the bar. "Here, look at this, Nemy-girl."

I turn off the lights underneath the bar, and turn the paper around to look at it. There are pictures of tile and carpet samples on it, and I quirk a brow at him. "What's this for?"

"My house. Which ones do you like?"

I study the samples. "Kind of hard to tell when they're just pictures."

He holds out a pen. "Mark the ones you like."

"Okay." I take the pen and place an X on the corner of the Travertine tile and the Italian grotto photos. Then I study the carpet. "I can't choose any of these without feeling them."

"That's fine," he says with a nod. "What kind of carpet do you like?"

"Not Berber. I have a dog and his toenails get stuck in the loops and pull up the whole row."

"Well, what colors then?" he asks while he scribbles lines through one of the pictures—obviously Berber.

"I don't know," I say with a shrug. "It depends on the colors in the house. I like earth tones."

He looks up at me. "So, like tans or browns?"

I shake my head. "Brown is too dark. Tonk is all white."

"Tonk?" he asks, his eyebrows rising with the question.

"Yeah, my dog—Tatanka."

He chuckles and shakes his head. "You named your dog 'Buffalo'?"

"Shut up." I slap him on the arm.

"You keep slapping me like that and I'm going to think you're hitting on me."

"You wish," I say stupidly . . . and fucking slap him again. Seriously? Am I five or something?

He grabs the center of my corset at the top and drags me forward until I'm standing between his legs. His eyes glint wickedly, lingering on mine, the low light reflecting in his dark pupils. His fingers slide out of the corset and take the zipper. I swallow my heart as the zipper slowly moves down its track until he finds the cherry halfway down, just beneath my breasts. His face dives between my breasts and he plucks the little bastard cherry out with his tongue. Just the touch of that tongue against my flesh makes my knees weak. Clancy's left arm quickly wraps around my waist for support.

I laugh nervously, my hands gripping his shoulders, as he spits the cherry onto the bar. His tongue touches my skin again and slides all the way up to my neck. When he reaches my ear, he whispers my name, and I lose any control I had.

I turn my head to the side, sliding my hands up into his hair, grabbing a fistful of those soft black waves. As my mouth covers his, his tongue slips past my lips to dance with mine, and I feel a rush of heat over my body that climbs from my legs to my head in two seconds flat, flushing me with the lust I've felt for him since the day I walked into his bar. His arms lock around me, pulling me closer, and I am in the heaven that is Clancy as his kiss devours me.

"Holy shit," says Scott, stopping dead near the entrance. It startles the hell out of me, and I break away from Clancy and quickly zip up my corset.

Clancy turns around, but I see his glare. "What do you need, Scott?" The tremor in his voice tells me he's about to kill his general manager.

Scott stammers. "I-I forgot something . . . in the office." He points to the back of the club.

"Well, go get it," Clancy snaps, his words harsh.

I grab my coat and pull it on, snatching up my purse and slinging it over my shoulder. Clancy turns back to me, his expression moving from anger to disappointment in a blink. He lets out a soft growl and closes his eyes.

"I really should go," I say, looking away from him.

"Probably a good idea," he replies, not looking at me.

Scott walks out of the back, and I jump and head for the front door.

"I'll go out with you." He looks confused, but nods and leads the way. Before going around the corner, I look back at Clancy; he's sitting on the stool exactly as I left him. Yeah, I don't think I could handle a rejection like that, either. I want to say something to him, but the words won't leave my throat, so I walk out the door and drive home in a frustrated anxiety-driven mess.

I'm kind of disappointed Scott interrupted us, but I'm not entirely certain I'm up for what Clancy has to offer me, nor am I certain about what that offer may be. Oh, I know the sex would be great, but to repeat what I said to Killian, there's more to life than great sex. I want someone who will love me for the rest of my life, who will support me in my aspirations, and who will lift me up when I've stumbled and fallen without thinking about what he can gain from it or leave because he can't handle it.

Is that too much to ask? Am I being too dramatic?

Fuck, I might as well blog about it and see what kinds of answers I get. Maybe the Asshole will read it and get a clue. Not that I'd take his sorry-ass back or anything.

Son of a bitch.

9

I Will Possess Your Heart

Sunday evening drones on with customers here and there, and finally it's almost closing time. I'm thankful because after that shit with Clancy the night before, I just want to get the hell out of here and go home. He kissed me. Wait, maybe I kissed him. I'm so confused. We've barely said a word to one another tonight, once he showed up, which wasn't until I was into my shift a couple of hours. I wasn't even supposed to work, but I'd traded with Chris so I could have last Thursday off.

Sean the scary leprechaun shows up at the last minute, topping off my wonderful evening, and Clancy is in his office gathering paperwork or whatever the hell he does back there.

"'Ello, lass." He takes a seat at the empty bar.

"It's closing time," I say, my voice clipped. "Make it quick." I cross my arms over my chest. Then after realizing that only doubles my cleavage, I lower them and pick up a towel and glass. My hands should have something to do so I don't punch him for any comments he may be stupid enough to make.

His thick brow goes up in an arch. "Well, ye know wha' I like, lass," he says with a wink. I briefly consider throwing the glass, which really isn't a good idea.

"Unfortunately," I mumble and pour him a shot of Jameson, wondering just what in the hell he's doing here. I place the shot on the bar where he has to reach for it because I don't want him to touch me again.

He studies this action carefully. "Wha's got yer knickers in a twist?" He reaches for the shot after I pull my hand away.

"None of your damn business," I reply and return the bottle to its rightful place on the shelf behind me. When I turn back, he's finished the shot. "You done with that now?"

"Perhaps you should jus' leave the bottle on the bar, Nemy."

I arch a brow and place a hand on one hip. "Oh really? Plan on staying long?"

He shrugs. "Depends. Is Clancy 'round?"

"He's in the office." I grab the damn bottle again and put it on the bar.

He reaches for it, his eyes flicking to my left hand as I pull away. "Where's yer ring?"

I look down and want to slap myself for forgetting something so minor, but so huge. "I guess I left it on the bath counter at home."

He nods once and leans forward after pouring another shot for himself. "Ye wanna 'ear a funny story?"

I roll my eyes. "What?"

"A friend of mine asks 'round about a lass who says she's engaged and 'e discovers tha' she isn't. So it makes the friend wonder why the lass would say tha' if it weren' true, y'know? Makes 'im wonder why she wears a ring."

"How is that a funny story?"

He shrugs and tosses back his shot. "Maybe she's jus' playin' 'ard to get."

"Doubtful. Maybe she just isn't interested in dating anyone, so she wears the ring to deter men."

"Maybe she 'asn't found the right man yet."

"Maybe she's been through two already and they were both shitheads." This is really starting to make me uncomfortable, on top of annoying me. I hope Clancy comes out soon because Sean gives me the heebie jeebies.

He grins and slaps the bar; the noise makes me jump a little. "Ah, tha' could be it, lass." He pours himself another shot and drinks it. "So, do ye think this lass would go out to a nice dinner with mah friend?"

"No," I reply. "I don't think she would if she's not interested in men right now."

"Even with no strings?" he asks, and pours another shot.

"How many of those you plan on drinking?"

He pauses and reaches behind him, and then flops his wallet on the bar. The leather opens with a quick flick of his fingers and he pulls out a couple of twenties and lays them on the bar in front of him. "How many'll this get me?"

"Well, you've drank almost half that," I say and step forward. "You'd better leave me a good tip." Normally, I wouldn't say this to a customer, but Sean's not my normal customer.

He drinks the fourth shot and pushes the glass and bottle toward me. "Tha' a good enough tip for ye, lass?"

I smile, probably for the first time all night. "That's a nice tip. Thank you." I put the bottle on the shelf and wash the glass, and then reach for the money. His hand traps mine over the cash in a movement so fast it startles me.

"Have dinner with me, Nemy," he says. "I'll be a perfect gentleman."

Somehow, I don't think that's possible. I swallow the lump in my throat. "No, thank you."

He winks. "Someday, lass, you and me are enjoyin' a fine meal together. I've got plenty o' time to wait." He slowly removes his hand from mine, and I pull away with the money.

"You'll be waiting a long damn time, Sean."

"'Tis fine. I'm good at waitin' for things I want."

I swallow hard because the look in his eyes is just plain evil, and not that delicious Clancy evil. Straight up E-V-I-L.

"Sean, stop fucking with my bartender," Clancy says as he walks up. The jovial look on his face contradicts the anger in his eyes, which tells me he either saw what happened or heard the conversation. "What are you doing here? We're about to close."

"Can't a fellow Irishmen just stop in 'n' say hi?" Sean says as he swivels the stool toward Clancy.

"And he can have a drink or two as well, but he'll have to leave when the bar closes" —he looks at his watch— "which is right now." He looks up at me and points at the register. "Make the last transaction and close out, please."

I walk over to the register to do exactly that.

"I'll walk you out, Sean," Clancy says and stops in front of him, waiting.

Sean snorts with laughter. "Ye're keepin' her for yerself, aren'cha?" he says when he stands.

"No, Sean, I'm just keeping my bartender busy until she's finished with her duties." Clancy nods toward the door. "She has a job to do and probably homework to finish, which you're keeping her from."

"Homework?" Sean asks. "What the hell for?"

"You'd have to ask her," Clancy says, and moves him along with a hand on his shoulder, guiding him toward the door. Before passing the end of the bar, Clancy drops a folder on it before they walk outside.

I finish up quick so I can leave and not be left alone with Clancy very long, but he stalls me when he returns.

"Stay a minute," he says as I walk around him.

I pause, my coat half on, and he finally looks up from whatever paperwork he'd brought out.

"I need to talk to you, and it'll give Sean time to leave the property."

Oh crap, but he has a damn good point. I pull up a barstool and plop my cute little ass on it, waiting. Everyone has left and it's now just the two of us sitting in the dimly lit room. My nerves are wreaking havoc on me, and I have to remind myself to breathe because I'll become overly anxious and pass right the fuck out. And boy, does Clancy make me overly anxious. *Breathe.*

Clancy finishes what he's doing, closes the folder, and looks at me with a heavy sigh. "What the fuck—"

"Chuck?" I ask lightly.

He frowns.

"Sorry." I can't stop a little giggle from escaping my throat. "Do you know that when he's around, you have a bit of an Irish accent?" Which gives my body chills in a good way.

"I don't doubt it," he replies, with a hint of the accent. "My father's is still pretty thick."

"Were you born there?" I ask, making a desperate attempt to deter the real topic of this discussion.

He nods. "And raised there until my early teens."

"Oh, kind of like I was raised in New York until my early teens."

"And somehow we both ended up in the desert." He turns toward me, resting one arm on top of the bar. "Now, can we talk about last night?"

I freeze where I sit and stare at him, and I clear my throat. "Look, Clancy, I really don't want—"

"What are you afraid of, Nemy-girl?"

My eyes widen. "I'm not afraid of anything."

"Ri*iii*ght," he replies. "That explains the deer in the headlights look." His fingers tap the bar a few times. "Why'd you walk away from me last night?"

"Because Scotty walked in."

"Uh huh, what's the real reason?"

I bite my lower lip, look away, and pinch the bridge of my nose. "Because I don't know if I want that."

"The commitment or the sex?" he asks and touches my arm.

My eyes rocket to his face, shock nearly knocking me off the barstool.

He reaches out quickly and snatches my arm, pulling me back toward the bar. "Wow, Nemy-girl, didn't think that'd throw you that hard."

"I . . . I . . ." I draw in a deep breath and raise my hands. "I can't have this conversation right now."

"Why not?" He slides off his barstool, reaches across my lap to the other side, grabs the edge of my seat and swivels it, moving it with him until my back is against the bar and he's directly in front of me. "I think this is the perfect time for this conversation."

"What are you doing?" My nervousness may reach levels that aren't safe if I wish to continue breathing . . . or stay conscious. I lick my dry lips.

He grins and places a hand on the bar on either side of me. "Trying to figure out what makes you tick."

My chest rises and falls rapidly. I swallow hard as my eyes dart around, trying to find my escape, which only makes his grin spread wider. Ducking under his arm isn't an option because of the confined space between us. I'd end up knocking him backwards. I study his build . . . bad idea; it's got my body heating to temperatures that could melt steel. There's no way I could knock Clancy out of my way from this position.

Hmm . . .

He jerks his head toward the front door. "If you want to run, there's the door. I'm not stopping you."

I cock an eyebrow at him. "You kind of have me trapped by those ripped arms of yours, big guy."

He leans closer, damn near doing a push-up against the bar, his biceps flexing. I can see—entirely too well—his fantastic upper body beneath his tight shirt. He's been hidden away in his office most of the evening; I haven't been close enough to notice the über-tightness of the fitted poly-nylon-whatever blend . . . oh my God, can he *get* any closer to me?

"So does that mean you're not going to run again if I kiss you?"

I fan my face. "Did you turn the air off or something?"

"It's sixty-eight degrees in here, as always, Nemy-girl." He moves close enough for me to feel his hot breath float across my cheek. His cologne drifts into my nostrils; that damn dizzying scent.

An image flashes through my mind, the one of us on the bar . . . or stage . . . or on the sofa in his office.

"Oh, hell." I grab his face and pull him that mere inch or two to my lips. His legs slide between mine as he presses me against the bar, his right hand tangling into my hair to cup the back of my head, angling it for the maximum effect of his heated kiss. My right leg hitches on his left hip, and when he presses against me, I can feel just how much he wants me.

I also feel a sudden vibration against my inner thigh and jerk.

"Shit," he whispers against my lips and draws in a deep breath, as though taking in my scent to savor it. He stands, leaving me breathless, and reaches into his front pocket for his phone, flipping it open. "What?" His brow creases. "Where are you?" He steps back. "Just stay there. I'll come get you." He runs a hand through his hair. "No, Brennan, stay put. I mean it. I'm on my way."

I bite my lip as I look up at him. "Everything okay?" I can see the concern on his face.

He shakes his head as he closes his phone and steps around me. "I have to go."

"Okay," I say, disappointed, and push myself off the barstool. I adjust my jacket and smooth back my hair, wanting to kick myself for not controlling my damn libido once again.

He studies me a moment, pausing in that realm of indecision: does he finish with me or go to Brennan, whoever he is? Wait, what was his brother's name? Brennan sounds familiar. "Have dinner with me tomorrow night."

"I have homework," I reply as I pick up my tote. "Big project."

"Do it before dinner."

"You can't be serious." I look up at him as I swing my bag over my shoulder and can see disappointment in his eyes. "I'll probably start work on it tonight."

"Okay, can you take a break and go to dinner later?" His brow arches.

"Maybe," I reply and head for the front door. "Call me."

Crap, what am I doing? I can't have dinner with my boss. *Why the hell not, Nemy? You just almost had sex with him.* The little voice in my head needs to keep her opinions to her damn self.

He locks the door, and we walk into the small parking lot, where he beelines straight for his car with a quick goodnight. I climb into my own vehicle to discover a note sitting on my windshield, fluttering in the small breeze. I pluck it off and shut my door, turning the key in the ignition and locking the doors out of habit. A quick flick of a button turns on the dome light so I can read the chicken scratch.

I'm good at waiting for things I want.

I swallow hard and look up to see Clancy pulling out of the driveway in a hurry.

"Fuck."

I slam my car into gear, drop the parking brake, and peel out of the parking lot, wanting to get the hell away in case Sean's still there. He knows my car. That scares the shit out of me.

From now on, I think I'll bring my Glock to work.

10

Another Hole in the Head

My right eye cracks open to glare at the ringing cell phone on my nightstand. Whoever the hell is calling me at this hour—before noon, which is entirely too damn early—better have something important to tell me or I'm going to kick their ass. I groan and snatch it off the table.

"What?" I say, answering in my normal *you-just-woke-me-up* cranky tone.

Teagan's voice hits me hard enough to jolt me awake completely. "Get over here, *now*!"

I sit up in bed. "What's wrong?"

"That son of a bitch" —she growls in the pause and I hear a door close— "fucking . . . just get over here."

"Your place?" I climb out of bed to search for something to wear, pushing aside the previous night's clothes with my foot and pulling my Chucks out because I sure as hell am not wearing flip-flops when there's a potential emergency.

"No, Jada's," she replies and I bolt upright and stare into my closet. "Can you be here in twenty?"

My eyelids flutter. "Uh, yeah. Let me get dressed."

"Good. Hurry." She hangs up, leaving me baffled. But when Jada's involved it means James is too. I throw my phone on the bed and dress with a speed that'd surprise any human being. After fastening my hair in a half pony-tail, half bun, I grab my keys and purse and head out the door. Then I turn right back around and run in the house to grab my phone that I'd left on the bed.

All essentials—phone, purse, keys—with me now, it doesn't take long to get to Jada's apartment, and about fifteen minutes later, I pull into her parking lot. I am, however, lacking the most important element of caffeine, so I'm not quite awake yet. I park in the nearest space to her apartment because the tone in Teagan's hurried words tells me the potential for the shit to hit the fan is extremely high. Leaving my purse in my car tucked beneath the seat, I climb out and speed walk to Jada's door. Teagan swings it open in a rush before I can knock.

"Jesus Christ! You scared the shit out of me," I shout as I jump back a step.

"Sorry," she says and shoves a small duffle bag into my arms. "Here, take this to your car."

"What the fuck is going on?"

She tips her head toward the open apartment door and shakes it quick; we can't discuss it right now. She grabs another bag off the floor and steps out, shutting the door behind her. I head down the sidewalk after she nods in that direction. When we reach the pool area, I breach the silence.

"You gonna tell me what's going on or do I have to guess?"

"It's a goddamn convoluted mess and she won't tell me anything yet, but unless the doorknob raced up to smack her in the eye, I'd say the son of a bitch beat the shit out of her." She rubs her face; looking as exhausted as I am.

I stop walking. "Are you fucking serious?"

She stops too and looks at me. "I'd been trying to reach her all weekend and nothing, so I came over an hour ago. She wouldn't open the door until I threatened to get the landlord. So we're getting her the hell out of here before the jackass gets home because I'm sick of this shit."

If Teags wants to get Jada away from James, Jada must look pretty bad this time around.

"Where is he? I'll fucking kill him."

She grabs my arm, pulls, and we start walking again. "Nemy, just don't. He's dangerous."

"So I'll get Kennadi to help me."

She snorts. "Yeah, that's just what I need, to bail you two out of jail for slicing the fucker up. When you and Kennadi get together, it's like a fucking hurricane and there isn't shit anyone can do about it. Not to mention that it won't do any good. You know how deep he's got his claws in her. I packed this shit with her protesting the entire fucking time. It's going to be hard enough getting her to agree to leave the damn apartment so she won't end up dead."

It's my turn to snort. "Knowing him, it'd likely be in a ditch somewhere."

"Or the town lake," she says.

I open the trunk of my car and shove the two bags in, which is about all I can fit in the tiny space. "She staying with you?"

"Yeah, that's my plan," she replies. "I thought it might be best because he doesn't know where I live."

"He doesn't know where I live either, and I have a dog."

"True, but I'm closer to her work."

My eyes widen. "What about her work? He could show up there."

Teagan shakes her head, the sun highlighting her red hair in vibrant rays. "I already made her call. She's going to take a few days off and has already told them why. Her boss is pretty cool and will likely tell the jackass he fired her or something."

I let out a brief sigh of relief. "Okay, that's doable."

"Yeah," she says, and then she looks around. "C'mon, we need to hurry."

I close the trunk and walk with her back to the apartment. "Where is he anyway?"

"At work," she replies. "Left an hour or so before I got here."

The calculations spin through my mind as I try to figure out just exactly how much time we have. "Roughly five or six hours then? That'll work. It's going to take at least an hour to get her out of here."

"Agreed," Teagan says, and opens the door.

We find Jada sitting on the sofa in tears. When she looks up, I have a hard time not taking a step back. Jesus. The bastard did a number on her face. Her left eye, nearly swollen shut, portrays all the colors of an Arizona sunset, and a nasty gash scores her inflated lower lip. Both injuries are about a day old. My adrenaline shoots through the roof and my hands clench into fists.

But I don't say a fucking word because what wants to come out of my mouth is useless right now.

Teagan and I sit on either side of her, our arms wrapping around her as she sobs. We comfort her as best we can, but Teagan wants to get the hell out of the apartment. Me, I'm all for sticking around so I can do to James what he's done to my friend. If I hadn't left my phone in my purse, I'd already be dialing Kennadi.

I decide to broach the topic, even though she might not want to talk about it. "What happened, Jada? You two had split as of Thursday night."

She draws in a deep shuddering breath and sags like a ragdoll. "He came back the next night. Wanted me to take him back. Took me to dinner. Everything was fine." She trembles against my arm, recalling the memory. "Then Saturday night he cornered me, wanting to know who I fucked when we went out Thursday night. I told him no one, but he wouldn't believe me and just kept asking all night." Again, she shudders. "Then last night he just lost control." She shakes her head. "I shouldn't have gone out with you guys. Then this wouldn't have happened."

"Bullshit," I say, unable to stop myself.

"No, really, Nemy," she says. "If I just don't do anything to upset him, he's fine."

I cock my head to the side. "What, like breathing? Come on, Jada, it doesn't matter what you do, he's a woman-beating jackass who will never fucking stop."

She starts crying again. I realize it's going to be a long day, and I need to tone it down a notch or two. Several minutes pass that have Teagan twitching because she thinks James is going to walk in at any given moment, and Jada finally stops crying long enough for us to begin our coercion tactics.

"Jada, we need to leave," Teagan says softly. "We have to leave now."

Jada's frightened tired eyes look from her to me, and I say, "It's okay, chica. We're taking you where he can't find you."

"He always finds me," she says in a hoarse whisper. She sounds like she's been awake all night or longer.

"He won't find you," I insist. "We won't let him." I grasp her hand and hold it tight in promise of my words. She sobs again and drops her head against my shoulder. It's all I can do to control the tremor of anger surging through me so she doesn't feel it. I mouth to Teagan, "We need to get pictures." She nods, letting me know she'll take care of it later.

An hour passes by as we sit on the couch consoling our beaten friend. I hold an ice pack against her face as Teagan and I continue to talk to her, encouraging her that it's best if we all leave together.

"We have to go," Teagan says again and lightly runs her scarred fingers down Jada's arm. "You're not safe here."

"I'm not safe anywhere," Jada whispers against my shoulder, which is now numb because the ice pack sits between it and Jada's face.

"You will be," I say and slowly get her to her feet. "What else do you want to take with you?" I toss the ice pack to Teagan, who shoves it in her purse on the floor.

Jada's eyes flit back and forth around the room in nervous movement before she finally shakes her head in doubt. "Teagan packed my clothes."

"I'll grab the rest," Teagan says and runs into the bedroom.

I look down at Jada. "Anything else? I can fit a few things in my passenger seat."

"My books," she says. "I can't leave my books."

"Okay." I look around and spy the bookshelf. You've got to be kidding me. "Um, I don't think I can fit those in my car."

Teagan walks back out with a handful of clothes on hangers. "What?"

"She wants to take her books," I say and nod toward the bookshelf.

Teagan's mouth drops open when she gets a gander at the double bookshelf loaded with R. A. Salvatore, George R. R. Martin, and God knows what else. "Shit. Um, boxes?"

"You got any, because I sure as hell don't," I say.

"I have some of those banker's boxes," Jada says softly. "Will they work?"

"Perfect, where are they?" I ask and as soon as she tells me, I run to get them.

After packing half the bookshelves, which is all we can fit into the boxes, and loading them into Teagan's truck—thank the gods she has a damn truck—we get ready to leave. A reluctant Jada squeaks about something and runs into the bedroom right as we're heading for the front door.

"I swear to God, if she locks herself in there, I'm kicking the fucking door down," I say and spin around. Halfway to the bedroom, I run into her in the hall.

"I forgot this," she says and holds up an old stuffed purple bear with frayed ribbons and one eye missing.

"Seriously?"

Her brow makes an attempt to knit together, but the bruising around her eye won't allow it and she winces from the pain. "My mom gave me this. His name is Otto." She cradles Otto against her chest and it wrenches at my heart to see her like this—so fragile and childlike.

"Great, any other friends you need to bring?" I ask, and Teagan slaps me from behind. "Sorry. Can we go now?"

Jada nods, puts on her giant bug-eye sunglasses—now I know why she wears them—and steps out the front door. Teagan and I follow, and Teags locks up the apartment. I'd have left the damn thing wide open so the son of a bitch would think someone kidnapped her or something—wait, that wouldn't work. He'd just end up playing wounded man or some bullshit and it'd be all over the news. Okay, so I'd leave it unlocked and hope someone discovered it.

"Meet you there," I announce as we head to our vehicles.

I'm in desperate need of caffeine and Jada deserves some sort of treat, so I stop at *Starbucks* on my way to Teagan's place. When I arrive at her apartment—I swear, I think I'm the only one who owns a house—the two of them have already unloaded the truck. It's mid-afternoon by now; I'm tired and hungry, so I picked up some food too.

Several hours later—and after loading Jada up with ibuprofen to bring some of that swelling down in her face—finds us debating which movie to watch as Teagan and I sit on the floor in front of her enormous DVD collection. Teags figures a movie might keep Jada's mind off everything that's happened, until I suggest we watch *Sleeping with the Enemy*.

She glares at me and whispers, "No, we're not watching *that*."

"Why not?" I ask. "Maybe it'll give her some ideas about how to handle this shit."

She just growls at me. Then, in a whisper, "I'd rather kill the shithead myself."

I giggle. "Okay, how about *Enough* with J-Lo?" I ask and try to control the smirk that wants to appear.

She slaps me on the arm and I gasp. "I can't believe you just hit me in front of Jada!"

Her eyes go wide as regret drifts across her face. "Shit."

I laugh. "Oh, stop it. I'm kidding." I backhand her shoulder in a quick slap.

"Bitch," she says and starts skimming the DVD collection again. "Help me pick a damn movie already."

I reach forward and snatch a DVD off the shelf. "Hey Jada, you ever seen *Avatar*?" She seems to like the fantasy shit, considering all those books we packed. When she doesn't answer, I half turn to look back at her. She has her head down, her hair hiding her face again. "Jada?"

She lifts her eyes, sees what I'm holding up, and shakes her head.

"Is that a *no you haven't seen it,* or a *no you don't want to watch it?*" I ask as Teagan stands up and walks into the kitchen for popcorn.

"We can watch it," she says in a voice so low I can barely hear her.

I pop the DVD into the player and crawl across the floor to the sofa, where I pull myself up to sit next to her. My arm stretches out across her back until my hand reaches her shoulder, and I gently pull her toward me. "Come here, baby girl. Let's disappear into another world for a while."

Teagan comes back into the living room with a bowl of popcorn, sets it on the table, and then drops onto the sofa on Jada's other side and pulls the tiny girl's legs up into her lap.

"I can't believe I got myself into this situation," Jada whispers as Teags massages her legs and feet.

I gently brush the hair away from her swollen face. "Shh, you aren't alone in this, chica."

"That's right," Teagan says. "We're right here with you, and we're going to help however we can."

Jada just nods slowly as she stares at the screen and watches the previews. I look at Teags and ask her silently if she got pictures. She nods and I indicate that I want her to send them to my phone. She nods again, grabs the remote, and starts the movie while we wait for Echo and Katy to stop by. They're going to pick up Jada's car for us so we don't have to leave her alone for any amount of time. Jada alone would be very bad right now.

The difficult part has yet to come—keeping her away from James. If we're not careful and vigilant, she'll run right back into the bastard's arms.

By the time I get home, it's well after midnight and I'm exhausted. All I can do is collapse into bed after feeding Tonk. Right as I drift off to sleep, I remember that Clancy was supposed to call me and take me out to dinner.

Shit. I didn't even check my phone.

I sleep like the dead for several hours, waking up only a couple of hours before my shift, so I don't get a chance to check my messages until I'm on my way to work. Jada's whole situation has my head a complete mess anyway. Of course, there are a few messages from Clancy regarding dinner. Now I feel like shit.

One message is from Teagan, detailing how we're all taking turns watching over Jada while she's off work. Today is Echo's turn.

When I start my shift, Clancy's nowhere in sight.

"Hey, Scotty," I say when Mr. General Manager appears near the end of my bar. "Where's the boss-man tonight?"

"He'll be in later," he replies. "Had to take care of some personal shit."

I nod and go about my bartending duties, wondering in the back of my mind what personal shit Clancy has to deal with. Maybe it involves that Brennan person who called Sunday night, interrupting the little interlude of lust that I can't get out of my damn head.

When Clancy does finally show up, he beelines for his office. I try to get his attention by waving my hand in the midst of mixing a drink, but he doesn't see me and disappears behind the door. I really need to talk to him about why I didn't answer the phone last night or return his calls, but this looks like it might be a difficult task, especially since he leaves the club again.

Later in the night, I have to talk to him because I need the coming Thursday off for Teagan's birthday. It's a long shot because that's only a couple of days away, but it's worth a try. I send him a text, hoping he'll at least answer that.

I really need Thursday off! I send, emphasizing my desperate need with three exclamation points in hopes that it'll get his attention.

Nothing. Nada. Zilch. Son of a bitch.

He responds about thirty minutes later. *I need you there.*

It's Teagan's birthday, PLEEEAASE??? I'll get Chris to work.

I don't know what he's doing out in the world, but another damn thirty minutes passes by before he answers. *Fine, Anna. You'll have to work Sunday to make it up.*

Fuck, I hate that name, and I cringe upon seeing it on my screen.

I scowl at the phone and type, *Thanks,* and then get back to work. I am *not* happy. He's stopped calling me Nemy-girl, and he's the only one who says that. Do I even bother to explain the whole phone mess at this point? Why'd I have to be so goddamn exhausted and not check my phone last night?

My phone buzzes once more and I find a text from him that says, *You can have Monday off.*

I stare at my phone, contemplating the next text to him. *Clancy, about last night–* but then Chris interrupts by telling me I have a customer. That's what I get for sulking against the cooler. I slide the phone into my pocket just as Mr. Impatient slams his hand on top of the bar. I give him a glare that has the bastard upright and stepping back within two seconds.

"What do you want?" I snap. He meekly gives his order and I retrieve it for him quickly before wallowing against the cooler for a good long while, debating on whether or not I should send the message I'd started earlier. Eventually, I decide that's a conversation that needs to happen in person, so I discard it and stare at Candace as she dances on the stage in her seven-inch heels. I often wonder how these girls can even stand in those shoes. It boggles the mind.

It's going to be a long fucking night. Clancy's not talking to me, probably because I didn't call him back, and I'm bored out of my damn mind without him here.

That alone says a hell of a lot. Shit.

11

3 Libras

Cherry climbs up on a stool and leans over while I'm at the other end of the bar making a drink. "Okay, what the hell is going on?"

I look up at her and get a full view of her double-D breasts underneath the skimpiest shirt I've ever seen. "Jesus, woman, would you put those away?"

She laughs and crosses her arms over her chest, which only serves to double her cleavage, and then rests her elbows on the bar. "Scotty says he caught you two going at it the other night. Now Clancy's not even here tonight and you're miserable. What happened? You look like hell."

I just shake my head because I really don't want to talk about it *or* the reason I look like hell.

"Come on, Nemy, talk to me."

My eyes flick up to meet hers. When I return from taking the drink to my customer, she's shooing someone away, and turns her attention back to me with raised eyebrows, anticipating what I might say. "Really, Christine, just leave it alone."

"Ooh, my real name. This must be bad." She leans in closer, her ass sticking up in the air, which has a few men drooling. "No, I won't leave it alone. You two have been playing footsies for like a year now, and then Scott tells me what he saw, and now you're all busted up about something and Clancy's nowhere in sight."

"I'm not busted up about anything," I insist. "And *footsies*, really?"

She grins. "Did you blog about it? I haven't been able to get onto my computer lately." Cherry's the only girl at the club who reads my blog.

"What's wrong with your computer?" I ask, trying to avoid the subject of Clancy.

"It's not hooking up to the internet," she replies.

"Did you reset the modem after the storm last night?" I ask and look at the guy a few stools down from her. I nod at him and he gives me his order. Fuck, I have to walk down near my boss, as Clancy's made a brief appearance, but I can tell he won't be here long enough to have that much needed talk.

"No, I don't know how," she answers.

I hold up a finger to her, and then head to the other end of the bar, trying desperately to not look at my boss. I sneak a glance a few times, but realize he's not looking back. I reach the cooler, open it, and pull out a Bud Light. Cherry's smiling when I look at her. "What the fuck is that look for?"

"He watched you walk all the way down here," she says with a giggle. "I guess it's not as bad as I thought."

I force out a breath. "Whatever. On your router, there's a place in the back that looks like a hole, where you have to push a button. You'll need a pen or something small like that."

She eyes me. "Did you blog about it?"

I shrug. "Kind of."

"What did you say?" she asks impatiently with a little bounce. That must've looked great from the other end.

I tell her about the whole 'things I want' thought, which coincidentally, is the name of that particular blog, and she nods in agreement. I'm not even going to bother telling her about the other night and that I stood him up for dinner last night because I had to rescue my friend from a woman-beating asshole, all of which I chose *not* to blog about. Not that I had time for that last night.

"Any comments?"

"Several," I reply. "There was this one anonymous person who made an interesting comment too, totally different from the rest."

Her eyes light up. "Ooh, what'd it say?"

I bite my lower lip as I think about it. "The comment asked if I was willing to give the same, and then it said it is entirely possible to have such a situation, but only if both parties involved are willing to commit to it."

"Wow," she says and pulls back a little. "Did you reply to it?"

"Damn straight. I told Anon I'd happily commit to someone who isn't going to end up treating me like shit, but it'll happen anyway, so why bother."

Cherry laughs. "You go, girl. Did Anon reply back?"

"Yes, the fucker. It's obviously a man. He asked how I would know a man's going to treat me like shit when I won't even try." I rub my right temple to soothe the oncoming stress headache. "Seriously, I don't want to get hurt again. That last one about killed me. You saw me. I looked like shit for weeks!"

"And dropped about twenty pounds," Cherry states with a nod of her head.

"Well, stress is the best diet ever invented, isn't it?" I say, and grab a plastic cup to pour myself some water.

"No shit," she replies, and then her eyes light up again. "Hey, you don't think it was Clancy who was leaving those comments, do you? Did you reply again?"

I quirk a brow at her and glance down at him. "Yeah . . . I mean, no, I don't think it was Clancy, but yes, I replied back, saying it wasn't worth the effort and the broken heart, totally contradicting my wishes, mind you."

She giggles. "When did all of those comments take place?"

"The blog had been up half a day, I think."

"And when did Clancy go all weird on you?"

"Saturday night, when I walked out the door with Scott."

Cherry gets serious. "Did you check the comments yesterday and before you came into work tonight?"

"He seemed okay Sunday night, maybe a little off from lately, but tonight . . . ." My mouth drops open and I stare at her. She's absolutely right. The first comment came within a few hours of me posting the blog Saturday night. The others came on Sunday before my shift, which might explain why he acted the way he did Sunday night, trapping me against the bar and such. I haven't been able to check them today yet, but maybe he's reacting to my last comment on top of not calling him back. I knew I'd screw this up. Fucktard of the Year award right here over my head, please.

"Holy shit, Cherry, you surprise me every fucking day."

She winks at me. "It was Clancy, sweetie." She hops down and wanders off to Manny the DJ, who is setting up her song for the next stage dance.

But what if it wasn't? I sneak another glance at him and catch him looking as Nine Inch Nails' *Closer* starts to play for Cherry. No, it is NOT called *I wanna fuck you like an animal*. And really, I must talk to that woman about her song choices because that particular one is like the stripper's national anthem—every one of them uses it. I turn to watch her, and I'll be damned if I can't dance like *that*. I know the moves, but I'd like to reserve them for someone special, who's incidentally not talking to me right now for whatever reason. God, I'm stupid.

On top of all this, my days off are all over the damn place lately. I need some sort of schedule back in my life before I lose it and truly go psycho. I am so blogging tonight . . . and rechecking those comments for closer inspection.

I'm able to get out of the club earlier than usual, since Clancy's not around the rest of the evening and I don't have to worry about being alone with him. I head straight home to my waiting laptop. Hell, I'm just happy Sean didn't decide to make any kind of appearance tonight. I'm not certain I could've handled that after all this shit with Clancy and Jada.

Comfy clothes are necessary for homework, blogging, and such—a tank and around-the-house jeans, which means they're riddled with holes. I call them my Sunday jeans too.

The laptop buzzes to life while I fix myself a nice glass of wine and cheese and crackers for a snack. I love a good hearty red wine like cabernet or merlot. My family still owns a vineyard in Italy, and some of the best wine comes from there. I got this bottle in a sampler case as a Christmas gift. The last time I visited the vineyard was when I was a teen, but I haven't been back since. I should renew my passport and visit again. Uncle Ant (Anthony, in case it's not obvious) would love to see me, I'm sure.

I eat some creamy Havarti on buttery club crackers while waiting for the browser to load the homepage, and I'm off like a shot, surfing my way to my blog. I want to reread those comments, so when the page loads I click on *Things I Want* and scroll down. There's a new one at the bottom, also from an Anonymous commenter. It says, *then you don't deserve him,* posted late last night. Ouch! That stings. I do deserve Clancy. I click on [post comment] and type, *you're right, I don't* because I'm pissed about several things, mainly the comment, but also his giving me the cold shoulder tonight and not giving me the chance to explain what happened.

As Cherry said, I'm a damn dramatic Italian princess.

I start a new post on my *Foxy's Den* blog. Now what was I going to write? I click through the notes in my phone. Ah yes, there it is: *bitch about schedule.* I can't say anything about Clancy because he's possibly reading my blog, but he doesn't think I know that, so I'm going to bitch and see what happens.

Hey, you never know.

Teagan calls as I type away about my schedule and how I'd like at least one consistent day off.

"How's she doing?" I ask in regards to Jada.

"Okay, I guess," she replies. "Echo was perfect today. I'm so glad she had the day off."

"Good, I can't take her until next Monday now, unless you want me to watch her Thursday day." I reach for my wine. My hand hits the edge of the glass and it starts to wobble. I end up knocking the fucking glass over, jump up and scream in horror as wine splashes all over the keyboard of my laptop, which scares the hell out of Tonk, who was nestled in a bundle beside me on the couch. I unplug the laptop quick and press the power button, but it's too late; smoke rises from between the keys, and I can hear the sizzle.

Meanwhile, my phone is on the floor and Teagan's shouting.

I pick up the phone. "Oh. My. God. The fucking motherboard just fried into computer hell on my laptop."

"What the hell happened?"

"Shit. Jesus. Fuck." I stare at it for I don't know how long before I begin pacing, biting on my fake nails, circling the coffee table while Teagan talks me down from the oncoming anxiety attack. Finally, I sit in front of the toasted laptop and stare at it some more, like that's going to help bring it back.

This is the proof that I'm utterly addicted to my computer and the internet. I completely melt down and sob as Tonk licks up the wine from floor, table, and laptop. When I'm off the phone with Teagan—and she only lets me go because I've stopped crying and she could tell my breathing is closer to normal—I clean up what little mess there is and grab one of my spiral-bound notebooks, outright disgusted I have to revert to fucking storyboarding and writing my blog posts on paper. I have several blank notebooks originally intended for journaling, which I'm not very good at, and I haven't used one in the two years since I got the laptop.

I plop down on the sofa again and groan as I flip open the notebook. The laptop taunts me and I snatch up my phone to call support. They transfer me to someone who can help, who's just so helpful in telling me about a fifty gigabyte online storage that does me absolutely no good right now. Techie dude hooks me up with shipping my laptop in and an approximate return date, and when I'm done speaking with him I hang up the phone and lean back into the sofa.

"Damn it." My laptop will be gone for a week or more. That's going to make me crazy. Not to mention I won't be able to do any homework. My professor is going to kill me.

12

How You Remind Me

It takes all of one day to get me to that breaking point of insanity. I'm a damn mess at work, dropping everything I lay my hands on, breaking glasses here and there, and stumbling over my own feet. Another glass goes down, right in front of Clancy during a rare appearance. Luckily, it didn't break. Addiction is a bad thing.

"Fuck," I growl and clean it up. Once that's done, I press a hand against my right temple to stop the headache that's about to envelop my brain. I don't know if he's noticed, and right now I don't really care. I'm completely flustered.

He does notice because he asks, "Are you okay, Anna?"

Calling me by my first name just makes it worse, and I wave a hand, dismissing his question, and walk away to cash out a customer whose drink I didn't spill all over the bar. I won't receive good tips tonight, and it's Wednesday, so we're not quite dead but not really busy either. Another customer wants a bottle of beer, so I head over to the cooler to grab it. The edge of the opening in the cooler meets my head because I've leaned over too far. Clancy slides off his stool and comes around the bar. My throbbing head now has a full-on headache with a very sharp pain stabbing behind my left eye.

"What's going on with you?" he asks and takes my right arm in hand.

I shake my head and pull away by taking two steps back. "Nothing." I turn around to head to the other end of the bar and trip over my own damn feet. The beer flies up into the air, and I plummet to the mats on the floor and land hard on my arms. A second later, the bottle hits and shatters, and I quickly cover my head to save my face from glass fragments.

Beer sprays all over me and a sharp pain shoots up my left arm.

Clancy runs over and kneels next to me. "Shit, Anna, are you okay?"

I want to sob, but I hold it back and push myself up, with Clancy's unwanted help, to a seated position. I lean gingerly on my left arm, but it hurts like hell. My face contorts in pain and I bite my lower lip.

"Anna?" he says as he glides his hand down my right shoulder and arm.

I jerk my head up and look him dead in the eye. Then I raise my right hand and punch him solid in the center of his chest. He falls back hard against the cooler, eyes wide with shock as he sucks in a breath. He never expected that one and I have a pretty mean punch. He's now rubbing his chest as his shock turns into—I don't know what that expression is because I've never seen it before.

I just might get fired for this.

"Ouch, what the fuck was that for?" he snaps at me.

"Prince fucking Charming, my ass," I retort. I grab the ice bin above me and use my good hand to pull myself up. I stomp toward the restroom on the other side of the club to clean myself up, but as soon as I reach his normal seat, he comes up behind me and grabs my right upper arm. I protest. He walks me around the bar and into the back, and doesn't stop until we reach his office. He fumbles with keys, still holding me, as though he's afraid I'll bolt. Once he unlocks the door, he swings it open and points inside at the small couch.

"Sit down," he growls.

"I'd rather stand, thank you," I reply, even though I'm in a great deal of pain. It's my defiant nature.

He pushes me inside and I stumble. "Sit down," he yells, still pointing at the couch.

I glare up at him. "I do not respond to commands like that."

Clancy steps forward, sweeps me into his arms, and drops me on the couch. He turns back to the door and slams it so hard I'm certain everyone heard it over the music. He stomps to the filing cabinet and pulls a first aid kit from the top of it, and then comes back to sit next to me. He pops the first aid kit open and rummages through it.

I notice blood on my jeans. I raise my left arm to look at the damage; a huge chunk of glass protrudes from my arm, wedged underneath about two inches of skin. Its sharp point sticks out on the other side. Blood runs in rivers to my elbow and drips.

That's when the pain really hits me. He grabs a bottle of water from his mini fridge and a clean towel from on top of it. He drapes the towel over his lap and my arm over the towel, and inspects the glass fragment. I can see worry in his eyes. His thumb and forefinger take the fragment between them. He pulls the glass out. My gasp of pain stops behind my clenched teeth, and I close my eyes.

"Oh God, now it really hurts."

He moves the towel under my elbow and twists the water bottle's cap off with his teeth. Bloody water pours down my arm and onto the floor and my jeans. He shoves the bottle into my hand and presses the towel against the cut. I scream and try to move, but his hand on my knee keeps me in my seat.

"It fucking hurts!"

He looks into my tear-filled eyes. "I have to clean it, Nemy-girl, to make sure there's no more glass. You've been breaking shit left and right all night."

I suck in a strangled, whimpering breath, and blurt out, "I'm sor-r-r-ry."

"Shh, it's okay," he says softly.

The towel is soaked with blood. He throws it to the concrete floor and snatches another clean one from the top of the fridge.

"Pour the water on the towel," he says, trying to distract me.

I lift the bottle and pour, shaking. He steadies me with his left hand.

"Keep your arm up."

I raise it again, not realizing I'd lowered it.

"Good girl." The wet towel presses gently against my skin once more, and he dabs in careful motions.

I drop the empty bottle on the floor.

To my surprise, I'm not having an anxiety attack; my breathing has calmed and I'm able to watch him now. Normally, I'd be way too freaked out by something like this. I have to wonder why that is. Shock, probably. His eyes flick up now and then to mine.

"We should go to the hospital," he says.

I shake my head. "I don't wanna go to the hospital." My head hurts, and I wonder if I hit it on the floor when I fell.

"You might need stitches."

"I don't wanna go to the hospital," I repeat as someone knocks at the door.

"Hold this against it," he says and presses my right hand against my arm. He opens the door.

"Is she okay?" Cherry asks, worried.

"She won't go to the hospital."

She peers in and her eyes take in the details, and then return to Clancy. "I'm almost done with nursing school, Clancy. Let me look at her."

Clancy steps to the side, lets her into the cramped office, and quickly shuts the door again. She sits next to me in her skimpy school-girl outfit.

"Let me look, baby," she says in a sweet tone I've never heard come from her before. I let her take the towel and pull it back. "She's going to need stitches on the one side for sure," she says while looking up at him. "I can do it."

"Check the kit," he replies and sits on the edge of his desk, crossing his arms over his chest and his legs at the ankles.

I watch her as she fumbles through the kit. "I didn't know you were going to nursing school."

She looks up and smiles. "Sorry I didn't tell you, but I didn't want anyone to know." Her smile dims when she notices the pout on my face. "Really, baby, I'm sorry. I should've told *you*."

Cherry gets me cleaned up and stitched, and Clancy takes over so she can go back to work, or so he can be alone with me again. I'm not entirely sure which it is.

"You should still get an X-ray, at least," Clancy states as he bandages my arm per Cherry's instructions.

"I'll go tomorrow," I reply.

"I suppose . . . ."

A long silence enfolds us as he finishes up and puts the kit away, and I stare down at my arm. "*That* tattoo is ruined." A bolt of pain shoots through my head and I close one eye. A slow breath leaves my lips.

"Still in a lot of pain?" he asks and sits next to me again.

I nod. "Oh yeah." I don't think I've broken anything because I discover that I still have pretty good movement after wiggling my fingers, but I'll get the X-ray in case there's a small fracture or something. "My head is killing me too."

He leans back, opens a drawer in his desk, and pulls out a bottle of Maker's Mark. "Here, try this. It'll be faster than over the counter drugs." He takes off the cap before handing it to me.

I don't even flinch; I just grab the bottle and take about six swallows. This expensive bourbon whiskey is not meant to be drunk so fast, but he's correct about it working faster.

"Careful," he says and takes the bottle from me after I tip it up again. He takes a swig of it himself, and then caps it and sets it on the desk

I wipe my mouth. "God, I hate whiskey," I choke.

"Bourbon," he corrects.

"Whatever, it's the same thing."

He slips his hand into mine and caresses my fingers. "Are you going to tell me what's going on?"

I shake my head, not in answer, but in awe of my stupidity and carelessness. "I don't know."

"Why didn't you answer your phone the other night?" he asks, but then quickly adds. "I mean, if you really don't want to do this—"

I hold up my right hand. "I couldn't answer that night and didn't get your messages until I was on my way to work last night."

"Why, what happened the other night?" he asks and leans forward, concern washing over his face.

"Had to rescue a friend from her abusive boyfriend." My head's starting to feel a little foggy. Boy, that stuff sneaks up on you fast.

"Oh, shit. Nemy-girl, I'm sorry. You tried to tell me last night, did you? And I just ignored you and left."

My eyes meet his. "Why are you calling me that again?"

A huff of breath leaves his nostrils in a short silent chuckle and he rubs his chest. "I figured out you don't like Anna."

I shake my head.

"What else has you all flustered? You're not acting like yourself at all."

I think about the night's events and what precedes them. "You wouldn't believe it."

"Try me," he says, still caressing my hand.

I give him a half-cocked smile. "I killed my laptop by spilling a glass of wine on it."

He blinks rapidly. "You're breaking shit in my bar and slice your fucking arm open because of your laptop?"

"Yep," I bite my lower lip, quickly letting it go with a pop. "Ridiculous, isn't it?"

He stares at me a moment. "No, not really. All of your homework is on there, and you said you had a big project due. I can understand not being able to access it causing this kind of reaction."

My eyes flick up to his in surprise. "Really?"

He nods. "Can you storyboard and write on paper until it's fixed?"

"I tried; nothing's coming to me," I say with a shake of my head. "And I don't have time to go to the school computer lab."

The Clancy smile hits his cheeks; the one I haven't seen all night, and he laughs.

"You've a serious addiction there, Nemy-girl," he says and oh my God is that accent thick. I think he did it on purpose. He lifts his hand and pushes my hair back behind my ear with his fingers. "Why do you think you don't deserve me?"

Eyes wide, I stare at him. "You can't change gears on me like that. It's not fair."

"Answer the question."

"You've been reading my blog."

"Yes, I have for a long time now," he replies and the smile reappears. "I like the name."

"Are you my anonymous commenter?"

"Well, if I told you that, I wouldn't be anonymous," he says. "Now answer the question."

"Why, you said it first."

"I wanted to see what you'd say to it," he says and pauses, looking at our hands briefly before his eyes lock on mine again. "You disappointed me."

That hits the center of my chest so hard I want to throw up. Being a disappointment to Clancy is the one thing I've never wanted.

"Yes, well, I tend to do that a lot when it comes to men," I say. "Besides, I knew it'd piss you off." Shit, I just said that.

His right brow arches. "So you knew it was me then?"

"Uh, not really," I say and try to pull my hand away from his, but he clutches it tight. "I wasn't sure if it was or not. Just guessing and . . . fuck."

He lets out a short laugh and shakes his head. "Oh, Nemy-girl." He takes my chin in his hand. "You are the worst liar on the planet."

"No surprise there." I meet his eyes. "So, if you read my blog, you probably got that Prince Charming thing, huh?"

He laughs and rubs his chest again. "Yeah, I'm just glad it wasn't my face you hit."

"I couldn't do it," I say, and grin. "It's too pretty."

He laughs. "You can punch."

"Yes I can, and you can take a hit." I tilt my head back and roll it from one side to the other. The warmth of the Maker's Mark filters through my body. "Can I go home?"

"Not until you answer the question."

I'm silent for a while, but he waits. "I don't want to get hurt again. I don't need another man falling out of love with me after so many years, and having to start over once again. I can't do it anymore."

His face moves closer to mine. "Nemy-girl, men who can't love your creativity, along with the rest of you, are not worth having."

"Well, I know that *now*," I reply.

Closer, those delectable lips come, so close . . . . "I love your creativity."

I refocus on his eyes and stare hard into those emeralds. "You don't have to live with me. You don't have to endure lonely hours while I sit and work all hours of the night. *That* is the deal-breaker. *That* is what makes them go away. They don't realize it's like a second job to me." I can't believe he just said to me the one important thing I've wanted to hear and I just riddled it with holes.

He nods. "Okay, you can go home now." I look at him in question and he nods again. "Go on. I'll call you later to check on you, and I'm taking you in for the X-ray tomorrow."

I open my mouth to protest, but his fingers lift my chin in a quick movement.

He leans forward, his lips hovering over mine, the smell of bourbon between us. "There isn't a question, so there isn't an answer. *No* is not an option." He gives me a quick kiss on the lips and stands to help me up. "Do I need to have someone drive you?" he asks, and I wobble a bit. "That'd be a yes. Let's go." He leans over his desk and picks up a thin black portfolio, and then he turns back to me and opens the door. "Maybe I'll just drive you myself."

"You don't have to," I say and run into the doorjamb. "Ow." Without thinking, I rub my shoulder with my left hand, sending a burst of pain through my damaged arm. "Ow."

He laughs as he steadies me. "How much of that bottle did you drink?"

I stumble into the hall. "Equivalent to eight or nine shots, I think, maybe, I don't know," I reply and bounce off the far wall. "Okay, maybe I can't drive." Cherry walks through the door, coming in from the club. "Cherry!" I yell and throw my arms around her neck. "Ow!"

The look on her face is incredulous. Her eyes flick to Clancy when she catches me. "What did you do to her?"

Clancy laughs. "Apparently she drank about nine shots of my Maker's Mark in two swallows."

Cherry's mouth pops open. "She hasn't eaten anything all night!"

Clancy's frowns. "Oh, that's bad."

"Oh my God, Clancy," she admonishes.

I reach up and caress her face. "Shh, Christine, it's okay." Then my eyes wander down her frame to view the six-inch heels on her feet and I grin when I look her in the eye again. "Damn, those things make you as tall as me."

"Help me get her out there," Clancy suggests with a nod to the front. Cherry wraps her arm around my waist while Clancy takes my left arm at the bicep, and we all go through the door together sideways. He points to a stool next to the bar and they walk me over to it and sit me down. "I'm going to take her home. Watch her a minute so I can tell Scott what's happening."

Cherry nods and he walks away. She looks down at me and shakes her head. "Oh Nemesis, you're trouble."

I giggle at the name she used because I don't hear that one often. I wrap my arms around her tiny waist again. "I love you." I jerk my left arm back a bit. "Ow."

"Hasn't quite taken full effect yet, has it?" she asks with a giggle.

"Don't worry, I'm getting there." My head is resting comfortably on her ample bosom and I crane my head back to look up at her. "Please don't let him take me home. I don't know what I might do to the man."

She giggles again. "Maybe you *should* go home with him. You've got enough liquid courage in you."

"That's what I'm afraid of," I say and lay my head down once more.

"Don't worry," she says while running her fingers through my hair. "Clancy's a perfect gentleman."

I look up again and grin. "You didn't see him unzip my corset Saturday night with that evil little glint in his eyes."

"And why, pray tell, did he do that?"

I giggle. "He got the cherry out."

She laughs hard, but stops in a hurry when Clancy returns to us.

He eyes her with piqued curiosity.

Cherry just grins and helps me to my feet. "Come on, girlie. Off you go." She passes me over to Clancy. By now he's holding my coat and bag, and he throws the coat over my shoulders and takes my arm.

"Wait, wait, wait," I say as I turn into Clancy in an attempt to get back to Cherry. My right arm goes up, and after hitting his arm a few times, I finally get it right and beckon her closer with my fingers. "I want to tell you something."

"What is it, baby?" she asks and steps close.

My head tilts to the side uncontrollably and I whisper, "I want you to know that you and Angelina Jolie are the only two women I'd fuck."

She giggles and covers her mouth as her eyes dart up to Clancy, who's rolling his eyes and chuckling at my statement. "My, Nemy, I've never seen you like this." She leans forward to whisper in my ear.

"Well then come home with me. Clancy won't mind."

"Come on, let's go," Clancy says and tries to turn me around. I stumble into him.

"Go on, Nemy," Cherry says. "Before you embarrass yourself."

I look back at her. "I don't think it's possible to embarrass myself further . . . farther . . . further?"

"Oh, yes it is," she states and pushes me forward. "Go home. I'll call you tomorrow."

When we hit the entrance to the club, Scott snickers at me, so I flip him off. He laughs outright this time and I lunge a step toward him. He flinches back into the wall and I almost head to the floor again.

Clancy grabs me once more, catching me before I fall flat on my face. "No fighting."

"He started it," I say as he drags me through the door.

He gets me out of the club and into his car, and I drop my head back against the seat. He climbs in and gets the car started, and then looks in my direction. "You okay?"

I nod a little sluggish and open my eyes. "Did I just tell Cherry I'd fuck her?"

"Yes, you did," he replies with that fucking devilish grin of his.

"Wow," I say and lean my head back again. "You're in trouble."

Clancy just laughs and drives out of the parking lot. I think it's somewhere around midnight, but I can't be certain. The night's getting a little fuzzy and I find myself staring at the car's ceiling for a good portion of the ride. Damn, that bourbon is strong.

Will I blog about this? Probably not. I don't have a fucking computer anyway.

13

Something I Can Never Have

We go through a drive-thru and I eat some nasty cheeseburger at some point during the ride home. I don't usually eat fast food, but when I've been drinking I crave the grease and nastiness of it. I just don't always give in to the craving. I think it was Clancy's idea anyway.

When we pass the airport, Clancy taps my arm because I probably look like I'm sleeping. "Which exit?"

I crack open an eye to see where we are and discover he's passed Priest already. "Rural," I reply and look at the lights that stretch across the two Tempe Bridges. One of the bridges is ancient; the other is about twenty years or so old. My eyes flick up to see the star and wise men that have sat on top of A Mountain every Christmas I can remember since we moved here, and nostalgia sweeps through me because I won't be spending the coming holiday with my family. Not that I've spent any holidays with them in the last few years. I'm not even sure where mom and dad are right now because I haven't spoken to them in a long time. I should probably ask one of my brothers. One of them is bound to still communicate like the good little Catholic boys they are.

Clancy takes the exit for Rural and I direct him through Arizona State University and downtown Tempe. I live in an old neighborhood, one filled with a ton of college students, in a house I inherited from my grandmother. My dad had the house built for her in 1952.

I absolutely love my house. It's a tiny three-bedroom, one bath, painted white with brown trim, and sits on a very large lot of land. Tonk loves it too, but he hates the pool and runs from me anytime I go in for a swim. I guess I've tried too many times to drag his ass in there, but I need to be sure the damn dog can swim and find his way out.

He can.

Clancy pulls onto my long barren driveway and parks the Beamer. I stumble trying to climb out of the vehicle, and he takes my right arm to help. Then he leans in beside me to grab my bag while I pat down my coat pockets searching for the keys. He pushes me aside so he can shut the car door as I drag my keys from a pocket, and he locks his beautiful car and sets the alarm. I start to lean a bit too far to the right and Clancy grabs my arm again with a shake of his head and a chuckle.

"Come on," he says and leads me to the front door.

I attempt to force the key in the lock, but it's just not going in. After a few more attempts, while Clancy laughs behind me, I hold the keys up. "Ah, wrong one."

Clancy laughs again.

"Shut up." I slide the correct key in the deadbolt and turn it. Then I repeat with the doorknob, and the door creaks open.

Tonk waits for me, happily wagging his tail. For him, this is usually a sign of happiness, but when Clancy steps in behind me, I see an adjustment in the wag as his ears go straight up. That's bad. A low rumble sounds in Tonk's throat, and I step in front of him and touch his head.

"It's okay, Tonk," I say and pet him. I turn back to Clancy, who's placing my bag on the sofa, and I hold out my hand. "Give me your hand." Clancy does so and I pull him to me. He stumbles because I've pulled so hard. "He's okay, Tonk." The dog takes a step toward us and raises his nose to Clancy's hand while I'm holding it. Then he sniffs and it takes a minute before he's calmed down and Clancy can pet him. "He's my protector."

"I can see that," Clancy replies. "Can I move now?"

I giggle while pulling my coat off. "Yes."

"Good." He turns away from Tonk after running his hand over the top of the dog's bulky head.

When I turn around from hanging the coat on a hook, he's reaching into my bag. "What are you doing?"

He pulls out the portfolio and beckons me over with a nod of his head to the side. "Come here." He sits down, and I sidle past him, stumble a little and fall down next to him on the sofa, my legs twisting like a damn pretzel. I untangle them and try to sit up straight without much success. Damn couch.

Clancy sets the portfolio down, clicks a button and opens it up. It's a goddamn laptop.

"Holy shit, that thing's thin," I say, astonished at the slim design. "I want one!"

Clancy chuckles and turns it on. He then looks at me, his head tilting down and to the side, which has his hair just flowing perfectly over his shoulder in onyx waves. I lick my lips.

"The rule is no food or drink near it," he says. "Got it?"

I frown. "What do you mean?"

"I'm letting you borrow this until you get a new one."

"Mine'll be back next week sometime, I hope." There's a little too much excitement in my voice for that, but whatever.

"Well then, until yours is repaired."

"Really?" I ask, eyes growing wide.

"Yes," he says with a nod. "No food or drink."

"Gotcha." I watch it hum to life. "Why are you doing this?"

"Because if it's going to take a week or more for you to get your laptop back and be able to work, you're going to cost me a fortune in broken glasses and medical bills." He smirks. "I'll write down the password for you."

I look into his green eyes and smile. "Thank you."

He nods. "Can't stop the work flow. The power cord is in your bag." Then he leans back against the sofa and stretches his arms out across the back while the computer boots up. There's a look on his face as he watches me that I can't quite decipher, probably due to the Maker's Mark. "Nice place, Nemy-girl."

I smile again. "Thanks."

"Paper?"

"Huh? Oh!" I put my hand out for my bag. He hands it to me and I sift through it to find my notebook and a pen. I pass them to him, and he writes something down, folds the paper in half after ripping it out of the notebook, and places it on top of the notebook with pen and sets them all on the coffee table. Then he starts to scoot to the edge of the sofa, hesitating briefly mid-way as though he doesn't feel like moving any further.

"I have to get back to the club before Scott freaks out, since there's no one bartending," he says and amazingly that wasn't a jibe at me. "I'll call you tomorrow and take you back to get your car, okay?"

I nod as he forces himself to stand, and I rise to meet him. "Thanks again, Clancy."

He smiles and turns to me, and runs his hand down my right arm. "No problem. Just don't fry it like you did yours." He leans over and kisses me on the cheek, and then turns to the door. "Night."

"Night," I say in a stunned daze. Did I really have a conversation with him in his office about us? Crap. Once he leaves, I walk over and lock the door. Then I return to the sofa, sit down, and I reach for the folded piece of paper. There's only one word written in handwriting too beautiful to be a man's, taunting me because he's left now.

Nemy-girl

"Holy shit," I say aloud and look at the laptop. I run my fingers over the mouse pad, type in the password, and then I wait for it to finish loading the desktop. Clancy has wallpaper. One of my online profile pictures sits in the center of the screen; one that doesn't really show a clear image of my face as it's mostly hair, but there it sits and I'm slack-jawed upon seeing it. I turn around and peer through the blinds to find he's already backed out of my driveway. I won't be able to discuss this tomorrow with him because the bourbon will have worn off. But hey, I can work now and I'm so going for it once I upload everything from my online storage.

Nemy is a very happy girl . . . and not one fucking bit sober at this point. Maybe I shouldn't work on my project. Blogging, it is!

It's around noon when I wake up with a splitting headache, which approximates to about ten hours of sleep, since I passed out around two in the morning. That's perfectly normal for me—the ten hours of sleeping, not the alcohol-induced passing out or the splitting headache.

I get a call from Clancy around three in the afternoon and his voice has a dread to it that resonates in my ears once he tells me what's happened. "Your car was stolen."

"Fuck," I say because my registration was in the damn car and it has my address on it. My Glock was in there too. This doesn't make for a very happy Nemy-girl. I tell him not to bother with coming to get me, since I have no fucking car to pick up because now I have to call the police and my insurance company.

He argues. "I *am* coming to get you because I'm taking you in for an X-ray."

"Oh Jesus, Clancy," I say with a roll of my eyes. Yeah, like he can see that on the phone.

"Don't roll your eyes at me."

I stiffen and look around my living room. "Did you plant a camera in my house last night or something?"

He laughs. "No, but that's not a bad idea."

"Seriously, you don't need to come over. My arm is fine."

"Just want to be sure," he replies. "I'll be there in ten minutes."

I scan the clock. "What? You can't give a girl time to get ready?"

"If you stop talking, you'll have plenty of time to get ready," he says with a laugh.

I growl at him, and say, "Fine, bye." I can hear his laughter when I hang up on him. I'm still in my around-the-house jeans and a tank top, no bra, not the best thing for Clancy to see me in right now. Not to mention I'm not wearing any make-up and my hair is pulled back in a bun. I have to make a decision. Make-up and hair first. By the time I'm finished with hair and make-up, my doorbell rings. Has it been ten minutes already? Jesus. I run out completely forgetting I'm not wearing a bra and only the tank and jeans, and I open the door.

"I still have to change," I say in a hurry while turning back to the bedroom.

"Nice pants, Nemy-girl," he says with a chuckle when he steps inside and closes the door.

"Hush," I reply and disappear down the hall. Tonk moves in to greet him while I change, and in a few minutes, I'm dressed and ready to go.

"Wow, a woman who can be ready in fifteen minutes," he says. "I'm impressed."

"Doesn't take much to impress you," I quip.

He smiles and his eyes give me the once over. "I kind of liked the tank top and other jeans."

"Shut up." If he were any closer to me, I'd smack him on the arm. I grab my bag from the sofa and head for the door instead.

He drives me to an imaging place in Mesa, and after they take their pictures, don't see anything wrong with my arm just like I thought, I return to the lobby with a smile on my face.

"We're good to go," I say to him when he stands.

"Nothing's broken or fractured?"

"Not a thing," I reply. "Now, I have to call the police about my car."

Clancy pulls a card from his shirt pocket. "Call this officer." He hands it to me. "I didn't know all of your information on the car. He's expecting a call from you."

"You called the police?" I ask and stare at the card.

He shrugs. "It did happen on my property. I just thought I'd get a jump on it for you."

"Thanks," I reply and look up at him as we're leaving the imaging place. I run into a corner of wall and grunt. "God, seriously, you'd think I was still freakin' drunk."

Clancy laughs and takes my left arm in hand. "You're an accident waiting to happen, woman."

"No kidding."

He safely leads me outside. "Didn't you work on anything last night?" he asks as we walk to his car.

"Yes and no, but it doesn't mean I'm not a klutz at times." I walk up to the passenger door, digging through my purse for my phone. "Besides, I don't even remember what I worked on. I should go look at that later." He unlocks the door in the midst of laughing at me, and I dial the number on the card.

"You wrote a post."

I look up at him over the top of the car. "I did?"

He nods.

"What was it about?"

"You professed your undying love for me."

I knit my brow for a millisecond before I say, "Oh, shut up."

Clancy laughs and the officer answers as I'm climbing into the vehicle. "Hi, my name is Anna Mussolini, and my boss says you're expecting my call about my Saturn that was stolen last night from The Fox Den?"

"Mussolini, huh?" the officer says.

"No relation." I honestly have to say that every time I tell someone my last name. It's annoying as all get out. I should have just kept my married name for all the trouble the maiden one causes me. Of course, the maiden name does have its perks.

"Do you have the VIN and plate numbers?"

"Yes, hang on a sec." I search through my purse again. "Here it is." Once I'm done giving the officer all the information he needs, I hang up and my stomach growls. "I'm hungry."

"Where would you like to go?" Clancy asks.

"I don't know. Sushi sound good?"

Clancy nods. "Delicious."

"There's a RA restaurant on Mill by my house."

Once we arrive at the restaurant, we grab a booth and order drinks—a White Russian for me and a Maker's Mark on the rocks for him, which sends a shudder through me upon hearing it—and we look over the sushi menu together.

"How's your arm?" Clancy asks, dipping an edamame pod in soy sauce.

"Itches," I reply. "Thanks for reminding me because I'd forgotten all about it."

He chuckles as he pulls the pod out of his mouth and drops it in the bowl. "No problem."

I stare down at the table. "I can't believe my car got stolen. This sucks." I look back up at him. "Think it was just a random car theft?" Growing up with my family, my mind will perpetually go to that place, always questioning who, what and why.

He sets his drink down and looks at me from under hooded eyes. "I wanted to talk to you about that." He stares at his glass as he turns it on the table in a slow circle. "Nemy-girl, people leave my property alone, so I'm wondering if maybe you pissed someone off."

I give him a shocked look and put my hand to my chest. "*Moi*? Never."

He laughs. "Ri*iii*ght."

"Okay, seriously, not to the point of them stealing my car. At least, I don't think so."

"Do you think it could have been Jeremy?" He studies my face like he's trying to memorize every detail. "I mean, you haven't taken his calls, have you?"

I frown. "I'll kill him if it was." I bring my drink toward me and take a long pull on the straw. "Besides, that asshole left me, remember?"

"But did you do anything afterward that would've pissed him off?"

I shrug. "It's possible. I have a bad temper." I bring the past events into the forefront of my mind and laugh. "Oh yeah, I forgot about that."

Clancy's right brow pops up. "What?"

I giggle. "I . . . um . . . burned a bunch of his stuff that he left behind, some of which included collectible Hot Wheels and vintage pin-up posters. Teagan helped me. She likes to play with fire."

"Ouch!" Clancy says. "Remind me not to piss you off."

"Well, he left them behind, so they must not have been too important to him. I found the picture I'd taken a few months ago and sent it to him."

"He knows where you work, right?"

I nod. "Yeah, I started two weeks before he left, remember?"

"Yes I do," he says softly while staring into his glass, and I'm not sure what to make of the tone in his voice. It sounds like a bad memory hit him.

I grab my drink again. "Well, whatever, either way I'm without a damn car."

"Care to borrow one of mine? It'll be cheaper than a rental."

I look up at him. "How many cars do you have?"

"A few," he says with a shrug, and then grins. "You can borrow the truck."

I know he's talking about that old beater because he knows I've seen it.

"I need something reliable, thanks," I reply.

"It is reliable. Just because it looks like crap doesn't mean it won't run for you."

"And something with heat too." I grab my drink for a big sip. At this rate, I'll be buzzed before the food comes out.

"It has heat."

I take a large mouthful of White Russian that is much bigger than a sip, and swallow. "Sounds like it'd be a gas guzzler."

"It's not too bad." He snatches another pod from the bowl. "I keep my vehicles running smoothly." He then pauses before putting the pod in his mouth. "Though it's nothing like driving that little Saturn of yours. Might take you a while to get used to the power." The pod disappears, except for the end he's holding.

"Oh right, what's it got in it, a three-fifty?"

His right brow quirks up and he swallows his food. "Yes it does."

"Then I can handle it." He's still giving me the same look, which now translates to an 'oh really', little shit. "I'll have you know I'm a car girl. I've had numerous Bugs and have taken their engines out and apart many times."

He chuckles. "That's not a car; that's a grocery-getter."

"It's a fast car when you drop a twenty-two hundred cc engine in it." Now both eyebrows are up. Good, I've shocked the man. "Besides, that little Saturn had turbo. That's why I bought it and not the Solstice."

My eyes drift to my watch.

"In a hurry?" Clancy asks and takes a sip of his drink.

"Girls' night out, remember? It's Teagan's birthday."

He nods. "That's right." A smirk hits his lips. "Where are you going?"

"I don't know," I say with a shrug. "They never tell me until I get in the car."

"Why's that?"

I smile. "So I don't bitch about it."

"Do you bitch a lot?"

"Constantly."

"You don't so much at work."

The server brings the wontons and rolls to our table. I ask for another White Russian and smile again. "I'm a wholly different person at work."

He grins. "I'm noticing that."

We stare at each other a moment, until I'm uncomfortable and look at the table. "Anyway, I need to be home in an hour so I have time to get ready."

He chuckles. "To primp yourself for your man-hunt?"

I bark out a laugh that was probably too loud for the setting. "Oh, I have no intentions on hunting anything tonight."

Clancy doesn't say a damn word; he just sits there grinning like a little boy. It makes me wonder what in the hell is going through his mind. My new drink arrives and I snatch it up for a sip.

"No man-hunting," he finally says. "Why is that?"

I shrug. "Just not interested in anything right now." I'm praying to God he doesn't bring up Saturday and Sunday nights, but I should be so lucky. I finish my drink in two large swallows and order another one while he stares at the table and picks at the edamame.

Silence stills between us, trapping us in a bubble as other patrons continue their chatter. The clink of ice against glass and the clack of wooden chopsticks from the two dueling behind me fill the air. Welcome to college town.

Surprisingly, he doesn't broach the subject of our relationship . . . or whatever the hell it is.

Once we've finished our meal, Clancy pays—I made several attempts to snake the bill from his hands, to no avail—and we leave the restaurant to walk back to his car. Unfortunately, we have to walk past Fascinations—an adult store—on our way because it's two doors down from the restaurant.

Clancy grabs my arm, bringing me to a halt in front of the store. "Need anything … for tonight?" he asks while nodding at the shop.

"Shut up!" I yank my arm out of his hand.

His laughter travels down the street, it's so loud, and he catches up to me as I walk away. "Come on, let's go inside."

"No. I don't need anything in there."

"*Mar sin é*?"

I turn my head quickly. "What?"

"Is that so?"

I nod. "Yeah, I have . . . never mind." He does *not* need to know about my massaging showerhead or B.O.B.

This produces loud laughter and he bends over from it. "Oh, shit." He straightens and jumps in front of me, walking backwards. "Tell me what you have, Nemy-girl."

Shit. I push him. Ah hell, maybe it'll shut him up. "Who needs a man when one has a massaging showerhead? Besides, I already have a toy and it works just fine, thank you."

The shocked look is all I need to feel satisfied, along with the little stumble in his step, and that little boy grin hits his face in full force. "I don't know what to say." Yep, I have rendered the man speechless. Awesome. He hops to his left and does a quick turn to walk beside me again. "You've surprised me, Nemy-girl."

"Thank you," I say with a nod as a short bow.

He leans toward me. "All men aren't bad, you know."

That came out of nowhere. Sneaky bastard.

"The ones I keep finding are." I look both ways and start to cross the street.

"It's not the ones you keep finding. It's the ones you keep choosing."

"Which is exactly why I'm not choosing any more of them," I say once we get to the other side of Mill Avenue.

He takes my hand. "What if a man chooses you?"

Oh shit. "The ones who choose me are usually creepy or have something weird going on," I say when we near the tavern Teagan works at that sits on the edge of Hayden Square Amphitheatre. I can't get my hand away from his; he's holding it tight and fast.

"Like?"

"Like owning a strip club," I quip, but would love to say 'Like Sean.' Yeah, he's a damn good example of creepy.

He chuckles. "And what if that man were to not own a strip club?"

"Yeah right," I say with a laugh. "Then I'd have to concern myself with some other weird aspect of said man."

"But what if said man doesn't have any?"

We pass the tavern and he still has hold of my hand. I'm thinking I may not ever get it back.

"That alone is strange and curious," I reply.

"You're impossible to please."

"In more ways than you know," I reply with a grin. "Someone commented on my blog recently and said that I'd be waiting a long time if I wanted what I'm looking for in a man."

"I don't doubt it with your high standards," he remarks. "And I saw the comment."

"You must have another computer at home then."

He nods. "Of course, I wouldn't have loaned you my laptop otherwise."

"Thanks," I say with a small amount of sarcasm.

"No problem." He gives my hand a squeeze. "I just would've had to buy you a new one."

"Oh, shut up," I say as we near the garage. "I wouldn't have allowed you to do that."

His laughter hits the garage and echoes. "I don't need your permission for that."

"Oh, so do you buy the other girls gifts?" His car is in sight.

"I helped Christine out with nursing school," he replies.

My mouth drops open in shock. "Really?"

He nods while I'm staring up at him. "Yes. She doesn't belong in my club."

"No, she doesn't, but I didn't think . . ." I stop myself from going any further with that statement.

"What, that I didn't notice that about her?" he asks. "Christine comes from a wealthy family and had a little falling out with them."

"Yeah, I know," I say when we reach his car.

He turns to me. "I know you do. It's the only reason I said it. Otherwise, I don't discuss my employees' personal lives with others."

"Does she have to pay you back?"

"Down the road, yes. We have a contract, at her insistence because I didn't ask her to pay me back."

He didn't ask for repayment? Wow. "That was really nice of you, Clancy."

"Thank you." He stretches out his arm, pointing to the passenger side of his car. "Get in, Nemy-girl. I'll get you home so you can get ready for tonight."

"Thanks," I say and walk to the door.

When Clancy drops me off, he doesn't get out. He just gives me a quick kiss on the cheek, tells me to have fun tonight, and then he drives off with a wave. I guess a real kiss is just wishful thinking. Didn't we make up?

I walk inside shaking my head.

Jesus, I don't even know what I want anymore.

14

Not in Rivers, But in Drops

The girls pick me up in a limo again and the first thing Echo asks is, "Where's your car?" Katy is with her tonight. Sweet. Too bad I don't need a wing-girl, but holy shit, Kennadi made it out.

"Got stolen last night from the club after Clancy drove me home."

"Motherfuckers," Kennadi spits, which is unbecoming of her beautiful features, but hell, I swear too, so fuck it. "I'd kick some serious ass over that. Any clues as to who the little shits are?" Her hand slides into the right back pocket of her Dickies pants, searching for her knife, I'm sure, but she comes back empty-handed. This leaves a sneer on her face. Kennadi doesn't like not having her knife with her, and she can't have it on her person where we're going. Truthfully, I'm surprised she hasn't hidden it in her boot . . . which she probably has. I shake my head in reply and smirk at her frustration.

Alanna passes a drink down to me. I throw it back and gag. "What the fuck is this?" Alanna shrugs, but I see Jada holding up the bottle. "Seriously, are you trying to kill me?" It's Jim Beam. "Whose idea was it to bring that shit?"

"Steal that from asshole?" Kennadi asks Jada, who smirks, just a little. Jada's with us because it's Teagan's birthday. Otherwise, she'd probably have stayed at the apartment and one of us would have stayed with her.

Teagan busts out laughing and slaps my knee. "God damn, Nems, what's got you in a mood, and what the hell happened to your arm?"

"My car has me in a mood." I look down at the fresh bandage. "And I fell last night behind the bar and a piece of glass went through it. Fun."

"Don't you clean up every night?" Echo asks.

"Yes, but I'd been breaking shit all night because I was all freaked out about my stupid laptop getting fried."

Lillian giggles. "Oh Nemy, what are we going to do with you?"

"Take me out and shoot me before I kill myself," I reply, then glare at Kennadi. "Don't even think about it." She smirks, and they all laugh, which pulls a chuckle from me. "Where to tonight?"

Teagan grins. "We're going to Dos Gringos again, since you had so much fun the last time."

"Wonderful, but I'd rather hit the Irish pub next to it. I hope that guy isn't there again. That's all I fucking need right now." I look at Teagan. "He came to my work and asked me, in front of Clancy, if I wanted to fuck. Seriously?"

"Did you?" Kennadi asks, twirling a lock of burgundy hair around her pale finger. She and Teagan could seriously be twins, I swear. "Wanna fuck him, that is."

"No, she wants to fuck Clancy," Alanna says.

Kennadi's grin beams across her face. "Better hurry up with that shit before I make a trip down to your club."

"Kennadi, as much as I love you, girl, I'd fucking kill you if you showed up at my club." I smile sweetly at her and she laughs. "You'll be wearing that knife of yours and I don't mean as an accessory."

Katy laughs loudly, says, "Omigod!" and then covers her mouth with her hands.

Alanna laughs and says, "Wow, jealous much, Nems?"

"Shut it," I reply.

"So, how are things going with Clancy?" A little devilish grin stretches across Alanna's Latino-Irish face that I'd really like to slap the hell off.

"Places I don't care for them to go." This gets all of their undivided attention, so now I have to tell them *everything*. Bitches. I really need to learn to keep my mouth shut, but maybe it'll keep Kennadi away from Clancy. Yeah, I doubt that too.

After I've told them all that's happened recently, Teagan starts doing a little dance in her seat. "Ooh, Nemy's got a boyfriend."

I glare at her. "Say it again, Teags, and I'll kick your ass." She sticks her tongue out at me. "Watch it. There are two lesbians in the car."

"Oh yeah, and I love tongue," Katy quips. "Sure you know how to use that, Teagan?"

Teagan flips her tongue up and down at Katy, and then says, "You've got a woman."

"I'm sure she'd enjoy it too," Katy replies with a smirk.

I laugh. "Watch out, Katy, she might hurt you."

Katy shrugs. "It's cool, I like pain." She is one odd cookie. Katy is akin to a little Goth girl with straight black hair, pulled up in two ponytails, and she's decked out in purple and black plaid, black fishnets, and purple Doc Martens that rise to her knees tonight. She could be my twin with her black pageboy haircut, except she's shorter than me.

Kennadi laughs. "Hey, I like her, Echo."

"You can't have her," Echo replies and grabs Katy's hand. Whenever Kennadi's around, it's best to keep an eye on your significant other or they'll end up with her someway, somehow. I wasn't joking about the thing with Clancy. I'd seriously kick the girl's ass and I'm not even certain I want the man yet. But this is one of the reasons that Kennadi isn't a BFF. I tend to not get along with bitches like her—the boyfriend-stealing kind. However, the fact that, aside from the SO stealing, she's just like me has me cool with her. Besides, she hates drama queens as much as I do and has no problem kicking one's ass.

During this exchange, I'm watching Jada take drink after drink from the Jim Beam bottle. "Somebody take that shit away from her."

Lillian snatches it from her grasp.

The next time I see James, I'm kicking his ass. Jada's still meek as hell, even though she moved in with Teagan. The man is *not* happy about it, either. He's left threatening messages on Teagan's and Jada's voicemails. So far, we've been able to keep Jada from him. I'm not sure how much longer this will be possible. She's starting to crack.

Maybe I should just have my dad take care of him. No, bad idea. Jada's got to learn how to do some of this herself without us cleaning up her messes constantly.

The limo pulls up to Dos Gringos and we all filter out. As usual, men gawk, we ignore as we file into the club, and I grab a table and a server. I know about half of the bar and wait staff by now. The next thing I do is scan the crowd for Killian because I don't like surprises. He gets me anyway by coming from behind and slapping my ass. I must've missed him on the patio. Damn it.

"Don't do that," I snap while turning around. "You almost got punched."

He laughs. "Oh, but to be punched by you, Nemy, would be a good thing."

I quirk a brow at him. "Into a little S&M, are we?"

"Into whatever the hell you like."

I let out a heavy sigh with a roll of my eyes. "You're not fucking me, Killian. Get that through your hard Irish skull already." This is getting old. "And don't you ever again ask me in front of my boss if I want to fuck! He nearly killed you."

"I'm just fucking with ya," he says and laughs hard. Jackass. "I noticed he has a thing for you."

"Right, like anything's gonna happen when I keep fucking it up," I reply and shake my head.

"Never know," he says and pulls his damn phone out to text someone.

"Dude, I think that thing may need to be surgically removed from you. Are you texting my boss or what?"

He grins and downs his beer. "I'll be right back." And he wanders off.

Weird.

The server brings the first shots and drinks, and I raise my shot glass. "Happy birthday, Teagan!"

We're having a grand time as the night moves on, dancing and drinking. Even Jada shows a glimpse of her old self, pre-James, now and then, which has my hopes up. More men than I can count hit on us, and with my rejections—the most sarcastic I can come up with—they crawl away with tails between their legs, which Killian finds hilarious.

"That amuses you, huh?" I ask as I bump into his arm and almost knock his phone from his hand. Good lord. I'm a bit tipsy by now.

"Only because it's not me looking like a jackass at this point," he replies with a chuckle.

I laugh—well, no, cackle would be more apropos—and hit him on the arm. "Hey, you're not so bad, Killian." He gets a gleam in his eye. "Don't go there."

Out of the corner of my eye, I spot a friend. "Hayden!" I so have ADD, especially when alcohol factors into the equation.

"Nemy!" he shouts back and his arms circle my waist when he jumps over to me. The man has a ton of energy. I want just a smidgen of it so I don't have to sleep ten goddamn hours.

"It's Teagan's birthday," I tell him and he grins.

"Cool," he says and runs off to the bar. He's probably getting her a shot of Jameson—one of his many drinks of choice. I'm wondering what the hell he's doing in Scottsdale because he's rarely up here unless there's a bike ride going on—bicycles, not motorcycles. The man will ride sixty miles just for the hell of it. Insane.

I lean back across the table. "Alanna, Hayden's here!"

"Where?" she asks and looks around. She has a crush on him. Hayden is a few inches shorter than I am, has sweet blue eyes and light brown hair with a bit of grey distinguishing his beard.

"Went to the bar, probably to buy Teagan a birthday drink," I reply and stand straight again. I suddenly jump when my phone rings. "Jesus." I pull the phone out to see who's calling me.

"You really shouldn't leave that thing on excite," Teagan remarks.

"Ha, ha," I say while answering the phone because it's Clancy. "Hello?" I can't hear him. "Hang on." I finish my drink fast and head for the patio. "Hello?"

"I tweed chew to some bin," Clancy says.

"What?" I ask, because that phrase just doesn't make any sense.

"I need you to come in," he yells into my ear and I quickly pull the phone away.

Then I bring it to my lips and shout back. "Are you fucking kidding me? Do you know how much I've had to drink?" The people around me laugh and I'm just so overjoyed to be their entertainment. "Tell my boss I'm too fucked up to work," I say and hold out the phone.

They all shout the phrase in unison. Seriously, I could've done that. Oh wait, I just did.

"Did you hear that? It's not gonna happen," I say. "You knew this was girls' night out!"

"Would you stop yelling? *I* can hear *you* just fine," he shouts in a huff.

"Sorry, I've had quite a few shots of multiple things. And some beers, I think."

"Are you okay?"

"I'm fine." I wave my hand, like he can see that. "The girls got a limo. No driving for Nemy tonight. Oh wait, I don't have a car anymore." The people near me find that funny. "And several people are laughing at me now. Am I being funny?"

"Funny-looking, Nemy-girl."

"Smartass. I must be something because several guys seem to want to fuck me tonight."

"Don't put down your drink!"

"Thank you, Captain Obvious!" Laughter once more ensues from the tables surrounding me.

"Do I need to come rescue you?" he asks. "Go someplace quieter so I don't have to yell."

I look around and walk over to the gate. "I'm gonna step out for a bit," I say to the bouncer, and he nods and laughs at me. There's no cover, so it really doesn't matter what I do as long as I don't bring alcohol with me. "Okay, I'm away from loud-ass music now. What's up?"

"Seriously, Nemy-girl, do I need to come down there?" His tone is much softer now, but I hear an echo.

"No, I can handle it." I step next to the street and lose my footing on the curb that seemed much farther away, and I stumble. "Whoa! Fuck!"

A muffled laugh comes through the phone. "What's happening?"

"I almost fell into the street."

"I'm coming down there," he says, and judging from his tone, if I can be any kind of judge tonight, he's serious.

"No, you're not. I don't need a babysitter!" I mean, hell, my words aren't even shlurring yet. Wait . . . .

"Sounds to me like you do, what with guys wanting to fuck you and all."

I sigh heavily. "Why are you calling me? You can't need someone at" —I look at my phone to check the time— "midnight? Are you serious? You're closing in two hours!" By this time, one of my many suitors has found me and stands near the entrance, and it's not Killian. "Shit," I say in a hushed tone.

"What?" Clancy asks.

"Guy who wants to fuck me found me again," I tell him, cupping my hand over the phone and my mouth.

"Probably has something to do with that getup you're wearing." Tonight, it's another backless shirt showing off my Fuck-me Art.

It takes me a minute to comprehend that remark, but I turn in a circle, shock certainly written all over my face once I realize what he said. I don't see him. It's not like the man is hard to miss. I bring the phone back up, and say, "Where are you?"

"Behind you," he replies, and his voice is in stereo.

I spin around to see him walking up from the bar next door. "Mother. Fucker!' I say into the phone. He laughs, closes his phone, and slips it into his pocket. "How'd you know I was here?" I ask into the phone.

He steps up to me, takes my phone and pushes it down into my pocket. "I didn't until I saw you through the window." I'm slack-jawed as I stare at him. His fingers touch beneath my chin and lift. "Close your mouth, Nemy-girl."

My mouth shuts, and as soon as I have my faculties about me, I reach up and hit him on the arm. "*Motherfucker*!"

His delicious evil grin spreads across his face and he leans over. "You already said that."

"Bastard," I say, and he laughs.

He takes my arm and loops it around his. "Come on, do a shot with me." He leads me back inside. This deters the guy who wants to fuck me. I just shrug at him. I don't know what else to do, but I know I don't want to go anywhere with *him*.

The girls' eyes grow wide when I pass by our table with Clancy. "Who's that?" Teagan mouths. They've never seen him because the girls don't venture into my bar. Usually because they're working too, but also because my place of work is closer to downtown Phoenix than Tempe.

"My boss," I mouth in return, but unfortunately, my voice doesn't wish to remain silent. I can see Kennadi's brow go up on the right as she checks him out from head to toe and smirks. I glare at her.

Clancy chuckles and leads me to the bar while Teagan gives me thumbs up. She's insane. He then orders two Irish Car Bombs, and I look at him incredulously.

"You can't be serious."

"You're fine," he replies, and his grin widens. "For now."

I lean against the bar and face him. "Are you trying to get me drunker?"

He laughs and then shrugs. "I just want to do a shot with you. We've never done a shot together."

"I believe the Maker's Mark could count as a shot." My right brow goes up as I eye the beautiful man, who is much more beautiful when I've had a bah-jillion drinks in me. "Who are you here with?"

"No one," he says with a shake of his head. His hair moves gently against his shoulders and he's wearing a shiny black shirt, opened about halfway down his chest. I lick my lips because my tongue just wants to play all over *that*.

Oh God, I'm drunk. The dangerous flirtation is about to go code orange. "Why aren't you at the club?"

He looks down at me and smiles. "I get to have a night off now and then too."

"So what are you doing down here?" It's just too weird to be a coincidence.

He nods toward the Irish bar next door and says, "My friend owns that place. I go in and visit him from time to time, since I have a silent interest in it." Then he leans over. "Sorry if I messed with you, but I just couldn't resist." His freakin' eye twinkles. "You're cute when you're pissed."

I surprisingly don't roll my eyes this time, but instead give him a shy smile.

This really gets his attention. "What's that, Nemy-girl?"

"What?" I deny what he's thinking, though I really want to kiss him again. Actually, right now I'd like to do a hell of a lot more to him.

His eyebrows rise into his forehead. "I think somebody wants me. Maybe I could get you to strip for me tonight, given the right amount of alcohol."

"Shut the fuck up," I say and grab the drinks as he throws a twenty at the bartender. He laughs and I raise the Guinness and shot, which has a mixture of Bailey's Irish cream and Irish whiskey.

"Hold up," he says and takes his glasses in hand. "Bet first?"

"On what?"

"Who can finish first," he says. "Obviously."

I let out a short laugh. "You do realize I'm a bartender, right?"

"And I own a bar. Should make this interesting."

"You own a strip club and I've never seen you drink outside of a few times in the last year. So, what's the bet?" I ask, and quickly add, "And don't say anything about stripping."

His nose crinkles in a mock growl, and finally, he concedes with a shrug. "How about a kiss then?"

I smirk. "You've already kissed me."

"Yeah, but I want another one."

I draw in a breath through my lips like a backwards whistle, and then close my mouth. Oh, the possibilities of what could happen with that kiss considering my current condition. My tongue moves back and forth inside my mouth while I think about it, the surgical steel bar clicking against my teeth.

"You're taking too long. A kiss, it is." I open my mouth to protest, but he stops me. "Nope, too late."

"How is that even a good bet? Either way, we kiss each other."

He shakes his head. "No, if I win, *you* kiss me, however you like, even if it's just a peck on the cheek. If you win, *I* kiss you, however I like. There's a difference. Unless, of course, you'd like to revert back to the stripping thing."

Laughter leaves my lips in a hurry, giving it an almost nervous quality, and I'm not even thinking about how that bet works out. If I were sober, I'd say it was a bit backwards. I shake my head quickly. "Nope, I only strip—"

"—in the bedroom, I know," he finishes. "And that's just fine by me." He winks.

Oh. My. God. Clancy's totally hitting on me. In public. He wasn't like this earlier today. What the fuck? Okay, so we've shared a couple of moments of pure passion, but nothing's happened since then and his kisses have only been those annoying pecks on the cheek. I was beginning to think he really wasn't interested. My eyes flick to the left to find my friends all gawking at us. I can't give them any kind of facial expressions because Clancy will see it. Crap. They seem to figure out my predicament and Alanna and Teagan are both nodding with smiles across their faces in expressions that say, "Do it!" Of course, they can't hear what Clancy and I are talking about, but they are well aware of his little bets.

Clancy peers over his shoulder and they immediately stop. He chuckles. "Your friends are all for it. Come on, bottoms up." He drops the shot into his beer, and I quickly do the same. The glasses go up and I can hear the girls hitting the table in rhythmic vibrations in their excitement. Guinness is a thick beer, so it's not easy to chug, but I manage to get it all down in a short amount of time and set the glass on the bar. The shot glass clinks against the pint glass. I hear it a second time while wiping my mouth, and I realize I've won. Wait a minute, what's the bet?

Holy fucking shit.

Clancy doesn't miss a beat. He sweeps me up in his arms and plants a hard one on me that sends my mind reeling when his tongue slips past my lips. I can hear the girls whoop and holler, but very soon, all sound disappears until it's just Clancy and me. My hands slide up into his soft hair as his lips work against mine, and he presses me against the bar and bends me over it backwards a little. His hand glides up my left ribcage, underneath the barely-there top, and his thumb moves in gentle motions, massaging my skin. Fire races through my body like mercury in my veins—every ounce of me realizes what it wants . . . *now*. His lips pull back and he bites my lower lip, and then he smiles with that evil glint in his eyes and takes a step back.

He glides his hand down my face and he softly caresses my cheek with his thumb. "Have a good night, Nemy-girl," he says and walks away. I can do nothing but stare after the man as he leaves the bar.

Wait, why is he leaving?

"Motherfucker," I whisper as I brace myself against the bar for support. I don't trust my legs at this point, and Teagan and Alanna run over to me. Kennadi just strolls.

"Oh my God," Teagan shouts and grabs my arms. "That was Clancy? He's fucking hot!"

I just nod, still dazed by the whole event.

"Yummy," Kennadi says and licks her lips.

Alanna laughs. "Look at her! Holy shit!" She slaps my face lightly. "Wake up, chica!" My eyes flick to hers in a rapid flutter of eyelids. "Wow, I've never seen you like this."

I shake my head and finally reach up to slap my forehead. "What the hell?"

Kennadi laughs as Lillian strolls over with Echo, Katy and Jada. "Hell, any man who can do that to you is worth a fucking try," Lillian says.

I shake my head again. "He's my boss."

"I don't think he cares," says Echo with a grin, and Katy giggles.

"Shut up, both of you."

Jada suddenly squeaks and runs away while the rest of us look at one another in bewilderment. Teagan and Alanna catch the abrupt change in my eyes because I see the cause of that squeak, and when I lurch forward, their arms fly out to grab me.

"No, Nemy," Teagan shouts. "You'll get us kicked out of the bar this time!"

"It'll be worth it," I growl and struggle against them. I've got James in my sights and nothing short of them chaining me to the bar is going to stop me.

I see Kennadi reach for her back pocket once again, and I break free and head straight for the poor excuse for a man while they holler after me and follow. My stride slows when I approach him and it catches him off guard, and right when he smiles and is about to greet me (I hate the way he looks at me), my right fist rounds and clocks the shithead in the jaw. Spittle hits his friend in the face when his head makes a sudden turn, jaw open, a little blood, and a tooth, I think. He stumbles back a step or two and comes back glaring mad.

"You fucking whore!" he screams while clutching his jaw.

I don't even notice the hands taking hold of me and move to kick him, but I get turned sideways and my foot misses his fat head by mere centimeters. Being not quite the gentleman that he is, James swings back at me and catches me in the right side, hitting my ribs before Kennadi punches him in the side of the head. I think I hear a couple of ribs crack, or at least feel it, as James swings an arm around, knocking Kennadi into a few patrons with his elbow to her jaw. My knees give and I drop to the floor, sucking in a strangled breath. The bastard can punch; I can't believe Jada's still alive. Teagan screams at him and tries to pull me away. The other girls are screaming too. Alanna rakes fingernails down his arm in attempt to grab him, but he pushes her back hard enough that she trips over my legs and hits the floor. I drop to the side and kick him in the shin, which brings him to one knee. One of his friends attempts to pull him up, but he yanks away from him and drops to his hands in front of me. The look in his eyes has a carnal reflection to them and tells me this isn't over by a long shot.

"You're mine, bitch," he growls before pushing himself up. Security arrives—a little late, not surprising—and assesses the situation, but I don't care by now because I've just proven in public what I've known for a long time: James holds no qualms about hitting a woman. Hell, he just took three of us down. I despise men like that. Of course, I did hit him first, but I know many men who still won't hit a woman, even in that situation.

Killian rushes over, pushing his way through the gathered crowd, and he touches my shoulder. "Nemy, what the fuck?"

My head cranes up to look at him. "Woman-beater." His face flushes with anger. Good, Killian's a good man. Teagan's still kind of diggin' him for whatever reason.

"Where's Jada?" Lillian asks in a panic as Killian pulls me to my feet.

"I bet she's in the bathroom." My eyes flick to James again, who's leaving the club with a security escort. If he hadn't returned the punch, I'd be the one getting escorted out.

Teagan snaps her fingers in front of me. "Nemy!"

My eyes return to her. "What?"

"Leave it alone," she says. "You don't know what he'll do." Her eyes search the crowd around us until they fall on Kennadi. "That goes for you too." Kennadi just shrugs and plays innocent. She's so far from it.

"No," I reply and move forward. I hear Killian's "oh shit" as I push past them and can feel fingertips against my shoulders.

"Oh, fuck it," Teagan says. "She's gonna do it. We may as well kick the fucker's ass."

Kennadi hops forward. "Hell yeah!"

When I reach the gate, the bouncer stops me. "Ma'am, not a good idea," he says, shaking his head because he knows what happened. I glare up at him and then turn my eyes to James, who's standing on the sidewalk, taunting me. The bouncer's concern is that I'm a woman. It's justifiable.

"Come on, Nemy," James goads, wagging his fingers at me. "I'll take good care of you, just like I did that little bitch friend of yours."

My eyes dart back to the bouncer's dark face. "Honestly." I hold an arm out to point at James.

He looks from me to James and back to me. "I can't let you do it," his deep voice replies. He takes stock of the people surrounding me, and then leans over. "But if you were to go through the other entrance, I wouldn't be able to stop you."

James doesn't hear the last part and I'm smiling at the bouncer with my eyes. "What's your name?"

"Dennis."

"Thanks, Dennis," I reply and turn on my heel, ignoring the pain in my side. I'm a woman on a mission, damn it. Everyone around thinks I'm letting it go, including James, with exception to Kennadi, of course because she thinks like me. I step inside and turn back to see which way he's heading, and then I make for the other entrance.

Teagan runs up beside me as I steal a glimpse of Killian on his phone. "What are you doing?"

"Sneak attack." I continue to push my way through the bar. "Echo, go check on Jada and get the limo. Katy, go pay the tab." Both girls nod and run off. Lillian and Alanna are still with me, as is Kennadi.

"He has friends with him," Lillian says.

"Yeah, I know, but did you see the look on their faces when he hit me? They didn't seem to like it much. I've never seen those guys before so they aren't *good* friends like those assholes in his little posse."

"This is insane," Teagan says. "Everything's always so damn chaotic around you."

"Stop talking. You're killing my mood." Kennadi stays silent because she's thinking the same thing I am.

Teagan huffs out a breath and we get to the front door. I peer out and turn to the four of them. "You gals ready?" We lost Killian in the crowd. Apparently the phone call was important.

Alanna is the first to speak. "I'm with you, chica, after the asshole threw me to the floor."

"Nemy, really, are you sure about this?" Lillian asks, hesitancy in her voice.

"He's going to talk her into coming back, you know that. He's done it every time they've split. We've *all* seen the bruises now, haven't we, Teags?"

Teagan nods.

"Okay, fine," Lillian says.

My hand rests on Lillian's shoulder. "If you don't want to be a part of this, go help Echo." I can't have her being any kind of hesitant when this happens.

I push the door open and step outside with Teagan, Kennadi, and Alanna behind me. It's still the same street; just a different section a little bit north of the other entrance through the patio. We round the corner and see James. He looks back and laughs, turns around, and his friends try to stop him, which makes me feel even better. James takes three large steps before I swing and clock him in the eye as Teagan hits him in the left side and Alanna kicks his right knee. He goes down and Kennadi knees him in the face and grabs the back of his head, pulling him forward again. She then slams her fist into his upper back when he bends over, and I stomp on him when he hits the ground.

"Stay. Away. From Jada!" I shout.

"Fuck you, bitch," he grunts and grabs my ankle. He pushes me back using my own leg and yanks me forward, causing my other foot to twist, and I fall to the ground.

"Shit!" I yell and hit the ground hard.

Once I'm down, he crawls over me, grasps my swinging arms and forces them to the brick sidewalk. He doesn't seem to care that the others are still beating on him, but by the time I get a chance to look, his friends have locked them up, arms at their sides as they kick and scream. Alanna actually throws her head back into one guy's face and breaks his nose. Kennadi struggles with another and throws punches in a flurry, knocking the guy to the ground.

James' face closes in on mine. "Nemy, you're one stupid bitch."

I arch my back in a quick motion to throw him off me, but he doesn't budge.

"All you need is a man to control you."

"Fuck off," I snap and spit in his face.

He returns that gesture with a head butt, which throws my head back to the bricks.

My eyes close tight and I'm seeing stars.

Then someone pulls him off me. I try to sit up and the world spins out of control, and that has me dropping back to the ground. I can hear the scuffle, but I can't look now. Then I hear, "Kick his ass, Clancy!" from Teagan. I smile a little, but I'm pissed that I allowed myself to get into this debilitating position. Alanna runs over to me and helps me sit up. My vision fades in and out, and in between the black spots, I see Clancy pummeling James into oblivion, kind of like he did with that dude that tried to rob us in the parking lot. I also see Killian and a few of his friends circling, throwing a punch anytime one of James' friends gets near him and Clancy.

And oh my God, is that Sean watching from the shadows? I squint, close my eyes tight, and reopen them to find no one where I'd thought I'd seen him. My eyes return to Clancy.

"Oh fuck," I say weakly as my head pounds. "Stop him before the cops get here."

Clancy gives him one last kick and tells his friends to drag him away. Killian helps with a second kick and shouts something I can't comprehend. Then Clancy runs back to me and kneels in front of me. "Nemy-girl?" His eyes dart back and forth between mine.

"She might have a concussion," Alanna says. "Her head hit the sidewalk pretty hard."

Kennadi walks up, flexing her hand. "Shit, I broke a damn nail."

It damn near has me laughing, but I'm too dizzy.

"What am I going to do with you?" He looks at Alanna, Kennadi, and now Teagan. "I'll take care of her. You three attend to your friend." Clancy nods forward and their eyes follow his to Jada. I look back to see the horrified expression that crosses her face as Kennadi waves at her and smiles.

I grab Teagan's arm. "Don't let her go back to him."

"I won't," she replies and looks at Clancy. "You sure?"

"I got it, don't worry," he replies. "She'll be fine."

The three of them run off to get in the limo as Clancy picks me up and carries me to his car he parked crooked on the side of the road. He must have been driving by and saw the fight. Clancy gets me in the car and drives off right before the police arrive, but not before I think I see Sean again, hiding in the shadows. Fucking creepy.

Yep, won't be able to go back to that bar for a while.

15

Baby Did a Bad Bad Thing

Clancy takes me to his house, which sits in a little art district near Old Towne Scottsdale. For the life of me, I can't figure out why he wants a new house because he lives in a neighborhood I adore. It's difficult to buy a house there because hardly anyone ever sells. All the houses are unique in their artistic custom designs, and his looks adobe style, but I can't see it very well at night and my head throbs like a mother.

He keeps me awake for a long time, holding an icepack to the back of my head, and we watch a few action-packed movies. I keep trying to doze off, but the son of a bitch won't let me.

"You can't sleep." He lightly taps my cheek.

"I can't help it," I reply in a hoarse voice. "Besides, I think that's old medicine. I just can't take anything but Tylenol." He's wrapped a blanket around us while we sit on his over-sized sofa in front of a gigantic flat screen television. The room is dark, save for the flickering screen, which didn't really help my headache all that much at first.

"Is the Tylenol working?" He runs his fingers through my hair.

I nod carefully.

"Just stay awake for a little while longer, so I can be sure." He leans forward and kisses my forehead.

"Ouch," I say, because it's right where James hit me with his hard head.

"Sorry. How about this?" He kisses my right temple.

"That's better." I snuggle close to him for warmth.

"Don't get too comfortable."

"Um, that's gonna be impossible with you." What can I say? The truth comes out after a night of drinking.

His smile presses against my temple. "Whose ass did I just kick tonight?"

"James," I say. "Jada's ex-boyfriend, who beat her."

"Ah, the one you rescued her from. Good," he whispers. "I feel even more honorable then."

I giggle. "I thought you'd left."

He shakes his head a little. "Just went back to my friend's bar to say goodnight. I was leaving when I saw the fight."

"How much did you see?"

"Enough for me to want to kill the man."

"I started it," I whisper into the blanket.

"That doesn't surprise me." He pulls me closer, wrapping his arm around my shoulders. "But it doesn't give him the right to hit a woman."

My phone buzzes on the coffee table. It's now five in the morning, so I know it's important because no one calls me at that hour. Clancy reaches out to grab it and hands it to me.

"Hello?" It's Teagan checking up on me, and she informs me Jada is passed out. "Is she pissed?"

"No, but she thinks the asshole might retaliate somehow," Teagan replies.

I'm not surprised by this information, but I am concerned because he didn't get picked up by the police either. "Okay, thanks." I get off the phone with her and tell Clancy what she said.

"He won't come near you or Jada again. I swear my life on it."

I crane my head back to look into his eyes. "Sounds like something my dad would say."

He smiles. "Then I'd like your dad."

"I need to get a new gun," I say out of the blue. Damn alcohol. "Mine was in the car."

"You were carrying in your car?" He tips my chin up so he can look me square in the eye.

"Yeah, I've been a little on edge lately," I reply, and decide in my inebriated condition that it's a good idea to tell him about the note Sean left on my car and that I've seen him twice at the nightclub now. His whole body goes rigid, which tells me that probably wasn't a good idea.

"I'll loan you one of mine," he says through clenched teeth.

"I may have some broken ribs, by the way." I figure a subject change might calm him down because it feels like he's about to go kill Sean.

"We already took care of that, Nemy-girl," he states, staring at the television.

"When?" I ask and look up at him again.

His eyes flick down to me. "About three hours ago. You screamed when my arm pressed against them. You're wearing a bandage around your ribcage."

My hand slips under the blanket and my shirt to find he's correct. "Wow, I don't remember that." I look up at him. "So, you put this on me?"

Clancy stares at me for a bit. "Yes."

"Did my shirt come off?" I ask, and he nods.

"Well, you pulled your shirt up a bit too high," he says. "How much did you have to drink tonight?"

I'm too tired to blush, so I let out a sigh and close my eyes.

He chuckles and caresses my left cheek. "It's okay. I'm going to win your heart one way or another. I'd eventually see them." I start to slip out and he lightly taps my face with his fingers. "Wake up." He waits for me to look at him. "They're beautiful, by the way."

"Mmm, thanks." I lay my head against his shoulder until he taps my cheek again. "I'm awake."

"Right," he says.

"Really, I'm just daydreaming."

"About?" He takes my hand in his, fingers sliding between mine and interlocking.

"You," I whisper, and he leans a little closer to kiss my temple once more. If I had the capacity to really think, I wouldn't have said that, and I'd be attempting with all my might to find some excuse not to want to be here in his arms and having him kiss me and take care of me.

Damn it, I feel too comfortable, which leaves a bad feeling in the pit of my stomach. Something will fuck this into oblivion; I just know it. Right now, my heart leads my actions and words. It's when my brain gets involved that everything becomes completely fucked up.

The following week, Clancy's joking is in careful moves and phrases because he knows I still hurt. No attempts to throw things at my cleavage, in other words. I might actually find the energy to punch him if he were to do that. My ribcage still aches a bit on the right side, and I'm wearing the bandage under the corset, although I don't really need it because the corset doesn't allow my torso to bend. It's probably better than the bandage.

"They found your car, right?" Clancy asks.

I'm making a drink at the station next to his normal seat that he's not sitting in. Instead, he's standing behind the bar, annoying the crap out of me.

"Yeah. Totaling it too." My poor baby. I worked hard for that car, damn it.

"Ouch," he replies. "That much damage, huh?"

"No sign of the gun, either, which is probably a good thing."

"Not registered, I take it."

I just nod once because I'm too depressed to talk about my stolen car. Although, the night after the fight with James, Clancy let me drive his Volvo S60 home. It's a nice little car, and brand new at that, which makes me nervous as all hell while driving the damn thing. It still has that new car smell, with a hint of Clancy's cologne. I take a deep breath every time I get in it.

"So, Nemy-girl," he says as he leans forward, practically over my left shoulder. "Since you punched James in the face, does that make him your Prince Charming?"

He's standing next to me because he won't let me do anything by my damn self. I'm not used to receiving so much help from a man, so I'm a bit snappish.

I turn my head and glare up at him. "That is *not* funny."

He smirks. "Why are you so crabby tonight? Are you in pain?"

"You're helping me too much. It's weird to me."

He leans over me and his hand touches the small of my back. "Get used to it. If you're injured, I'm going to take care of you."

My brow arches and I look into those green eyes. "Even if I'm like incapacitated for several months?"

"Absolutely."

"That's not normal," I say with a shake of my head.

His hand reaches for my chin and he turns my head to face him. "Maybe not for you, but it's perfectly normal for me."

I've been incapacitated for several months before, only to have the man in my life walk out on me during my worst moments in time. I have a hard time believing Clancy won't do the same when it comes right down to it. That'd be my trust issues with men.

"I need to take care of some paperwork in my office. I'll be back out in a bit. Don't lift anything and call me if you need me or ask Scott."

I nod and my eyes follow him the length of the bar as I mix a drink for the guy two barstools down. I'm hoping the scary leprechaun doesn't show up while he's gone because my gut still tells me something's off about him, aside from his lack of ability to take no for an answer. And seeing him during that fight with James was weird too. Why was he there again? Because of me? A shudder trembles through my body.

Clancy's still a bit tense too, ever since Sean walked into the bar that first night. He's constantly checking the front door anytime someone walks in. He didn't really do that before. I keep his borrowed Beretta in the glove box of the

Volvo—a place where I can easily reach it—and it goes in the house with me every night after work. I kind of miss my Glock, though. I'm not real keen on the Beretta.

A little while later, a nice looking, well-dressed man steps up to the bar in front of me. I look up from cleaning a glass. "Can I help you?"

"I'm looking for Mr. Dolan. Is he here?" His eyes wander studiously around the club, but don't linger on any of the girls. Now *that's* dedication to your job . . . whatever his is, unless he's just not into women.

"May I tell him who's here?"

He turns back to me. "Bernard Raymond," he replies. "Attorney."

"Okay." I start to put down the glass. A lot of attorneys, judges and such visit the club, so there's no question in my mind about what he wants.

"For Mrs. Dolan," he adds and looks around some more.

That jolts me and the glass drops into the ice bin and breaks. Fuck, and I mean that on many levels.

"Um, I'll go get him for you," I reply distantly and throw my towel in the bin so I remember the broken glass. I'm surprised I even think of it. The walk to the back has me in tunnel vision because I can't see anything but that damn door, and when I walk through, all I see is his office door. I knock and wait with more patience than expected.

Clancy opens the door and smiles. "What do you need, Nemy-girl?"

"There's an attorney with two first names here to see you," I say in a distant fog and point toward the front of the club.

His brow creases. "Really?"

I nod and turn away from him to go back to my bar, and he quickly shuts his office door and catches up to me.

"Did he say why he was here?" He opens the door to the club for me.

I walk through, shake my head and keep walking, still with tunnel vision. When I pass Mr. Raymond, I point back to Clancy, who offers his hand.

"Mr. Dolan?" the attorney clarifies as he shakes his hand.

"Yes, how can I help you?" Clancy seems mystified, and so am I because he's never mentioned a wife in the last year. That's how private he keeps his life. Maybe I'm misreading and the attorney's here about his mother, but that wouldn't make any sense.

I pick up the towel and lay it flat on the side counter so I can place the broken pieces of glass on it. I'm also doing this so I can eavesdrop.

"Bernard Raymond, Mr. Dolan, attorney for Amanda Dolan." Clancy sheds several layers of pigment and his eyes flick to me. I'm staring at him, questions certainly in my eyes he can't answer right now, and he takes Mr. Raymond's arm in hand and points to his office.

"Let's speak in private, shall we?" He ushers the attorney back.

Yeah, that is so a wife or an ex-wife reaction.

I continue to clean out the ice bin, melt the ice and have Scott refill it for me. Then I start wiping everything down and cleaning up the rest of my bar. I reach down and grab my bag and coat, and call Scott over. "I have to leave, Scotty. It's important."

He stares at me a minute before saying anything. "Um, okay. I can take over for you, I guess."

"Thanks, you're a sweetheart," I reply and give him a quick kiss on the cheek. I run out the door before Clancy can return to the club with Mr. Raymond, and I get in his borrowed Volvo and drive home. I'm not really feeling anything at the moment; I'm just dazed by the surprise. Clancy has a wife? It figures; just as I was starting to give in to the man. The fact that her attorney is present doesn't even cross my mind, or why he's possibly there. *Wife* is the only word I can see. I did say *almost* perfect, and I refuse to become the "other woman."

This is why I hate men.

About halfway home, my phone rings. I pick it up to see who it is, and I set it right back down without answering because it's Clancy. I can't talk about this right now. He calls five times in three minutes and leaves a voicemail each time he calls. I still ignore the phone as it rings a sixth time when I take the Priest exit, and a seventh time when I turn on University. The phone chimes again with a voicemail. My hands shake against the steering wheel, and I try to keep it together so I can make it home without getting a speeding ticket, or crashing, or having an anxiety attack while I'm driving this fucking car that smells like *him*. What the hell did he do, pour his entire bottle of cologne in the car?

I get inside my house and quickly drop down on the sofa, spreading my fingers through my hair as I try to control my breathing because it's killing my ribs. Thank God I discovered this shit before I fell too hard for the man, but hell, I've been falling for him for the last year. Had I let this go any further, he could have shattered my heart just as bad as Jeremy did, if not worse. I don't think I could handle worse.

I draw in a final deep breath, which hurts like hell, and let it out in a straggle of short puffs. I don't know how long I've been sitting here because I'm staring off in a trance, wondering how I allowed myself to fall for his charm even though I fought it the entire way.

Fuck.

There's a soft knock on the door and my head snaps to the side, but I don't say anything. The knock comes again.

"Nemy-girl, I can see you in there."

"Go away, please." I realize I didn't lock the door. I jump to my feet as painlessly as possible and run over to it, but he's already turned the knob and enters. I take two steps back as he closes the door behind him. "Please, Clancy, just go away."

"No," he replies. "Why did you leave?"

I look at the floor and turn around.

He walks up behind me and places his hand on my shoulder, which I shrug off. He lets out a long sigh. "Nemy-girl, Mr. Raymond is a divorce and child custody attorney."

I spin around on my heel to face him, arms crossed over my chest. "You're married?"

He holds up a manila folder. "Did you see her at my house last week?"

"That's not the point. You're married!" The type of attorney Mr. Raymond is crosses my mind again. "Do you have a child too?"

He lets out a short laugh, barely audible, hardly visible, and he looks me in the eye. "Does it matter, really?"

"You never told me," I reply in a hurt-filled voice. "Of course it matters."

"It matters that I'm married?"

"No," I say with a shake of my head. "You didn't tell me, but yes, it would matter if you were married."

"I'm sorry. But I'm not married any longer. She hasn't lived with me in several years." He holds up the folder again. "Do you want to know what this is?"

I tilt my head. "I don't need to see the divorce paperwork. It just hurts, like you don't trust me or something. Trust is important, Clancy."

He smiles and cups my face with his hand. "You've been pushing me away since the day I met you, and even more so since Jeremy left you. The only time I ever get anything . . . *real* out of you, is after you've been drinking."

I swallow hard because it's the damn truth of it. "This is really hard for me, to get close to you after being hurt so badly. You're my boss on top of that."

He leans over and drops the folder on my coffee table, and then he places a hand on each of my hips and pulls me close. "I'm not your boss right now."

"Yes, you are."

He cups my face again with his hands and leans over. "You're impossible," he whispers and gives me a quick kiss on the forehead. Then he takes a step back and heads over to the sofa, dragging me by the hand with him. "I've been divorced for five years. How about you?"

I sit next to him. "Uh, about the same."

"I might have a daughter, but it's hard to say right now. I'll need proof."

"Paternity test?" I ask, and his grip tightens on my hand.

"Yes." He looks me in the eye. "Now, let's discuss some other pending issues."

"Like?" A tremble of nervousness makes its way through my body.

"The Monday after the holidays . . . ." Monday is now my consistent day off. Apparently, he read my blog because I was able to finally post that one I'd been working on the night my computer fried.

"What about it?" I turn a little to face him and he's grinning.

"Well, we can begin the day with lunch, then move on to look at the house, and then I'd like you to have dinner with me." I quite visibly swallow the lump in my throat and he chuckles. His hand squeezes mine again. "Don't be afraid."

"I can't help it," I reply.

"Why?"

"Because of the way you make me feel," I say and crinkle my nose. Jesus, I haven't even had a damn drink tonight.

He chuckles. "Pain killers apparently have the same effect as alcohol."

"No shit, but my mouth has a mind of its own. They wore off a couple hours ago."

"Wait, so you're stone cold sober right now?" That evil Clancy grin spreads over his face after I give him an affirmative nod. "And how do I make you feel, Nemy-girl?"

"Can I plead the fifth on that?"

"No," he says.

"Damn it." I look at him, and I'm certain the look says it all, but he's still waiting for an answer. "Fine, I've fallen completely in lust with you and want to do ravenous things to your body." It's really hard to say that with a straight face.

His head falls back with deep laughter that rumbles through my body, bringing it to life in areas that have lain dormant for some time now. Then his left hand leaves the back of the sofa and glides up my arm, leaving a trail of goose bumps in its wake. By the time he reaches the back of my neck, my body is about to hit thermo-nuclear meltdown, and he gently pulls me forward. I'm helpless when it comes to this man, so I just fall into him.

"I feel the same way," he whispers, his lips brushing against mine.

His right hand slides around my waist to pull me forward and over him as our lips meet. I just happen to be wearing the fucking zipper corset. However, I wouldn't mind so much if he decides to unzip it now.

"You should take some more pain killers," he whispers against my lips.

I pause and pull back a little as I stare into his eyes. "Why, are you planning on hurting me?"

He chuckles and smiles sweetly. "I don't want to." Oh, the double meanings this man gives. We are not talking about my ribs. Clancy sees my apprehension at the idea of a real relationship and rubs my neck and shoulder with his left hand. It relaxes me in ways I'll never understand. "Look, I understand there will be many nights when you'll feel the need to be isolated. I'm fine with that."

"So were the others at first," I whisper.

"I'm not the others. I understand your need to create the things you do. It's much like my need to paint."

"You paint? What do you paint?"

He smiles. "Lots of things. My point is while you're working, I can paint." He tilts his head. "I'm going to assume from your reaction of when I asked to see something of yours that the others didn't."

I shake my head. "Not their cup of tea, I guess." Then I hold up a finger. "Wait, no, my ex-husband looked at a couple of things."

"But not Jeremy."

I shake my head again. "He wasn't interested in anything I did."

"Damn shame he didn't recognize your talent and couldn't support you in it." His eyes flick to the left wall. "Who painted that?"

My eyes follow his to the large oil painting hanging on my wall with its splashes of whites, browns, reds and oranges, and a woman twirling around at center stage. Mariachis sit on chairs behind her, as well as two other women.

"Originally, it's the Spanish Dancer by John Sargent," I reply with a proud smile. "But that's a copy and I think the background may be added by the new artist."

"And who's your favorite artist?"

"Oh wow, that's a tough one. I love van Gogh and Picasso and Degas and Dali and . . ."

He laughs and gently pulls me closer. "See, I needed to find out too."

I giggle and his lips take mine in a heated kiss. He's got my head so whirling with those kisses and his touch that I completely forget about the wife—*ex*-wife—and child.

"So, are we together or not?"

He grins. "You tell me."

I bite my lower lip and stare into his deep green eyes before I answer him with another kiss. His hands travel up my back, pushing me closer to him and crushing my chest against his.

I gasp in pain after trying to maneuver into a better position to take advantage of his body beneath mine. My ribs still hurt like hell, so our playing doesn't last long before he leaves to go back to the club, since I left before my shift was over and it's Chris's night off.

Damn it. This is going to take for*ever.*

16

Let It Die

James vanishes into thin air one day and none of us can figure out what's happened. His incessant phone calls just cease. It's got Jada all kinds of freaked out, which irks me, but I get it, I guess. Maybe not.

It's my turn to spend one whole day with her, which happens to be the day James doesn't call at all for the first time, of course. It's outside the norm for her routine, so she notices it right away. I guess the guy had some sort of weird schedule about it. Figures. Overbearing control freak.

"I wonder why he hasn't called yet." She twirls a lock of her jet black hair around her finger and stares at her phone.

"Who the fuck cares? Can we go get Starbucks now? I need caffeine."

She sighs heavily. "God, Nemy, you're so addicted. Find a different way to wake up."

I cock an eyebrow at her. "Did you seriously just say that to me? You can't possibly be my friend if you'd deprive me of the one substance on this planet worth living for."

She rolls her eyes. I must be wearing off on her. "Oh fine. You're buying, right?" She smirks, which produces a cute little dimple on each cheek. Haven't seen those in awhile.

"Oh, there you are," I quip. "I've been wondering when I'd see you again."

"Shut up." But she giggles, which has me smiling. My little porcelain doll has returned, even if just a little.

I pull myself off the sofa and grab my tote. "Let's go. It's happy hour."

"Starbucks has a happy hour? I didn't know that."

"Damn straight, they do," I say and head for the door. "C'mon, woman, before I fall asleep."

We get in my—Clancy's—car and Pink's *So What* starts playing. I'm about to change it when Jada says, "Hey, that could've been the theme song last week."

"Ha, ha, funny," I say, but it's true. James picked a fight—okay, *I* picked a fight—at the bar that night, but it's cool to see Jada making fun of it. I was worried how she'd react to me after that. "Hey, Jada—"

"Don't," she says. "I'm glad you did it. Really."

"You sure?"

"Yeah." She takes a deep breath. "I know you're trying to protect me and all, and I appreciate it . . ."

"But?"

"*But* I kind of need to do this a bit on my own without you guys all suffocating me." She turns to face me. "I mean, I love having you all around me, but I don't have one moment of privacy."

"Ever consider why we're doing that?"

"You're afraid I'll run back to him," she admits. "And you should be afraid of that. I don't trust myself, but look" —she holds up her phone— "he hasn't even called today."

"I don't trust that. It could just be one of his games."

"Maybe," she says softly and stares at her hands.

"Sorry, but I'm not giving him even the slightest benefit of doubt, chica," I say as we pull into the parking lot. "Inside or drive-thru?"

"Inside," she replies. "Then we can sit on the patio or something, for the fresh air."

I smile. "Good idea."

As soon as we're settled on the patio, a text message from Clancy hits my phone, which must light up my face because Jada's splits into a wide grin.

"Clancy?" she says with an arched thin brow.

"Yeah." His text: *How's Jada?* I shoot a text back at him, telling him she's *just peachy, and no, that wasn't sarcasm.* He responds with *And how's my fave hot bartender?* Oh boy. *I'm just fine too.* His next message has me heated: *Yes you are, and one of these days I'm going to show you just how fine I think you are.* ☺Yes, he added a fucking smiley face, but I can see the evil glint in his eyes and the wicked grin spreading across his face all in my mind. That's what's got my temperature rising. Meanwhile, my stomach has butterflies flitting about just with this minor digital conversation. I can only imagine what I'd be feeling if those words were to my face, which would likely turn red from embarrassment. I've been trying with all my might not to be alone with the man lately because the lust will take over and as much as I *want* him, I don't want to rush things. Call me crazy. I mean, what if he really is my Prince Charming?

"He's really got a hold on you, doesn't he?"

I look up into Jada's eyes that show wisdom beyond her years. "Yeah, I guess he does." I put my phone down and lean forward. "It's just . . . shit, I don't even know where to begin when it comes to him."

She smiles sweetly. "Nemy, you're falling for him. Be happy."

"But what if—"

"No, don't do that," she warns. "Don't *what if.* That shit doesn't factor in. Not with Clancy. Not after what I saw that night at the bar. He is all about *you.*"

I run a hand through my hair. "When did you get so smart?"

"I've been paying attention, even when you think I'm not." She grins and sips her latte.

I crack a smile. "I guess so."

Amazing how someone can see what's going on in others' lives, but can be completely oblivious when it comes to their own.

Jada receives a call two days later from the Mesa Police Department about James, wondering if she'd seen him within that timeframe. Teagan's freaking out and calls me immediately, like I had something to do with the asshole's disappearance.

"You and Kennadi didn't go anywhere near him, *right*?" It's not a question, really. It's a demand in Teagan-speak that says *you bitches better tell me the truth.*

"Swear to God, Teags," I reply. "Haven't seen the bastard since that night I punched him." And as far as I know, Kennadi's been damn busy since then. "What happened? Are they saying? Did they find a body?"

"Why do you want to know if they found a body?" she asks sharply.

"Because then I'll know Jada is safe!" I pause and reflect on the statements I just made. "I didn't do it! I have an alibi, damn it."

"Oh yeah? Who?"

"Jesus, woman, do you really think I'd risk my entire life on that asshole?" Now I'm getting pissed that she's even considering my involvement. "You want Clancy's number? I've been at work with exception to the other day when I was with *Jada*."

A heavy sigh comes over the line. "I'm sorry, Nems, it's just crazy right now. They're questioning the hell out of Jada and me, and they want to talk to you and Kennadi . . . and Clancy."

"Clancy? Why?"

"Because he beat the shit out of him that night before we all left," she says. "There were witnesses."

"Oh, fuck." My throat tightens. Could Clancy have . . .? No. I won't think about him like that. Although there was that statement he made that reminded me of my father. "I gotta go, Teags."

"Clancy?" She's asking a slew of questions with that one word.

"I'll drop by after work," I say and hang up quickly. I know better than to talk any more in depth about shit like that on a cell phone. Hell, I probably said too much as it is. Shit.

When I arrive at work, I check with Scott to see if Clancy's around. He points to the office, so I head straight back, not even stopping to leave my stuff behind the bar. Once I'm standing outside his office, I swallow the lump in my throat and knock.

The door opens and I'm slapped in the face with his cologne. My eyelids flutter a second before my eyes meet his and I notice the grin on his face.

"Hey, I was just thinking about you." He steps to the side to let me in.

I walk past him and wait for him to close the door.

"Forget to put your stuff away first, or were you just dying to see me?" Bad choice of words, and I wince. He catches it. "What's wrong?"

"Uh, have you seen James since that night at the bar?" I'm still holding all my crap. I'm not sure why. Maybe it's so I can make a mad dash for the door and get the hell out of the club. Call it growing up in a mob environment and the need to protect myself.

His brow arches, as he's noticed my body language. "No, I haven't." He steps around the desk, offering me space. "Why don't you sit down?"

"Maybe I don't want to," I say, clutching my tote so tight that my knuckles are turning white.

"Fine, don't sit down then," he says and drops into his chair. His hands go up behind his head and rest there, locked in place, as he kicks his feet up on the desk.

Reverse psychology. Bastard. I look behind me and then sit on the sofa. We stare at one another in silence for a long time. I can't speak because I just don't know what in the hell to say. He finally breaks the silence.

"I got a call from Mesa PD today."

I feign surprise. "Oh, did you?"

He smirks. "Isn't that why you're in here and have the death grip on that Gucci tote of yours?" He nods at my bag.

I let go of it and set it aside. "Promise me you haven't seen him."

He looks me dead in the eye. "I promise."

"And no one you know has seen him, right?" Yes, I just pulled a Teagan on him.

"Correct," he says. "As far as I know."

I let out a sigh of relief and rub my hands together, working through the anxiety. "I don't know a lot of details, but I'm thinking he might be dead."

"Strong possibility, since he hasn't shown up for work in three days," Clancy says, and my eyes rocket to his face. "The police told me."

I relax a little again. "Oh, okay. Do they have any ideas as to what happened?"

He shakes his head. "Not yet, but they're checking every place he's been known to frequent, and looking at anyone who's had contact within the last month or two."

"Really? God, that could be a lot of people." I bite my lower lip, thinking about that night. They might even question Killian, if that's the case. He was there during the fight.

"I'm their primary suspect," he says suddenly and drops his feet to the floor as my mouth falls wide open. Then he leans forward on his desk. "Of course, they haven't come right out and said that just yet, but I'm expecting a visit very soon."

"How can you be so calm?"

"Because they have no proof, Nemy-girl," he says in such a soothing voice that I'm inclined to believe him. Hell, with that voice, he could tell me he's the Pope and I'd believe him.

"No, just witnesses of you beating him into a bloody oblivion that night."

"I take it you haven't talked to them yet."

I shake my head, and then wonder why they haven't called me. "What if they think I did it?"

He chuckles. "I don't think that's the case."

I arch a brow. "Why's that funny?"

He shakes his head, stands, and moves over to the sofa next to me after moving my stuff out of the way. "Unless your last name becomes involved in this, they have no reason to believe you've done anything."

I frown. "Shit, that's just what my father needs. Oh my God, he'll be so pissed at me." I drop my face into my hands. Then I realize what he said and look back up at him. "Wait, you know about my family?"

He grins. "Nemy-girl, you can't walk around with a last name like that and not have anyone recognize it." He holds up a hand as my mouth opens to protest. "Regardless of your little disclaimer. All it takes is a Google search, woman."

"Shit."

He laughs.

"I'm so glad you find this amusing."

"You don't recognize my last name, do you?" he asks, taking one of my hands in his.

"Should I?"

His other hand brushes my cheek before slipping behind my neck and pulling me forward. "I suppose not."

I lick my dry lips and he smiles.

"Can I have my kiss now? I've been waiting for hours."

He pulls me into the kiss and everything just melts away . . . until someone knocks on the door. "Perfect timing." His sarcasm is not lost on me because I'm the fucking sarcasm queen.

When he opens the door, I catch a brief flash of badge and gun and uniform, and my whole body tenses. It's an involuntary reaction from growing up with my dear old dad. I still can't get past it. They see me sitting on the sofa, so I force a smile and wave.

"Anna Mussolini?" one asks.

I hop up. "Yep, that's me."

"We'll need to question you too," another says. "Would you come with us, please?"

"I'm just starting my shift."

They look from me to Clancy, at each other, and then back to me, like they don't know how to answer that.

"Scott can cover you and call Chris to come in if he has to," Clancy says. "Come on, Nemy-girl, let's go with the nice officers and get this over with."

I scoff at him, grab my tote, and walk past all of them and through the door. "Can I drive myself at least?"

"My apologies, officers, she's a stubborn woman," Clancy says from behind me.

"Don't do that," I shout back and open the door that leads out into the club.

"And a handful," he adds, to which the officers laugh. Great.

17

King of Fools

Detective John Jacobs takes me to an interrogation room where I sit and wait for*ever* alone. They've taken Clancy to another room. Jesus, you'd think we'd been arrested. A short time later, I'm joined by Jacobs, who walks in and drops a file on the table. It's mine.

"Where is James Peterson?" he asks.

"I don't know," I say.

"I think you do."

"I'm pretty certain I don't."

"Come on, Anna, or Nemesis, isn't it? Talk to me," Jacobs says.

"Not without my attorney present."

"Why would you need an attorney if you're innocent?"

I tilt my head and smile. "Do you think I don't know how this works? You obviously know who I am, which means you know my family."

"Very well, in fact."

"Then cut the bullshit."

"Do you have any idea as to how much trouble your boyfriend is in?" he asks, dropping his hand to the table a bit more forceful than I think he intended.

"Is that supposed to scare me?" I ask and lean forward. "Neither of us have seen James since he attacked me. When did he disappear?"

"Three days ago."

I sit back. "And you're just *now* looking for him? Jesus. I'll remember not to call you when someone goes missing."

He growls at me and leans on the table. "We've been looking for him for the past two days. It's standard procedure. The trail leads to you."

"I don't see how."

He withdraws a baggie from his pocket and drops it on the table. "Look familiar?"

I lean forward, look at it, and sit back again. "Yeah, I have a pair of earrings like that." It's the ten-gauge set that looks like the number nine.

"Missing one?" James ripped one out of my ear. Luckily, it didn't rip my ear open.

"Lost it the night James broke my ribs. Wanna see the doctor's report?"

"You certainly like to fight, Anna," he says and flips open the file. "Disorderly conduct, assault; oh look, assault with a deadly weapon, but you got off on those, didn't you?"

"Had a good attorney," I say with a smile.

"More like they were coerced into dropping the charges."

"There's no proof of that," I reply. "Besides, all that stuff was ages ago, when I was still a minor. I've been a perfect angel since then."

He closes the file, and then he leans forward, placing his arms on the table. "Anna, tell me where James is."

"I. Don't. Know. I found out he was gone when Teags called me earlier today to tell me how Jada's doing."

"Jada, that's the girlfriend, right?"

"Yes, but I believe 'ex' is the term now. He'd gone missing a few days ago. Hadn't called her since four days ago. That's all I know."

"Do you think your boyfriend would know where he is?"

"Why would he know? Aren't you questioning him too?"

We stare at one another for about thirty seconds, his anger growing because he's not getting the answers he wants, which I don't fucking have, while I sit nice and calm and concentrate on my breathing.

"I'm not saying anything else, unless you intend to arrest me and I can speak with my attorney," I state and look away from him.

He grabs the baggie and the file and leaves the room. The only reason I can come up with for his determining the earring belongs to me is Jada. My stomach knots and I feel sick, but I make myself look bored, uninterested. Deep down, though, I'm worried about Clancy. I haven't been in a police station in twenty years, but the rules don't change. I know how to act. I learned real fast the first time they caught me. Dad was furious with me, not so much for the craps game, which I'm surprised Jacobs didn't mention, but for the fact that I was caught.

They finally let me go and I'm happy because I don't have to call my brother Joey. I make several attempts to inquire about Clancy before leaving, but they won't help me and shuffle me off to the lobby, where I stand frustrated and wondering if they're still questioning him. Worry is right up there too because he'd said he was possibly their prime suspect. The *what if*'s start filtering through my mind again.

And why should I recognize *his* last name?

One of the faults of being a mafia princess is that dear old dad tends to protect you from *everything*. In fact, it wouldn't surprise me one bit if dad knew where I worked and had Clancy checked out, regardless of the fact that we haven't spoken in several years.

"Oh my God," I say aloud and pull my phone out. I call my brother Octavian, who would possibly know Clancy's last name if there's any sort of miniscule relation to the mob. He picks up on the third ring.

"Well, well, if it isn't my long lost sister." His voice is heavily laden with his thick New York accent—Brooklyn, to be more precise, which means in about five minutes, I'll be talking like him because mine will return.

"Funny," I say. "Nice to hear your voice too."

He laughs. "What's up, sis?"

"Do you know the last name Dolan?" I bite one of my fingernails in anticipation of the answer.

"Seriously?" So not the answer I expected.

"Yeah." I start heading for my car, quickly jaunting across the street.

"Anna, they're like our family, only the Irish version."

That stops me in my tracks. "Fuck."

"Why?"

"I'm kind of dating Clancy Dolan," I say, then quickly add, "Don't tell Papa!"

A loud burst of laughter comes over the line and I pull the phone away from my ear a bit. "Oh my God, Pops is gonna kill you."

"I know! Please don't say anything," I plead as I begin walking again.

"What's it worth to ya?"

"You suck, you know that? I can't believe you'd blackmail your own sister."

"Doesn't change anything," he says. "What'cha got for me?"

"Oh, like I have anything you'd want, asshole."

"I'm sure you can think of something," he says. "Hey, how's school going? Done with that yet?"

"Oh, hell no," I reply. "Still have like two semesters left, I think."

A police car drives by and blips his siren. Asshole. "What the hell was that?" Octavian asks.

"I'm at the police station in Mesa," I reply and want to instantly hit myself.

"What'd you do now?"

"Nothing," I say. "Swear."

"Ri*iii*ght, I'll believe that when I don't get a fucking report across my desk with your name on it." He works for Joey, trying his level best to stay out of the family business, but I know he dabbles now and then. Our dear mother knows nothing about her baby doing so and never will. It'd kill her.

"It's nothing. I just had to come in for questioning about my friend's ex-boyfriend's disappearance, is all." Can I at least *try* to keep my damn mouth shut? Jesus.

"Dead?"

"They believe so. They're questioning Clancy still, I think."

"Did he do it?"

"No!"

He sighs. "Look, Anna, Clancy's not an angel and hasn't been for a long damn time. You be careful."

"That'd explain Sean."

"Sean who?"

"I don't know his last name. Some Irish guy with a thick accent. Looks like he just got out of prison."

"Jesus, hang on." I hear the phone clunk against the desk. He comes back on the line in a bit. "Anna, what the fuck have you gotten yourself into?"

I'm all kinds of offended with that question. "What are you talking about? I just tend bar at Clancy's club and barely started dating the guy."

"Sean 'Leprechaun' Delaney, one nasty mother fucker who just spent fifteen years in prison for armed robbery and manslaughter."

"Ooh, I knew there was a reason he gives me the heebie jeebies. He's creepy looking too. And seriously, his nickname is Leprechaun? That's hysterical."

"You're just his type, you know," he says. "You steer clear of that asshole. I'm serious. His last girl only survived because he went to prison."

"I have no desire to be his girlfriend." I don't bother to add that Sean certainly seems to desire me. "Besides, Clancy would probably beat him into oblivion like he did James a week ago. Shit. I mean . . ."

"Just fucking great. Don't wait for Clancy. He may be in there awhile if they think he did it."

"I really don't see why they'd think that," I say. "Has he been convicted of anything over the last five years?"

"No, he's kept his nose clean. Sean's probably got it in for him, though. Clancy's brother started that job with him fifteen years ago, but Clancy pulled him off at the last minute, which is why the shit went bad fast."

"Oh, wow." Then I remember the call Clancy got one night. "Hey, would his brother's name be Brennan, by any chance?"

"That's the one," he replies. "Why?"

"Something bad happened to him recently. I don't know what, but I remember Clancy getting the call and he had to leave in a hurry."

A groan filters through my earpiece. "Be careful, Anna. Retribution is our family business and you know what Pops will do if something happens to his only daughter."

"Yeah, right. We haven't spoken in ages."

"Doesn't matter," he says. "You're still his only daughter. It'd be the one time he'd go to prison."

"Thanks for the guilt trip. I'll be careful, promise. I gotta go. Talk soon?"

"Yeah, sure. Love ya, sis."

"You too."

Well, that was a font of information I didn't expect. Now I *really* want to talk to Clancy. I peer back at the station and consider my options. He could be in there for hours, maybe even overnight if they really want to be assholes about it. I look at the time and see that I can get a few hours of bartending in if I just head back to work, so I climb into the car and call Scott on my way out of the parking lot.

Of course, who shows up within my first hour there, but Sean? Now I'm even more freaked out by him after Octavian's little info dump on me earlier. Lovely.

He winks at me as he sits at the bar right in front of my usual spot. "Nemy."

"Sean." I force a smile and place a shot glass in front of him. Then I reach for the Jameson and pour.

"Thank ya, lass," he says before picking it up and tossing it back. He hits the bar and shoves the glass forward. "'Nother."

I oblige and stand back to watch the intriguing display of masculine stupidity. This time he howls a little. Really? "Having a good night?" I ask and arch my right brow.

"Oh yeah," he says. "Go' a bit o' a problem out of mah way for a spell."

"Well, I suppose that's a good thing, right?"

A gleam hits his eye as he settles his gaze on me. "Aye, 'tis, lass."

"Wonderful," I say and turn on my heel to walk to the other end of the bar. I hope he decides to leave soon because quite frankly, I just don't want to deal with him tonight.

Two in the morning clocks in as I'm cleaning up my bar and Clancy still hasn't returned, nor have I heard from him. I keep checking my phone. Sean left an hour ago, so I'm able to clean up in peace, with exception to a couple of dancers wanting drinks. Once I'm finished, I grab my stuff, say goodnight to Scott, and head out the door.

It's exceptionally cold tonight, about a week before Christmas, and I pull my pea coat closed tight and flip up the collar, since I forgot my damn scarf. When I step around the corner of the building, I see Sean leaning against the Volvo. He has his legs crossed at the ankles and his bulky arms crossed over his chest. The leather jacket he's wearing strains against the muscle mass beneath it. I almost stop walking and turn back to have Scott escort me out, but he sees me and if I did that, he'd know he gets under my skin. Can't have him realizing that. It'll make everything ten times worse.

A smile flits across his lips and he cocks his head to the side, his eyes scanning me up and down. I attempt not to visibly shudder in revulsion and pull my keys out of my coat pocket.

"What are you still doing here?" I depress the unlock button on the remote. The lights flash twice and the driver's side door unlocks.

"Waitin' for you," he responds, but doesn't move.

I arch a brow at him. "Any particular reason, or are you my new stalker?"

He laughs. "Tha's a good one, Nemy." He leans forward, invading my personal bubble. "Jus' makin' sure you get to your car safe."

"And how interesting it is that you know my car when I've only had this one for like a week." I slip a hand into the door handle and pull. Then I toss my tote inside. "Especially since this is the first time I've seen you in the parking lot."

"Jus' here to protect ya, lass. Wouldn' want some looney comin' out the dark to scare ya."

I let out a short laugh. "You don't know who I am, do you?"

His brow goes up. "Who would that be, love?"

A grin spreads across my face. "I'm Don Michael Mussolini's *only* daughter."

"Is that so?" he replies, his voice going a bit high pitched with the typical Irish accent, which is weird considering how deep his damn voice is.

Normally, I wouldn't throw the name thing at someone, but a guy like Sean would know the name and respect it, especially if he's any type of mafia or has been to prison. I give him a short nod and open the door wider to climb in. "Yep, so you might want to remember that."

He pushes away from the car and turns toward the door, grabbing the top of it before I can close it. "Oh, you can bet'cher sweet fine arse I will, lass."

"Lovely." I look up at him. "Now, if you'll excuse me, I have homework to finish and need to get home."

He grins. "Goodnight then, Nemy."

"Night, Sean."

As I pull away, I make damn sure he's still in the parking lot and not getting in a vehicle to follow me. Apparently, I need to carry my gun—Clancy's borrowed gun—into the bar with me. Too bad that's illegal.

18

Foxy, Foxy

It's Christmas night, and I have to work. I'm fine with it because I haven't spent the holidays with my family in a few years. Last time was right after my divorce, and my father didn't say a word to me the entire time. So I decided to not ever go back during holidays. In fact, I haven't seen Papa since that day. I'd thought about moving to Italy to get away from the drama. I could live on the vineyard with my uncle and his family. I can't think of a more perfect place to work on my projects. All that Bisaccia scenery. Hell to the yeah.

Of course, that'd require me moving away from Clancy. Yeah, so not gonna happen.

The club's been decorated all Christmas-y since Thanksgiving, which I find rather strange, but the girls look cute in their Mrs. Claus and elf costumes for the night. Actually, they're quite hilarious and I'm having a hard time not laughing, even though my ribs are better now. Some of them are even playing the *Santa Baby* song and now the damn thing will be stuck in my head for the next two weeks. We're also busier than I expected. I'd say it's sad, but here I am too.

Clancy's sitting in his usual spot at the end of the bar, and the man is wearing a goddamn Santa hat, which about kills me every time I turn around. He even has a red shirt on—silky and shiny. Jesus. I can't really make fun, though, because I'm wearing a bright red corset, by request and with much animosity from me. I refuse to put on the antlers I found waiting for me when I came in tonight. I figure it might have something to do with Clancy wanting to mount me.

The police kept him a good portion of the night for questioning a week ago. I guess they're still looking at him as a suspect, but he hasn't said much about the whole episode, which kind of has me worried. It also means I'm keeping him at arm's length now. I do *not* need a man who is like my father. No siree, I don't.

He crooks his finger at me, beckoning me. I walk down to him, stifling my laughter, and lean against the bar. "What's up, Santa?"

He chuckles and pats his thigh. "Sit on my lap and tell me what you want for Christmas."

"Good God, no. You don't want to hear what I want for Christmas, Santa." All of which involves him and me and several hours of . . .

Yeah, my plan is so not working.

"Wow," he says. "Now I really *do* want to hear it."

"Not gonna happen," I say with a shake of my head. I am not indulging the man's fantasies tonight. No way.

"That's just cruel." His eyes scan the club and then settle on me again. "Make us a couple of drinks."

"You can't be serious."

"Oh, I am," he says with a grin, the evil glint appearing.

"Okay, what do you want?" I grab a couple of short glasses.

He shrugs. "You decide."

It's my turn to grin. "You got it." I scoop ice into the glasses and set them on the bar. Then I grab the Vanilla Stoli from the back bar and another (no, I'm not telling what it is), pour both in each glass and finish it off with a splash of Coke. It's the Dirty Russian's version of a Dirty Russian. Yes, that's my photographer's nickname, well, because he's Russian. I don't ask about the dirty aspect because I'm not certain I care to know.

My brow jumps when I place the drink in front of Clancy. "You'll like this. It tastes like candy."

He takes a sip and the grin spreads. "That's dangerous." He saw the alcohol that went into it. You can't really taste it, so the drink can sneak up on a person if they're not careful. Kind of like that jungle juice shit. He holds his glass up. "Merry Christmas, Nemy-girl."

"Merry Christmas, Clancy," I reply and the glasses clink. I don't have the time to sip mine and let it water down, so I drink it fast, throw the ice in the sink, and wash the glass. Clancy follows my lead and sets the ice-filled glass on the bar. "Want another?" My lips have twisted up into a devilish grin.

"Only if you'll have one with me."

I scan the bar, reach out and tap my fingers in front of him, and then grin. "Give me a minute." I have a couple of customers. Chris is working tonight too, and he's not happy about it. He keeps grumbling, so I take the brunt of the customers so he's not a crab-ass to them. He's more like a bar back for me tonight. Once I'm done, I head back over to Clancy and make another round for us, sans ice.

"You *did* eat tonight, right?" he asks while I mix the drinks.

"Yes. Had a nice pasta dish I learned how to make from my grandmother. You know what that means?"

"What?" He takes the drink from me.

I tilt my head to the side. "If we continue drinking, you're in trouble because I can drink a lot when I've had pasta!"

He laughs. "Well, alright then."

"Of course, I do need to drive home tonight." I bring the glass to my lips.

His head tilts up. "You can always come home with me."

I lean over and smirk. "You're not to that point yet."

"Seriously?" he asks, and I nod. "You sure enjoy kissing me."

Damn it. I got nothing. Oh wait . . . "My brain was overwhelmed by pain," I quip about our last encounter and stick my tongue out before walking away to help someone.

"Oh yeah, that was it," he shouts.

I don't make another drink for a while, and when I do, Clancy brings up going home with him again. The man just won't let it go.

"You're obsessed," I say when he pulls me to him.

That evil glint sparkles in his eye, and he lets out a short laugh and stands, pushing me back. "Chris, take the bar for a minute."

Chris nods, even though the look on his face says, *what the fuck*?

Clancy ushers me around the bar and into the back where his office is. He pulls his keys out, unlocks the door, and opens it. "After you."

I'm a bit leery about what he's up to, but I step forward, and he follows and closes the self-locking door behind him. Oh, this could be a bad situation. I turn around in front of the desk. "Am I in trouble or something?"

His eyes gleam with danger when he grins at me. "Oh, you're in trouble, all right." He takes a step forward, closing the small gap between us, and he slides his arm around and behind me to move objects on the desk to the side. Then he lifts me up as his face slowly makes its way up my shoulder and neck, and he plops me right on the desk and stands between my legs.

I suck in a small gasp, and whisper, "Holy shit."

He chuckles against my skin as his lips travel up my neck to my jaw and finally hover over my mouth. "Nemy-girl, tell me to stop and I will."

At first, I can't speak, and he stares into my eyes, waiting. I swallow the gi-normous lump in my throat, and whisper the only excuse that comes to mind, "I'm still having issues with the fact that you're my boss." I know, it's getting old, but it's the only thing I can think of to stop him. Clancy's not one I want to be a *wham bam thank you ma'am* kind of night. *Bow chicka bow wow,* maybe, with all sorts of kinky . . . I shake the lusty thoughts from my head, but it's too late. My body's burning up.

His face pulls back a little, and a devilish smile spreads. "Well, I could fire you, but then I'd be losing the best bartender I've ever had."

I roll my eyes for the umpteenth time of him making this statement. "Please."

"Besides, if you work for me still, you can keep an eye on me, right?"

My eyes widen at the fact that he actually heard me that night so long ago, *and* he'd said *that would be a turn-off for you* when I commented about what a woman wouldn't want. Holy shit. "Um . . . I really don't know, Clancy."

The short laugh comes again. "I need to stop giving you time to think about it, it seems," he says and presses closer. "Maybe this will help you figure it out." His hand slides up my back, into my hair, and he pulls me just a little forward into the kiss. My body, of course, wants to slam him against the wall and fuck the hell out of him, and my brain starts to shut down all logic while his other hand presses against my lower back, pulling my hips forward while he's kissing me just like that night at the bar.

Okay, I'm about to fuck Santa Claus. That is not a good picture in my mind! I snatch the hat off his head and throw it God knows where.

The doorknob jiggles with the sound of keys making their entrance into an unknown land, and the door opens. Clancy kicks a foot back and slams it into the door. Scott yells. "I'm busy," Clancy says at my chin because his head has dipped down and turned a little to the side.

"Okay," Scott replies in a painful tone that has me wondering what happened. "Can I have my hand back?"

I stifle my laughter, and so does Clancy.

"Sure. Sorry about that."

"It's good," Scott says through clenched teeth and slides his hand back out the door.

Clancy kicks the door shut again, and his eyes return to me. "Well, Nemy-girl?"

I look into those beautiful eyes and smile. "I think I'm lucky it's not after hours."

His eyebrow jumps. "That you are." His grin grows wide. "Tomorrow, you're going to dinner with me."

I shake my head. "I have to work tomorrow night."

"Well, now you don't," he returns.

"Are you serious? Friday is my best night!"

"Are *you* serious?" he asks. "You make almost forty grand a year!"

I grin. "Actually, I make more than that, and it's because you keep losing bets . . . and I get really good tips."

His face moves closer once more. "Maybe I lose on purpose." His brow jumps again. "Ever think of that?"

"You'd better not," I insist as I recall the night of that kiss. "That'll ruin the whole thing for me."

His laughter is deep, and I can feel it rumble through my body. "Well, we wouldn't want anything ruined for my little Nemy-girl, would we?" His lips go to my neck again.

A soft moan leaves my lips. Wasn't there something about him and my dad? "I don't recall making a decision."

He chuckles against my flesh, which has my body going crazy again. His hand leaves my back and reaches for something on the desk. Then he slowly pulls away from me and holds a box in front of him.

"What's that?"

"A gift. I saw it the other day and thought you'd like it. Merry Christmas."

Ooh, presents. I take the box from him while adjusting my seat on the desk, and I open it to find a seriously kick-ass leather bondage corset. Buckles and straps down the front and back in black. "Oh, this is cool."

"Yep," he says with a nod. "That's the reaction I knew I'd get."

I check the tag and find it's my size. "You're a smart man."

"Yes, I am." He grins.

"How'd you know my size?" I turn it around and place it against my body to check the look. Clancy doesn't respond, so I look up at him to find an arched brow with a look that says, *seriously*? I giggle because the man does own a gentleman's club, after all, and has been around enough women to be able to eye one's size.

"Are you going to try it on?"

"Not right now. Especially in front of you."

He laughs. "Modest, huh? I like that, but I have seen your breasts."

"Don't remind me." I shake my head slowly. "Modesty is the reason I'm behind the bar, and not on the stage."

"Oh, you've considered it?" he asks with a chuckle.

I shake my head more quickly this time. "Absolutely not!"

Clancy steps forward again and places a hand next to each of my hips when he leans into me. "This is why I'm interested. You're smart, you're funny, and I will *never* see you on that stage."

I fold the corset in my lap and pick at it. "Amanda was a stripper, wasn't she?"

He's silent for a moment before he finally nods.

"Why'd you marry a stripper?"

"I was young and stupid," he replies.

"Oh man, do I ever understand that."

"I know you do."

I just have to ask it again because he never really answered me the first time. Well, he didn't know at the time. "I know we kind of talked about this, but do you have a child?"

He bites his lower lip. "As you know, I just found out about it when Mr. Raymond visited. She's insisting the child is mine."

My eyes blink in rapid flutters. "How old? Boy or girl? How could she not tell you?"

"*She* is three months old, and the bitch didn't tell me because she's a fucking bitch," he replies. "I'm not even sure the kid is mine."

Wait, the math on that doesn't work out. "How long—"

"Five years," he replies. "We were trying to reconcile, but it didn't work out, and then you walked into my bar."

"Did she cheat on you?" I ask, and he nods again. Well, that explains the whole *I don't fuck or date strippers* statement.

"I'm doing a paternity test."

"And if she is yours?" I'm a little nervous about his answer.

He shrugs. "I'm not sure what I'll do."

Clancy sees I've tensed regarding the subject.

"Don't think that I'll ever leave you for any reason," he says. "Especially to go back to that bitch."

I swear, the man can read my fucking mind. That alone should scare me. I shrug. "I didn't think Jeremy would ever leave me, either."

He lifts my chin and his nose touches mine. "I remember the hell he put you through. I remember the countless sleepless nights and the dark circles under your red, swollen eyes. I will never do that to you."

"You won't make me cry, huh?" I give him a half-smirk, but he stays serious.

"I don't intend to make you cry . . . ever," he insists.

I roll my eyes. "That's what they all say."

His chuckle sounds almost pitying, but now he knows I'm kind of joking around.

My eyes focus on his and we stare at each other for a long time. I could stare into his eyes for the rest of my life. Finally, I say, "Can I get back to work now before Chris chases all the customers away?"

He grins, and he gives me a quick kiss on the nose. "Sure, but one of these days you and I are going to finish what we start without interruptions from work or anything else."

I giggle because I just don't see that happening. When he steps back, I hop off the desk and place the corset on top of it.

"Not going to take it with you?"

"I can't walk out there with this thing."

He laughs. "Okay, I'll remind you before we leave."

I nod and head for the door. "You coming?"

"In a minute," he says, so I walk out and shut the door behind me.

I can see what he's doing now. He's moving at my pace so I don't freak out and run. I'm not sure I want to run away from him now.

Holy crap.

✯ ✯ ✯

At the end of the night, which is early because it's Christmas, I clean up and cash out as usual, finishing everything I need to do, and while I'm doing all of that, after everyone else has left, Clancy retrieves my gift from his office. He hands it to me and I stuff it in my tote. Then I pull my jacket out and put it on, and I grab my bag. "Are you done?"

"No. I still have a few things to do, but I'll walk you out if you're ready to leave."

I nod, and he grabs his keys. "You're usually finished by now," I remark as we head for the door. "What else do you have to do?"

"Some paperwork," he replies, and unlocks and opens the door for me. "Important paperwork."

I step out into the chilled air and pull my coat closed. "On Christmas night? Do you need help?"

He smiles and his hand takes my elbow. "No, I'm good, but thanks. What time should I call you tomorrow?"

"I should be up around one or so."

We step up to my car—*his* car—and he leans over to kiss me. "I'll call around two to give you a chance to wake up." Then his lips touch mine and I don't even think about it. I just kiss him back. When he pulls away, I unlock the car and throw my tote inside, onto the passenger seat. I slide down into the car, careful not to hit my damn ear again, and once I'm sitting down, I look up at him.

"Please be careful when you leave tonight," I say, a hint of worry in my voice.

He smiles and steps to the side to lean in. "Always, Nemy-girl." He gives me another quick kiss, and then stands and shuts the door.

I start the car to get the heat going, pull out my iPod, and search the playlists. I have a few different ones just for driving, some for when I'm working on homework or drawing, and some for different moods. I select "Driving Late" with a vast assortment of hard-hitting songs that'll keep my ass motivated, and of course, Flogging Molly is on that playlist. I set it up, put the car in gear, wave to Clancy, and drive away. I see him enter the club, mainly because I stopped and waited for him to do so, which left a happy little grin on his face, and then I head home.

I'm kind of nervous about several details. Not so much the house thing in the next week, but the dinner and the child—definitely. It's been a long damn time since I've been on a real date. Christ, if he keeps kissing me like that, he'll have me in bed within the week if I'm not careful.

Should I be punching Clancy in the face about now? Damn.

I pull into my driveway and shut the car off. Tonight's drive seemed a little faster, probably because my mind is filled with fantasies about Clancy. I grab my tote from the passenger seat and something catches my eye. When I turn my head toward the seat, I get a full view of the present left for me. I smile because the single red rose is beautiful, and I pick it up and climb out of the car after retrieving the gun from the glove box. Clancy's a damn romantic. Who'd have thought? This definitely squashes my nervousness about dinner on Monday. He's going to need a much bigger surprise to get me over the nerves about the child.

I walk inside my house, close the door behind me, and pull the note off the stem. Familiar chicken scratch graces the paper and my heart stops as I read the words.

You and I will share a fine meal together soon, Nemy. I always get what I want. Sean.

I reach for the door with a shaky hand and quickly lock the knob and deadbolt. I drop the note and the rose, and run through the house, checking every door and window with the Beretta in hand. Once I'm somewhat satisfied and feel a little secure after having Tonk search the entire house with me, I grab my phone and call Clancy, but he doesn't answer. I try a few more times, but all I get is his voicemail. My heart races faster than it ever has and I open the laptop and email Octavian to see if he can find any more information on Sean the scary leprechaun. He won't get it until morning because he's likely sound asleep by now, having put the kids to bed hours ago and cleaned up after the day's Christmas festivities.

I cover my face with tired hands, the gun still in one hand. I wish I had some family here to run to right now, to protect me, but they're all somewhere else that would require a plane trip.

My hands are graced with the wetness of rarely shed tears. I can't start showing weakness now. It might get me killed, since I don't really know what Sean's plans are yet. I wipe my eyes and draw in a deep breath, and then I pick up the laptop and start searching for anything about Sean. My brother's search would be more in depth, but hey, I may find something. I need to have a reason to shoot first. The police can ask their questions later.

19

Winter Solstice

I finish my search, coming up with only what looks to be a botched robbery fifteen years ago and I'm guessing that's the incident where Sean's brother died. Due to subtle comments here and there, not to mention my brother's little info dump on Clancy too, I scour the newspaper article for Clancy's name and find nothing. Thank. God. However, Sean and Connor Delaney are all over that article and a few others. Connor was shot by police, who interrupted the robbery, and Sean ended up being sentenced to . . . well, what do you know, fifteen years. Explains his lack of social skills. I can't find anything else on him, though. Nothing that would signify my being in any kind of danger outside of what Octavian told me on the phone and what I've experienced already. Of course, I'm still taking heed because I know for a fact that evil isn't always center stage for the entire world to see. Just because it looks like a leprechaun and talks like a leprechaun, it doesn't mean it can't act like the little fucking demon it is.

I stare at the wall for a smattering of minutes when I'm hit with the need to write something. Blogging is a form of writing, so I do that and put up a small piece I wrote just for Clancy.

Around three in the morning, my phone rings.

"Something's happened at the club," Scott says. "I got a call from the security company." He's the general manager, so he gets the calls too.

"Was it bad?" In the back of my mind, I'm wondering why he's calling me to tell me someone's potentially broken into the place. Unless it's burned down. Shit, I hope not.

"It's not good." He's silent for a space of heartbeats. "Nemy," he says and pauses, which has the warning bells going off in my head. "Clancy was still inside."

My whole body freezes as dread runs through me. I struggle to breathe. "Is he . . . okay?"

His voice is grim. "He's at Scottsdale Osborn. Beat up pretty bad. Not sure what all happened yet."

I gasp. That hospital has the top trauma center. Only the real bad cases go there and with the club's location, St. Joe's or even Phoenix General would be closer.

"How bad?" I run into my bedroom for shoes. I don't have time to change out of my holey jeans and tank.

"Don't know other than what I've told you. I haven't talked to him, not that he's talking right now."

I gasp into the phone and drop to my bed. Oh. God.

"Sorry, Nemy. Look, just get to the hospital and check on him. I called because I know that's what he'd want me to do and you'd want to know."

Breathing has become difficult and everything is fuzzy around the edges.

"Nemy?"

I drag in a deep breath and attempt to focus. Clancy. Hospital. Go. "I'm here." After a moment's thought, I ask, "Do they have any clues as to who it was?"

"No," Scott replies. "But they have the video from the security system. Nothing was really stolen, except for maybe some liquor. All the night's cash is still there. He'd already deposited it in the safe."

I double-check the hospital.

"Keep me updated," he says.

"You too." I hang up the phone, grab my coat and purse, and run out the door.

The drive into Scottsdale is horrifying, only because I'm so worried and freaked out, but it's only a fifteen minute drive. When I reach the emergency room, they give me the drill, so I have to tell them I'm his fiancée. The nurse at the front desk pauses before letting me in and I walk at a fast pace to the next nursing station. They point to his room and I walk quickly down the hall, checking each room as I follow the numbers, passing several occupied curtains along the way. When I finally reach his room, I see why the nurse paused. A tall blonde-haired woman stands beside his bed, holding his hand. She looks like white trash gone rich in her tacky thrown-together high-priced outfit. Long manicured nails in bright red tip her fingers, and her hair looks like it would go up in flames if someone lit a cigarette within a three-foot radius of her. I also call girls who look like her Guidettes. Rare to see one on the west coast.

She scans me with blue eyes when I step into the room, and she gets this little smirk on her face that I want to slap right the hell back off. It probably has something to do with my outfit. "Who are you?"

I give her my best fake smile. "Nemesis."

"What kind of name is that?"

"A good one."

She laughs. "Oh, are you one of his dancers?" Strippers never call themselves strippers, except for Cherry.

"No. I'm one of his bartenders."

Her waxed-too-thin eyebrow goes up. "Now why would his wait staff feel the need to show up?"

I don't answer, but instead step up to Clancy's other side and take his right hand. Both of his eyes are black and blue, he has tubes going in everywhere I can see and I'm certain a few places I can't see, and his face is cut up but sutured. "Holy shit."

"It doesn't look so bad on the outside."

I quirk a brow at her because the bitch must be blind.

"He has some internal stuff going on, though."

"Like what?" I squeeze his hand gently to let him know I'm there.

She has to think about it. This may take a while. "Um, something happened to a lung and kidney, I think."

Seriously, why is she even here? "Where's the doctor?" I turn around to look out.

"He's supposed to be by again soon."

Thank God because I'll never find out any information from this twit.

"I'm Amanda."

I raise my eyes to her. "I know who you are." I run my fingers along Clancy's palm in a gentle sweeping motion to see if I can stimulate movement.

"His wife," she continues.

"Oh, I thought it was ex-wife."

She doesn't appear happy at my knowledge of this. "Well, yes."

Clancy's fingers move a little against mine and I smile.

"What are you doing?" She peers over him.

I don't answer and look at his face. His eyes flutter open and he looks right at me, and then he attempts a smile, God knows why, but it disappears when he sees her.

A nurse walks in, thankfully ceasing any conversation with Amanda. "Ah, good, Mr. Dolan. You're awake." She walks around to where Amanda is and has her move so she can check his vitals.

Amanda groans and stomps to the far wall, outright pissed she had to move while I still stand beside him.

The nurse looks at me. "Are you his wife?"

"No, fiancée."

"I'm his wife," Amanda states. The nurse's eyes flick from me to Amanda and back to me before a smile touches her lips.

"Ex-wife," I say.

"Well, Mr. Dolan, you've had an interesting evening, haven't you?"

He moans his answer.

"Are you in pain?"

Clancy nods.

Once she's done checking him, she smiles again. "We'll see what we can do about getting you something for the pain. I'll have to check on what they've already given you."

He nods slowly and his eyes flick to me as the nurse leaves.

I lean over him. "Who was it?"

He shakes his head.

"Who? Did you recognize them?"

He shakes his head again, and I'm at a loss as to who it could have been if his property is "protected." It has me wanting to ask exactly where that protection was while someone beat him to a bloody pulp. Clancy's fingers tighten around mine, like he knows my thoughts and is afraid I'm going to do something stupid.

"Looks like it's my turn to take care of you." I give him a wink. This time, the smile does appear, at least in his eyes, and it warms my heart.

Amanda rushes back to his side and grabs his other hand. "Clancy, baby, I'm here for you."

Oh, for the love of God. I roll my eyes and watch as Clancy attempts to regain his hand. "Why are you even here?"

She gets snotty with me. "We have a *child* together."

"Maybe." I stop there because it doesn't need to be discussed like this in front of Clancy, and because the doctor walks in.

"Good morning, Mr. Dolan. How are you feeling?"

Clancy's right brow goes up a fraction of an inch and he closes his eyes.

Doc's looks from me to Amanda and he chuckles, but doesn't say a word about what he may think. "Nurse Reba says your vitals are good. Are you allergic to anything?"

Clancy slowly moves his head back and forth.

"Good, I'll get you something for the pain."

"What's going on with him, Doctor?" I ask, since blonde twit here couldn't tell me anything. Don't get me wrong. I don't think all blondes are stupid. Echo is actually quite intelligent, but this woman . . . well, Jesus.

"Well, he had some internal bleeding, a class two hemorrhage, around the kidneys, but we were able to take care of it with a saline drip. They hit him pretty good there. The gunshot didn't hit anything vital."

"Gunshot?" I ask wildly. "Where?" I glare at Amanda for not telling me about it.

"In the shoulder here," he replies and points it out.

I nod and refocus.

"But that's about it other than some bruising and cuts. He's a lucky man."

"No lung issues?" I ask, just to be sure.

"At first, we thought so, but he's fine. He was unconscious when they brought him in and had some trouble breathing. It's his heart that concerns me because of his age. Ran a CT scan and an MRI, but everything looks good. He's just beat up and shot." He looks at Clancy as I withhold a burst of laughter wanting to explode from my mouth. "No more fighting off burglars for you, Mr. Dolan."

Clancy groans.

I've always loved doctors with a sense of humor. "He says no problem."

"He's lucky he doesn't have any broken bones, as badly as they beat him. But he'll need some supervision once we discharge him. Could take a day or two."

"No problem," I say and pat the back of Clancy's hand. "He's a strong boy."

"It's a good thing," he says. "We'll observe him for a few more hours and then they'll probably move him upstairs later today."

"Thank you, Doctor." I smile at him.

Doc nods and leaves the room.

"I can take care of him," Amanda insists.

I look at Clancy and nod upward once, asking the silent question. He moves his head once to the right in answer. "It's okay, Amanda. I owe him anyway."

"Well, I am his wife," she states . . . again.

"He doesn't want you to, Amanda." And I don't want to watch them do whatever they're about to do as a small team comes into the tiny room. "I think I'll step out for a minute." It's too crowded in the small space and I can't handle it.

Amanda joins me in the hall amidst a row of curtains containing beds and patients behind them. I think someone just moaned. "You think you've got your claws in him?"

I look at her fingernails again and then smile at her. "I'm not the one with claws."

She splays her fingers out in front of her and smiles. "Yeah, these babies will claw your eyes out."

"Sweetie, you two are divorced and have been for some time. Go home to your baby girl, because you really don't want to fuck with me."

"Just protecting my interests."

I raise a brow at her. "What interests?"

She grins. "The club."

"What about it?" I ask as the nurses file out of the room.

Amanda turns her head, raising her shoulder to her chin, and smirks at me before bouncing back into the room. Wow, she is a fucking bitch. When I step back inside, Clancy's hoarse whisper travels to my ears.

"Go home, Amanda. I don't want you here."

"Just making sure you're gonna live," she quips and picks up her purse. Her eyes flick to me, run the length of my body, and rest on my face once more. "Nemesis. What does that mean anyway?"

See what I mean? Dumb.

"Enemy." I give my best all-knowing smile because the stupid bitch doesn't realize I could very easily kick her ass. She probably fights like a girl anyway.

She shoves her nose in the air, and her heels click against the linoleum as she walks to the door. "Call you tomorrow, Clancy-baby."

"Please don't," Clancy whispers.

I watch her leave, holding back the compulsion to visibly shudder with disgust and tackle her to the ground, and I then turn to him. "You can't seriously have married *that*!"

He lets out a half-laugh, half-groan. "She wasn't like that before I married her, and I was stupid enough to think she loved me." He clears his throat and I reach for the cup and pitcher on the rolling table. Both are empty. "Bitch. She's the reason I don't like blondes anymore."

"I'll be right back." I head out of the room before the statement hits me. And here I thought blondes were more his type. Guess not anymore. Thank you, Amanda!

I have to ask one of the nurses if Clancy can have ice chips, and where I might find them, and then I return to his room. I pull an ice chip out of the cup and lean over him. "Here, this will help your throat."

Green eyes stare at me as he takes the chip into his mouth. "Thanks."

I nod and stand straight again. "Was it just one guy, or were there more?"

Clancy reaches for my arm and pulls me to the edge of the bed, wanting me to sit down. "Started with one; ended up being several. They didn't even ask for the cash. There was another purpose and that was simply to" —he coughs and groans— "beat me up for whatever reason."

I give him another ice chip. "Try not to talk too much, sweetie."

His eyes flick to me and smile with a little twinkle. "Sweetie?"

I grin. "Don't get excited. I call everyone that."

"Still sounded good," he replies and squeezes my hand. He has a strong grip, which is good because he won't be spending a week in here. "So, when are we getting married?"

I laugh. "Hey, I had to say I was your fiancée or they wouldn't let me back here."

He nods. "So . . . when are we getting married?"

I decide to change the subject. "You're lucky nothing's broken."

Clancy's eyes wash over me and he smiles as his hand breaks from mine and opens my coat. "You didn't even change."

"I was worried about you."

He pulls me down by my coat collar and kisses me with more strength than I thought he'd have right now. "You should go home and sleep."

"I'll be fine," I say against his battered lips. "You'd be surprised at how long I can stay awake. Besides, I've only been awake for fifteen hours. I'm not even tired yet."

He lets out a heavy sigh, which looks like it pains him to do. "I don't want to be here."

"Where would you like to go?"

"Home with you."

I give a warm smile and touch his cheek. "Well, that's not going to happen for a little while, so how about a land far, far away?"

"A story?"

"Sort of." I lean in to kiss his forehead.

Clancy gives me the go ahead with a nod and I close my eyes to bring forth the memories. "When I was a little girl, we once visited my uncle in Italy—he has a beautiful vineyard there. I remember one day, walking down the rows of vines, the sun shining brightly—its warmth felt wonderful on my skin—I came upon a baby bird near one of the old scattered trees that grew defiantly within the vineyard. I knelt down and inspected the bird carefully, thinking maybe it'd broken a wing or something, but it seemed to be okay."

He smiles. "It didn't have a broken wing? Maybe it just fell out of the nest."

"Don't get ahead of my story." He chuckles and I continue. "Knowing that I shouldn't touch the bird because then its mother wouldn't claim it—which I now know to be false—I carefully picked it up with the skirt of my dress." I glare at him for raising an eyebrow at me. "Yes, I wore a dress. Hush. I was like seven."

He chuckles. "I'm just trying to imagine you in a dress."

"You're lucky you're in pain, or I'd smack you."

"What happened to the baby bird?"

"I took it back to the villa to show my dad, who scolded me for picking it up. I explained to him that I couldn't just let it die there in the field. He smiled sweetly at me, as a father does with his little girl, and picked up a linen napkin. Then he took the little bird from my skirt and asked me to show him where I found it. We walked out through the vineyard until we came upon the tree, and he told me to climb after spotting and pointing out the nest. So I climbed up into the tree and looked at the nest where all his little brothers and sisters were, and my dad climbed up behind me, opened the linen napkin, and scooted him out into the nest. It was then that I noticed my little bird's feathers were different, like a different color, so I asked my dad why. He said, 'God made him that way so you'd be able to recognize him when he's all grown up, *figlia mia*. And I was satisfied with that answer, being only seven."

Clancy smiles at me and runs his fingers down my arm.

"We spent the whole summer at the vineyard, and one day I walked out to the tree as part of my daily routine to check on the bird. When I got there, I found him perched on the edge of the nest. He looked down at me, and then jumped out of the nest. It was as though he'd been waiting for me so I could watch him fly."

"And he flew, I assume?"

I nod. "Yep, he flew . . . and then a cat jumped out of the tree and took him to the ground as I watched in horror."

"Oh shit." Clancy grips my arm in the midst of trying desperately not to laugh.

"That was the day I learned about death." I stare down at my hands. Then my eyes flick up to meet Clancy's. "I gave him a name, you know."

He smiles. "What did you call him?"

"Octavian, because he reminded me of my youngest brother," I bite my lower lip. "You see, a year earlier we were driving upstate—I think we were going to Connecticut—and during the drive, Octavian stopped breathing. We sped down the highway, my mom in a panic and yelling at my dad, my dad trying to calm my mother down, but it's no use because Octavian's not breathing. My other three brothers aren't making things any better by trying to peer over the front seat to see what's happening, so my dad starts yelling at them. Meanwhile, I'm just sitting in the backseat trying to decipher the chaos, and I didn't understand it because I was so young."

"So what happened?" Clancy asks, his grip not softening in the slightest because he can tell this is difficult for me.

"We get to the hospital and they rush inside with Octavian, leaving my oldest brother in charge of the rest of us. A long while later, they come out of the hospital with Octavian, and he's fine. He's breathing, he's healthy, and he's even happy. God's given him a chance to spread his wings and fly." Tears fall down my cheeks and Clancy reaches up to wipe them away. "So, one Octavian survived, but the other one didn't, and the day I learned about death was the day I realized that could've been my brother instead of a bird."

Clancy just stares at me, his thumb caressing my cheek, wiping more tears away. "That's one hell of a lesson for a seven-year-old to learn." He pulls me to him in a hug and cradles me against his chest, which is probably bruised as hell, but he holds me tight. "I'm sorry, Nemy-girl."

"No, Clancy, I'm sorry," I reply in muffled words against his neck. "I'm sorry I've been such a stubborn bitch with you, but the thought of losing you tonight scared the hell out of me." I pull back and look him in the eye. "I'll stop being so damn stubborn. I want the chance to spread my wings and fly."

His hands cup my face and he pulls me down into a kiss. "It'll take a hell of a lot more to kill me than a bunch of thugs or a ratty cat."

I giggle against his lips. "God, I hope so."

"I just wish I'd left with you last night," he whispers into my mouth.

"Me too," I whisper in reply and kiss him.

This took entirely too long for me to realize. I know, I'm an idiot.

20

You Do Something to Me

It's dawned on me Clancy's nights off are always—and I mean *always*—the same as mine. So, I'm making a decision to break one of my most important rules, and if it doesn't work out, I'll have no one to blame but myself.

He'd better not fuck me over. I might end up in prison. Like my father, I've done a good job of staying away from that fortress.

On a side note, I'm still trying to figure out how a mafia Don stays out of prison all his damn life. They must be hiding something from me.

The hospital discharges Clancy the next day (evening, really) and after making a stop at his house for some things, he comes home with me because I have an animal to take care of and he doesn't. I'm so exhausted at this point because I haven't really slept much aside from a quick cat nap or two in a very uncomfortable chair in his hospital room.

I settle him into my more comfortable bed after helping the man strip to his boxers (his body is in Oh-My-God shape, even when he's all banged up), and then I grab a blanket and my favorite pillow. He catches my arm before I leave his side.

"Where are you going?" he asks in a groggy voice.

"To sleep on the spare bed." My own voice sounds tired. "I don't want to disturb you."

"Bullshit. You're tired as hell. Sleep in your own bed."

He's not letting go of my arm and I stare down at him. His eyes, still surrounded by black and blue, open in slits to look up at me.

"Are you sure?"

He nods a little and pulls me forward, and I almost fall on him.

"Jesus, Clancy, be careful."

He chuckles. "Come to bed, Nemy-girl."

I throw the pillow back on the bed and spread the blanket out over him. "Give me a minute." Then I take care of some things around the house, and once I've finished, I return to the bedroom and watch him for a minute before trying to figure out just what in the hell I'm going to wear because I don't have pajamas.

"What's the problem?" he whispers, eyes still closed.

"Nothing." I kick off my shoes and socks, and push my jeans down. Then I turn off the light and climb into bed behind him.

He reaches back with his right hand to find mine under the covers, and he slowly turns over to face me. In the darkness, I can't really see the bruises and cuts on his face, but I can see those eyes and they warm with a smile. "Thank you."

"For what?" I'm still lying on my back, my head turned to him.

He brings my hand up and kisses the back of it. "Caring."

"Um . . . like I'm not going to care about you after all we've been through."

His grasp tightens on my hand. "Finally got you into bed," he whispers and winks at me.

I laugh and watch his eyelids grow heavier with each passing second. "I don't think these were the circumstances you were aiming for, though."

Mmm hmm." His eyes don't open again and I think he's fallen asleep, so his voice startles me when he speaks again. "Goodnight, beautiful."

"Night, Clancy."

It doesn't take very long for his medication to kick in, rendering him fast asleep. I rescue my hand from his and turn on my side, and I watch him sleep for a long time before falling off to sweet slumber myself, but not before a very large dog hops up on the bed and curls up between our legs.

During the next week, I have Chris fill in for me the first two nights and I have Monday night off, but Clancy's doing well enough for me to go in Tuesday and Wednesday nights. He doesn't really want me to because it's New Year's Eve, and I told him about the rose I found in the car, but he makes me promise I'll have Mike or Scott escort me out after my shift.

Tonk takes good care of him, keeping him warm by curling up next to him no matter where he is, and by the time I get home Wednesday night, Clancy is fiddling around on his laptop with the dog at his side. My laptop came back from the shop—finally—the day before.

He glances up at me as I walk through the living room and head into the kitchen. "Did Sean show up tonight?"

I cringe upon hearing the name, but answer, "No," and continue to mumble a *thank God* as I pour myself a glass of wine.

Clancy clears his throat. "Any *surprises* waiting in your car?"

"Nope." I walk into the living room. "Maybe he gave up. It *has* been a while."

He just shakes his head, and I can practically hear the thought he doesn't want to voice—*Sean doesn't give up.*

I move Tonk off the sofa and glance at the screen when I sit down next to him before sipping my wine. "What'cha doing?" I catch a glimpse of Amanda's name in the email he's working on and look away quickly because I'm not really the prying type. Okay, I am, but not in this instance. Amanda has called incessantly every day, sometimes three or four times a day. It's beginning to annoy the hell out of me.

"Emailing my attorney," he replies and hits send.

"About what?" I pretend not to have noticed her name.

He leans back against the sofa. "About Amanda and Sable."

I choke on my wine. "Who the fuck is Sable?"

"The paternity test came back positive. Sable is my daughter."

"Oh," I say because I have nothing else. Well, I do have one other thing. "She named her *Sable*? What kind of name is that?"

"A stupid one." He looks at me and then his eyes flick to my wine glass.

"It's nowhere near your computer." I hold it over the arm of the sofa.

"I can smell it from here. What is it?"

"You can't have any. You're still on meds."

He chuckles. "Just let me taste it."

I stare at him a moment and decide a taste will be fine, and I hand the glass over to him. He sniffs the bouquet, swirls the wine in the glass, watches the legs, and then tips the glass up for a small sample. He actually knows what he's doing and not faking it, which doesn't really surprise me. Eyes closed, he savors the wine, and a smile touches his lips after a few seconds. "This is good. What is it?"

"It comes from my family's vineyard in Italy," I reply and take back the glass. "It's one of the specialty merlots."

He looks at me. "Where in Italy is this vineyard?"

"It's in Bisaccia, north and a bit east of Naples. Beautiful country."

He nods, as though remembering the story I told him in the hospital. "I bet it is. I've never been to Italy."

"Oh, you should go. It's so wonderful. I'd like to move there someday."

"Is that so?" he says as his right brow goes up. "Perhaps we could take a trip there soon."

"I'll have to save up the money." Not really, because I have a nice little chunk in my savings account I've been saving for that rainy day, but he doesn't need to know that.

He smirks. "You do that."

I bite my lower lip and decide to return to the previous subject. "So, what are you going to do about the kid?"

He drops his head back against the sofa. "I don't know." Then he brings his head back up quickly. "I mean, Amanda wants child support, but wants to retain all parental rights, not even giving me visitation. She's being a royal bitch about this, which is par for the course with her."

"And you want to be a part of Sable's life?" I'm bit nervous about the outcome of that. I'm not sure I'm ready to have a baby around, not at the beginning of this whatever the hell it is thing with him.

His green eyes study me closely. "I don't know. Do I?"

My eyelids flutter. "Why are you asking me?"

"I need to know where we stand so I can make a decision. Were you serious about spreading your wings?"

I swallow the lump in my throat. "Um . . ."

He leans toward me. "Nemy-girl, if you want a child, I can give you one."

My eyes blink in rapid motion. "What? You can't be serious."

"I'm very serious." His face moves closer to mine.

"Do you really want to involve a child in our fairly new relationship?"

He arches a brow at me. "Let me ask you this, would you have dated me if I'd already had a child, regardless of age?"

"Well, yes, but that's not the point."

"It's precisely the point. A child isn't going to make a difference in how we feel about one another."

Damn it, he's right. I let out a frustrated sigh and stare at the coffee table.

He takes my hand and pulls it over to his lap. "Look, Nemy-girl, I can pay Amanda what she wants and walk away from it all—her, the child, everything. Or, I can take responsibility for my daughter and make sure she's raised in a loving environment . . . and right now, she's not in that environment."

I frown as I look up at him. "What do you mean?"

"Amanda is a meth addict and tends to spend many a night out drinking and getting high, thereby leaving the child at home . . . alone."

This floors me, that a mother could do such a horrible act. It floors me even more that she's getting away with it. "And how do you know this?"

"I've had her followed ever since Mr. Raymond visited."

My brain begins its theorizing of the past month's events regarding myself, with thoughts bouncing and rolling all over a pinball board until I hit the bonus. I turn my face so I'm looking directly at him. "Have you had *me* followed?"

For a split second, he looks away.

I gasp. "You have!"

"It's not what you think."

"It doesn't matter what I think the reason is, you had me followed. Who is he? What's his name? I want details."

He grasps my hand tighter. "I only had it done because of Sean. I wanted to be sure you were safe. He's not a pleasant fellow."

"So, you don't think I can take care of myself then?"

He lets out a heavy sigh. "It's not that. It's never been that."

"God, you're just like my dad," I say in a clipped voice.

"I'll take that as a compliment, considering who he is."

I glare at him. "You shouldn't!" I yank my hand out of his grasp and stand after placing my wine glass on the side table. As I walk around the coffee table, I run a hand through my hair. "Do you know why I went back to my maiden name?"

He shakes his head as he watches me closely from the sofa.

"Because everyone and their goddamn grandmother know the Mussolini family name . . . *everyone*. Sometimes, it's a blessing. Other times, it's a curse."

"Do you think I want you simply because of who you are?"

I stop pacing and turn to him. "That's just it, Clancy. I don't know when it comes to men like you, men who know my family and are involved in the same business."

He stands abruptly, staring me down from across the small rectangular table between us. "That's not the case." His demeanor is calm, but I can hear a touch of anger in his voice.

"How can I know? For all I know, you could want to make a name for yourself within the business."

"Have you done a search on me yet? Have you figured out who I am?"

"Yes," I reply. "I called one of my brothers."

He leans forward. "And what did you find?"

"That you've kept your nose clean for the last five years. That you pulled your brother off that job with Sean, which is why it went south."

"Anything else?"

I shake my head.

"Then tell me exactly why I would go to all the trouble of keeping my record clean if I was interested in making a goddamn name for myself." He runs his hand through his hair out of frustration. "I'm just a businessman, Nemy. I just want a quiet life with the woman I love and to raise a family. That's it. I don't care what your last name is, but I can tell you who will care . . . Sean. If he doesn't already know who you are, he'll find out soon."

"Fuck." I close my eyes at my own stupidity. "I told him."

Clancy steps around the table and comes to my side. "Because you thought it would protect you."

I nod and he wraps his arms around me.

"In most cases, it would. No one would be stupid enough to get within twenty feet of you without raising some hairs. But Nemy" —he raises my chin so I have to look up at him— "Sean's not your average gangster. He has no fear. He has no morals. He doesn't give a fuck about anyone but himself, and he doesn't care who he hurts along the way to get what he wants."

"What does he want?"

"You, plain and simple." He kisses my forehead. "I can see it in his eyes when he looks at you. I've seen that look before."

"What's any of this have to do with Amanda and Sable?"

"Nothing," he replies. "You tried to start an argument over a non-existent topic to put a wedge between us because you're afraid of what that child will mean if I get full custody."

"No, I'm a bit weirded out because after knowing you for a year, a woman suddenly appears and she's your ex-wife, and now there's a kid involved and you want me to help you make a decision that'll highly impact my life. I'm not ready for that. We've barely figured out what this thing" —I point to him and then to myself— "is between us."

"You think too much," he says calmly with that damn accent.

My hands go to my hips as I step away from him. "I can't help it! A child would be a dramatic change!"

He frowns. "I thought you wanted children."

"Oh my God, you are not listening," I say and rub my face. "I do want children, but not like this." Memories flood my mind—the miscarriage, the man I'd dated briefly who had a child . . . the pain of it all. What if Clancy gets his daughter and then decides he doesn't want me down the road? It's not like that's never happened to me before.

I don't realize I still have my eyes closed and start to sway from the oncoming anxiety attack until Clancy catches me. "No fainting. You need to deal with this."

I shake my head slowly back and forth. "I can't," I whisper.

He takes my face with his left hand and forces me to look at him. "You have to."

Tears blink away and fall down my cheeks as a long silence encompasses us before I answer. "He stopped loving me. Just stopped. How can somebody do that?" It's hard to say who I'm talking about because it covers several men. But I can suddenly breathe again.

I can see the anger flash in his eyes before they go soft as he wipes a tear from my cheek. He reaches for my left hand and pulls it up between us. His thumb moves the engagement ring back and forth.

"Did Jeremy give you this?" When I nod, he works it off my finger and throws it across the room, and then he leans forward. "I'll buy you a new one, if you want." Then he kisses me and, with his lips on mine, the pain and hatred that fractured my heart vanish and I feel whole again. "I want you in my life, Nemy. And I will never stop loving you."

I look up at him. "And I want to be there now, but you can't throw something as huge as a child at me and expect me to be all peachy fucking keen with it."

The noisy air-pull that signifies he's irritated comes through his nostrils, and finally, he shakes his head. "That's it." He slips his arms around me in a quick motion and he lifts me.

I press against his shoulders with my hands as he walks into the hall. "What are you doing? Be careful, Clancy. Don't hurt yourself."

"I'm doing something I should've finished several weeks ago," he replies and steps through my bedroom door. "Instead of letting you walk out on me." He lowers me onto my bed, positioning himself above me, staring into my eyes. "You see, Nemy-girl, I've learned something about you. If I give you too much time to think, you run scared, so I'm not doing that anymore."

"Clancy—"

"Hush," he replies and kisses me again.

Clancy's kiss is like a rare wine, subtle, yet overpowering, and I'm helpless, held in its trap of seduction while his soft lips work against mine. He runs his hand along my right leg, bending it so he can reach my foot, and he flips my tennis shoe off and pulls down the sock, discarding both to the floor. That same hand slides back up my leg, over my hip and waist, and up my side as his lips explore my neck. I let out a sigh, and I can feel his lips curve against my skin when his left hand repeats the removal of my footwear.

The leather corset I'm wearing tonight has frog hooks in the front, and his fingers nimbly work them open one at a time. I open my mouth to say something, but I get two fingers over my lips as he shushes me and returns to his work. I would tell him there's a faster way to get the damn thing off, but I'm kind of liking this way, so I stay quiet. He pulls the corset from beneath me and throws it behind him. I hear it hit the floor, a soft muddled thud against the carpet. He hesitates at my waist, trying to decide if he should go up or work on my jeans. He chooses the jeans and once he gets them off, he pulls his shirt over his head and throws it aside.

Oh dear God, that body. Broad shoulders tapering down to muscular arms—he looks even better after a week of healing. His pecks flex in turn and I must be drooling because he grins and leans forward. Sweet Jesus, he's got like the perfect V thing going on with that six-pack and his jeans hanging low on his hips.

His tongue slides up my stomach and I shiver. I run my fingers through his soft hair, pushing it back because it's hiding his face from me. Those green eyes meet mine as his tongue flits around my nipple, and it pulls a long overdue sigh from me. The necklace he's wearing—a dragon's tooth, he calls it—rests gently against my skin between my breasts, cool to the touch while his warm lips devour me.

I help him take his pants off in a euphoric daze because I'm enjoying the sensation his touch brings me, and I've forgotten all about our conversation once I see the length of his erection. Call me one-track minded, I don't care. He slips his fingers under my lace panties and slides them down, and then he returns to that place a man hasn't touched in months with perfect little circles over my clit.

I gasp. "Clancy?"

His lips curve against my skin. "Shh, just let me take care of you."

My back arches when I gasp again, and his lips continue their seduction, gracing my inner thigh before he moves on. His tongue slides up my slick folds that are wet with anticipation of taking him into me, and I'm already so close to orgasm because I've wanted him for so long.

"Oh my," I say in a sigh when his tongue plunges into me, sending me close to the edge of bliss. I clutch the bedspread with one hand, my other hand reaching down for a handful of that gorgeous hair of his. My hips undulate, bringing that tongue closer to my core again, and I let out a moan that hasn't left my throat in anything but solitude in ages.

He gently lifts me, hands sliding beneath my hips and lower back, and he turns me on the bed, and then lies next to me. I'm still a bit nervous about his condition, but he stops those thoughts when his right hand glides over me, caressing me with the gentlest whisper of a touch. He slips his hand around my side and pulls me on top of him in a motion that has me never doubting his strength again. I kiss him ferociously, devouring those lips and that long beautiful neck of his while his hands slide down my back and rest on my rear. One hand raises and slaps against my cheek with a quick *thwack*, sounding like a whip. It pulls a giggle from me and I look into his smiling green eyes. He laughs and pulls me down to him.

"Nemy-girl," he whispers. "I've waited so long . . ." He gently nibbles my earlobe before his lips meet mine once more in a heat of passion, his tongue slipping into my mouth while my hand takes his head, forcing him to stay where he is for the moment because I love kissing him.

Clancy's hand clasps my shoulder, his other behind my neck and into my hair. He drifts down my arm with light fingertips until they jump and he reaches my waist, and then they rest on my hip, pressing firmly into my skin. I raise my hips and lower myself until I can feel the tip of his shaft enter me. He pushes into me, raising his hips, and I bite my lower lip and sigh because oh my God that feels damn good. When my eyes flick to Clancy's face, his eyelids close and his head presses against the pillow. He digs into my hips with his fingers as I move gently on top of him, savoring each breathless moment of him being inside me.

He raises his hips again, only this time he rolls me onto my back, and he covers my breast with his mouth while his hand slips under my thigh, raising my left leg for a better position. Clancy's teeth close around my nipple and he pulls tenderly until it leaves his mouth and snaps back. A short moan escapes my lips before it's cut off by a gasp of breath.

"Sweet Jesus," I barely manage to get out, and really, I didn't intend for it to be voiced.

Clancy returns his lips to my neck, slowly running along my jaw line with light feathery kisses, and he finds my mouth once more while we move in perfect harmony I never thought was possible. Slow gentle movements of the lover who already knows your body, having tasted it several times over. My heart races, my breath catching every time he pushes himself deeper into me. His lips brush over my nipple once more and a shudder ripples through me. Sheer ecstasy, as my body reacts to his touch. My breath comes harder, faster, until it suddenly stops, keeping me frozen for that split second before I'm engulfed, drowning in it.

I cry out his name, one hand clutching the sheets on the bed, the other digging into his back with my nails. My head swims with emotion, thoughts, pleasure, and the scent of him, my Clancy, sending me reeling in a downward spiral as his orgasm joins mine.

He collapses against me after my name leaves his lips on a whisper, and I wrap every limb around him and hold him tight. I don't intend to ever let go of this man.

What seems hours later, he holds me in his arms and nestles his face against my neck, breathing deeply, satisfied, and I can feel his mouth move gently against my flesh.

"I'm sorry I threw the whole kid thing at you," he whispers in the curve of my neck.

"And I'm sorry for implying your intentions. I really do want to do this with you, but I need to see where it's going to go before introducing a child into the mix of chaos surrounding that which is my life."

He chuckles at my wording. "It'll go as far as you want to take it, Nemy-girl. I'm yours." He draws in a deep breath and when he exhales through his nose, it flutters across my neck and tickles a little.

"I'm so not used to this."

He lifts his head, stopping to kiss my cheek on the way before looking into my eyes. "Neither am I."

"Have you even met Sable yet?" I ask because he's talking about getting full custody of the little girl.

"Yes, for a brief moment. She's beautiful."

Oh, I can see the proud father twinkle in his eyes.

"It'll take some time to get her. She's not going to appear in my arms tomorrow."

"How long do you think?"

He shrugs. "Maybe a few months or more. This state tends to lean toward the mother, as do most. I'll have to prove she's not fit."

"How are you going to do that?"

"Not only have I had her followed, but the men following are documenting in every form possible. They have proof of the night she left Sable home alone all night."

Now I'm getting angry again. "What kind of mother does that?"

"Not a very good one." I think he's happy I'm pissed because there's a little gleam in his eyes.

"The whole night is photographed, including the John she fucked in her car."

I blink. "Did you call the police?"

"I'll handle it, don't worry. I have a child support hearing coming up soon anyway."

I'm used to statements like that first one from my childhood, so I don't think twice about it, but I'm thinking about the second part. I growl softly. "Take Sable away from the bitch with whatever means necessary. I'll deal with my own shit."

He moves his face closer to mine, until our noses touch. "You mean *we'll* deal with your shit."

I smile at him and give him a quick kiss. "I have a few concerns."

"You mean aside from this not being the best pillow talk?" He smirks at my glare. "Tell me." He traces the side of my face with his fingers.

"Well, how are you going to prove you're fit to care for her? I mean, there's the club and all. A judge might not like that. It's one thing if the kid's already in your custody, but it's entirely different when you're trying to get custody."

"I have a plan for that," he replies and winks. "Not to worry."

This brings a comment Amanda made to mind. "What's Amanda's interest in the club? She mentioned it."

He frowns. "She owns a small part of it."

Shock fills my face, I'm sure. "Okay?"

He laughs. "It was part of the divorce. The reason she was at the hospital was to see if I would live, or more beneficial for her, die. If I die, she inherits the club." He sees the concerned look on my face and shakes his head. "I've already discussed it with my attorney. He's drawing up the papers now to change things and buy her out."

"Wow, you were young and stupid." I grin.

He slaps a hand against my hip. "Hush, you."

I giggle and raise my head to kiss him. It's a nice long and slow one before he pulls himself away with a sigh, and I just have to say I love that I do that to him. He licks his lips afterward and gazes into my eyes.

"What would you think if I sold my portion of the club to her instead?"

"If that's what you want to do. Would she go for that?"

"I think she will," he says. "Amanda's very money motivated."

"I'll have to find a new job. What are you going to do?"

"I don't know. Maybe I'll retire." He gives me a grin that reaches his eyes.

"How much is the fucking club worth?"

"A lot because it has a liquor license attached to it. Around seven figures."

"Holy shit."

"Any more concerns?"

I nod. "Please tell me you'll rename her." If Sable were older, I wouldn't suggest it because it could damage a child's psyche, losing their identity, so to speak. However, she's just a baby.

He laughs again. "Damn straight. She's young enough." He leans in and starts kissing my neck. "Will you help me with a name?"

"Sure." I'm swept up in his kisses for a moment. "She's healthy, right? I mean, if Amanda's an addict . . ."

"She's perfect," he says.

"What does she look like?" I'm hoping nothing like Amanda.

"She looks like me," he replies, and then smiles. "And a little like you, actually."

"Shut up."

"Seriously, she does. When I saw her, my first thought was that this would be what our baby would look like."

"You're making me nervous again."

"Don't be nervous," he whispers in my ear after noticing I've tensed a little. "I'll take care of everything."

"I think you need to take care of me again."

His head pops up with a devilish little grin spreading across his face. "Abso-fucking-lutely." He kisses me, then rolls to the side, pulling me on top of him, and I grin at the man beneath me.

"I said *you* take care of *me*, not the other way around."

He laughs and slips a hand around to the back of my neck and pulls me down. "Oh, I can take care of you from here."

Oh my.

21

Head Like a Hole

Over the next month, I've had to deal with Amanda every time she shows up at the club, which has been several times. One night, she even brings Sable with her. Stupid bitch. Honestly, doesn't the woman have a fucking sitter? I keep checking my mental calendar for the child support hearing. God, why do these things have to take forever?

Sable is a little darling. Amanda stupidly sets her car seat in front of me to retrieve something from her over-the-top Louis Vuitton purse. Yeah, I don't think I need to say anything about white trash leaving the trailer park here, and she *is* thin, like straight out of Apache Junction thin. That place is like the meth capital for the state.

I pull Sable from her seat to hold her. She takes to me right away, and I don't want to put her back when Amanda yells at me for holding her. Her gripe is that she'll want to be held more often. Jesus, woman, get a fucking clue. She's a *baby*. She *needs* the personal attention.

Clancy notices how Sable takes to me too. She has his eyes and his black hair. I perform a little test on her to check her reactions, essentially checking her development process while I'm holding her. All of my brothers have kids, so I've been around babies. I've just never been one to hold a stranger's baby or freak when I see one and *have* to hold it. I'm not that kind of girl. Clancy notices my little test as well, and as soon as Amanda leaves, he turns to me.

"Well?"

I look at him in the midst of mixing a drink. "What?"

"Is she okay? I saw that little test of yours."

I giggle. "Amanda wasn't doing meth during the pregnancy, but that would have been painfully obvious. Sable is a bit thin, though. I don't think she's feeding her enough. There's definitely neglect there." I hand the drink to the man in front of me. "But something like fetal alcohol syndrome will be a little different. Does she drink a lot?"

Clancy has to think about it for a bit before answering me. "Only when she's stripping, as far as I can recall, and she hasn't done that in a long time."

"So, is Sable a little goodbye sex present?" I don't know how else to phrase that.

Clancy laughs. "I've been waiting for you to ask about that."

"Wasn't my business before."

"I suppose you could call it that. It was just the one time, and I was in a bad place."

My eyes flick to him. "Don't feel you have to justify it."

"I'm not. I just want you to know it only happened once."

"Okay." I pick up the tip the man left me and walk down to place it in the jar, and then I return to Clancy. "How long before she owns this place? I'll need to start looking for a new job."

"How about you don't look for a job and just work on that magazine idea of yours instead?"

"Are you kidding?" I say. "I'll go nuts."

He chuckles and shakes his head. "Trust me, you won't."

"Why, because I'll be taking care of a baby?"

He frowns. "Now don't think I'm going to do that to you, Nemy-girl." Then he sees my little smirk and his eyes narrow on me. "Oh, you little bitch."

I giggle and toss a cherry at him, which goes right down his shirt. "Goal!" I shout, jumping up and down.

He flies off the stool, knocking it over, and comes after me.

"Shit." I turn and run down the length of the bar, only to find myself trapped at the end. He wraps his arms around my waist and lifts me off my feet before I can turn around. "Clancy, stop, I have to work!"

He sets me back on my feet and rests his chin on my left shoulder. "Not for much longer."

I turn my head to the side. "Really?" I can't stop it, that gnawing feeling in the pit of my stomach which tells me something is just not right with this whole situation.

"What's wrong?" he asks. "I thought this would make you happy."

I shrug it off, considering it my over-active mind. "Nothing's wrong. I'm fine."

"No, you're not," he replies and turns me around. "Tell me."

"It just doesn't feel right. I don't know. Could just be my imagination."

He smiles and kisses my forehead. "Well, if there's one thing I've learned from you, it's to trust your feelings. I'll be cautious. I still remember your last words to me on Christmas night."

I shake my head and look down. "Don't remind me of that."

He lifts my chin. "You've saved my life and have come to my side when I needed someone. I don't forget these things easily. And before you say anything, yes, I would do the same for you."

I don't doubt this now. Clancy's been at my house a lot over the last month, not to mention that night he took care of me after my fight with James.

"Besides, that stay in the hospital is what changed your mind about me."

"That's true." Technically, it was right before I'd received the call that he was in the hospital.

"Would you two stop playing kissy-face," Cherry shouts over the bar.

I stick my tongue out at her, and then reach up around Clancy's neck and pull him down for a kiss. The club disappears for a long moment, and when he pulls back, he lets out a moaning sigh. I can't give him a hard time for it because he does the same damn thing to me.

"Back to work," I say and slap his chest.

"Ow." He jumps out of my way. "When are you done with school?" I hear Clancy ask Cherry as I help a customer.

"Tomorrow's my last day." She plucks a cherry from the fruit tray. The cherries always disappear when she's working, and I have to wonder at times if this is a special diet she's on. She loves them, and I'm certain it had something to do with her chosen stripper . . . er . . . dancer name.

"You still need to do an internship, right?" Clancy leans on the bar, but his eyes are on me.

"Yeah, the school's supposed to help us find something."

"I have a friend who's a doctor," Clancy says. "You could probably work for her."

"Wow, really?" There's a little gleam of happiness in her eyes. "If you'd said *him*, I'd be leery about it, but since it's a woman . . ."

"I'll call her tomorrow."

"I just love you, Clancy." She bounces up on the bar to lean over and gives him a kiss on the cheek.

"Watch it, now," he says and glances my way. "You might make Nemy-girl jealous."

I turn my head to him and smirk. "She's the only one I'd trust with you."

"That's because she's the only one you'd do *other* things with." He is so lucky he didn't say the real deal. I'd have to kick his ass later.

My eyes narrow on him in a mock attempt at glaring at the man, but he sticks his tongue out at me and continues his conversation with Cherry, which I can no longer hear because I have to go to the other end of the bar. When I return, Cherry has a wide grin on her face.

"Okay, what are you two saying about me?"

"Oh, newbies," Cherry says and jumps off her seat to go work.

"What did you say?" I ask the grinning man standing in front of me.

"Nothing."

"You're a terrible liar." I slap him on the ass before tending to the new guys who just came into the club. He returns the slap when he walks by me to go sit down and it makes me jump a little.

The next day, Clancy calls his doctor friend and she finds a place for Cherry . . . er . . . Christine in her practice. She's so excited about it she jumps into his arms for a big hug. I just laugh at it and continue about my business. She'll be starting on the following Monday, so Clancy and I plan a big party at the club for Friday night, which will be her last night. Clancy even advertises it, so we're bombarded with customers. Cherry is a favorite, and her last night draws probably the biggest crowd I've ever seen at the club. It finds Chris, Clancy and me all behind the bar serving. I think it's the first time I've ever seen him tend bar.

Amanda shows up, with Sable, and it irks the ever-living hell out of me. There are too many people in the club and it's too loud to have a baby in here, not to mention that she shouldn't bring a baby to a goddamn club in the first place. Thank God for the smoking ban, or this place would be filled with second-hand smoke. Not a good thing for a baby to inhale . . . or me, for that matter. Clancy's pissed too, so he suggests Amanda take her to the office when she refuses to leave. I see the sly little grin she gives me while hooking her arm through his when they walk the length of the bar. Fucking bitch. I do not question what she's up to, either, and they are gone for a good amount of time before Clancy returns pissed off to holy hell.

I try to contain my laughter. "She try to fuck you back there or something?"

"Yes," he says with a very visible shudder, which makes me smile.

Then Amanda appears in front of me on the other side of the bar. "Nemesis, I'd like a drink." Clancy runs away . . . the chicken.

She can't even *ask* for the damn thing. I throw her a fake smile, and ask, "What would you like?" How about a Cement Mixer, or maybe I could just beat you about the face for a while? A Cement Mixer is a very nasty drink because it curdles the second it hits one's mouth.

"Something strong."

"Plan on drinking a lot tonight?"

She leans over the bar and smiles at me. "The second I fully own this bar, you're fired."

"Cool," I reply with my own little smile. "Now answer the damn question."

"As a matter of fact, I do."

"Wow, you should get the Mother of the Year Award then."

She glares at me, and then stands up on the edge of the barstool so she can get closer to me. "Fuck you, bitch."

Ah yes, and the trailer trash comes out. That didn't take much. She swipes a claw at me and I lean back out of reach, laughing. Clancy rushes over.

"Sit down, Amanda!" Then he looks at me. "Give her a Diet Coke." I nod and fill a glass for her while Clancy goes back to his end of the bar, but still watches us with caution.

"One Diet Coke," I say and place it in front of her. Amanda's eyes flick to Clancy, and whatever she wants to do quickly falls by the wayside. I have a feeling it involved me wearing that drink. I tend to a few others while she sits sipping her soda and watching me, and finally, Clancy decides it's best if we switch places. Fine by me, but that doesn't stop her from watching me.

About ten minutes later, I meet him at the cooler. "Someone should check on Sable. I mean, I know she's safe in there, but look at Amanda. She's not even concerned about her."

He nods. "I was just thinking that. I'll do it, since that bitch isn't going to." He runs off around the bar and into the back, and Amanda doesn't even notice it. She has a strange gleam in her eyes after coming back from the bathroom. Shit, the bitch is stoned. I hope his hired hands are getting these photo ops. Oh wait, no cameras allowed inside the club.

My phone vibrates and I jump. Then I pull it from my pocket to find a text message from Clancy. *COME BACK HERE!* Scotty's standing near the end of the bar and I tell him to cover me as I run to the back. The office door is shut, so I knock. Clancy quickly opens it while holding Sable in his arms.

"Nemy-girl, I don't think she's breathing," he says in a panic.

I move the blanket from around her face and see her lips are turning blue. "Jesus, Clancy, call fucking 9-1-1!"

"The children's hospital is right up the street."

"Wait, wait, wait," I stammer. "There might not be time. Let's put her on the desk." He steps back and I take her from him and carry her over. I check her heartbeat—it's there, but faint. Her breathing—nothing. I look to see if something's stuck in her throat—can't tell even with a swipe of my finger. If something is stuck, it's lodged there deeper than I care to put my finger. Clancy's wringing his hands while watching me and it's making me nervous. I pick her up again, place my hand at her neck for support, and lay my arm across her lengthwise. Then I turn her over, aim her head down a bit and hit her back with my other palm just hard enough to dislodge anything that might be stuck. Something shoots across the desk and hits the floor, and I quickly turn her over again. She's still not breathing. Fuck. I lay her on the desk and begin CPR—my mouth covering both her nose and mouth, and I give short puffs of breath. Very soon, a baby's wail hits my ears and I pick her up and cradle her against my chest. "Okay, now we can go to the hospital. Find whatever she spit out."

Clancy jumps behind the desk and he is pissed when he rises, holding a little bag in his hand with a small white rock.

"Are you fu . . . freakin' kidding me?" Sable's still crying, and I bounce a little and pat her back.

"I'm going to kill her," he growls.

"Bring it with. No, wait, they'll think it's ours. Son of a . . . monkey."

Clancy shakes his head. "We don't have a choice." He rounds the desk and grabs my arm. "Come on." We go out the back door so we don't have to go through the crowd, and we get in the car, heading straight for the hospital. He hands his phone over to me. "Text Scott. Tell him what's going on, and tell him to call the freakin' police on that b . . . witch."

"They'll arrest her." I flip the phone open. "She's stoned already."

"Good. It'll help my fu . . . case."

I scroll through his contacts, find Scotty, and send the text. He sends back *WTF?* I reply with *I know! This is Nemy, BTW.* It is not easy texting while holding a crying baby in one's arms in a moving vehicle. "You need a child seat."

"One thing at a time, Nemy-girl."

I close his phone and move Sable around to check on her. She's still crying a little, but it's winding down. Her big green eyes stare up at me, looking scared, and I shush her and rock her gently. "It's okay, *mi hija.*" She responds well to my voice and I start humming. When I look up to see how far we are from the hospital, I catch a smile on Clancy's face. "What?"

He glances at me and I can see the smile has touched his eyes. "I love you."

Oh, hell. I just smile at him.

He pulls into the emergency room entrance, driving right up to the doors. He jumps out of the car and runs around to open the door for me, and then he helps me out and we run inside.

We've explained what happened, they're checking the bag and running tests on Sable to make sure the contents didn't seep through, and I'm leaning against the wall, my head back, eyes closed, trying to keep my breathing calm.

Fucking meth. I'm going to kill that bitch if Clancy doesn't get to her first.

I feel his arms slip around my waist and I open my eyes.

He presses his forehead against mine, and whispers. "Thank you."

I give him a short nod and make some sort of sound that's akin to *no problem*. Bless his heart, he doesn't say those three little words again.

However, this doesn't stop my mouth. "I love you too."

Fuck, did I just say that?

A doctor approaches us right after. "Excuse me, Mr. and Mrs. Dolan?"

"Yes," Clancy says before I can correct the doctor on our marital status. "Is she okay?"

"Yes, Mr. Dolan. If you hadn't performed CPR, I'm not certain she would have made it here. You did a good job."

"Oh, it wasn't me." He looks at me with a proud smile.

"Well, Mrs. Dolan, you did very well. More mothers should know First Aid and CPR."

"Oh, she's not—"

"She used to work with kids, so she had to have the training. Have the tests come back yet?"

"Yes, they have," doc replies. "Lucky for her, none of the drug got through."

"Thank God." I breathe a sigh of relief.

Doc's eyes flick from Clancy to me and back to Clancy. "Child Protective Services are going to want to speak with you, though."

"That's fine," Clancy replies. "My ex-wife is being arrested as we speak, I'm sure." He looks at me. "Do you still have my phone?"

I pull it out of my pocket and hand it to him.

"I'll check with my manager to be certain."

"Very well," doc says. "Once you're finished, you can come back to see her. Mrs. Dolan, you may follow me, if you'd like."

I hesitate and Clancy nods in the direction the doc is heading. "Go on. I'll be back in a minute."

I follow the doctor back while Clancy texts Scotty, and the doc leads me right to her. My heart aches upon seeing her with tubes and IVs all over her little body. "I thought you said she was okay."

"She is, Mrs. Dolan," doc says. "She was a bit dehydrated so we put her on a saline drip. She's also undernourished. Does she stay primarily with the mother?"

"Yes, but Clancy's trying to get custody," I say. "He doesn't even have visitation."

"I see," he replies. "And how did she end up in your care tonight?"

"Stupid woman brought her to the club." I look down at myself. I'm wearing the bondage corset Clancy gave me for Christmas. "You don't think I dress like this every day, do you?"

He chuckles. "Well, no, Mrs. Dolan."

"Please stop calling me that. I'm not his wife."

Doc's eyes flick to me. "That's surprising."

"How so?"

"Well, to be honest, with the way you came in with little Sable, I thought she was yours." He smiles at me. "Until I heard the story, that is."

I look at him, all the while thinking *I wish she was.* "Can you run some other tests on her?"

"Whatever you like. I assume you want to check for things like FAS?" He's only asking that because Amanda's former job was mentioned during the story. Well, and then there's the meth rock Sable choked on.

"Precisely. I need to know what I'm dealing with."

He smiles again. "Of course, and if I do find something?"

My eyes meet his. "Then I know what I'm dealing with."

His smile spreads across his cheeks, touching the corners of his light blue eyes, and he nods and walks away. I think I just got doc's approval. My fingers slip into the little crib and I rub her tiny hand.

Clancy touches the small of my back, and then wraps his arms around me and peers over my shoulder at Sable. He tilts his head toward mine. "Think they'll give her to me tonight?"

"Don't know. They can be a real pain in the ass, but you are her father, so they might."

"I just don't want her to go back to Amanda."

"Neither do I." Yes, I just said those words.

We stand and watch her for awhile, and finally, a woman from CPS arrives to speak with us . . . well, with Clancy. She's already heard the story, has talked to the police, who are now charging Amanda with child abuse because the bag was in Sable's mouth and she was sucking on the damn thing. After confirming Clancy is Sable's biological father, she sets up a home appointment for the following week. Yes, it can happen that fast. They prefer a child stays with family. On the other hand, they could have just taken her into foster care, which would have sent me through the goddamn roof because it takes forever to get your kid out of that system.

I'm certain that Clancy passing their little drug test helped matters too.

By the time we return to the club, it's almost two-thirty in the morning. Scotty's still ushering out guests and wants to know all the details, but we can't tell him because we have to grab the car seat base out of Amanda's car and put it in Clancy's car so we can go back to the hospital to pick Sable up and take her home. Clancy pulls his tire iron out of the trunk and breaks her window to get into the car.

"Are we going to your house or mine?" I watch as he struggles with the seat in the back of his BMW. Yeah, little bastard thieves stole my car, but didn't touch his while it sat here for a whole week. Go figure. So where was this damn protection when he got beat up? Eventually, someone's going to answer to me for that.

"I was thinking yours, since you have Tonk." He stops what he's doing and looks up at me. "Is he okay with kids?"

I giggle. "Yeah, he loves them. She'll give him something to protect."

"Good." He continues his struggle.

"Oh, honestly, man. Let me do it." I reach forward.

He lightly slaps my hand. "Get, you."

I sigh dramatically. "Men never want help."

"Hush," he replies and finally gets it right. When he goes to stand, he hits his head on the car. "Damn it."

I lean into the car, across the back seat. "Want me to kiss it and make it better?"

He peers down and sees my grin. "I've got something for you to kiss."

"Right," I say with a laugh. "Not with a baby in the house tonight."

He growls. "Come on, let's go."

"I'm driving my own damn car. You can follow me once we leave the hospital."

He nods, shuts the back door and opens the front to climb inside the car. I've already grabbed what I need from inside the club, so I walk over to my car, get in, and follow him to the hospital.

It is going to be a long fucking night.

22

We're in This Together

We stop at the store on the way home to buy supplies for Sable: diapers, formula, a blanket, and some toys (I've veered off my normal path to hit the 24-hour Super Wal-Mart, where they have *everything*). Thank God I have siblings too, because Clancy is clueless, but right now I'm wandering around the store looking for the man. I find him near the furniture. He wants to buy a crib.

"Oh, come on, it's four in the morning."

He turns to look at me. "She needs something to sleep in."

"I have a bed in the spare room. We can put pillows around her so she won't roll off, *if* she's even rolling yet."

His right brow goes up.

"Don't give me that look. I've done it with my nephews."

"I'm buying a crib," he says and looks at them again.

I look at Sable, who's sitting safely in her car seat in the cart. "Your daddy has lost it." I wiggle my finger at her. She's actually in pretty good spirits and giggles a little, even though she had IVs poking her not so long ago. I'm sure there will be bruises there in a few hours, and I'm quite surprised she's not cranky or sleeping, considering the time. This gives me a little clue on her possible sleeping hours. At this point, she should be sleeping almost through the night. "Can you say da-da?"

Clancy turns to me. "Should she be able to speak yet?"

"You're hopeless. She's four months, right?"

He nods.

"Well, she's starting that stage developmentally, so we need to talk to her a lot and praise her every time she makes an attempt. Repetition, you know."

He sighs. "I'm glad you know this shit . . . I mean, stuff."

I laugh and push the cart past him. "Since you're stuck on which crib to buy, I'm going to go pick out some clothes for her."

"Okay, come back when you're done. I'm sure I'll still be here."

Half an hour later, I finally get him out of the damn store and we head to my place. Watching Clancy stuff the crib box into the trunk of his car was quite hilarious. The damn thing barely fit and ended up hanging over the rear bumper. Good thing he carries rope in the trunk.

I'm exhausted by now because it's about my bedtime, but I sit on the sofa holding Sable and feed her a bottle while Clancy puts the crib together. What's bothering me at the moment is Sable isn't trying to hold the bottle, and God knows when the last time was Amanda fed her, aside from that little bag of meth—bitch—and the hospital fed her a long while ago.

Clancy looks up at me now and then, smiles ridiculously, and then gets right back to work. Once he's put the crib together, he drags it into my room.

I rise from the sofa and follow him.

"Uh uh," I say, rocking Sable in my arms. "Put it in that room." I point to the next room.

His eyes flick to me, and he chuckles. "Yes, ma'am." Once he has it squared away on the free wall that shares with my room, he covers the mattress, puts a blanket down, and takes her from me. Her little eyes are trying hard to stay open, and Clancy kisses her forehead. "Okay, little one, time to sleep." He lays her down, watches until she nods off, and then closes the door a little before joining me in my bedroom.

I've already stripped down and climbed into bed, and he follows me. His arms wrap around me and pull me close, and his face nestles in the curve of my neck while one hand glides across my stomach.

"There's a baby in the next room," he whispers.

"Yes, there is."

"How long do you think she'll sleep?"

"A couple of hours, maybe. I don't know her sleeping habits, so it's hard to say." I reiterate my thought on how long she *should* be sleeping.

I can feel his mouth twist into a smile against my skin. "You told me you love me."

"So I did. I must've been tired."

His head pops up so he can look me in the eye. "Is that an excuse?"

"Yep." I smile at him.

He grins. "I'll take what I can get." He presses his lips against mine and the whole world disappears while he makes love to me. I may be exhausted, but his touch consumes me to the point I don't care how tired I am. I need him. We remain as quiet as possible and just as we start to fall asleep, I hear Sable cry.

"That didn't last long," he whispers.

I look at the clock. "An hour, maybe a bit longer."

"I'll go." He pushes himself up.

"Check her diaper," I say as he pulls his boxers on. "That's probably what it is."

He goes into her room, changes her, and returns to me thirty minutes or so later. I don't really know because I've fallen back to sleep, but I feel him climb into bed and slip his arm around me.

The next time Sable cries, which by the way, is a barely audible whimper, I get up and slip on my robe, and go into her room. When I see her, my hand flies up to cover my mouth, forcing the laughter in because what I'm looking at is the funniest damn diaper change I've ever seen in my life. "Wow, how in the heck did he put that on you? I think it's on backwards." I lift her out of the crib. I can't even describe what I'm seeing, it's so bad. "Daddy needs to take a parenting class." I change the diaper and take her into the kitchen with me.

The sun is up and it's late morning. Tonk is at my hip, inspecting the new creature in his midst. I shoo him away.

"You did that hours ago." He stands fast and licks her foot. This gets her attention and she tries to look down at him, but doesn't have the neck strength to do so and her head lolls to the side before I can move it back to my shoulder. I grab another blanket from the bag sitting on the table, unfold it one-handed, and lay it on the floor in the center of the kitchen. Then I lay her on her stomach. Tonk lays down face-to-face with her and she makes many attempts to look up at him. "Good boy, Tonk. Help her out there."

Clancy stumbles into the kitchen wearing only his jeans as I prepare a bottle for her. He rubs his eyes, looks at Tonk, and chuckles. "That's a funny sight."

"There's a camera on my desk," I say over my shoulder.

"Oh, definitely." He steps over them to go into the office, which was once a carport. When he returns, he gets down on the floor to take the picture. Then he hops up and shows it to me. "Nice, huh?"

"Beautiful." It's a perfect shot because Tonk stretches his neck out and Sable gets her head all the way up for that split second, and they're nose to nose when Clancy takes the photo. "Why are you up?"

He slips his arms around my waist and he kisses me on the cheek. "I didn't want you to do this by yourself."

"You are a rare breed, Mr. Dolan." I kiss him back.

"I know." He takes the bottle from me. "Come here . . . what did you call her . . . *mi hija*?"

"Yes."

"Think of any names yet?" He lifts her, and then settles her into his arm and places the bottle in front of her. She doesn't reach for it and he moves it closer.

"I might have a few." I walk over to the small table and sit down. "I was attempting to match the sound, but nothing came to me aside from objects and fairytales, and one horrible name."

"What about Anna?" He's sitting in the only other chair. His eyes flick up to me and he smiles.

"No. I hate it; so will she."

"You hate your last name more than your first."

"Yes and no."

"How about Mary or Maria then?"

Maria is my middle name. I tilt my head. "Why are you trying to name your child after me?"

He smiles. "Because you're the woman I want to spend the rest of my life with."

"Oh, wow." I bite my lower lip. "Are you sure about that?"

"Positively, absolutely, definitely certain."

I draw in a deep breath.

"You're not going to get scared of all this and run away from me, are you?" He's teasing.

I shake my head. "Nah, I don't run away . . . usually."

He chuckles.

"What are you going to do about the club now? I mean, Amanda's certainly staying in jail or something."

He shrugs. "I'll figure it out. All that matters right now is this little one."

I'm silent for a bit and he looks up at me.

"You're just as important to me too, Nemy-girl."

"Oh, I don't doubt that," I reply with a smile. "You showed me how important I am earlier, even though we're both exhausted." Sable tries to turn her head. "She's done. You have to burp her now." He moves her into position and I jump up and grab a kitchen towel, and throw it at him. "You might want to put that on your shoulder, dork-mo."

"Thanks," he says and does so with no mention of the name I called him.

"Antonia," I say, pronouncing the name with emphasis not on the *o*, but on the *nee* sound, like *Ann-toe-NEE-ah*.

"That's pretty." He pats her back. "Toni for short?"

"Yeah, I like that." I smile at him. "It was my great-grandmother's name."

"Then it's perfect." Sable burps and spits up on the towel. "Okay, that is disgusting."

I giggle. "You're a man. I thought you'd appreciate a good burp."

"I do, but without what came with it." He cradles her in his arms again. Then he pulls the towel off his shoulder and wipes her mouth in a gentle sweep. "Is it normal for the back of her head to be so flat?"

"Well, she's spent a good portion of her life so far in that car seat. We'll just have to not do that so much. She needs the attention anyway, since her mother couldn't seem to find the time to give it to her."

Clancy nods and coos at her. "I should probably give Scott a call and tell him I won't be in tonight."

"You mean *we* won't be in."

He looks up at me. "You can go in."

I shake my head. "Not after that diaper disaster I saw when I went in to get her this morning."

He chuckles. "It was dark and I was tired. Somebody wore me out."

"Whatever. Just admit you have no clue what you're doing. It'll be so much easier."

"Not so. I have three nephews. Trust me, changing a girl is easier. I was half-asleep when I did that this morning."

"Uh huh." I inform him of the parenting classes.

"Yeah, I should do that. It'll help me get her, huh?"

"Can't hurt, especially if Amanda hasn't taken them, which I doubt, considering. What's really going to help you is what happened last night, although I'm a bit leery about the club."

He agrees with a nod. "I know you're worried about the club factor, but you don't need to be. I'll make some calls today. Shouldn't be a problem."

"Why don't you ask Scotty if he wants it?" I stand. "Want some tea?"

"Please," he replies while rocking Sable. "That's a really good idea, Nemy-girl. Damn, you're a smart woman."

"Watch your mouth." My hand flits across the top of his head. "Put her down on the floor again. It'll help her learn to hold her head up."

He leans over and places Sable on the floor on her stomach. "Okay, you're not smart."

I laugh in silence, preparing the teapot, and once I've placed it on the stove, he wraps his arms around my waist again. I'm thinking he's going to say something, but he doesn't. He just kisses my neck, and I close my eyes and lean my head back against his chest.

I let out a long sigh and end up biting my lower lip because Clancy's hands wander inside my robe. Sable's high-pitched shriek disrupts the silence, and Clancy looks back at her and chuckles. We both turn around to find Tonk's head right next to hers, and she's trying to pull on his ear. The dumb dog loves every second of it too. Damn, she's a happy baby. How'd that happen?

"Go make your calls."

He smiles at me, and then leans over to kiss me before heading out of the room to retrieve his phone.

I step over Tonk and reach into the bag for a toy we'd bought, and then I place it on the floor next to her. Tonk inspects the toy and Sable makes another attempt at holding her head up. I'm not certain of her birth date, so I can't figure out exactly where she should be in her development. Wait, Clancy said it at the hospital. I kneel down next to her and tickle her cheek. "Why aren't you able to do that yet, *mi hija*?"

She coos, and I smile and return the coo to her.

"Da-da," I say to her and she shrieks again. I lay down next to her and her arm rises up, and then I notice a scar on the inside of her bicep. "What's this, *mi hija*?" I pick her up and raise her arm so I can inspect the little half-moon. "Son of a monkey."

"Ah," she says with a squeak.

"That's right, *mi hija*, ah." I stand up and carry her into the living room where Clancy sits on the sofa. "Baby?"

Wow, I just called him that.

"She has a scar right here." I point to it. "Looks like it could be from a fingernail."

He stretches out his arms and takes her. Then he beckons me closer and takes my hand, places the tip of my thumbnail against her arm, and then releases my hand. "Get the camera."

Oh joy, more possible abuse. I grab the camera after removing the whistling teapot from the stove, we take a few photos, and I take her from him again because now he's calling his attorney back. I lay her on my lap, supporting her completely because she won't be able to bear weight for a good long while, and make faces at her as Clancy talks on the phone. Then he calls Scott next, and they discuss my idea. Scott is happy about the prospect of owning the club, but wants me to help him interview a new bartender if I'm going to potentially leave. I nod at Clancy and Sable tries to grab her foot. Clancy chuckles, gets off the phone with Scott, and leans back into the sofa.

"Thomas is putting together all the necessary paperwork to strip that woman of her parental rights. In fact, he thinks he can talk to the judge today."

"It's Saturday," I say.

"Yeah, and?"

"You can get through to a judge on the weekend?"

He eyes me a moment and smiles. "Yep."

"Nice. I'm going to have to put a fence around my pool soon."

Clancy grins. "Let's go look at that house today."

"Why do you want to sell your beautiful house? I love that neighborhood."

"Really? I didn't know that."

I nod. "I wanted to buy a house in there, but they never sell, and then my grandmother left me this one."

He contemplates a moment as Sable attempts to grab his finger. "Well, how about I just rent it out, and you rent yours out too?"

My eyes flick to his. "Seriously?"

He nods and leans closer. "We've practically lived together the last month."

"I know. But actually moving into your new house . . . That's totally different."

"*Our* house, not mine," he corrects.

I stare at Sable a moment while bouncing my legs a little. "You're the one buying it."

"And you're the one designing everything inside," he returns with a raised brow.

I turn my head to him again.

"Why do you think I've had you help me choose from the samples and pick the elevation?"

My mouth opens and closes, and opens again, but I'm speechless.

He laughs.

"You've . . . you've . . . been—"

"Planning this? No." He shakes his head. "I've been hoping." He reaches up with his hand to caress my face. "Come on, Nemy-girl, live happily ever after with me."

I regret the Prince Charming comment now. Damn it.

"There's no such thing." I look at Sable. "You are *not* being read princess stories." She giggles. If only she knew what I was talking about.

"You've come this far with me, and there's even a child in the mix now, and look at how you're handling it. What's another step?"

"It's a big step."

"Alright, let me ask you this" —he takes my hand in his—"If we stay in our respective houses, how often would I be here?"

"I'm guessing quite a bit."

"I'm saying every day and night because I want to be with you."

"Okay, and?" I turn Sable on my lap so she's lying within my right arm.

"We could put your name on the title too."

"Wouldn't I have to qualify for that? That house looked awfully expensive."

He laughs. "Don't worry about qualifying. Just say yes."

My eyes flick to his. "What am I getting myself into?"

"A relationship with a man who's not going to leave you because of your dreams. And one who loves every aspect of you . . . including your right cross."

I laugh, and he scoots closer to me and kisses my cheek.

"I love you, Nemy-girl. I have since the day you walked through the doors of my club."

"That's kind of creepy."

He chuckles. "You would think that."

"Okay, fine. Show me the dang house."

Jesus effing Christ, did I just become domesticated? Fuck . . . I mean, fudge.

Foxy's Den

Fairytales vs. Reality

January 31, 2011

You know that part in the fairytales where the girl is so happy because her Prince Charming has rescued her from her miserable life, and the birds are singing, animals rejoicing, and it's like she's floating on clouds? Yeah, I am so there right now. Not that my life was really so horrible or anything, but right now Mr. fucking Perfect and his wonderful daughter are something I've always wanted, and they're here in front of me and a part of my life.

Don't worry, reality will hit me soon enough.

After looking at the house—which I fall in love with—we stop at a little restaurant in North Scottsdale, which is only open for breakfast and lunch. We bring the car seat in carrying Sable because she can't sit up yet. Clancy gets a call from his attorney during the course of our meal, and he has a happy little grin on his face when he hangs up.

"It's done," he says.

I have a hard time not choking on my Panini and end up coughing a little. "Huh? So fast? Is that even possible?"

The grin spreads. "I know people."

"Jesus, I guess so. Do you still have to do the visit with CPS?"

"Nope. After we're done here, we'll swing by Thomas' office. I need to sign a few things."

I'm stunned. "Who the hell do you know?"

"Just you never mind and finish your meal," he says, which tells me either he can't say it in public, or it's none of my damn business. Considering Clancy's type of business and the clientele I've seen come through the club, I'm betting on the former. Musicians—famous ones, movie stars, and yes, politicians of many levels, to include attorneys and judges. There you have it.

"Christ, do you know anybody in media?"

"Maybe," he replies, which I did not expect. He leans over to check on Sable, who's sitting between us. "Hi, my little Toni-girl." She giggles.

"Is that done too?"

He looks up at me. "What, her name? It will be soon."

I narrow my eyes on him. "When we get in the car, you're telling me who you know."

He chuckles. "Of course. I have nothing to hide from you." His eyes go back to Sable, now known as Toni. Got that? Okay, good. I'll still be confused for a while. He picks up the pacifier she spat out and puts it back in her mouth.

"Okay, I was wrong."

"About?" He goes back to his plate.

"You kind of know what you're doing with her."

He chuckles. "Thanks for that." He takes the last bite of food from his plate. "I did help raise my little brother, and his sons."

"How old is your brother?"

"Your age." He leans back in his chair and watches me. "And man was Brennan ever a handful."

"He's the one who called you that one night."

"Yeah, got himself beat the heck up over a woman."

I stare at him a moment. "I'm not sure I want to even know." I finish off the Panini and wipe my mouth. "Ready to go?"

"Yes." He picks up the check, which we have to pay up front. Then he pulls his wallet out and drops a ten-dollar bill on the table while I pick up Sable—Toni.

Once we get in the car, I'm on him. "Alright, spit it out."

He laughs at me. "The judge Thomas spoke to earlier?"

"Yes."

"You've met him before."

"How many times have I met him?"

"Several," he replies with a grin. "He's quite the regular. *Loves* Cherry."

"Who doesn't?" The evil glint hits his eyes. "And don't you say anything about me."

He barks out a laugh, and Toni (Jesus, this is going to be a bitch) mimics him with a loud laugh of her own. I peer back at her and smile.

"You do realize the process you just completed in one day takes weeks for anyone else to complete. Months even." I'm still a little shell-shocked by it and find it rather impossible.

"I'm well aware of the process. But Amanda was in jail and therefore, couldn't do a darn thing about it."

"Wait, what do you mean she *was* in jail?" I'm a little taken aback. The man is surprising me left and right today. "What did you do?"

"I had Thomas bail her out."

"On the condition she sign Sable—I mean, Toni—over to you?"

"Precisely. And before you start thinking too hard, I did not force her to make the decision. Thomas laid out the plan to her, told her what the charges would be, that I would get custody no matter what, she would spend several months in prison, and she is no longer eligible to purchase the remainder of the club from me, or inherit it in the event of my death." He stops at a light and looks at me. "Amanda doesn't want to go to prison. She's been in jail before. I've offered her a nice little lump sum to disappear."

I blink twice as I stare at him before the light changes. "Um, wow." I look out the window and he pulls into a corporate parking lot.

When he parks the car, he turns to me and touches my arm. "Nemy-girl?"

I turn to face him again.

"Are you okay?"

I bite my lower lip. "I'm just in shock, that's all."

"Well, don't be. Amanda's answer was precisely this: *fine, I don't want the damn kid anyway. She's been a pain in my ass ever since I had her.*"

My mouth drops open as shock and anger fill up inside me. "She said that?"

He nods. "She did. Now, let's go see Thomas, okay?"

I agree and climb out of the car.

I discover a bit more about Amanda, especially after listening to Thomas and Clancy talk. Clancy gave her about six figures, at the low end because she's just that stupid, and she signed over all parental rights to Sable—Toni—without batting a false eyelash, and at the jail when Thomas went to bail her out. Thomas handed her a check, got her in a cab, and sent her on her way to God knows where. I hope I never see the stupid bitch again. I'm still astonished they were able to work things so fast, and believe me, my mind rolls through all sorts of scenarios best suited for mobster movies than real life, and I do *not* want to think those things about Clancy. I know, I know, *almost* perfect and I already know he's a mafia-type guy. I wish I could change that aspect of him. I've had about enough of the mob shit after growing up in it. But damn it, I love the man, flaws and all.

23

Feelin' Love

Toni's been quite the little handful the past few weeks and can now push herself up on her hands. Yep, I really need to get the fence put in because the house isn't being built fast enough and there's a dog door in my back door. She has a bit of trouble moving forward, though, so that should stall things for a bit. We've been so busy with her I don't even miss work when I'm not there because she's got my schedule full day and night. Clancy still shows up at the club now and then, but not when I'm there because one of us is always with Toni. That may sound a bit like I'm complaining, which is kind of true because he's part of the reason I enjoyed the job. The issue is the extreme change of it all by adding a child into our fairly new relationship. It's not like I was pregnant for nine months—God forbid—and had time to prepare for this. Oh, like that could happen anyway.

Scott and I interview a few bartenders at the end of the next week, and we decide on one who I think will do well because she's actually a lot like me. Scott mutters something along the lines of *go figure*. Smartass. Clancy laughs at him during our morning meeting before the club opens as Toni attempts to scoot across the floor on her belly.

"Come on, *mi hija*."

Her little hands move a small distance.

I scoot my chair out so I'm in front of her and put my hands down to beckon her forward. "Come on."

She inches forward a bit more, and then falls back to the floor and looks up at me.

"Good girl!"

Clancy scoops her up and kisses her cheek. "That's my Toni-girl!" She lets out a loud giggle and Clancy puts her back down on the floor.

Scott's shaking his head. "This is just fucking weird."

I shoot a glare at him. "Watch your mouth!"

He cowers a little. "Sorry, Nemy."

"So, are you going to hire that chick, or what?"

"Yeah, she's the best candidate. I really wish you'd reconsider, though."

"You can't afford her," Clancy interjects.

I laugh and Scott glares at him. "Nah, I think I'm done bartending for a while, but you'll still have me for a few weeks."

Scott sighs. "Okay, fine. I guess we're done here, then."

"Don't be sad, Scotty," I say and smile as Clancy walks away.

"Ha! You always thought Clancy was joking when he'd claim you were the best." He leans forward. "He wasn't."

I tilt my head to the right. "Well, I've moved on to greener pastures."

Scott leans over the table. "I hope they stay green for you, Nemy." That was almost a whisper, and my brow goes up.

"What's that supposed to mean?"

He shakes his head and sits back. Clancy reappears and picks up Toni. "You ready? Toni's appointment is in thirty minutes."

I jump to my feet. "That's right." I look at Scott and extend my hand for a shake. "Good luck, Scotty. I hope you find success."

"Or success finds me," he says with a laugh.

"I'll be in later tonight."

"Okay." He yanks me forward in a hug. "Be careful," he whispers in my ear.

"Always." I pull away and produce a smile, though my face doesn't wish to go that route. During the ride to Toni's doctor, my mind attempts to figure out just what in the hell he's talking about. Why do I need to be careful? Is there something I need to know about Clancy that I don't already know? Fuck. Why do people do that?

"You okay?" Clancy slips his hand over mine.

"Yeah, I'm fine. Just thinking about stuff."

"Such as?"

"Oh, you know, my mind is always running through ideas." It's not really a lie, right? I won't say anything just yet, not until I've sorted Scott's words out in my head.

"Got any for the next project?"

I laugh. "I have several started."

"Maybe when we put Toni down for her nap, you can show them to me and I can help you decide."

"That's actually a good idea." My mind starts to wander again. It drifts to the one thought that's always in my fucking head—*you can never truly know a person*—since that one's happened to me twice now. Third time's the charm, right? Clancy has won my heart—something I didn't think could ever happen again—and now I'm concerned with the fact he could just as easily shatter it, all because Scott said those two little words—*be careful*. What the fuck?

"Nemy-girl," Clancy says with a snap of fingers.

"Huh?" I focus on him. "What?"

"We're here." He opens his door. I get out of the car and he retrieves Toni. We then walk toward the office building. "Something certainly has you preoccupied."

"Yeah, sorry about that."

We walk through the automatic sliding doors, stop in front of the elevator, and he lightly touches my cheek with his child-free hand.

"I hope it has to do with me."

I smile at him and the doors open.

We step inside and he pushes the button for the doctor's floor—third, I think—and then he leans over and whispers, "Maybe you could put on the zipper corset tonight."

I grin. "You wanna stop and pick up some cherries on the way home?"

He chuckles. "Oh yes."

We finish up with Toni's doctor appointment—she's fine; it was just a check-up. Then we head home after stopping at the store. Yes, cherries.

After dinner, we put Toni down for a bit, and while I'm cleaning up, with Clancy's wanted help, there's a knock at the door.

I look up at him. "Expecting someone?"

He throws the towel on the counter and runs to the door without saying a word.

I finish what I'm doing and head out of the kitchen to find Cherry . . . I mean Christine in my living room. "What are you doing here?"

She flashes me a big smile and throws her arms around me. "Your man has a special night planned out. I'm here to watch Toni."

"Shut up." I look from her to Clancy, who nods and has that evil little glint hitting his eyes. Then it dawns on me; it's Valentine's Day. "Well shit, let me go get ready!" Christine laughs at me as I run into the hall. I turn back quickly and look at Clancy. "Wait, I'm supposed to work tonight."

"I got you the night off," Clancy says.

I bite my nail and grin. "Am I wearing *that*?"

"Yes." He walks toward me. "Come on, move." He pushes me into the hall and into the bedroom.

"Where are you taking me?"

He's putting on another silky black shirt. "You'll see," he says rather smugly.

"Bastard," I whisper and finish up. Then I check my hair and make-up.

Clancy whispers something to Christine before we leave.

"What'd you say to her?"

"Nothing," he replies.

"That was *not* nothing. She giggled."

"I guess you'll just have to wait to find out."

I'm not going to get anything out of the man, so I may as well sit back and enjoy the ride, and wonder exactly where he's taking me when I'm wearing a leather corset . . . and a skirt. I can't believe I even have the damn thing on because I rarely wear skirts. I'm also wearing a leather jacket because it's cold outside, and I have these boots on I like to call Fuck-me boots. They have about a five-inch heel and rise to my knees. I look like a hot biker bitch, which I'm certain Clancy just loves right about now, but I'm glad we're not on a motorcycle. That would be a bit difficult . . . and cold.

We drive up Scottsdale Road, through Old Towne Scottsdale. He better not be taking me to Dos Gringos, but there it is, coming up. I turn to him and open my mouth to say something.

"We're not going there," he says, shutting me up. "We're going next door."

"You're taking me clubbing on Valentine's Day?" I'm teasing a bit . . . just a bit.

"You didn't even know what day it was until Christine showed up."

"That's true. Sorry. I don't usually remember stuff like that."

"It's fine." He parks the car. "I don't really care."

We head inside and toward the bar where I shed my jacket. Clancy waves the bartender over when I sit on a barstool, and the guy heads toward us, the smile on his face spreading with every step.

"Drew, this is Nemesis."

"Hi," I say and put out my hand.

"Good to meet you." Drew's eyes give me a quick scan as he shakes my hand. "So you're the beauty he keeps talking about."

"You talk about me?" I tease Clancy as I look up.

He's leaning against the bar sideways and his shirt is open enough to expose part of his chest. "All the time." He winks.

"Shit, he's been going on about you for a fucking year." Drew quickly steps back so Clancy can't hit him.

"Don't listen to him," Clancy says. "He's a drunk."

"Most bartenders are," I quip.

Drew laughs and leans on the bar. "What can I get you two?"

"Let's start with an Irish Car Bomb," Clancy suggests, and Drew nods.

I grin. "Are you trying to get me drunk tonight?"

"Now, why would I do a thing like that?" The evil glint hits his eyes and I laugh.

"Oh boy, what do you have in store for me tonight?"

He just grins and Drew places the drinks in front of us. Clancy picks his up and holds the shot ready. "What's the bet tonight, Nemy-girl?"

I shrug. "I don't know. You've already kissed me and we've had sex. What's left?"

The sinister grin spreads over his lips. "I can think of one thing."

"I am not stripping for you."

He chuckles. "Oh, yes you are because there's nothing left."

"Bullshit. I bet you can't hit Drew in the forehead with a cherry."

"That doesn't work for me."

"Tough shit."

"You're so damn stubborn, woman." He drops the shot in his Guinness. Then he slams it back quickly.

I follow him and set my glass on the bar. Before I can even wipe my mouth, Clancy leans over and kisses me. It still weakens me and I'm very happy I'm sitting down this time.

He pulls back with a bite on my lower lip and smiles as he runs his hand up my thigh. "I love you."

"Ditto," I say with a grin.

He chuckles and orders more drinks.

After a few shots and a couple of drinks, I hop off the stool. "I'll be right back." I give him a quick kiss on the cheek.

"Don't be long." He slaps my ass before I walk away.

I look at Drew and point to the back. "Restroom?"

"All the way back."

The place is rather busy for Valentine's Day night and I work my way through the crowd with care. I get ass-grabbed and the fucker is lucky I didn't catch him. I swear, this is one of the many things I hate about men. I know I haven't been in much of a man-hating phase lately—it's Clancy's fault—but there are still things that drive me nuts. Like when Clancy brushes his teeth. He brushes each one separately for about a minute—I'm not kidding. It takes him for*ever* to get out of the bathroom. At least he's not a freak about his hair, like most men with long hair. Okay, that wasn't a man-hating issue. Sue me.

I start to head back to the front of the bar, but someone grabs my arm before I can turn the corner, and when I look up at the guy, I'm a little surprised at who I see.

"Nemy," he says and steps forward, cornering me against the two walls. He's grinning in an evil way that Clancy's eyes never reach.

"Sean. What are you doing here?" I peer over his shoulder to find no one can really see me behind this behemoth of an Irishman. Not fucking cool.

"'Tis an Irish pub, lass." His grin stretches across his scary leprechaun face. "'n I'm Irish."

"You seem to like this part of town." I try to hide my nervousness, but don't know if it's working.

"Well, a woman I fancy seems to visit it often enough." He leans closer.

I swallow my heart. "Oh yeah? Who is she? Maybe I know her and can help you out with that."

His cheek touches mine as his lips approach my ear. "Oh, ye know 'er quite well, lass."

"Oh," is all I can say.

He runs his fingers up my arm. "Damn, ye look mighty fine tonight."

"I'm here with someone."

"Yeah, I saw 'im." His eyes lock on my chest as his fingertips continue a trail up my arm. "Ditch 'im and come with me."

"I don't think so." I brace my hands against his chest. "Would you please stop touching me? I'm taken."

"Like it matters, lass."

Men like Clancy make me nervous. It's not that I think I don't deserve him because I damn well do, but it's the fact that I'm tired of getting my fucking heart stomped on over and over, and he is one I could actually see spending the rest of my life with, more than I could with Jeremy and Garrett (that's my ex-husband).

Creeps like Sean piss me off on a level beneath the surface fear. Deep down, he's a bully. He probably bullies all women, much like James, and I hate that shit. It really makes me want to shake the shit out of Jada for falling for the stupid manipulation game James put out.

I consider my situation. I'm wearing a skirt. Why did I wear a fucking skirt? Sean is the type who doesn't give up once he starts. I know what he wants to do to me. I'm not stupid. There is no way to talk myself out of this situation.

He's standing close enough, so I bring my knee up hard. He's expecting it, of course, and blocks me with his leg. I could go for the head butt, but I remember what happened with James, so I ram my thumbs into his eyes. He screams and backhands me across the face. Lucky shot, and my head hits the wall to the side, but not too hard. I kick at his legs, and then push myself forward from the wall and barrel into him with my shoulder. I can move a mountain when needed. Jeremy was a large man, and I could move him back a few steps from a standing position. Not many people could do that to him, but I knew his weaknesses. We both fly through a group of people and hit the floor, me on top of him. I quickly sit up and start punching as fast as I can, hitting any part of him I can, which just so happens to be the bastard's ribs because he's covering his face with his arms. I feel the crack beneath my knuckles. It feels good. Someone catches my left arm in mid-swing and pulls me from the floor. I stomp on Sean's ribs one last time before I'm turned around and face to face with Clancy. He pulls me through the crowd and sits me on my barstool. Then he leans over, grabs my face and turns it from side to side.

"Are you okay?" I can see the fire in his eyes. He wants to kill Sean, but he's not going to do anything with so many witnesses around.

I nod. "Just pissed off."

Clancy turns around and stands in front of me as security walks by dragging Sean out the door. He's protecting me. I find it a bit amusing and endearing. Right now, I'm so glad Sean doesn't know where I live. I feel a hand on my left shoulder, and when I turn to look, Drew nods at me. I nod back because he's asking the same question Clancy just asked me. Then Drew places a couple of Jäger shots in front of me, and I smile at him.

I touch Clancy's back and he turns around. "It's a good thing you get special parking."

He nods, picks up the shot, and throws it back. Then he sighs. "Why is it when I'm out with you, you always seem to get into a fight?" He's teasing me.

"I didn't start that one," I say and take my shot. "And you technically weren't *out* with me the last time."

He chuckles and peers out the window. "He'll be out there for a while."

"No doubt." I wave to Drew.

Clancy pulls his barstool around and sits in front of me, taking my hand in his, saying in silence what he doesn't want to say aloud as he looks deep into my eyes with concern washing over his face.

"He wants to fuck me."

"More like rape you."

"Yeah, that too," I reply.

His hand squeezes mine. "Women don't survive . . . when he rapes them."

I swallow the lump in my throat and look down at his hand clasping mine. "What can we do?"

"I'll think of something," he says. "Soon."

I start thinking about the fight with James and how Clancy ended up in the hospital. I've never really thought about it until now, and I'm wondering if it wasn't some random break-in, but Sean. The security video didn't show a clear enough image of Clancy's attackers. He upgraded the cameras after that. But I remember Sean all schoolboy giddy once I returned to work.

After about thirty minutes pass, I look at Clancy. "Can we go yet? I'm not really in the mood to be here now."

"Sure." He tips Drew as I stand and pull my jacket on. We're careful when we step outside, and Clancy scans the whole street before we even make a move for his car sitting right in front of us. Then we get in and drive off. I notice he's paying special attention to his mirrors tonight.

"Are we being followed?"

"Not as far as I can tell."

He makes a left on Osborne and watches his mirrors again. I don't question where he's going because I figure he's just trying to keep us safe. I find myself watching my mirror too. Next, he turns north on Hayden and heads back up to Indian School Road. He's making a loop, but I'm curious why he doesn't just hit the freeway and take it back into Tempe. I sit in silence, surprised I'm not aching anywhere from the fight. Clancy turns on Miller heading south. Yep, a circle, sort of.

"Okay, we're good." He turns on the street heading to his house.

"Why are we coming here?"

He smiles. "You'll see."

Okay, I guess I'll see.

I climb out of the car and when he opens the front door, the fragrance hits me. I peer into the living room and step inside. The lights are low, soft music fills the air, and there are roses everywhere.

"What the hell?" I turn to him when he shuts the door and locks it. "I thought you didn't care."

"I lied," he replies with a grin. "Sue me." He slips his hands over my shoulders and pushes the jacket off me, and then those hands slide around my waist and he pulls me close.

"How long have you been planning this?"

He bends forward. "About a year."

I look down before he can kiss me upon realizing just how long he's wanted me to be his. "I feel like shit now. I didn't do anything for you."

He ducks down, presses his lips against mine, and lifts my head during the kiss. "Mmm, you're here, aren't you? That's all I need and want."

"So why'd you take me to the bar?" I ask when he kisses my neck. I move my arms around his shoulders.

"To throw you off."

I giggle. "Did a damn good job of that."

"Mmm hmm," he hums against my skin. The vibration of his voice ripples through my body and I shudder with excitement. He pulls back and takes my hand, and he leads me into the kitchen where a bottle of champagne sits on ice.

"Wow, all this for me, huh?"

He grins, pops the bottle open, and then he pours the champagne into two flutes.

I hate to ruin this beautiful moment, but I need to know. "Did you see Sean enter the bar?"

"No," he replies. "I was a little shocked to see it was him you were beating on."

"He backed me into a corner and wouldn't leave me alone. What the hell was I supposed to do?"

He hands me a glass. "I think you handled it quite well, Nemy-girl. But I don't care right now. My only thought is you."

"Yeah, but . . ."

Two fingers move over my lips and he shushes me. "Would you stop, please? I'm trying to be romantic."

I giggle. "Well, then you need to try a little harder if I'm thinking about anything."

He slips a hand around to the back of my neck and he pulls me forward into a sweet kiss. I almost drop the glass. "How's that?"

"I'm good." I lick my lips. "No thoughts but those of you."

He smiles. "That's like magic."

"Only you have the power." He takes my glass from me after we both take a drink and he sets it down, and then he lifts me and sits me on the counter. His hands run down my thighs and back up under the skirt. Okay, this is why I wore the damn thing, and it has a nice little zipper on the side, which he finds fast. All I have on under that is a pair of lacey boy shorts—his favorite. "Left the cherries at home."

"I don't need them." He closes the small gap between us, reaches for the corset's zipper, and he kisses me again while the zipper inches down.

My legs lock behind him and I slide my hand into his hair, the other inside his shirt.

He's grinning when he pulls back. "Mmm, you can keep the boots on."

"If that's what you want, baby." I nibble on his chin.

He slides me off the counter and carries me out of the kitchen. My corset is still on, skirt practically falling off, when he sets me on my feet in the center of his bedroom. Then he steps back and moves toward the bed, turns, and sits on the edge of it facing me. His eyebrows jump a few times, and my hand flies up to cover my mouth. A small giggle escapes anyway.

"What music would you like, Nemy-girl?" His eyes veer to my right, looking behind me.

I turn my head to find a fucking floor-to-ceiling pole, and I laugh. "Oh my . . . well . . . ."

"How about this one?" He clicks a button on the remote in his hand. I hadn't noticed it lying on the bed before he picked it up.

I grin, zip my corset back up, leaving the skirt the way it is, and head over to the shiny pole as he leans back on his hands and watches me with that evil glint in his eyes. It's also spread across his divine face.

The music is soft at first, seductive, and I let it take me in its trance. My fingers wrap around the pole and I swing slowly around it. I wrap a leg around the shiny metal and slide down in a dip and spring back up with the first word as Paula Cole's sultry voice seeps from the speakers.

I move to the center of the room and slowly approach him, my prey for the evening, with a strut that matches the music's beat. I grasp the zipper of my skirt while Clancy's beautiful green eyes watch intently. The skirt falls to the floor. His grin spreads slowly across his face and I take the corset's zipper between my fingers, stop about halfway down, slide my hands down my torso and thighs, and bend at the knees. I rise in a slow motion and turn using my right hip with the beat in a swirl of my pelvis until I've completed a full circle, my eyes staying on his as much as possible as my hair flips when I turn my head.

I step up to him, and run my hands over his shoulders when I lean over, my hips still moving with the beat, and I slide down his body. As I come back up, my tongue slips inside his half-open shirt and drifts along his skin all the way to his neck. He moans softly and I can feel him shudder beneath my tongue. Then I push him backward onto the bed and step back. I turn and walk away as he pushes himself back up, and I stop with a hop and plant my feet more than a shoulder's width apart. I turn my head to the side to peer at him over my bouncing shoulder, and I bring my finger up to my mouth, moving my hips back and forth in a semi-circular motion.

Clancy licks his lips.

I face him again, place one foot on the bed next to his hip, and the corset's zipper slowly descends its track. Clancy's fingers snake their way up my leg, and when they reach my thigh, I slap the back of his hand.

"Not yet," I say and let the corset fall to the floor.

"To hell with that." He grabs my hips and pulls me forward.

We tumble onto the bed and he soon has me on my back, lips and tongue moving against my flesh in gentle sweeps, teeth taking my skin between them and sucking before letting the flesh snap back. I gather the material of his shirt at the shoulders, slowly inching the hem up little by little until I have it, and I pull the shirt over his head. He braces himself above me and withdraws one arm at a time. I toss the shirt to the side and slide my hands around his neck and shoulders as he lowers his chest to mine. Then those soft lips touch my neck and he devours me. My head swims in a sea of seduction.

"That's the best striptease I've ever seen," he whispers, and I giggle.

I never should have told the man I wouldn't strip for him, but hey, I did tell him only in the bedroom.

24

You Know I'm No Good

A month later, Toni's trying hard to crawl, but she definitely has the rolling thing down pat. I've had to baby-proof the whole house. Not fun. My relationship with Clancy has evolved nicely too, and the house we're buying is about half finished.

Christine loves her new job as a nurse and the doctor hired her after one month of internship. I've gone out with the girls a few times, one of which Clancy had to practically push me out the door. Too many guys hit on me when I'm out and I just don't want to deal with it. I'm not wearing my ring anymore, which makes it worse, and which I still haven't found since Clancy threw it across my living room. So, one day—that'd be today—I decide to move furniture around to find it before Toni does and chokes on the damn thing.

I pull the chair away from the wall and look behind it. Nothing but dust bunnies back there and one of Tonk's chew toys. I pick it up and throw it behind me.

"Hey," Clancy says, and I look back at him. He's holding the chew toy.

"Oh, sorry," I reply with a giggle. I ignore his next little *uh huh* comment and go back to looking for the ring. I slide the bookshelf out and look behind there. Still nothing and it's dark, so I can't see very well. "You did throw it in this general direction, right?"

"I think so."

Toni's bouncing on her butt in her playpen in the kitchen. Her neck strength is finally getting better and she's holding onto the netting for support. "Ah-da," she shrieks.

"I'm right here," he tells her and peeks through the archway. "Boo!"

Toni and I both giggle, and then Clancy laughs, watching her. "What?" I ask as I slide between the shelf and the wall to reach back into the corner.

"She fell over." When he sees my head snap back, he adds, "She's fine."

I let out a little breath of relief and go back to my search. No, I will not become an over-protective mother, stepmother, whatever. "That's her favorite word now." I'm talking about *boo*, not *ah-da*.

He agrees with a nod. "Find anything yet?"

"No." I then snap my hand back because it feels like a bolt of electricity bit me. "Ow!"

"What happened?" He moves closer to me.

"Something bit me, I think. Shit, it hurts." I resist the urge to shake my hand.

"Let me see." He takes my hand, touching the spot by accident while lifting it, and I yank my hand back with a scream. "Sorry. Let's try that again."

I point to the spot and he looks at it, but there isn't any swelling and only minimal redness. Now it feels a little numb and tingles. My breathing starts to labor a bit because I don't know what it was and that freaks me out a little, especially in this state.

"Calm down."

Toni shouts something from the kitchen.

I look up. "Did she just say ma-ma?"

"Sounded like it, huh?" Clancy inspects my hand and I look down as I go to push myself up, which is when I discover my perpetrator. I scream to holy hell and climb like a goddamn monkey onto Clancy—my arms wrap around his neck; legs around his torso.

"Jesus, Nemy, what the hell?" He stumbles back, my weight throwing his balance off.

"Kill it!" I shout and point at the creature over his shoulder as I cling to him. "KILL IT!"

He unlocks my legs and arms from around him, which is a serious chore, and steps forward to look at it. Then he grabs an empty mason jar he'd used to drink out of earlier and scoops it up.

"Fuck me, it's a bark scorpion." He takes my arm and drags me into the kitchen, and then sets the jar down on the counter.

I walk in a wide semi-circle around the area, which is tough to do when Toni's playpen sits in the center of my tiny kitchen.

"Oh stop, it's not going to jump out at you."

My hand goes under the faucet, forced there by Clancy, and he adds some soap to wash the sting.

"Uck uck uck," Toni says.

My head tilts to the side and I glare up at the man. "Good one."

He chuckles. "I don't think she's quite at the repetition stage, babe."

He's right, thank God. I close my eyes and sway a little. "Is it bad that my vision is blurring?"

"Okay, we're now going to the hospital." Clancy slides the jar off the counter, and then he grabs the lid he discarded before filling it with fluid earlier and covers it. "Hold this," he says and pushes it into my hands.

"No!" I shout and the jar tumbles between my hands.

He catches the jar and forces the fingers of my right hand around the glass. "It can't get out. Hold it!"

I whimper; he turns around to grab Toni.

"Come on." He grabs my arm and walks me to the front door. "On duty, Tonk." We walk out the door because he doesn't have time to lock it, or doesn't think about it as he drags me to his car. The hospital is right down the street and around the corner, like in the same neighborhood.

I'm crying and so freaked out by the pain, I'm having an anxiety attack. Clancy tries to calm me down, but it doesn't work for once and I'm wheezing to the point that the hospital staff is now on alert and they're giving me shots of God knows what. It doesn't take long to get my breathing stabilized, and soon after that, the pain numbs until I'm lying on the bed with Clancy at my side, his hand on my shoulder while Toni's little eyes are bright and wide-fucking-open because of all the new sights to see. She has a lock of his hair in her mouth and chews on it.

What a great way to remember Toni's first time calling me ma-ma. I'm so fucking thrilled I have to tie this damn scorpion sting to it. Don't mind me. It's the shots they've given me in the emergency room, whatever those were. Wait, did I say that shit aloud?

Clancy's laughing at me. "Stop thinking, Nemy-girl. You have no control over your mouth."

Apparently so. "You might want to take her out of here then, because she's gonna hear every swear word we've neglected to say around her."

He looks at Toni and pulls his hair out of her mouth. "Mommy's funny, isn't she?" She giggles and slaps her hand against his shoulder a few times.

My head spins, and though they've shot me up with who knows what, the anxiety kicks and screams at me. Oh my God, I'm a mother. What if I turn out just like my mother?

Jesus, what has happened to my life?

Clancy doesn't say anything, so I don't know if I said that one aloud or not. Shit, I hope not. Wait, did I say that aloud too? I cover my face with my hands. I want to scream.

☆ ☆ ☆

After we've put Toni to bed, and are in bed ourselves, Clancy pulls me close to him. "Are you not happy, Nemy-girl?"

"What? Why would you ask me that?" I say and look into his eyes. There's a sad quality to them I've never seen before. Wait, no, I've seen it once before. Oh shit. What did I do?

"Something you said today at the hospital," he replies. "I'm sure you thought you were just thinking it."

My eyes close and I sigh. "I was drugged up, Clancy."

"Doesn't mean it's not true."

"It doesn't mean it *is* true. I don't know. Maybe I'm bored." My eyes open and I quickly add, "Not with you or Toni, but because I'm not working, and I haven't really created anything like I used to. It's been a couple of months, and I haven't signed up for classes again. It's an intellectual thing." It's only been a week since I left The Fox Den.

"I didn't force you to quit. I let you make that decision. You could've still worked for Scott."

"I know," I whine. "But then I wouldn't have time for you or Toni. I'd be too tired, and besides, it wouldn't be the same working there if you weren't there. It wouldn't be fun and would become an actual job. That's what I hated about those last few weeks."

He smiles and trails his fingers around the edge of my face and pushes my hair back. "Why don't you start up the magazine you showed me?"

Hey, that's not a bad idea, but . . . .

"I won't have time for that soon." Toni will be walking soon, maybe, which also means she'll wear us both out and I won't be getting laid for a while. Fuck. I hope he has more of those Valentine ventures planned. I may have to plan some my damn self.

"You'll have plenty of time to get it started. I can help you with it, if you'd like."

"Put some of your artwork in it?" He hasn't really had time to paint lately, either, so I think he understands me.

"I would love to."

I smile at him. "I love you."

"I love you too," he says and kisses me. Toni sleeps through the night now, so Clancy makes damn certain I get the attention I need. He chuckles against my skin. "I've gotten you out of your man-hating phase." He is so fucking proud of this fact.

"Nah," I say while his lips travel to my breasts. "I just don't hate you."

"You let me know when that starts to happen, and I'll turn it around real quick."

"It's a deal." I'm still trying to find that flaw in him. Maybe the only flaw he has is that he's essentially a hitman, and he hasn't done that in some time. Right now, he's making me forget about my finger, and that's all that matters.

A week goes by and I'm fully recovered from the scorpion sting *and* we've had the house exterminated, even though it's very rare to find a scorpion in Tempe, especially where we're at. Neither of us wants to take any chances with Toni being so young. That whole thing has really freaked me out and I twitch for a couple of days afterward. I'm also a bit cranky lately and certain foods I like taste funny to me. We found the ring too, right where the damn scorpion was hiding. It's like the creepy-crawly was guarding the blasted thing. He won't be guarding anything now.

Five days later, we're on our way to look at the construction on the new house, when I get a call from one of my girlfriends.

"What's up, Teags?" I say while Clancy drives north on Loop 101. "Don't forget there's cameras up ahead here." He remains silent and has learned to ignore these little reminders for the most part, because he knows by now I just have to say them. It's not that I think he's incompetent or anything. The words just fucking come out and I am helpless to stop them. Jeremy failed to realize this and usually got annoyed with me. Then I realize they took the cameras out. "Never mind."

He still says nothing, but I can see the grin on his face.

"No, not you, Teags. Talk to me. Shut the eff up! When? Really? Well, thank God for that. Okay, call me later. Bye." When I turn to Clancy to relay everything Teags told me (not that he really cares, but he has become my best fucking friend—how d'ya like that for a BFF? Fuck that forever shit), I find him withholding his laughter, his lips pressed together in a thin line. My brow rises and I tilt my head. "What's so freakin' funny?"

He glances at me. "Have you ever listened to yourself when you talk to one of your friends?"

I roll my eyes. "Oh, shut up."

He laughs aloud, which wakes up a teething Toni.

Background noise can only reach a certain decibel before it wakes her. My head falls back with a sigh. "Wonderful." I turn and lean back to her. "It's okay, sweetie," and I put the pacifier in her mouth. She spits it back out. I rummage through the diaper bag and pull out a toy she started chewing on the day before. She and Tonk now share chew toys, which has Clancy laughing and me throwing away a good number of toys, or at least washing them thoroughly before giving them back to her. "Here, sweetie." She knocks it from my hand, and I sigh again. She has not been a happy baby lately.

"You need to put that stuff on her gums," Clancy suggests.

"I can't do that from here." I'm stretched as far as the seatbelt will allow. "And don't tell me to ride in the backseat with her. I'll get carsick."

"I didn't say anything about the backseat." His voice is über calm with the slow head shake. "Do you want me to pull over?"

"Yes, please." When he does, I get out and move to the backseat to take care of her, where I discover she also needs her diaper changed. Clancy leans over the back seat and watches me, and my eyes flick up to him now and then. I'm confused because the evil glint is like a goddamn beacon in his eyes. "Please don't tell me this turns you on."

He chuckles. "Actually—"

"Just stop, I don't want to know."

"I wasn't going to say that. I'm curious about something."

I get Toni changed and back in the car seat, and then I rub her gums with the gel, even though the doctors say not to use it. I just put a little bit on to give her some sort of comfort. I let out a heavy sigh because he's still giving me that look. "What?"

"When was your last period? You have this glow about you I've never seen before."

My forehead creases. "Um, I don't know. Maybe . . . seven or eight weeks . . . ago." I gasp and look him in the eye upon realizing my crankiness and that I've felt a little nauseous recently. "Oh my God! It's been over two months! You don't think? I mean, I can't . . . I don't think." I freeze and just stare at him. "Clancy?"

He grins. "I think we'd better pick up a pregnancy test on the way home."

I quickly nod.

"Come on, get back up here so we can go."

I climb out of the backseat and into the front seat and shut my door. His fingers pluck up my left hand and he kisses the back of it. That's when it dawns on me.

"Oh no," I say, staring at my hand.

"What?" He looks down.

"Those shots they gave me and the Anascorp. What if I actually am pregnant? What could that do?" The hospital staff did ask me if there was any chance of my being pregnant, and I said the same thing I always say—no. It's been like ten years.

"Nemy-girl, don't jump ahead." He strokes my arm with his other hand.

"You know I can't help it." My right hand starts shaking.

He cups my face in his hands and pulls me forward until I can feel his breath on my lips. "Calm down."

My eyes dart back and forth between his. "I don't want to lose another one. I can't. It's so painful." My lower lip quivers.

Clancy pulls me into his arms and holds me tight. "I didn't know you'd lost one. I just thought you couldn't get pregnant." He kisses the top of my head. "We'll get the test and go from there. No sense stressing about something that isn't certain."

"My breasts are tender."

He chuckles. "I'm waiting for the test."

"I've had morning sickness too. Just didn't realize it and thought it was a cold or something."

"I'm still waiting to see that little plus sign, or whatever. Let's go look at the house and get that over with, and then we'll stop at the store, okay?"

I nod and he kisses the top of my head again, and I settle back in my seat as he starts driving once more.

I pick at my nails for something to do as my mind rockets through the thoughts. "I bet it was Valentine's Day."

"I'm sure it was. That was a fun night." His voice gets this husky growl and catches my attention as my body heats up.

I giggle.

Holy crap. I could possibly be pregnant.

While we're at the construction site, I don't even pay attention to what anyone's saying. I hold Toni in my arms and bounce a little, and stare at her, wondering what hell it's going to be to have two babies. Jesus.

Clancy ushers me back to the car and we leave. "That was quick."

He nods. "I have other things on my mind."

"Yeah, me too." I stare out the window for a good long while.

When we get home, I head straight for the bathroom with a pregnancy test in my hand. I come back out and Clancy sits at the kitchen table while Toni plays on the floor. She can sit up now and she throws a toy at Tonk's head. It bounces off and his eyes flick to the toy. It's lying about a foot away from him. He lifts his head and stretches his front leg out, clawing the plastic toy and dragging it back to him, making the whole scenario look like something out of a weird horror movie.

I laugh and sit down in the chair across from Clancy. He's watching me carefully and I place the test on the table. It doesn't say anything yet because it hasn't been long enough. Soon, my nails click against the tabletop and it attracts Toni's attention. She shrieks a giggle out and Clancy looks down at her and chuckles. My hand lays flat against the table, and we both look at the test again.

"Holy Shiite." I'm dumbfounded by the digital *yes* gracing the mini-screen. My eyes flick back to Clancy, who has a grin spreading across his face.

His brow jumps. "Well, looks like we'll have our hands full."

"Um, yeah," I reply and stand. "I need to call my doctor."

He sits back and grabs my left hand when I walk by. "I'd better put a ring on that finger now."

I look down at him. "Only do that if you *want* to, not because I'm having your baby."

He grins. "Maybe I want to, Nemy-girl."

Okay, I need to breathe.

25

Tura' Lu

Holy fucking shit, I'm pregnant! The doctor has confirmed it and she's not too worried about the corticoids the hospital gave me or the Anascorp because she requested a copy of my charts, but she decides to send me to a Perinatologist, which is a high-risk pregnancy doctor, just in case and partly because of my age. She's also found some underlying systemic issues with me after running some blood tests. Jesus. I get the first ultrasound done a week later. It's just a little sac and I can barely see the fetus, but it's there. I'm about seven weeks along, so yes, Valentine's Day it was.

I'm scared shitless too, because I lost the last one at nine weeks. Clancy won't let me do anything around the house now. I'm going crazy. Help!

Thankfully, Scott wants me to guest bartend now and then at the club, so he and I schedule that over the next few months.

I start designing the layout for the magazine on my laptop to distract my negative thoughts. Alanna has already agreed to do the photos, and so has Teagan, so I call up the Dirty Russian because he's a damn good photographer, especially when it comes to the pin-up girl shots. We set up a photo shoot date and I go back to my designing. Clancy sits on the sofa next to me after putting Toni down for a nap, and he leans over to look at my progress.

"Nice. I like it."

"Thanks." I move the cursor to insert a picture. I have some of his art already on my laptop and I click on one to place it within the pages. He painted one of me in an implied pose. That means I'm naked, but nothing really shows. I'm sitting on the bed with my head turned to the side, one arm crossed over my chest to cover my nipples, leaning back on the other arm, legs bent and crossed, and the camera angle is just right. The Fuck-me boots are damn prominent, though. He took the photo on Valentine's Day and painted the portrait shortly thereafter. It's hanging in the bedroom now.

He leans closer and kisses my shoulder. "That's my favorite one."

"Mine too," I say and grin.

He slides his hand over my belly and rests it there. "I can't wait. I didn't get to experience all of this with Toni."

I draw in a deep breath and let it out slowly. I'm trying very hard not to think negative thoughts when regarding the pregnancy, but it's so damn difficult. It'll be much easier once I've passed the ninth week. Yeah, I know, I'm kidding myself.

"Stop worrying. It's not helping the situation."

"I know. I'm trying."

Clancy's phone rings and he snatches it off the coffee table. "Hello?" He abruptly sits up. "Well, take care of it."

My eyes flick to him and back to my computer.

"I don't care how you do it. Never mind. I'll be there in a bit." He closes his phone and turns back to me while I tap away at the keyboard, and he leans over to kiss my cheek. "I have to go help a friend with something."

"Who and what?"

"Drew. He's having some issues with one of his employees."

"Why is that your problem?" I look at him.

He smiles. "I'm a silent partner, but he refuses to let me remain silent sometimes."

I chuckle. "What's the issue?"

"You just never mind and keep working on that." He points to my computer. Then he ruffles my hair.

"Hey, don't do that," I protest as he grabs his keys and stands.

He looks back at me when he reaches the door. "What are you gonna do about it?"

"Kick your ass later," I reply and stick my tongue out.

He chuckles. "Yeah, right." He opens the door. "By the way, I think Drew wants you to guest bartend too. I'll double-check with him. I'll be back soon."

"Have fun." I spend the rest of the afternoon working on the magazine, attending to Toni, and preparing dinner, since he's not home yet. He walks in right at six o'clock when dinner is ready, and he has a nice little bouquet of flowers for me. I think it's supposed to be an apology for taking so long. Not sure that's going to work on me.

"Sorry I took so long." He leans over and kisses my cheek. "It was a bit more difficult than I thought."

"Mmm hmm." I transfer the flowers into a vase and arrange them. I learned a long time ago not to question shit. Thanks, Dad. "Thanks. They're beautiful."

"You should look at them a little closer." A sly grin touches his lips.

My eyes flick to him, view that grin, and then I look back at the flowers. I spread them apart, searching the stems, and then I look in each rose until I find the one with a gift in it.

"Clancy!" I pull the ring out. Oh God, I just went totally girlie on that. Shit.

He takes my hand and takes the ring from me.

"Marry me, Nemy-girl." He pulls me close.

"Um, okay," I reply.

He chuckles. "That's not good enough."

"Are you gonna get down on one knee at least?"

He grins and drops to one knee. "Will you, Anna Maria Mussolini, be my wife, companion, and lover for eternity?"

"Smartass." I bend at the waist, leaning forward. "Yes."

He slips the ring onto my finger.

I study it. "Jesus, is the diamond big enough?" It's about three times the size of the one Asshole gave me.

"Is it?"

"Oh, like I care." I look him in the eye. "Please don't buy me a fur coat."

"Darn it, that was going to be my next purchase."

"Da-da," Toni says from her playpen.

He turns to her and plucks her out of it. "What, Toni-girl?" His tone is a playful one and kisses her little neck. She giggles and he does it again.

Teagan calls me later to inform me Jada is officially freaking out, as though she wasn't doing that before. I guess they found James' body. I say who the hell cares, and Teagan agrees with me, but only after she's left the room so Jada doesn't overhear her. Clancy bathes Toni, and while I'm on the phone with Teagan, I grab his keys because I left something in the car the day before. I walk outside, talking to Teagan the entire way, and get in the passenger side of Clancy's BMW. While I search around for the note I scribbled an idea on, I find a small piece of paper wedged beside the seat . . . and it has James' name and address on it.

"What the fuck?"

"What?" Teagan says.

"Oh, I found something odd."

"What is it?"

"Oh, it's just a piece of paper I didn't expect to find, that's all." The wheels turn in my mind as I attempt to figure out why Clancy would have this. I mean, hell, what if the police found the damn thing way back when they questioned us? It's not in his handwriting, either. "Hey Teags, I'm gonna have to call you back. I really need to find that note." She says goodbye and I hang up the phone. Then I sit there and stare at the paper I found. James' disappeared ages ago and his body just turned up. I shake the horrible fleeting thought from my head, but it doesn't wish to go away. I look around the car some more and finally find the note I'd come out to locate, and then I return to the house.

Clancy comes back to the living room after putting Toni down for the night, and he sits next to me. "Show me how much you got done today."

I hold up the piece of paper. "What's this?"

He tilts his head. "A piece of paper."

I look at it and turn it over. "No, what's this?"

"A name and address." He plucks it out of my hand. "Thanks, I was looking for that."

"Why do you have James' name and address on you?"

He stares at me a moment. "I was keeping an eye on him after he attacked you."

"You've hardly left my side."

"Okay, I was having someone keep an eye on him for me."

I'm not able to stop myself. "Would that someone be the reason he disappeared?"

He lets out a short laugh. "No."

"Are you sure about that? Because if there's something I should know . . ."

"Nemy-girl . . ." he leans forward, cupping my face with one hand, "you know all you need to know." I bite my lower lip and he chuckles. "Don't pout."

"Do you have any idea the havoc that little piece of paper would have caused had the police found it? You do remember they questioned us, right?"

"I remember." He shoves the paper in his jeans pocket. "And they didn't search my car."

"They questioned you all night!"

"And didn't have anything solid to keep me. Besides, I told them I had James' address and why, but I had an alibi the night he disappeared, so there wasn't shit they could do."

My mob-minded brain kicks into overdrive, and my eyes flick to his shirt. "There's a speck of blood on your shirt."

He looks down, and when his eyes return to me, he sighs. "It's not blood."

"Looks like blood."

"It's not."

I arch my brow at him and he shakes his head.

"Okay, I had a nosebleed earlier."

"So it *is* blood."

"Yes, but it's mine."

"You never get nosebleeds."

"I know, but I didn't want to worry you." His hand slips over my belly.

"I would think a nosebleed would leave more than a speck of blood on your shirt."

"Stop over analyzing. I leaned forward in time, with exception to one little speck."

"Why did you get the nosebleed?"

"It's the weather. My nose is all dried out and with spring here, I'm getting an allergy attack."

"I don't recall you being prone to allergies last year."

He chuckles again. "What the fuck is this, an inquisition? You are not going to let this go, are you?" He leans forward until I can feel his breath on my cheek. "I did not kill James."

"Who said anything about killing James? I certainly didn't. I'm just asking about the blood on your shirt. Who does that belong to?"

He draws in an irritated breath through his nose. His eyes dart back and forth, watching mine. "Do you really care?" His tone is full of serious *stop asking questions.*

I glare at him, and finally say, "No."

"Good, then the conversation is over." I open my mouth and he lifts my chin with his fingers and closes it. "It's over."

I stare at him a moment longer and then go back to my computer, keeping my mouth shut for God knows why. I don't usually let a man shut me up, but I'm not certain I care to delve into that any deeper. I've been running away from it all my life.

Damn it. Perfection slashed to ribbons . . . with a fucking bloody trail.

Not long thereafter, I shut my laptop down and go to bed. Clancy watches me leave the room and I hear his heavy sigh before I reach the bedroom. Then I get ready for bed and climb in, lying on my side, and I can hear him roaming through the house and turning lights off. Soon, I feel him climb into bed beside me, and he moves closer. He slips his hand over my waist and rests it on my belly after pushing my tank out of the way, and his lips touch my shoulder. I don't move or make a sound.

"I know you're not sleeping yet. You don't fall asleep that fast."

I don't respond.

"Nemy-girl, why are you mad at me?"

"I'm not mad," I whisper.

A silent laugh moves his body against mine. "Yes, you are." His lips move to my neck. "I'm sorry."

"You don't even know why you're sorry," I say. "Or why I'm mad."

"So you *are* mad."

"No, I mean . . ." I stumble and just want to hit myself. "Shit."

He pulls me back and stretches across me, his face hovering above mine. "Ask the fucking question I know is on your mind."

I shake my head. "No."

"You must have a million questions. You've never asked me about so many things. Like why I get a call and have to leave late at night. I think tonight's the first time you asked about anything."

I stare at him in the darkness. "I don't want to find the flaw in you."

"I can't be perfect, Nemy-girl." He brushes the hair away from my face in a gentle sweep. "I'm *not* perfect."

"Yeah, but that one imperfection seems really fucking big right now, regardless of what Octavian told me."

He smiles. "Well, it might be to you. To me, it's just a small part of my life. You and Toni are much bigger parts."

"I don't want to know how involved you still are." Dread rolls through me that he'll tell me anyway.

He grins and kisses the tip of my nose. "Are you sure?"

"Am I the only woman in your life?"

"Yes," he replies with conviction, looking me right in the eye without a single twitch or blink.

"That's all I need to know."

"If that's what you want, fine. But don't get mad at me if you inadvertently find out more, because I'm giving you this one chance to ask your questions."

Call me stupid, but I agree with that.

I'm an Italian princess. I know where my nose doesn't belong, and if I find something along the way, well, so be it. If Clancy's into some shady shit outside of what Octavian dumped on me, I don't want to hear about it right now, not when I'm trying to keep this baby.

However, I can't help myself. "Is it like a mafia thing?"

He's laid his head against my chest by now, and he chuckles at the question. "To your Italian mind, maybe, Ms. Mussolini."

"I know we've covered this before, but how do you know about my family?"

He lifts his head and perches his chin on my chest. "How could I not? Your family name has covered the headlines for the last twenty years."

"Try forty," I correct.

He chuckles. "Okay, forty years."

"How long have you known? About me, I mean."

He stares at me in the darkness, eyes glinting a little now and then from the intermittent light flashing on my phone. "I discovered it right after you interviewed with me. You should've changed your last name if you didn't want anybody to know."

"Yeah, Google search, right?" I shrug. "My father would kill me. Besides, most normal people wouldn't look it up and be content with my *no relation* comment, regardless of mob family or dictator."

He laughs. "You applied for a job at a strip club, woman. The thought that someone in a place like that would recognize your last name *had* to cross your mind."

"It did, but I just ignored the thought. I needed the job." I run my fingers through my hair. "I know you've kept your nose clean, but are you still involved in that shit?"

"Yes, but I keep a low profile." He lays his head back down, but turns it up so he can see my face. "Does it scare you?"

He's asking if what he's into scares me. I have to think about it. "Surprisingly, no."

"Good."

I sigh. "How'd he die?"

"I didn't kill James."

"Swear it on your life."

"I swear. I honestly don't know who did it. I'm sure a guy like him has many enemies, but it wasn't my family."

"Okay."

A silent void encompasses us as we stare at one another.

"Bullet to the head, right?" I'm teasing now. He remains silent. "Baseball bat?"

"You never relent," he says with a chuckle.

I slap his arm and it's loud. We both freeze for a moment, not breathing, and listen for Toni.

"Shush, you'll wake the baby."

"You shush," I whisper and look down at him. His chin is perched on my chest again. "I almost wish you had killed him so I could know if it was painful or not."

He studies me for a bit before responding. "How much have you seen?"

"More than I care to admit."

"The first time I saw your name was in a newspaper clipping. It was about Michael Mussolini's daughter. You're his only daughter, huh?"

"My father was named after his father, so there were two mob bosses named Michael Mussolini, and both of them had a daughter." I smile. "But very likely, yes, that was about me because my aunt was a perfect little Italian princess."

"I thought so."

I giggle. "That article was from when I was a teenager and got busted for a craps game, or something, at school. I don't even remember the whole story. The press had a field day with it because I'm a girl."

"Yeah, I think the headline was *Following in Daddy's Footsteps*, or the like," he says. "Anna Maria Mussolini, aka Nemesis. No wonder you're such a tough girl, growing up in that environment."

I quirk a brow at him. "It's just a façade. I'm really not that tough."

"Bullshit. I've felt your punch, remember? Why'd your family move to Arizona?"

"Same as any other mob family. I was in middle school. I started to rebel around that time. Got my first tattoo when I was sixteen. Dad wanted to kill me."

He chuckles and runs his hand down my arm. "How does he feel about your tattoos now?"

"He hasn't seen them. We haven't talked since I divorced Garrett and that was like six years ago. Good Catholic girls aren't supposed to get divorced, or get tattoos, or work in strip clubs."

"Good Catholic boys aren't supposed to get divorced, either, or do the other things I've done." He grins. "So, should we get married in the Catholic Church?"

"Fuck no." I know he's teasing a little, but he sounds damn serious. "We're both divorced. We can't get married in the church."

"Would it make your father happy?"

"Once he sees me looking like this? No. Let's not forget the fact you're Irish. That alone will kill the man."

The grin stretches across his face. "I bet I could win your father's heart."

I laugh. "Oh yeah, now that I know you're like two peas in a pod. He'll be fucking thrilled!"

"Normally, I love your sarcasm, but not at my expense."

"Oh, hush. Actually, he'd probably love you to death, even if you are Irish. He might overlook that flaw." I laugh and slap a hand over my mouth so I don't wake Toni. "Oh my God, that's your flaw!"

"Great." He positions himself on top of me, leans over, and his lips travel along my jaw toward my neck. "I'll have to search for your flaw."

"I can point them out for you." I close my eyes with a shuddering sigh as his feathery kisses grace my flesh.

"Nope, not there." He's at my ear and moves on to my neck. "Not here, either." The collarbone. "Nor is it here."

"Oh wow, are you gonna search every inch of me?" I giggle.

"You bet." He stops at my chest. "Mmm, not here." He inches the tank up and drops his face down to my stomach, his body sliding down my legs. "Definitely not here." He presses his lips against my skin. "Hey, little one."

I giggle again. "It can't understand you yet."

"I don't care." He continues talking to my belly. "Daddy's about to make mommy a very happy mommy. Hold on tight."

I have to slap my hand over my mouth again because my laughter might wake up Toni. Oh man, is Clancy ever talented. He got me out of my little whatever the hell that was mood, and yes, made me one very happy mommy.

Son of a bitch. I found a man who's just like my dad.

26

You Know What You Are

Michael Mussolini, aka my father, has never been officially charged with anything in his life. I know, it's surprising. He was quick on his feet when young, and quick to think when older. The Feds couldn't gather evidence against him for murder or anything like that, but they did find a few items of racketeering, though it was small time stuff. Aside from that, my dad's been pretty careful. The Feds were a little shocked when he agreed to testify several years ago against Vitto DeGrazzi, the Don back then, who was as old as the day is long and took over when grandpapa died. What the Feds didn't know was that it was all planned, and because it is in violation of the Principles of Federal Prosecution to use a RICO (Racketeer Influenced and Corrupt Organizations) count for plea bargains, they had to release Dad without charges after he testified. They haven't been able to get a thing on him since—not even tax evasion because he's real careful about that—and we moved shortly thereafter. It was a ruse to make the Feds think my father left the family, and they even helped us out, though Dad refused to change our name. Vitto died before going to prison, just as he wanted. The man was almost dead anyway.

Most people think Nitti is the Don—not the Nitti from the roaring twenties, but his son. In truth, my father leads the family, which Vitto turned over to him before he died. That makes me a fucking Italian Princess, which is exactly why I rebelled. I was supposed to get married to a nice Italian boy, make babies, and be a good little homemaker. First step in the rebellion—date only Irish boys. Dad still groans over it. I even married one—Garrett. Then, I almost married another one—Jeremy. The last one doesn't matter much because dad's still pissed at me for divorcing Garrett, even though he's Irish, and he never met Jeremy. Oh, and there's also the fact that I've never had children. He thinks it's some sort of protest. Jesus.

I've watched a man take a bullet to the head. I was twelve and quite the little Tomboy. That shit toughens a girl up real fast. I remember it vividly too. I ran into the warehouse looking for my dad because I'd gotten tired of waiting in the car, and I opened the door right when Vinnie pulled the trigger. My eyes blinked shut and I felt a splatter hit my face—just a light sprinkle, but blood-spatter nonetheless. When I opened my eyes, they were all staring at me, I think surprised I didn't scream and run like a girl would do. To my surprise, they stood and waited to see what my reaction would be. I thought I was in so much trouble. Then my father called my name.

"Anna."

I looked at him and stepped forward, obeying his beckoning hand.

He took out his handkerchief and wiped the blood from my face.

Arty was the first to speak, and with a bit of a chuckle. "It figures, your daughter is the one who can stomach it." Dad backhanded him for it. Arty lost a tooth.

My older brother, Donnie, couldn't handle the violence. He's an air traffic controller now. Go figure.

Dad continued to wipe my face after spitting on the cloth. "Your mama will have my hide for allowing such ruin to your pretty dress." I scrunched up my nose and dad laughed because he knew I hated dresses, but it was a special day, which was why we were back home. He and mom had a nasty argument that night after I went to bed when she found out what I'd witnessed. I will say that he never hit my mother once.

And I never waited in the car again.

"Wow, Nemy-girl, that's quite a story."

Toni bounces on my knee and I nod. He's silent for a while after that. I mean, where does one go from there?

"Have you ever killed anyone?"

Okay, I guess one goes there. I shake my head. "Beat the snot out of a few guys in the neighborhood who were fu . . . messing with one of the shops my dad protected." My eyes flick to his. "You?"

He nods, the motion slow and calculated while he studies my reaction.

"How many?"

He holds up one hand, all five fingers displayed. I'm waiting for the other hand to rise, but it never does.

"Okay. Not just random, right?"

"No." He's still studying my face.

"Would you stop examining me? I'm not going to freak out on you."

A smile touches his lips and eyes. "I've never told any woman about it, so I'm a little apprehensive regarding the subject."

"Yeah, well, ditto on what I just told you." I pause a moment, make a face at Toni, and then meet his eyes again. "I need to call my mom."

"Set up a lunch or dinner with them."

"If they're even here yet. They have a house here and one in California. They jump back and forth throughout the year, and then go back home too."

He takes Toni from me and sits her on his lap. "Go call her."

I bite my lower lip and stare at him. I really don't want to call my mom. It'll be thirty minutes of hell before I can even talk. I pick up my phone and dial as I walk back to the bedroom. She waits until the fourth damn ring to answer.

"Hello?" Her voice is sugar sweet, as though she doesn't know who the hell is calling her.

"Hi, Mama." It's about all I get out and embark on listening to the cavalcade of worrisome, tiring, *why can't you call your mother more often* jargon for the next ten minutes. "But—" and I'm cut off for another five minutes while she goes into *where have you been* and *what trash are you sleeping with now* bullshit. "I'm not—" I squeeze in before she begins the *why don't I have any grandchildren from you* phase. A-ha! "I'm pregnant." It takes her a minute to register my comment.

"What was that?"

"Mama, I'm pregnant." My stomach is in knots and I feel like I'm going to be sick.

"You should have a teenager by now." Like I don't fucking know that. "What kind of woman has a baby at your age?"

"I'm not even forty yet."

"You will be soon enough. Thirty-five in a few months—"

"I know when my fucking birthday is."

"Don't you talk to me like that!" Then she sighs heavily, as though I am such a burden on her. "Is there a father?"

"Obviously, or I wouldn't be pregnant."

Her growl comes through the line nice and clear. See where I get it? "Is he still around?"

"Yes, I'm wearing a ring." I hold up my hand to admire the giant rock on my finger.

"A wedding ring?" Of course she'd have to ruin the moment for me.

"Not yet. Just an engagement ring right now."

"Aye, Anna!" She continues to mutter curses at me in Italian. Oh my God, you'd think I was twenty. "Who is this man?"

"His name is Clancy Dolan."

She starts swearing again in Italian. "Another Irish boy? You will be the death of your father!"

"Jesus, Mama, it wasn't on purpose this time."

"Watch your mouth!" My mother likes to think of herself as a devout Catholic woman, even though she's married to Don Mussolini.

"I'm sorry. Are you and Dad in Arizona yet?"

She huffs. "Yes, why?"

I swallow the lump in my throat. "Because Clancy would like us all to have lunch or dinner together." I can hear my dad in the background, asking Mom whom she's talking to, and I tense up because I really don't want him on the phone.

"It's Anna," she tells him. "She's not married and pregnant." Now his Italian curses are flying over the line at me. She really could have phrased that differently.

"Mama, I'm getting married!" I shout because she has the phone away from her ear. Now I *feel* like I'm twenty, or even seventeen. Jesus. I draw in a deep breath to calm myself.

"Anna?" My dad's voice comes over the line and I freeze. "Anna?"

"Papa." All of my strength disappears when I hear his voice. He is my only weakness. Well, aside from Clancy.

"You are with child?" He's so old-fashioned.

"Yes. About seven weeks."

"And you will marry this man?"

"Yes, Papa." I nod, like he can see that.

"Tell me about him."

"Oh . . . um, well . . . ." I stumble over my words, not quite sure what to tell him about the man I love because he's my dad and he'll judge the minute he hears his name. "Um—"

"Is he successful?" he asks to help me out.

"Yeah, he's retired, sort of."

"How old is he?" His voice grows a tad toward anger.

"He's only five years older than me, Papa."

"Hmm, and what brought him success to be able to retire early?"

"He owned his own business. And he's very good at managing money, and he's . . . um . . . in the . . . in the *business*." I have to stress the last word so he'll understand.

"What's his name?" he asks both my mother and me. Mom answers first. "He's Irish?"

I hear him spit after saying that. By now, I'm lying on the bed, curled up on my side, holding my head.

"Why must you torture me like this, Anna? What could you possibly see in those Irish boys? Are you trying to send me to my grave early?"

"No, Papa. I just don't like Italian men." Oh, that was so not the right thing to say.

"So you don't like your own father or brothers?"

"That's different."

"Anna!"

"Just meet him and give him a chance before you condemn him, please. You gave Garrett a chance."

"And he wasn't good enough for you."

"He treated me like shit!" Bad move.

"Don't raise your voice to me, Anna," he growls. Yeah, I get it from him too.

Clancy stands in the doorway, watching me, listening to this wonderful conversation. If he's smart, he'll run screaming now.

"I'm sorry." Mom mumbles in the background.

"He wishes us to have dinner together?"

"Yes, he does."

Clancy sits on the bed and rubs my leg. He silently asks for the phone. I shake my head because that's a disaster waiting to happen. Clancy insists and I pull away by rolling over.

"When?" Dad asks.

"I don't know. Let me ask him." I roll back and Clancy leans over me. "He wants to know when regarding dinner."

"Give me the phone," Clancy says.

"No."

"He's right there, Anna?" Dad asks.

"Yes."

"Let me talk to him," they both reply.

I sigh and hand the phone to Clancy.

"Hello, sir," Clancy says. "Yes, sir. I do apologize for that, sir, but we didn't think she could . . . No, sir. Yes, sir, I do intend to make her an honorable woman." He's trying not to laugh at that one. "Absolutely. We can do that, sure. Is tomorrow night good for you? Tonight? I'll make the reservations, certainly. Mastro Steakhouse on Pima and Pinnacle Peak? Good, I'll have Nemy call you back with the time. Yes, sir. I look forward to meeting you and your wife. Here she is." He hands the phone back to me and leaves the room to call the restaurant.

I bring the phone to my ear and clear my throat. "Hello?"

"He has manners."

"Yes."

"Call your mother back when you get the time."

"Okay, bye, Papa."

"*Arrivederci*, Anna." And he hangs up the phone.

I'm shaking like a fucking leaf now. This is why I hate calling them . . . for anything. I can't even get off the bed, and Clancy has to come back to the bedroom to tell me the reservation time.

He sits next to me. "Now I see why you haven't talked to them in so long." He pulls on my shoulder and I fall into his arms. "Shh, it'll be fine." He strokes my hair.

I let out a nervous laugh. "Yeah, right." I look up at him. "You call them back."

"No. I told your father you'd call."

"Damn it. I don't want to get stuck on the phone with my mother for twenty minutes."

"So, you're not so tough when it comes to your parents."

"No, mostly just my father." I pick up my phone again and stare at it. "I was daddy's little girl, after all."

"Maybe you could just send a text," he suggests.

I snap my head to the side to look at him. "Are you kidding me? I'd never hear the end of that!"

He laughs. "Make the call and get it over with."

"Can the whole night be over already?" I ask and dial. This time the phone only rings twice. "Hi, Mama. Dinner's at seven." I fall back on the bed while she yaps away. "Mama—" and I'm cut off again. Jesus. Clancy chuckles and stands up to leave. I kick at him and he bends his legs in time for me to miss him completely. Bastard. "Now I hate you," I mumble. "No, not you, Mama."

Clancy grins as he peers around the doorjamb. "We'll just have to fix that later." His brow jumps and he disappears down the hall while I'm stuck on the damn phone with my gabby mother. She's not chewing me out anymore. Now it's more like girl chat because she wants to know all sorts of details about my life, since I haven't spoken to her in a while. I'm not sure if I'm comfortable with this.

"Can we discuss this at dinner? I really need to find something to wear."

"I suppose."

Toni shrieks when Clancy carries her into her room, and I close my eyes, waiting for it.

"What was that?"

I sigh. "That was Toni. Clancy's daughter. Long story. We'll discuss it at dinner."

She's silent for a moment. Then, "Fine. See you then, Anna." She hangs up on me and I drop my phone onto the bed.

"God, just kill me now, please," I say while Toni talks Clancy's ear off in the next room.

We arrive at the restaurant early so we can get Toni seated, and so I can order drinks for my parents. I really want a drink. I don't know how I'm going to survive this night without one, but no, I have to drink water.

Clancy leans close. "I'll let you have a glass of wine with dinner, if that'll help."

"Oh God." I cover my face with my hands. "Why did I call them?" Then I tug on the neck of the shirt I'm wearing—a long-sleeved black turtleneck to hide every single visible tattoo on my upper body. I have one on my neck as well, and it's barely covered by the shirt.

"You'll be fine, Nemy-girl." He doesn't know my parents, or he wouldn't be saying that.

"This stress alone could cause a miscarriage."

"Don't say that." He lifts his hand and his fingers graze my chin. He turns my head to face him. "I love you."

"I love you too."

He smiles and kisses me, and it calms my nerves . . . until I see them walk into the room. My blood pressure soars and it's suddenly very hot in this room.

My father is a very robust man, tall with black hair going gray on most of his head now, and he is dressed in Armani, of course. My mother is only a few inches shorter than I am and looks like Sophia Loren. I'm not kidding. Especially with the dress she has on tonight. She's dressed to kill, and I'm pretty damn certain she's wearing either Dior or Versace, as though they're heading to a Hollywood screening. It's an impression game for them, and I whisper that to Clancy before they get within earshot. He chuckles and then stands to greet them. Clancy has on a nice suit, comparable to the one my dad wears, and it receives close inspection from the both of them. I stand because I have to hug them or I'll be disowned . . . again.

"Mama, Papa, this is Clancy." I point to my parents. "Clancy, Michael and Claudia Mussolini."

Clancy shakes my father's hand and kisses my mother's hand.

Once we're all seated, them across from us, my mother leans over. "Who's this little darling?" She pinches Toni's cheek, who then pulls away from her. My father glares at me. Honestly!

"Antonia. We call her Toni."

Mom's eyes lift to meet my face. "That's Nonni's name."

"Yes, that's why we named her that."

Now her eyes blink in rapid motion to the point that I think the false eyelashes will flutter off. "Is she . . . yours?"

I shake my head. "No, Clancy was married before." I sigh heavily. "It's a really long story."

"Please, Anna," Dad says. "Amuse us with the story." I look at him, and then look at my hands, which sit in my lap.

Clancy clears his throat. "If I may?" Dad looks at him and nods, and Clancy explains the process by which we received Toni, and thankfully leaves out the whole strip club thing, but I know that won't last long because my dad will to want to know exactly what kind of business Clancy owned, if he doesn't already know. Even though we haven't spoken in a few years, I know Dad's had me tailed to keep an eye on me. He probably even knows exactly who Clancy is, which could be a tad frightening and is part of the reason I'm nervous as hell.

I pick up my glass of water and take a sip to quench my completely parched mouth.

"Ma-ma-ma," Toni babbles and my eyes flick to her. This silences the table for a moment and I lean over to her because she's holding her hands out. "Ma-ma-ma," she repeats and I go to reach for her.

Clancy's hand touches my arm. "No, Nemy-girl. She can stay there."

"It's okay." I pull her out of her chair, and I stand her on my legs. She cranes her head back to look at my mother, so I turn her around. All the sparkles on Mom's dress and her jewelry have caught Toni's attention. Finally, she sits on my lap and I bounce my legs a little. Mom watches me the whole time.

"Well now, looks like you're already a mother."

I nod and Clancy continues the story. When he's finished, the waiter takes our order, and the table is quiet for only a moment.

"Anna says you owned a business." Dad breaks the uncomfortable silence with an even more uncomfortable topic. "What was it that gives you the opportunity to retire young?"

Clancy clears his throat. "It was a bar."

"And how did you meet my Anna?"

"She worked for me." Clancy smiles and touches my thigh. "She's the best bartender I've ever had."

"Hmm, yes well, Anna's all or nothing." Dad's eyes lock on me. "I think it was a bit more than a bar, though, wasn't it?"

I turn away from his glare. Just as I thought, Dad's done his homework already. If Octavian told him, my youngest brother will die a horrible, painful death very soon, regardless of the story I told Clancy in the hospital.

"Yes, sir, it was."

"Please tell me my little girl did not strip for you," Dad says in a threatening tone.

"Oh, no, sir," Clancy replies quickly. "She was a bartender only. You have my word."

Dad stares at him for a short amount of time and finally nods, satisfied, probably because he's already gathered information and knows Clancy's telling him the truth.

Mom reaches across the table and grabs my left hand. She pulls it forward, nearly pulling Toni and me over the table. "Very nice, Anna. What is that, three?"

Clancy looks at her and smiles. "Try five."

Her eyebrows rise and she smiles as I turn to Clancy. "What's five? The ring?"

He nods.

"As in carats?"

He nods again. Jesus. I'm afraid to wear the damn thing now. Mom pats my hand and lets it go. It's a sign of approval for her.

"Do you still live in Mama's house?"

"Yes, I've remodeled it. You wouldn't recognize the inside." Toni starts pulling on my sleeve and I move quickly to push it back down so the tattoos don't show.

"Well, I'm glad it's getting some use. It's such a quaint little place."

I nod. "I had to have the trees out front removed because they died, but I replaced them with some nice citrus trees." Toni grabs my sleeve again and pulls it up.

Mom's eyes catch the ink. "Anna! Is that another tattoo?"

I roll my eyes. "Mama, I'm not a teenager anymore!"

"How many do you have now?"

Dad leans forward. He beckons my arm with his hand across the table. I reluctantly give it to him and he takes my hand, pushes the sleeve of my shirt up to my elbow, and turns my arm over to view the entire inked sleeve.

"Oh my," Mom says.

Dad's face starts turning red. "Anna Maria! Does the other arm look the same?"

"Well, no, it has different tattoos on it." I yank my arm away from him and push the sleeve back down.

Dad eyes Clancy. "You approve of those?"

Clancy must answer very carefully here. "She had them already when we met."

"But do you approve of them?" Dad's voice is stern, on the edge of threatening, as though Clancy had anything to do with my tattoos.

And seriously? It's not like I can get rid of an entire sleeve of ink.

Clancy smiles. "I think they're beautiful on her. If one were to study some of the pieces, one might find a bit of Luca Signorelli, whom I believe painted his masterpiece within the Duomo di Orvieto Cathedral."

Whoa! That was impressive, and there's a huge smile forming on my dad's face.

"Have you seen the Cathedral in person?"

"I wish I could say that I have," Clancy replies. "But sadly, I have not yet visited Italy."

Dad nods. "My brother runs our vineyard there, near Bisaccia."

"Yes, Nemy has told me," Clancy says. "We were discussing a trip there soon."

"She can't travel right now," Mom says.

Clancy nods. "Obviously we would wait until after the baby is born, since her pregnancy is high risk."

"What?" Mom turns to me. "Why are you high risk?"

"Medical conditions the doctor discovered recently." I lift Toni to put her back in her highchair when the appetizers come out.

Mom jumps to her feet and takes Toni from me. "You shouldn't be lifting a baby!"

"Mama, it's fine."

"I try not to let her do it," Clancy says with a chuckle. "But she's so stubborn."

Dad's boisterous laughter echoes through the restaurant. "Ah, he knows her well!"

I look back at my fiancé, who could likely become single very soon if he continues along that line of thinking. "Thanks for throwing me under the bus. I appreciate that."

He winks at me. Bastard.

Dad leans across the table, toward Clancy. "Have the two of you picked a wedding date yet?"

"No." I adjust Toni's dress after mom places her back in the seat. She's wearing a cute little black and white polka dot dress with a bow to match.

"Well, you must do it soon, before she shows," Dad says.

Oh God, no, please, don't start planning my wedding.

"Claudia started showing early with Donnie. What was it dear, four months?"

"Five. With Anna, it was six."

I don't like the smile she's giving me.

"We could have your wedding next month, Anna." Oh God, there it is!

"I'd rather go to Vegas."

"Nonsense." She waves her hand around. "That's hardly worthy of a Mussolini. Tomorrow, we'll go shopping."

"No, Mama, really, I don't want a big fuss over this."

"Weddings are for the family, not for you!"

"Exactly why I don't want one. It's too much. I'm not supposed to have any stress or I could lose the baby like I did the last one."

Mom goes silent and crosses herself. Oh brother. "I'll help you, Anna. There won't be any stress for you."

I roll my eyes and reach for my water.

"You should be drinking milk." She turns around and snaps her fingers at the waiter. "Excuse me."

"Mama, milk is too fattening." I wave the waiter away.

"You'll need the calcium."

"I'm on prenatal vitamins and taking extra calcium, Mama. I think my doctor knows what she's doing."

"Oh, and I don't, after bearing five children?" She has that mother tone I pray to God I never get.

"I didn't say that, Mama." I take a deep breath. Clancy places a hand on my back and rubs in gentle motions. It relaxes me a little. "Tell them about the house," I say to him so it gets the subject off me and the wedding. I reach for a jumbo shrimp and dip it in the cocktail sauce as Clancy tells them about the house we're buying. Dad is pleased and so is Mom when he describes it. "It's really beautiful."

Mom sits back in her chair and lifts her second Cosmopolitan to her lips. "It's about time you found a man who can take care of you."

"Mama." I tilt my head to the side. "I've done just fine taking care of myself."

Clancy chuckles. "I will take very good care of her, Mrs. Mussolini."

She waves a hand at him. "Oh please, call me Claudia." Then she leans forward. "When you've married my daughter, you can call me Mom."

Okay, so Mom approves of Clancy. This is good. The jury's still out on my father, but I think he may be coming around.

I don't know why this is so fucking important to me, but I suppose regardless of how I feel about them, they're still my mom and dad, and I need that damn approval.

"Clancy, we will have to sit down and discuss *business* soon," Dad says. "I have done a bit of research, but would like to hear it straight from the horse's mouth."

"Papa." I shudder at the word 'horse' coming out of my father's mouth ever since I watched the *Godfather*, and especially since Clancy's name is attached to that damn sentence.

"Of course, sir," Clancy replies. "Whenever you'd like."

"Tomorrow afternoon."

Clancy nods. "I will make myself available."

I don't know if that's good or bad just yet. It's been awhile since I've experienced one of Dad's "business" meetings, but considering I'm carrying Clancy's baby, I don't think Dad will hurt him. See, I can be optimistic.

The rest of the evening consists of Mom gabbing, and since she likes to talk so damn much, we all let her, but even Toni gets a few words in here and there. Well, not really words exactly. Mom thinks it's adorable and pinches her cheeks again. I think I've gotten past the questioning of the last six years of my life now, and my real parents have now taken their bodies back from alien invasion. Whew. That was difficult.

Now, why am I doing this again?

27

Just a Girl

The next day, my mother insists we go shopping. I loathe shopping of any kind, and especially with her. She always wants to go to stores like Nordstrom's and Neiman Marcus. I can't afford that shit. Well, maybe I can, but still, the women in those stores are less than helpful if any of my tattoos are showing, which are rather difficult to hide when there's one on my neck and it's damn near summertime.

Clancy has Toni with him and he's meeting with my father while Mom and I shop. We're supposed to meet them for an early supper later. I've decided to piss Mom off today and am wearing a small T-shirt with cap sleeves. The disgusted eye roll was totally worth it, as were the mumblings that followed. I should've worn a tank top.

My mom is fifty-five. She married Dad at seventeen, had Donato (Donnie or Dan for short) right away, immediately followed by Giuseppe (sucks to be him with that name, but we call him Joey), and then I was born when she was twenty, followed two years later by Anthony, and then four years later she had her little darling Octavian (don't ask). It sucked growing up with four brothers so close in age. If … *when* I make it through this pregnancy, I'm done, and I'll make certain they fix me too.

I'm hoping for a girl.

After browsing several stores, buying a few items, and looking at wedding dresses, where I didn't find *anything* I liked, we head over to Lo Cascio, a little family-run Italian restaurant in Tempe. They have great food there and my parents love the place. Clancy, Toni and Dad are already waiting for us, and the two men stand when we walk up to the table. I hug my dad and kiss Clancy on the cheek, and then I lean over Toni and kiss her on the top of her head.

"Find a dress?" Clancy asks when I sit next to him, a little evil sparkle in his eye because he knows I dreaded the afternoon.

I lean over and whisper, "Found a nice little black teddy."

He grins. "Mmm, did you buy it?"

"You bet. Picked up a few things, not much, but I can't do much until we settle on a date."

"How about the fifteenth?"

"Can't, that's Anthony's birthday. What about the following weekend?"

He nods. "That could work." He pulls his new phone out and opens the calendar. After skimming through, he nods again. "Yes, it's fine."

I quirk a brow at him. "Do you have some important appointments coming up next month?"

He grins. "Maybe I do."

"What date was that?" Mom asks.

"The twenty-second," Clancy replies.

Mom jots it down in her little notepad. She is the very reason I learned to carry one with me at all times. Mom writes a little, mostly poetry, but it's beautiful stuff. "Alright, Anna, we can go look at the other store tomorrow for a dress and stop by the printer."

"Okay." I try to withhold the whine from that one little word, but it's damn difficult. I lean over to Clancy again and whisper. "My feet are killing me from walking all over the damn place today."

"I'll take care of it later," he whispers back. "After Toni's asleep."

I sit up abruptly. "Oh, I almost forgot to tell you. Guess who I ran into at Neiman Marcus?"

"Who?" He takes a sip of his water.

"Amanda."

He chokes and quickly covers his mouth. "Amanda, really? What did she do?"

"Who is Amanda?" Dad asks.

"Ex-wife, dear," Mom replies. "Nasty thing. Dominic took care of her for us." Dad's brow goes up and Mom shakes her head.

"No, Papa, not took *care* of her." I roll my eyes and turn back to Clancy. "She was just being her normal bitchy self. She did demand Toni to be given back."

"Did she now?"

I nod. "She also made mention of" —I soften my voice— "having the ability to get more money or she'd sing like a bird."

Clancy's brow rises and so does Dad's.

"What does she know?"

Clancy shakes his head. "Nothing. We'll discuss it later."

"If we're going to discuss it later, it's not nothing."

He turns his head to me as if he's going to respond, but then decides against it and looks at my dad, who's arching a brow at him. "I'll take care of it."

"Might be wise," Dad says.

I look from one to the other of them. "Wow, you two have had a nice little discussion, haven't you?" The server stops by and places salads in front of us. "Did you order for me?"

"I did, Anna," Dad replies and digs in.

Clancy leans over to me. "I helped him," he whispers.

Thank God.

"Nemy-girl, let's go," Clancy shouts from the living room.

We're going to his dad's house for lunch today, the day after having dinner with my parents. Hey, it got me out of shopping with my mom again.

"I'm coming," I reply and hurry to pull my jeans up. He steps around the corner just as I'm buttoning them. These aren't going to fit me much longer.

"Jesus, woman, would you hurry? We're going to be late." Toni shrieks something while he's holding her and he coos at her. "I've already got the car running."

I button the last one and slip my feet into a pair of flip-flops. "I'm good, let's go."

We rush out the door, get in the car, and we're off to Scottsdale. Once I'm settled, I feel brave enough to ask him about his mom because he hasn't talked about her and totally side-stepped her in conversation recently.

"So, where's your mom?" I ask carefully.

His eyes flick for a mere fraction of a moment to me and then back to the road. "She passed away a few years ago."

I cover my mouth with a hand. "Oh my, Clancy, I'm sorry."

"It's okay."

"What happened? I mean, if you don't mind . . ."

"Cancer." There's a long silence between us before he adds to it. "It's the reason I quit smoking."

This shocks me. "You smoked?"

"Yeah." His fingers tap the steering wheel a few times. "For a long time too."

"I tried it when I was a teen, but it made me sick to my stomach."

"Good," he replies. "You didn't have to deal with the addiction then."

I don't know about that. I have my own addictions. Tattoos count as an addiction, right?

I look back at Toni, who is sound asleep already, and I smile because she's just so damn cute. It takes us about thirty minutes to get to his dad's house, and when we pull up, his dad and brother are standing outside checking out the car in the driveway.

"Ah, Brennan bought a new car," Clancy replies and turns the BMW off.

"Nice," I comment on the brand new candy apple red Corvette Clancy's dad Bran is leaning over for inspection. When Bran stands, I realize he's the man I saw leaving the piano bar with Clancy one day several weeks back. Interesting.

Brennan hops over to Clancy as he gets out of the car. "Check it out, bro. Sweet, huh?" Clancy nods as I climb out of the car and shut my door. Brennan's eyes flick to me and the smile on his face widens. "Is this the blushing bride I've heard so much about? Nemy, right?"

"Yes," I say with a nod. "It's a pleasure to meet you."

He walks around the car and embraces me in a hug. "Welcome to the family." He has a pretty fresh scar on the side of his face, and I have to wonder what happened to him that night Clancy got the call. It must have been bad.

Then Bran walks over to me. "Nemy, darlin', how are ye feelin'?"

"Fine, thank you."

He hugs me tight. "I can' wait ta meet my newest gran'child," he whispers in my ear before letting me go. Right now, I'm wishing Clancy had that Irish accent on his tongue more often because I love it. His dad's accent is thick like Sean's.

Clancy pulls Toni out of the car, in her car seat, and we head inside. And damn is Bran's house ever a nice one. Vaulted ceilings, expensive tile and carpet, granite countertops in the kitchen, all done in very neutral tones. I look through the giant windows into the backyard to find three boys running around in a very rough game of what looks like football.

Clancy leans over me and whispers. "They're playing rugby." I close my gaping mouth and look up at him. He grins. "Don't worry, they aren't being half as rough as they could be."

My eyes wander back to the boys. "How old are they?"

Brennan steps up and points at the tallest boy. "That's Patrick there. He's twelve." Patrick is lean with the Dolan black hair, cropped short around the sides and the back, but long on top so his bangs hang over his eyes. He looks like a little skater. "And that one" —he points to the next tallest boy, who has short black hair all the way around— "is Thomas, but we call him Tommy. He's ten years old." Then he points to the shortest and youngest of the three, a cute little redhead with freckles all over his pale face. "And that is Rupert—don't ask—and he's eight."

"Rupert?" I ask anyway.

"Yeah, his mom was on a *Harry Potter* kick at the time and thought he'd look just like the boy who plays Ron in the flicks."

I stifle my laughter, but Clancy chuckles and goes back to Toni, whose car seat is sitting on the nearby kitchen table.

"I know," Brennan says. "Poor kid, he's gonna have to live with that damn name the rest of his life. Crazy bitch wouldn't let me reason with her."

"So, may I ask where she is?" I watch the boys as Rupert and Tommy try to tackle Patrick and take him down, but it's just not working for them.

"I'm hoping Costa Rica or someplace like that," he replies, and then he looks down at me. "She left me for a damn cabana boy."

"Wow, I'm sorry." I try hard not to laugh.

He shrugs. "Eh, damn turning-thirty crisis thing, I guess. Don't know, don't care anymore. She's been gone for six years now." Just like Clancy, there's a hint of the Irish accent when Brennan speaks.

"How do the boys handle that?" I'm curious because I'm probably going to end up having some weird conversation with Toni in the future about her mother.

"They used to ask where she was a lot. But not so much anymore. I told them I didn't know, because you know, I really don't know where she is. I make sure to tell them she loved them so much, though. Don't wanna fuck up their emotional psyche or whatever. I'd rather have them pissed off at me and think she abandoned me and not them, you know."

"Yeah, I think I understand that." I feel kind of sad for the boys, though, not having their mom around. "Are you ever going to get married again?"

"They've asked the same question, and I tell them they are much more important to me than finding a wife." Then he looks me in the eye, and holy crap, he gets that same evil glint in his eyes that Clancy does. "Of course, if you have any single friends—"

"Brennan, who the hell would want to date you?" Clancy remarks while holding Toni against his chest.

Brennan swings around as Bran laughs from the kitchen. "Hey, I'm surprised you're dating anyone with that ugly mug of yours."

For clarification, Clancy and Brennan look a lot alike. I mean, so much so they could be twins if it wasn't for their age difference and Brennan's goatee.

"If I'm ugly, so are you," Clancy replies.

I move away from the window and try to take Toni from him.

He pulls away gently and shakes his head. "No, you know what the doc said."

"Oh, come on, I pick her up when you're not home." Shit, that wasn't a good thing to say, and his right brow arches. Damn it, now he's not going to leave me alone anymore.

"Go sit on the couch. I'll bring her to you."

I roll my eyes and head for the nearest sofa, and I sit down as Brennan beats a hand against the window.

"Oi, your Uncle Clancy is here!"

"Brennan! How many times have I told ye not to 'it the winder?" Bran growls from the kitchen.

"Sorry, Da," Brennan says as the boys all run to the door and try to squeeze through it all at once. "One at a time, you nimrods. Jaysus."

I giggle as Clancy passes Toni down to me. "You want something to drink?"

"Yes, please. Thanks, baby."

He nods and is quickly surrounded by boys encircling his waist. "Hey there, gents. What's up? Careful now, don't fall on my fiancée and baby."

This comment freezes them in their tracks and they all turn to look at Toni and me.

"Hi," I say with a smile.

"Wow." Patrick's eyes widen by the second. "She's got lots of tattoos."

"Yes, she does. Boys, I'd like you to meet Nemy and my daughter Toni."

"Nemy?" Tommy says. "What kind of name is that?"

"It's short for Nemesis."

"What's that mean?" he asks.

"Enemy, you dork." Patrick hits him on the shoulder. Tommy grabs the spot where he was hit and his face goes sour.

"Dad! Patrick hit me."

"Knock it off, you two," Brennan says from the kitchen.

"That's a weird name," Patrick says when he turns back to me. "Why would your parents name you that?"

"They didn't. It's a nickname. My real name is Anna, but I don't like it."

Rupert grins and sits on the couch next to me. "I don't like my name, either."

I turn my gaze to him and smile. "Oh, I don't know. Rupert is a very regal name."

He frowns. "What's regal?"

"Royal, like a prince."

"It is?" His eyes grow wide.

"Oh yes, it is." My recent history class filters through my mind. "Prince Rupert of the Rhine, I believe. And it comes from the name Robert. Many great men with that name, so you see, Rupert, your name is wonderful . . . and regal."

He beams from the comment and runs into the kitchen. "Dad, did you hear that? My name is REGAL!"

Brennan ruffles the top of his red hair as Rupert wraps his skinny arms around Brennan's legs. "Yeah, I did, buddy. That's cool." He looks up at me, nods a thank you and smiles.

I smile in return and adjust Toni in my lap. Then I hear him softly say, "I love her" to Clancy when he walks by with a drink for me.

Clancy smiles at him and returns to my side.

We enjoy a lovely meal and once the boys return outside, the three men join me in the family room. It's very weird to me being the only woman in the house too. I place Toni on the floor so she can get her scoot on across the carpet, and then sit back and cross my legs. Clancy runs a hand over my thigh and squeezes my knee.

Brennan shifts in his seat and looks at Clancy. "So, um, we need to talk about your ex."

"Kill already told me." Clancy closes his eyes. When they open again, he's watching Toni. Oh shit, does that mean . . . "You've taken care of it, I assume?"

"Yeah," Brennan replies. "You wanna know the ins and outs of it?"

Clancy shakes his head.

I realize by now my mouth has dropped wide open, and I quickly shut it. Amanda's dead? I just saw her yesterday. My heart sinks a little at the revelation. I mean, what if I hadn't told Clancy I saw her and the things she said? Would she still be alive? I may have seen a murder, but I've never been the cause of one.

Brennan says, "She overdosed."

"Fu—dge," I mumble and Clancy's hand squeezes my knee again. Brennan's eyes study me for a moment. So do Bran's. "I'm fine."

Brennan's eyes flick to Clancy, who nods. "Good." He leans forward. "We don't normally talk about this shi" —I hit him with a glare regarding the word that's about to spew from his mouth— "stuff, but you're a bit different, considering your pops."

I roll my eyes. "Yeah, good ol' daddy dearest." I feel sick to my stomach.

Bran speaks up. "I remember when you were busted for that craps game in school."

"Lovely." I turn to Clancy. "Do you have a scrapbook of my family somewhere?"

Clancy laughs and Toni cranes her head around as far as she can to look at him before she continues to scoot along the floor toward Bran.

Bran leans over to pick her up. "Come 'ere, granddaughter o' moine." She squeals in delight when he makes all sorts of crazy faces at her. It pulls a giggle from me, which isn't easy, considering what's going through my mind about Amanda.

"Excuse me," I say and beeline for the bathroom because I feel like I'm about to lose my lunch.

There's a knock on the door several minutes later. "Yeah?"

Clancy's calming voice seeps through the door. "Are you okay, Nemy-girl?"

"Fine. Just give me a minute." I stare at myself in the mirror, pat a little water on my face, and let out a huge breath, questioning why I can't escape this godforsaken life of mob and death. Do I really want to raise a child in this mess? She could turn out just as fucked up as I am.

He knocks again lightly. "Open the door, babe."

I hesitate a moment, my hand hovering over the knob, and finally, I turn it to let him in.

He steps inside and closes the door behind him. Then he reaches forward, brushing hair away from my face with light fingertips before his hand stops on my cheek. He cocks his head, concern sweeping his eyes as he looks at me.

"Talk to me."

At first, I can't speak because my heart seems to have lodged itself in my throat, but then I look up into his emerald eyes and say, "Am I the reason she's dead?"

The right corner of his mouth hitches upward in a half-smile. "No, she is the cause of her own death."

"But Brennan just—"

"It would've happened one way or another." His voice is soft, and he brushes his thumb along my cheek. Then he wraps his hand around the back of my neck and pulls me into him. "You've witnessed a hit, and yet, this bothers you." He kisses the top of my head.

"I've never been the cause—"

He pulls back, takes my head in both hands, and looks me in the eye. "You are *not* the cause. Please understand that. Amanda sealed her own fate when she opened her mouth yesterday."

"But if I hadn't told you—"

"She would have lived only a little longer. Trust me, Nemy, that woman would have overdosed by the end of the month anyway, or she would have said the wrong thing to the wrong person."

"So you just sped up the process for her?"

"Not me, but yes," he replies. "Do not let this sit on your conscience."

After staring at him a good long while, I nod my head what little I can while he holds it between his big hands, and he pulls me against him once more in a tight embrace.

We make our way back out to the family room where Bran holds Toni over his head, making those goofy faces at her. Once we sit again, he brings her down and sits her in his lap.

"How's the house comin' along, son?"

"Fine, almost finished," Clancy replies. "Should be done right after the honeymoon." He steals a glance at me. "That is, if Nemy still wants to marry me." He grins.

I slap his leg.

Bran chuckles. "Very good. And how are the wedding plans comin' along?"

"We still need to find a dress for her. Gonna check out a shop today after this."

Bran's eyes light up. "Ye can leave Toni with me, if ye'd like. I'd love to 'ave my only granddaughter 'round for a bit."

"Don't let the boys hear you say that," Brennan says.

"They've spent many nights with their grandpapa," Bran replies. "Last night, in fact. How are you getting' them home, by the way? Am I drivin' them?"

Brennan chuckles. "Yeah, you're gonna have to. The Vette's only a two-seater."

"Please tell me you still have the Range Rover," Clancy says.

Brennan cocks an eyebrow at him. "I'm not stupid, big brother. Jaysus."

Well, I've spent some good quality family time with Clancy's little clan and discovered Amanda is dead by way of a forced overdose. Yep, sounds just like something I'd experience in my own family. Wonderful. Feels just like home.

I think I'm going to be sick again.

We eventually get away and leave to go dress shopping, and I actually find a shop that has a black wedding dress in the store, though I'm not sure I'm up for twirling around in a damn dress now. However, I need to see the dress before making the decision, and yes, I am wearing a black wedding dress, regardless of my mother's feelings on the subject. She'd even put her hand over her heart and feigned a heart attack. Seriously? She's such a drama queen sometimes. I can't stand that shit.

And she wonders why I don't talk to her for months on end.

I try it on, twirl around in front of the mirror, and Clancy's eyes sparkle as he watches me from the chair. It's a strapless gown with a fitted bodice covered in lace and black pearlescent beads, and it has a full skirt with a decent-sized train. I'm all aflutter wearing it and the shopkeeper hands me a pair of black lace gloves to try on with it. That just makes it even better and I have to have it. Clancy tells the shopkeeper to ring it up when I return from the dressing room, and I jump in his arms and shower him with kisses. A few alterations will need to be made to fit my growing belly, and I can pick it up a week before the wedding, once I come in for a couple more fittings. Then I pick out dresses for the girls—nice ones, so they don't kill me—and we leave the dress shop to pick up Toni from his dad's house.

28

Weak and Powerless

The following week, Mom is not pleased when I show her the dress. I took it from the shop so she wouldn't have to trek down there, and because she'd give the shopkeeper a hard time about selling me a black wedding dress. He was rather cool with the idea.

"Anna Maria!" she says with much disdain. "How could you?"

"Here, Mama. I'll put it on for you." I pull my shirt off and turn to the dress, and I hear the gasp. I know this is for the back piece. "Oh, get over it, Mama. I have tattoos." I push my jeans down after kicking off my sandals.

"You're covered with them."

I glance back at her over my shoulder. She sits on the bed, holding her hand over her heart. Oh really, like my being covered with tattoos is going to give the woman a heart attack.

I turn around, unfastening my bra, and I look down. "I am not." I pull the bra off and throw it on the bed. "Do you see any here?" I point to my stomach. "Or here?" I point to my legs. "Just the one here." I point to my left calf and turn a bit so she can see it. "And here." Then I point to the top of my foot. "That's all."

She shakes her head. "*That's all,* she says. What did I do wrong, Anna?"

I pull the dress off the hanger, and I turn my head back to her. "You did nothing wrong, Mama. I just like tattoos."

"What are those going to look like when you're older?"

"They'll show that I've lived a good life and enjoyed the hell out of it." I grin.

"What about the jewelry on your navel and that one in your tongue?"

I shrug, turning. "I like that too."

"You can show you've lived a good life without all of that."

"Would you prefer I look like Giovanna Delveccio?" Giovanna *is* an Italian Princess, or at least looks like one. She's gorgeous with long brown hair, big brown seductive eyes, a slim body (I've had to work my ass off to keep mine in shape), and she was my best friend back home—until she stole one of my boyfriends. She's the reason I keep an eye on Kennadi. That was ages ago, and the last time I saw her (probably five years ago), the bitch was still drop-dead gorgeous.

"Pssh." Mom waves her hand. "I hear she's on the cocaine."

I snort. "*The* cocaine?"

"Whatever you call it."

"Really?" I sit on the bed with the dress in my hands, covering my lap. "Since when?" I have to know this because it'll give me a little satisfaction.

"A few years now, I think." She looks at me. "Put the dress on already. My breasts haven't looked like that in thirty years. I don't know how you do it at your age."

I laugh and lean forward. "They're fake, mama."

"Are they really?"

"At least I'm not addicted to drugs. You should consider that when you're freaking out about my tattoos." I stand again and step into the dress.

"This is true," she agrees. Finally. "Did you reserve the church yet? You might not be able to get it now."

I pull the dress up and shimmy into the bodice. "I don't want to get married in the church, Mama, and I don't think Clancy does, either."

She gasps again. "Anna!"

"Both of us are divorced and won't be able to and, since it's not that far away, I'll be surprised if they have an opening." I stop fiddling with the dress and look at her. "A minister will do just fine in an open setting."

"Did you schedule a minister yet?"

"Well, no. Haven't had the chance. I've been kind of busy with one baby already, and doctor appointments, and I'm still kind of working."

I get the stern mother look for that one. "Father Michael would be good. I'll call him when we're done."

"Mama, he's a priest."

She wags her finger at me. "If you're determined to wear *that* dress, I get to choose the minister or priest *and* the location."

This completely stops my adjustment of my chest in the bodice. "*And* the location? Mama!"

"End of discussion." I can't touch it any further. God, she's stubborn.

I zip the back of the dress up as far as I can, and she stands to finish it for me. Then I pull the gloves on and turn around. "Well?"

She takes a step back, studies me with those motherly eyes that scrutinize every detail, and wipes her right eye. Then she nods, albeit with reluctance, and steps forward again.

"How are you going to wear your hair?" She leads me to the full-length mirror and stands behind me before she starts messing with my hair, first pulling it up and then dislodging small locks around my face. "That's pretty."

I nod and can't say anything because it's just hit me I'm doing something I didn't think I'd ever do again, and I'm staring at myself wearing this beautiful dress.

"Anna, are you okay?"

I smile at her reflection. "I'm fine, Mama." It doesn't stop the water works, though.

She grabs my shoulders and hugs me from behind. "Oh, Anna, what is it?"

I wipe my tears and shake my head.

She smiles. "You have found your Prince Charming, yes?"

"He's not supposed to exist. Why does he exist, Mama?"

She leans her head against mine. "It scares you, doesn't it?"

My throat practically closes up, so I nod.

"Your father scared me too, dear. It just took you a little longer to find yours."

An abrupt laugh escapes me. "It took a year of flirtation for him to convince me."

She places her hand over the center of my chest. "Because your broken heart needed to heal."

I stare at her, wondering how she knew about that, until I remind myself who my father is and that he likely kept tabs on me down to every minute detail. I should hate him for that, but somehow, for whatever reason, right now I don't, I can't. I needed to hear my mom say that, and she knew she had to say it to me.

Either that or one of my brothers spilled the garbanzo beans, in which case someone's getting their ass kicked.

Mom's arm hangs around my shoulders; we stare at each other in the mirror. It's like a fucking Hallmark card picture.

This is the single most endearing moment I have ever had with my mother. It's winsome and sweet . . . "Okay, this is getting too mushy for me."

She laughs and steps back. "You always like to pretend to be the tough girl, Anna, but I know better." She wags that finger at me again.

I just *hmpf* at her and reach behind me. "Help me get this thing off."

After yet another dinner and saying goodnight to my parents, we head home. Toni is cranky and tired, but it takes forever to get her to sleep. Once she's off in dreamland, Clancy shuts down the house and comes back to the bedroom. I open the bathroom door and step out wearing the teddy I'd bought the first day Mom and I went shopping. Clancy grins, that evil glint hitting his eyes, and I smile. He's stretched along his side of the bed wearing nothing but boxers.

He bites his lower lip as I move toward him. I place my hands on the bed and crawl across like a cat until I reach him and climb over. His hands glide up my sides when I sit on top of him and lean forward.

"That is one damn sexy teddy."

"Thought you'd like it," I whisper and kiss him.

His arms tighten around me, and he rolls me onto my back . . . and his phone rings. He pauses in his seduction and looks at it.

"I have to get that," he whispers.

"Seriously?"

He leans over to pluck it from the nightstand. "Hello?"

I push myself up and bite his neck.

"Yes. What? I'm sorry, I'm a bit busy right now." He moves his head to the side, bringing up his shoulder in order to force my face away, so I decide to go another route. "No, I'd like to be there."

I let my hands slide down his chest to his waist and beyond.

"I suppose." He jerks and makes an attempt at escape, but I lock my legs around his. He grunts. "I can't right now."

I giggle softly and slide down, and my tongue flits around his nipple. He successfully suppresses the sigh and I'm impressed.

"Alright, but I have" —I bite him again, and he growls—"to take care of something first. Fine. Bye." He hangs up and looks down at me. "You are a bad girl."

I look up from beneath him and grin. "Gonna spank me?"

"I just might."

"Are you going somewhere?"

He nods slowly. "Don't worry, I'm gonna take care of you first." He lowers himself to me and returns the bite on my neck.

"You promised to take care of my aching feet like a week ago."

He takes a spaghetti strap in his teeth and pulls it down past my shoulder.

"I will." He grabs his phone and sends out a quick text message. "You have me for an hour."

"How much is that going to cost me?"

He grins wide. "About five bills."

"Ha! You aren't worth that much."

"Fine, you just lost a half hour." He pulls the other strap down, along with the top of the lingerie.

"In that case, I'd rather wait until you come back." I push myself up on elbows.

He chuckles against my skin and I let my head drop back. "How about now *and* when I come back?"

I giggle and fall onto the bed. "Okay."

Clancy reluctantly leaves an hour later and I lay in bed for a while, staring at my ring. The sheets barely cover me and a smile flits across my face because right now my life is perfect. I didn't think perfect could exist. What's that commercial? Yeah, I totally live in Perfection right now.

I hear a scratch and look at the doorway to my bedroom, and I figure it's Tonk, so I call out to him. Normally Tonk would run right in and jump on the bed, but he doesn't, which I don't find odd because he's been spending a lot of time in Toni's room protecting her. It gives him a sense of purpose, I guess. Maybe he moved in his sleep and his nails scratched the furniture.

"Tonk." Then I hear a faint growl. It's coming from Toni's room. I jump out of bed, throw my robe on, and creep around the corner. "Tonk?" He's looking at the window, and I see the shadows move.

The glass breaks, a shot fires, Tonk hits the floor with a yelp. Jesus, whoever it is knows about him. I snatch Toni from her crib and run into my bedroom with her screaming in my ear because the sound scared the crap out of her, and I shut and lock the door behind me. I lay her on the bed and run to my dresser. I attempt to push it in front of the door, but the damn thing won't move but an inch.

I can hear them climbing in now and I shove my body against the door while looking at Toni as she wails on my bed. "It's okay, sweetie." It is so not okay when I feel one of them slam into the door. "Oh God." I brace myself against it. The guy slams into it again and I hear wood crack. I jolt a little. "No." I can't get to my phone to call anybody and I don't have time to go for my gun, which has been in a fucking safe since Toni started trying to crawl.

He hits the door again and the wood splinters. I breathe deeply to keep myself focused. Then I hear mumbling on the other side of the door. *Please God, don't shoot me.* Two of them hit the door simultaneously and I fly forward into the nightstand. I grab my phone and reach for Toni, picking her up before quickly backing into the corner.

"Get out of my fucking house!" They're both wearing ski masks. The taller one steps forward and tries to take Toni from me. I kick at him and punch him in the face after adjusting Toni to one side. He wrenches my screaming baby from my arms and I reach up and backhand him with my left hand. The ring leaves a large bloody gash on his left cheek near his exposed lips. He passes Toni back to the other man, knocks the phone from my hand, which shatters to pieces when it hits the wall, and he returns the backhand. My head hits the wall and I start to slide down completely dazed. He then lifts me up and throws me on the bed.

His friend hisses at him while holding a screaming Toni in his arms. "We don't have time for that, *puto.*"

"We'll make time." He rips my robe open. "I have to pay the bitch back for my face."

"Aye, *Dios mio,*" the friend says. "You're gonna get us caught, *chingada.*"

I blink twice and thrust my foot into his stomach. He bends forward, groaning, and I push myself up and punch him in the head. As soon as he recovers from that, which is mighty quick, he draws his gun and places its tip against my forehead. He's still leaning over, grabbing his stomach.

His head tilts to the side. "What'cha gotta say about that, bitch?" he grunts in a hoarse whisper.

"Fuck you."

"Don't do it, fucker. Don't you know who she is?"

"Should I give a fuck?"

"Yeah, you should. She's Don Mussolini's daughter."

"Oh really?" His brown eyes flicker with a hint of evil. "Perhaps we should take her with us. I wonder how much he'd give to get her back safe."

"You wouldn't live long enough to spend it."

Nervous laughter leaves the other guy's mouth. "She'll kick your ass before you get her to the front door. I've seen the bitch fight . . . men. Besides, that's not why we're here, and *he* said not to hurt her."

The guy leans forward, his hand slips around the back of my neck, and he pulls me up, gun still placed against my head. "You gonna fight me?"

"Absolutely."

"Hold the kid out," he says to his friend, who complies. He then points the gun at Toni. "You still gonna fight me?"

My eyes flick from him to Toni. "Don't hurt her."

He smiles and turns me around, his arm across my neck. "I didn't think so." The gun trails down the side of my face and I close my eyes. "You're gonna be fun," he rasps in my ear. He beckons his friend forward and hands him the gun. "Keep the gun on the kid so I can fuck this bitch." He rips the robe back.

"Man, come on, what if her man comes back?" There's nervousness in his hoarse voice. They're purposely talking this way, in rasps and whispers, which means I'll recognize them if they use normal voices. "He said not to do anything to her, damn it. Just fucking grab the kid and go."

"Shut the fuck up!" His hand slides up between my legs from behind.

I distance myself in my mind, to keep Toni safe, to keep from experiencing this horrible nightmare, but I know who he is now. A guy named Artie, who frequented the club, and whom I turned down on many occasions. Motherfucker. I'm going to kill him. I open my eyes and look at the other guy's face, look him dead in the eye, a look that tells him I know who they are.

His eyes grow wide with fear. "Dude, come on, we just came for the kid." His voice is on the verge of panic. "We need to get the fuck out of here."

"Not until I'm done!" Artie pushes me forward to the bed.

My hands brace against the mattress. I'm still trying to figure out who the other one is. Who swears in Spanish all the time? Hector? No, maybe Efrain. Shit. Wait, did he just say they came for Toni? I smile at the little revelation because it tells me they won't hurt her. Artie grabs my hips and pulls them back. I lean over the bed, and as soon as I feel him against my thigh, I rear back and twist. My elbow catches him in the side of the head. It sends him careening into the nightstand. I jump up and kick him in the chest. He hits the wall once more.

"Stop!"

I feel the tip of the gun's barrel against the back of my head.

"You're both dead."

"Not if you want this kid to die," he replies.

Artie gets to his feet, pulls his pants up, and lurches toward me. After his fist slams into the side of my head, the lights go out as I head for the floor.

29

No, You Don't

I awaken in the dark room, lying on the floor next to my bed, which is right where I fell when Artie punched me. Thank God, because that tells me he didn't rape me in my unconsciousness. I don't even recall hitting the floor because my eyes went black halfway down. I move a hand to my throbbing head and squint to look at the time because my vision is blurred. The alarm clock sits sideways. I think an hour has passed, but I can't be certain since I can't see the clock all that well. My stomach hurts like hell too, and I don't know why. I grasp at the bed and pull myself up, and then I look down at my legs because they feel wet. My hand runs along my inner thigh and I drop to my knees upon seeing the dark substance on my fingers.

"Oh God, no." I'm bleeding. I scoot toward the cluttered nightstand and search for the house phone, since my cell is in bits and pieces all over the floor. I find it within the debris of what was once a lamp and struggle to dial the number from memory.

He answers after two rings. "Hey, beautiful. I'll be leaving in a minute."

Hearing his voice throws me into a rare moment of weakness and I lose it completely. I begin sobbing, barely able to choke out his name.

"What's wrong?" I hear him silence someone with a grunt. "Nemy?"

I can't speak. I can't get enough air into my lungs.

"Nemy, what's wrong?"

"They . . . they . . . took . . . Toni," I say between sobs. "I t-t-t-tried to s-s-s-stop them."

"Who took her?" Heavy breathing comes over the line, as though he's running. "What happened? Are you hurt?"

I sob again. "I'm bleeding." I draw in a deep strangled breath. "I think I m-m-might have lost the b-b-b-baby."

He growls and I hear a car door slam shut. "Stay put. Don't move." Tires squeal in the background. "I'm on my way, baby. Just hang in there."

I fall to the floor crying and he stays on the phone with me. I don't even realize it when he runs into the house until he's kneeling next to me.

"Jaysus, Mary and Joseph!" I hear another voice say with an Irish accent on his tongue. It sounds familiar.

Clancy scoops me up in his arms and lays me on the bed. "Nemy, what happened?" He smoothes the hair away from my face and covers me with a blanket.

"Two guys. Came in. Took Toni. One tried to rape me. Knocked me out. I woke up on the floor."

"There's a white dog on the floor in here," the other voice shouts. He sounds like an older man. "He's been shot, but he's still alive."

Clancy leans forward and kisses my forehead. "We're going to the hospital." He helps me sit up and it makes me dizzy. My head rolls to the side. I want to vomit. He leans down and picks my robe up from the floor, and he helps me put it on before lifting me. Then he carries me outside and shouts back to the other man. "Take the dog to the vet hospital for me."

Once he gets me fastened in the car, I grab his arm. "Tonk?"

"Taken care of," he replies and pats my hand.

He shuts the door and then runs around to the driver's side. "You're gonna be okay."

I sob again and cover my face with my hands; he backs out of the driveway.

"Hey, it's Clancy," he says into his phone. "Someone broke into the house. They took Toni. Nemy's been hurt. Tonk's been shot." A raised voice comes through the line. "I don't know who did it yet! I'll let you know when I find out."

I whimper.

"I'm taking her to the hospital—Tempe St. Luke's. I need someone to meet me there." He turns the corner onto Thirteenth Street. "Thanks." He hangs up, turns another corner, and then one more, and he pulls into the hospital parking lot.

My door opens and Clancy pulls me out. He carries me into the emergency room. The nurse looks up, sees the blood and makes a call. "She's pregnant," Clancy says when he hands me over to them. They start working on me right away, wheeling me back while the nurse asks Clancy a bunch of questions. "I don't know other than what I told you!" I hear him shout.

I don't hear any more, and when I open my eyes, Clancy is standing next to me, holding my hand in a tight grip. "Tonk?"

"He's fine," he says. "My dad took him to the vet."

"That was your dad?" I groan when Clancy nods.

"Anna," Mom's voice chimes in and she takes my other hand. "Oh, Anna."

I look at her and back to Clancy. "How long was I out?"

"A few hours." I detect sadness in his voice. "Nemy—" He stops and looks down at my hand. His lower lip quivers. I start crying because he doesn't have to say it. I've lost the baby. He falls down to me, holding me, his back rising and falling with each sob. After a few minutes, he gathers himself enough to whisper, "Who did this?"

"Artie Jones is the one who tried to rape me. I'm not sure about the other one. Efrain, maybe. They used to go to the club all the time." I start shaking. "Why, why would they do this?"

"They'll be dealt with, Anna," Mom whispers, stroking my hair.

"We have to find Toni."

"Already working on it," Clancy replies. "You just rest."

"I can't." I try to sit up. "What if they hurt her?"

Clancy and Mom push me back down. "Anna, you need your rest. Lie still."

"I don't think they're going to hurt her. I'm just waiting for a call."

"I'm going to kill that son of a bitch."

Clancy attempts a smile and touches the side of my face. "We'll catch them, don't worry." He looks at my mom. "I have to make a phone call."

"Go ahead, she'll be fine." She squeezes my hand. Once he's gone, she leans over me. "Papa is furious. Some of the family will be here this afternoon. Anna, they found a footprint on your stomach."

That's why my stomach hurt. Artie must have stomped on me before they left. I nod in silence. There's nothing really for me to say because for once in my life, I truly want someone dead and I have the family connections to get it done . . . and the part that scares me the most is I want to watch it happen. I haven't witnessed a murder in over twenty years. After that first time, Papa kept me away from that end of the business—the killing part. Guess he didn't want his little girl ending up like him.

Too late for that.

✯ ✯ ✯

A day later, the hospital discharges me and Clancy takes me home. He's cleaned up the mess of broken glass in Toni's room, ordered a replacement window *and* alarm system, cleaned up the blood in both rooms, and removed the shattered lamp. *Dexter* flits across the television screen as he mills about. It's my favorite show. I love a good serial killer. Must be a family trait or something.

Clancy comes out of the kitchen and sits next to me.

"Where's my ring?" I've been staring at my hand for several minutes now, recalling that moment of perfection right after he left before my world crumbled into oblivion.

"My guess would be they took it."

"Please tell me you had it insured." I look up at him.

He wraps his arm around my shoulders and pulls me close. "There's no police report, Nemy-girl. Don't worry, I'll get it back."

No police report. I'm surprised the hospital staff didn't get the police involved, since there was a fucking footprint on my stomach. "I don't care so much about the ring. I just want Toni back safe." I look down. "They threatened to hurt her. Pointed the gun at her. That's why I had to stop fighting."

He kisses the top of my head. "It's okay."

"I couldn't get to my phone *or* my gun, Clancy." I meet his eyes again. "There wasn't any time."

"Shh." He presses his lips against my head again. "It's not your fault, baby."

"Maybe it was Amanda, before . . . you know. Maybe if I hadn't said what I did to her—"

He lifts my chin. "It still would've happened because it wasn't her."

"Then who in the hell was it?" I'm completely bewildered and on the edge of a full-scale panic attack. "Who was the 'he' they were talking about?"

He soothes my panic by holding me close and whispering in my ear. Finally, he says, "We *will* find out who did this, and they *will* pay. I can promise you that."

Clancy's phone rings and he leans forward to pick it up, taking me with him. "Hello?"

I slide my hand that's behind him back out and position myself to lay down, my head on his lap. Tonk is on the floor in front of the coffee table. He has one of those buster collars on so he doesn't lick at the wound in his side. The bullet grazed his stomach. Clancy's dad, Bran, said Tonk almost died during the surgery, so I'm grateful he came to the house with Clancy, otherwise I'd have lost him too.

"Mm hmm."

My eyes water thinking about the baby, and Toni, and my beautiful Tatanka, and my hand slips over my stomach and rests there, though there's nothing to protect anymore. Not long after, Clancy's hand covers mine while he talks, his fingers sliding between each of mine.

"Five men. Go in *stile di milizia*. Take care to watch where the child is."

Stile di milizia means "militia style" in Italian. I didn't know Clancy knew Italian. I suppose if he's in the *business*, he would have to know it. Dad had a few Irish guys work for him. I only seduced one of them—the cute one.

"Call me when it's done." He hangs up the phone and sets it on the side table. What he didn't say aloud was for them to eliminate any others in the house, hence militia style.

My eyes flick up to meet his. "They found her?" My voice is soft, worried, wounded.

"They think so." He closes his hand over mine until my hand is a fist within his. "They'll be careful." He says that to calm my nerves about Toni getting possibly hurt.

I turn my head back to the television. There is nothing to do but wait for the call. My mind wanders to the thoughts in my head just before I heard the scratch. Perfection only lasts a moment, it seems. I turn my head again and look up at him.

"Why aren't you there too?"

His eyes flick down to me. "Too emotional. I'd slaughter everyone *near* the house."

"Me too."

I turn back to *Dexter*, wishing he'd go take care of this for us.

When the call comes in an hour later, I jump from the sound of the ring. Clancy squeezes my hand and answers the phone. I stare blankly at whatever we're watching now, but don't even know what the show is because I've been so distracted in thought. I totally missed Dexter's escape from certain capture yet again. I blow out a breath and turn my head to see his face.

Clancy hangs up and his worried eyes meet mine. "Toni wasn't there." His voice is soft, sorrowful.

The tears roll down my cheeks as my throat closes with fear. When I look up at Clancy again, a tear falls down his cheek as he stares at the television with a look that shows his sorrow, yet pure fury simultaneously. He's barely holding himself together and a tremor runs through him, transferring to me because I'm still leaning against him.

I force myself to speak. "Have they found Artie yet?" My voice comes out as a hoarse whisper, and I'm surprised he even understands me.

Clancy's mouth twitches. "Fucker's on the run because no one can find him. I'm sure word got to him that your family *and* mine are looking for him."

"There is no place he can hide." I growl. "It may take a while, but my father *will* find him. Papa always finds what he's looking for."

"As does mine."

His phone rings again, and he answers it without looking at the screen. "Yeah." I've only ever seen Clancy shed that many levels of pigment once before, but this time it's worse because he turns sheet white. He closes his eyes. "I understand." His eyes open again and he stares blankly at the television. "I'll be there," he says and hangs up.

"Where will you be?" I sit up. "What do you understand?"

He draws in a deep irritated breath and exhales slowly. "That was Sean."

"What the fuck did he want?" My voice raises an octave.

"He has Toni."

My jaw drops. "The *he* was *him*?"

Clancy shakes his head. "Can't be certain. He says he caught them and took Toni. Killed Artie for hurting you once he pulled the info from them."

I blink in a rapid flutter. "So . . . wait, Sean's a good guy? I find that hard to believe."

"So do I, which is why I'm not bolting off this sofa and out the door. He's up to something. It's just too goddamn convenient." He rubs his hand across his forehead and massages his right temple. "I've never trusted him."

"That's why you pulled Brennan off that job, huh?"

He cracks an eye open and looks at me. "How'd you know . . ." Then he lets out a chuckle and sits forward, pulling away from the back of the sofa. "Damn, Nemy-girl, you've known this long and you're still with me?"

"I'd already fallen for you by then." I slip my hand over his and grasp tightly. "You're stuck with me now."

He nods and lifts his phone again. "I need to call my da. This might get ugly, if he's up to what I think."

"Where and when are you meeting him?"

"At the club, in an hour." He skims his contacts and hits send.

"I'm going with you."

A startled look crosses his face, then territorial. "No, you're not," he says right as his dad answers. "No, Da, I was talking to Nemy. Look, we've got a situation."

I stand, look down at him as his eyes meet mine, and say, "I'm going whether you like it or not. Deal with it." And I walk around the coffee table to head into our bedroom to change into something more appropriate for fighting and kicking a leprechaun's ass because holey jeans and a tank top sure as hell won't cut it.

Then again, that might be a good distraction.

30

Hour of Darkness

Scott couldn't come up with all of the money awhile back when he bought the club, so Clancy became a silent partner and still has a set of keys. I have to wonder if this is how he's a silent partner in Drew's Irish pub too. How in God's name Sean would know Clancy still has keys is beyond me because Scott certainly wouldn't be stupid enough to tell him. Maybe Sean just doesn't realize Clancy sold the club. Whatever. The point is moot aside from the fact that we can get inside without a problem.

I'm in full stealth mode, meaning I'm wearing all black: a black long-sleeved turtleneck, black Dickies pants, and black Chucks. Okay, there's white on the Chucks, but whatever. I have my hair pulled back in a ponytail and braided too. Don't need it getting in my face.

Clancy's outfit is opposite from mine, as he's wearing a black T-shirt instead, and blue jeans. Sean's expecting him, not me.

"He insisted I stay behind?" I ask as we drive along the Loop 202.

Clancy nods. "Listen, I don't want you taking any chances, okay? You're still not healed from the attack and miscarriage."

"I'll be fine." I check my gun's ammo for the umpteenth time.

"Would you stop doing that? It's making me nervous and the bullets aren't going anywhere until you fire the damn thing."

"Sor-ry." I check to make sure the safety is on, and lower the gun to my lap. Apparently, we're both on edge.

The noisy air-pull drifts to my ears. "I'm sorry. I'm just worried about everything that could go wrong."

I slip a hand over his thigh and squeeze lightly. "Me too, baby."

Five miles later, his phone rings. His dad and brother are in position in case the shit hits the proverbial fan. I'm sure they have more men with them too. At least, I hope so because I doubt Sean will play fair.

Ten minutes later, we pull into the club's dark parking lot. Even the floodlight is off, which isn't normal. Butterflies start fluttering about in my stomach.

"I don't like this."

"Me either." Clancy turns the car off and turns to me. "I want you to stay here" —he holds up a hand to stop my protest— "because he's not expecting you. I'll leave the door unlocked. Wait for my signal."

His signal will be a text message that he's already set up in his phone to go to me, Bran, and Brennan. All he'll have to do is press a button. That's assuming he'll have the opportunity to do so.

"If I don't get that text in ten minutes, I'm coming in. Me and my little Beretta." All I need is a cockatoo, right?

He reaches for me; his hand slips behind my neck, and he pulls me forward for a kiss. Then he rests his forehead against mine. "Whatever happens tonight, know that you are the only woman I have ever truly loved."

I swallow hard. "Don't talk like you're not going to survive the night."

The corner of his mouth curves into a half-smile. "I love you, Anna Maria Mussolini."

"I love you too, Clancy . . . wait, what's your middle name?"

The full Clancy grin hits his cheeks. "Patrick."

"Clancy Patrick Dolan." I lift my hand and slide it up his neck and into his hair, and I kiss him fiercely because I just may not ever get to do that again. "Be careful."

"Always, Nemy-girl," he says and climbs out of the car.

"That's what you said last time and you ended up in the fucking ER."

He drops back down and looks at me. "Wait for the goddamn text, please."

I sigh and nod, and he shuts the door. Watching him walk into the club without me and possibly to his death wreaks havoc on my nerves and restraint, but I sit, and wait, and pray for the first time in who knows how long.

And as much as I don't want to be involved in my family's extracurricular activities, I made my own damn phone call when I went to into the bedroom to get ready. My dad and his buddies are hiding around here somewhere too. Clancy doesn't know that, but I let Bran in on it so he and Dad wouldn't shoot one another.

Ten minutes is a long fucking time to wait when you're worried sick about the love of your goddamn life. When I look at my Fossil watch—barely visible in the near dark—I discover my forever of waiting has only been two minutes. I'm never going to last another eight minutes. During my wait, I notice that Scotty's car is still in the lot, along with a black SUV. It must belong to Sean. Maybe I'll wander over there and flatten his tires.

I check my watch again. Seven minutes. Shit.

I get out of the car, shut the door quietly, and carefully scan the lot before making another move. I can feel eyes on me, but I know Bran and my dad are watching, so I ignore the feeling.

My phone vibrates in my pocket, startling me. It's a good thing I didn't have my finger on the trigger or I'd have gotten a shot off. I dig into the front pocket to retrieve the phone and answer in a hushed voice. "Bad timing."

"What are you doing?" It's Bran. "Get back in the car until he sends the message."

"I'm going crazy in the car. I figured I'd scout around a bit." An incoming call beeps in and I pull the phone back to see who it is. "Shit, that's my dad. Hang on." I switch over. "Yeah, Papa."

"Anna, get back in the car."

I roll my eyes. "I don't need to hear this from you too. Bran just told me the same thing and I'm not getting back in the car."

"Anna Maria—"

"Papa, I love you, but I'm hanging up now." I hang up on my dad, tell Bran pretty much the same thing and hang up on him. Then I slide the phone back into my pocket.

Now, where's my knife? I fasten the gun in my pant's waistline at my lower back and slip a hand into my only back pocket. I withdraw the butterfly knife Kennadi gave me for my birthday one year. Oh damn, I should've called her in on this shit.

With a double twirl of my wrist, the blade is free and ready to work. I sneak over to the SUV, the gravel crunching beneath my Chucks, and inspect the vehicle before deciding to slice and dice his tires. The thought that Sean's on the up and up hits me briefly, so I make the decision to free the air from only one tire . . . just in case I'm wrong about him. I don't think I am, but it wouldn't be the first time I've been a bad judge of character.

I go to check my watch again and can't see it because Fossil watches don't have backlighting—at least, the ones I buy don't—and I'm too far away from the street lamp. So I pull my phone out again to check the time. Four minutes. Still no text.

I spend the next few minutes making my way to the door, gently pulling the heavy thing open, and slipping inside as quietly as possible, which I'm certain has both my father and father-in-law-to-be in fits.

The entry is dark and the leftover scent of beer taints the stale air as I creep to the edge of the wall hiding the main entrance from the rest of the club. Damn Sean for bringing Toni here. I don't want her breathing in this crap.

Two men are talking, and from the sound of their voices, I gauge that they're near the bar. I listen carefully and recognize Clancy's voice immediately, but I don't hear anyone else aside from the evil little leprechaun. The discussion is . . . friendly? What the fuck? Was I wrong about Sean?

The entry is painted all black, so I'm hidden quite well . . . until the fucking door opens.

The ghost walking through the door beams when he sees me, and he roughly grabs my arms and yanks me out from behind the wall. "Hello, princess."

"I-I thought you were dead."

He pushes me forward. When I look toward the bar, Sean and Clancy both move with such speed I hardly see them draw their weapons.

"Well now, isn't this a nice surprise?" Sean says over his arm, gun pointed at Clancy's head. "I told ye to leave her at home."

"She's stubborn and you took her baby," Clancy growls, not taking his eyes off Sean for one second while he holds his gun on the scary leprechaun. "You can't keep a mother from her child, regardless of whether or not she gave birth to her."

"Kid's not hers?" Surprise hits Sean's face with a rapid blink.

"May as well be," Clancy replies. "Tell the thug to let her go."

"I don' think ye're in a position to be makin' demands."

I look around the bar. "Where's Toni?"

"In the office, safe," Clancy answers. He's still locked on Sean.

"I want to see her." I look directly at Sean. "Now."

He lifts a brow. "Demanding one, aren't ye? I hope ye're like that in other areas as well, lass." He jerks his head to the right, telling Artie to take me back. As we walk by, he grabs Artie's arm. "Show her quick an' get back out here."

Artie nods and follows me to the back.

The office door is propped wide open and I see Toni on the sofa in a car seat. I bolt for her, but Artie's arm stops me in the doorway.

"You've seen her. Now we go back."

"I can't hold her? I need to make sure she's all right."

I hear the click of a hammer being locked in place before the tip of the barrel presses against my temple. I'm getting about damn tired of this.

"Back to the front, now."

Before completely turning to head back, my eyes catch a glimpse of feet on the floor behind the desk, and I recognize the shoes. I gasp and place a hand over my mouth.

"Is he . . . ?" I just can't finish that sentence.

"Yeah, tried to be a hero." Artie grabs my arm and yanks me past him. "Now shut the fuck up and move."

He pushes me into the door and I slam against it, but thankfully braced for the impact with my hands. I already know Artie's the rough type. His breath on my neck warns me just how dangerously close he is. They don't know I have a gun yet, and I'm not inclined to let them know.

"Maybe I should finish what I started with you the other night." His gun trails down the side of my face as he presses his hand into the center of my back, holding me against the door.

"I don't think Sean would take too kindly to you raping me, dumbass. He's kinda got a thing for me."

"What he doesn't know won't hurt." He moves his hand around my side and squeezes my left breast.

I choke down the bile rising in my throat. "He told you to come right back. Do you really think he's stupid enough to believe any lie you'd tell him, or that he wouldn't check to see what's taking so long?"

He growls, lets go of my breast, and steps back. I decide not to hesitate and quickly open the door before he can push me against it again. I move fast, getting ahead of him a few paces and visibly shudder as I look back at him. Artie's not an ugly man, but that soul of his sure the hell is. Sean catches my non-subtle moves and quirks a brow at Artie.

"What happened?" Although he's looking at Artie, I know the question is for me.

Artie speaks up anyway. "Nothin'—"

Sean points his gun at Artie. "I wasn't askin' you!" He tilts his head to me.

"He wanted to finish what he started the other night. I talked him out of it." I place my hands on my hips and glare at Sean. "I thought you told Clancy you'd killed him."

He grins. "I did, didn' I?"

Artie is standing next to me when Sean puts a bullet in his brain. Blood splatter hits the side of my face, but just like when I was twelve, I don't flinch.

Shocks the hell out of me too.

31

Headstrong

Before Clancy can even take a step forward, Sean aims the gun at me. "Ah, ah, Clancy. Wouldn't want my finger to slip with this one now, would ye?"

I keep my hands on my hips just because it'll be faster to grab my gun when the opportunity presents itself. "Why are you doing all of this?"

"It's a wee bit complicated, Nemy. But we'll call it payback."

"Sean, Clancy didn't kill your brother."

He sneers. "He did, when he pulled his brother off the job."

"So what's your plan then? Are you going to kill him? Because, you know, that'll *really* get you into my bed."

Sean quirks a brow at me, then turns to Clancy. "Is she always like that?"

Clancy nods slowly. He's still got his gun aimed at Sean. "Look, Sean, we can put the past behind us and move forward like you said when you first walked into my club a few months ago, or you can kill Nemy and I'll kill you."

I glare at Clancy. "Excuse me? There will be no killing Nemy!"

"His gun's on you, babe, not me."

"Aye, but if I kill Nemy, you kill me, and ye're the one who's sufferin' the rest of his life." He cocks his head to the side and arches a brow, like he's got one up on Clancy. Sure as fuck sounds like it to me.

My attention moves to Sean. "Well, take the aim off me and put it on him." I wave my hand at him. "Go on."

He chuckles and shrugs, but aims his gun at Clancy again. "I can see she really loves ye, Clancy."

I wink at him, but he keeps a straight face. "Yeah, thanks."

"Who killed Scott?" I have to know. Maybe it'll stir the fire in my belly.

"I did when he tried to take tha' little one from me," Sean replies, stealing a glance at me and jerks his head to the left. "Why don't'cha go behind the bar and fix us a drink, Nemy?"

I cock a brow, but move between the tables, past Clancy, and around the end of the bar. "Jameson?"

"Yeah, that'll work. Three shots."

"I don't like Jameson," I say as I pull the bottle down. I have to turn sideways so he doesn't see the gun at my back when my shirt lifts to expose my midsection.

"It doesn't matter, lass. It'll likely be the last drink ye ever 'ave. When I'm done with the two of ye—and Nemy, I'll be spending quite a bit o' time with ye--I'm gonna put a bullet in that kid's brain too."

The shot glasses tumble from my fingers when those words leave his lips. They scatter across the bar and Clancy catches one without ever taking his eyes off Sean, trapping the glass beneath his left hand against the black surface. Damn, my man is good. He sets it upright and slides it across the bar to me.

"Thanks." My voice trembles and I swallow the lump attempting to block my airway. Right now is a bad time for passing out. I try to think of a way to distract him, or to get that gun off Clancy. There has to be something . . . .

"How about a Flaming Dr. Pepper? I mean, if I'm going to die, at least let me make us a killer shot." I wince at the words, and Clancy's too focused on Sean to react, but I'm sure he'd probably laugh at me.

"'Tis fine," he says with a wave of his left hand. "Just hurry it up. I don't 'ave all night." His hand drops to the bar. "Ye're arm's gotta be getting' tired by now, Clancy."

Clancy shakes his head a miniscule amount and I look at his elbow that's resting against the edge of the bar. I wonder what else I'm not catching when it comes to him and his subtlety.

"You could've had me taken out at any point over the last fifteen years," Clancy says. "Set it up through the network in prison. Why the wait?"

Sean grins. "I wanted that pleasure for myself." His eyes shift to me for a brief moment. "And am I ever glad I waited. Now I can take yers like ye took moine."

I stop pouring and raise a brow. "What's he talking about?"

"Amanda," Clancy replies.

"Amanda? Wait . . . she belonged to Sean?"

Clancy nods.

Sean slaps his hand against the bar. "She did, and he fuckin' stole her from me."

"You really didn't expect her to wait for you, did you?" Clancy cocks a brow at him. "The woman was a stripper, for God's sake."

"She really wasn't much of a prize," I reply a bit too loudly.

"Ye didn' know her, Nemy. And then he went and 'ad 'er killed."

"How the fuck does he know that?" I turn to Sean. "She'd have ended up dead no matter what, with her drug problem." Which is something I probably shouldn't have said, but shit, I'm not going to let him hurt Toni. I point to the office. "And that's her daughter back there, and you want to kill her too?"

The shocked look on Sean's face tells me he somehow didn't know that information, even though he discovered a bit ago that Toni isn't mine. "Tha' little one is Amanda's?"

"How do you not know that?"

"He's been in prison, Nemy-girl."

"Yeah, but it's not a deserted fucking island. He had to have had contact with someone."

"No one knew Amanda had a baby except the people in this club." Oh, that's right, she went out all night and left the baby home. Bitch.

"Jesus." I hold out my hand. "I need a lighter."

"What the fuck for?"

"*Flaming* Dr. Pepper?" I wiggle my fingers because I know he smokes. I can smell the nasty odor on him.

He hands me the lighter.

"Still want your Jameson?"

He nods and beckons the shot with his fingers. I slide it to his hand and one to Clancy, and I wait for them to drink.

For the Flaming Dr. Pepper, the Bacardi 151 sits on top of the rest of the shot for the three small glasses in front of me. Said liquor is the reason I can light the liquid. I pick up the bottle of 151, and the moment they drink their Jameson shots, I quickly pour a shot of the 151 in a shot glass I placed below the bar. They slide the shot glasses back to me and I place them below the bar.

Sean's standing practically in front of me; Clancy off a bit to my left. Clancy has seen me light Flaming Dr. Pepper shots before. He pulls his gun hand back a little.

"I have another quick question," I say before pushing the shots forward on the bar. Sean gives me the go ahead with a nod. "What could possibly make you think I'd come to you after you've killed my fiancé?"

Sean grins. "Tha's why you were s'posed to stay home, Nemy."

"Ah, you'd make it look like someone else—say Artie over there—did it and pretend you tried to save Clancy, right?"

"Tha' was the plan."

"Son of a bitch." I test the lighter's wheel. Sparks flicker and I look at both men. "Ready?"

Clancy nods once and Sean says, "Yeah."

"Could you at least put the guns down for this?"

Clancy moves first and slowly places his gun on the bar. Sean follows suit.

"No funny business," he says to Clancy.

"It's just a shot, Sean," Clancy replies.

They both turn to me. "Keep your hands where I can see them."

I place one hand on the edge of the bar and the other hovers over the drinks, lighter at the ready. The wheel sparks, a flame flickers to life, and I lower it to all three shots, hitting one at a time. I've spaced the shots out so the guys don't knock into them when they reach for one. Then I grab my shot.

"Show me how it's done, Nemy."

I sneer at him, blow the flame out, and drop the shot back.

He laughs and raises his to Clancy. "Bottoms up." They repeat what I did, but in that short amount of time, I grab the shot below the bar and toss it into my mouth.

Sean slams his shot glass on the bar at the same time Clancy does. He looks at me and I give him that evil smile he gave me so many months ago, even though the liquid burns the shit out of my mouth. The flame comes to life again and I spit the 151 over it. A large fireball swirls through the air, engulfing Sean's upper body.

Don't. Fuck. With. A. Bartender.

Clancy moves a hell of lot faster than I could have ever imagined. Sean's screaming, his entire head in flames, and I bring my hand around my back to grab the gun.

A shot fires.

Sean and his flaming head hit the floor.

My gun still points to where he was standing.

"Fire extinguisher." Clancy reaches across the bar.

It snaps me out of my daze and I hand the container over to him. Then I push up and lean over the bar to watch as Clancy puts out the fire.

I crinkle my nose at the crispy leprechaun's new look. "Is he dead?"

"Of course he is. I shot him."

Oh, okay then. "I was just about to do that. Why didn't you let me?"

Clancy kneels on one knee next to Sean. He's checking the wound in Sean's head. Nice shot. Right between the eyes. "Because you've never killed anyone before and I wasn't about to let you start."

"Aw, my hero." Honestly, I'm kind of glad he did that. He's been paying attention, knowing I have issues with the things my family does, which also means I have issues with the things his family does. Crap. I'd better get the fuck past this. Thing is, Clancy and I do make an honest living, regardless of his past and mine, if you can call a strip joint honest. Hey, there's nothing illegal about running the place.

I run to the end of the bar and around it right as my dad and Bran come in. "Hey, Dad." I pass Clancy quickly. "I'm going to get Toni."

"What happened?" Bran asks Clancy as they make their way over to him before I bolt through the back door.

When I come back out holding Toni in my arms, the men have all gathered around Sean's body, and there are a lot more of them than I thought there would be.

A short, stocky blond steps forward and kicks Sean's body. "Jaysus, nice shot there, Clancy." Where the fuck did that accent come from?

Clancy slaps his leg. "Going for your best, you know, Kill."

I stop walking and stare at Killian. Shock quickly turns to anger, and I glare at my soon-to-be-dead-anyway fiancé. "You *did* have me followed, you son of a . . . Oh my God, I'm going to kill you!"

He jumps to his feet. "Now, Nemy-girl, I told you—"

My free hand slices through the air sharply as I cut a straight horizontal line. "Don't you dare make an excuse!"

Killian steps forward. "Nemy, I was just—"

I point and give him the death look. "Shut up!"

Both men go silent. But of course, my darling father has to comment.

"You boys *did* know we called her Nemesis for a reason, right? I'd suggest everyone clear out—"

"Don't you start that, Father."

He shakes his finger at me. "And don't you talk to me in that tone, young lady."

That shuts me up.

Clancy claps a hand on Dad's shoulder. "I think we'll move in next door to you."

I growl. "I hate you."

"I'll fix that later." Clancy winks and steps close to me, placing his finger in Toni's hand. "Is she okay?"

"Yeah, she's fine." I kiss her forehead right as Clancy leans forward to kiss her on top of the head.

Then he moves his head around and kisses me on the cheek. "Nice job with the fireball."

I grin. "Did you know what I was up to?"

"I sure did. From the moment you mentioned Flaming Dr. Pepper."

"And this is why I love you. You're smart."

"Is that the only reason?"

I pause dramatically before saying, "Okay, you're cute too."

He laughs, and I am ever so thankful I'm hearing it.

"But I'm still mad at you, so don't get all happy."

He laughs at me again and slaps my ass before putting an arm around my shoulders and pulling me to him.

"Why didn't you take the shot earlier when you had the chance?" I'm talking about that brief moment in time when Sean had his gun on Artie.

"Because I didn't have the shot. If I'd shot him, he would have shot you, and I was trying to get out of this without anyone but Sean getting shot." He looks over to Artie's body a few feet from Sean's. "I'm kind of glad Sean shot him. Saved me the trouble, though I wanted to rip his head off once I realized he was the one who . . . ."

I touch his arm. "I know."

If he were to pull me any tighter, we'd be Siamese twins. Our fathers, after having given us a private moment, make their way over to us.

"Everything okay?" Bran asks.

"Yeah, Da," Clancy replies. "My girls are safe now."

Bran smiles.

"Anna," Dad says. "I'm very proud of you." The grin stretching across his face says it all, and I know Clancy's told them what went down tonight.

Yep, Dad's proud of me, which probably isn't something I should be happy about and Mom will flip over. Clancy's not dead, nor am I, and we have Toni back. That's all I care about right now. Life is good.

32

Feel Alive

Over the next couple of weeks, my life is beyond hectic, with wedding plans, a baby, a full-scale photo shoot, and prepping the magazine for its release just before the wedding. I know, I'm insane to try and pull all of this off, but apparently I'm happiest when my life is hectic and I don't know which direction I'm going. It doesn't leave me room to think about anything. I just go, go, go. My schooling is on hold until the chaos is over and I can return to a somewhat normal life, if one can call it that.

Actually, this is kind of normal, considering what our lives were a couple of weeks ago. The families took care of everything. They even got the police involved, since Sean killed Scotty *and* Artie. For Clancy, it was self-defense, so no charges were brought against him for killing Sean.

Clancy runs by the new house every couple of days to check on the build, and leaves me completely out of it unless he knows I want something specific and has questions about it. I am very thankful for this, and it *will* be done right before we return from Italy.

The wedding looms around the corner and family begins to arrive in droves. Blood family, extended family, friends—you name them; they come. My mother has made a very huge deal out of this and I never should have let her handle the guest list. God, what was I thinking? There are close to five hundred people on it between Clancy's list and mine, and my mother's list. Yes, let's not forget she has her own list.

I have ten bridesmaids. Well, technically nine and a maid of honor, but who's checking? Teagan is my maid of honor, and she screamed and tackled me when I asked her. Their dresses are black as well with pink underneath the lace bodice. Alanna loves it. Echo, not so much, but Katy likes it too. Anything black will make Katy happy. Kennadi is so not happy that she has to wear a dress, but she'll get over it. My girlfriends make up most of my bridesmaids, but mom slipped in a few cousins.

The groom, groomsmen and best man will be wearing black tuxedoes with pink ties and cummerbund. They're wearing black kilts with white barely visible in lines of plaid too. Can't argue with an Irishman about the kilt, but I just know there will be a photo of them with their kilts up and mooning the camera. No doubt.

This particular day, about a week before the wedding, I'm fretting about the magazine print. It's not ready yet, and it needs to be out the door in two days. There's an issue with one of the photos. It keeps doing this weird thing on my computer when I send the whole thing over to the printer and it disappears from within the pages. Yes, panic attack.

Clancy is on the phone with the printer because I'm too freaked out by now. "Try sending him just the photo, Nemy-girl. He says he can insert it and see what happens."

I take a deep breath and exhale. "Okay, I can do that." Fingers fly over keys and mouse pad, I upload it and hit 'send,' and then I hold my breath.

Clancy frowns. "He says he can't open it."

"Damn it." I hit my knee with a closed fist. "Okay, let me try to change the format. Maybe a PNG will work." Clancy relays what I'm doing to the printer and then waits. After a bit, I finally send it. "Have him try it now."

I pick at my fingernails in the silence, play with the rings on my fingers—I still don't have an engagement ring replacement—and sigh heavily, waiting for the printer's response.

"He's got it. Opens fine, inserting it into the magazine . . . and we're good to go."

I blow out a breath. "Thank God."

Clancy thanks the printer, talks to him about a few other details I'm not paying attention to, and gets off the phone. "Okay, that's now taken care of, what else is on the agenda?"

"A massage." I rub the back of my neck. "I'm so stressed."

His bare-footedness climbs up on the couch behind me and slides down. He slides his fingers up to my shoulders and pulls me back against his bare chest. My head drops forward and Clancy's magic fingers pull the stress from my shoulders and neck. He works his thumbs into my shoulder blades, making me push my chest forward. "God, that feels good."

Once the tension is gone, he slides his hands around my waist and pulls me back again. He kisses my shoulder in a soft sweep of his lips and trails those lips up to my neck. I tilt my head to the side to give him better access. A subtle sigh leaves my lips and he leans me to the left and takes me down on the sofa.

"I've got a way to relax you," he growls from my belly button.

I giggle. "Oh dear God, it's a good thing I'm not wearing white."

His laughter rumbles against my flesh and it sends a shudder throughout my body. Of course, this makes him pounce on me.

And then Toni cries in her bedroom. Ah yes, welcome to parenthood.

My stress level just shot back up.

"Mama," I scream from the bedroom of the villa at the Scottsdale Conference Resort. The make-up artist waits for me to stop moving around. "Sorry, continue." My mom rushes into the room.

"What is it, Anna?" she asks, out of breath.

"Breathe, Mama." My eyes move to their corners to view her. "Where's my veil? I can't find it."

"I'll have Papa check the car." She dashes off before Teagan has a chance to say anything.

"Jeez, Nems, she gonna run herself ragged."

"No shit, but she's happy as hell right now, so leave her alone."

Teagan laughs and adjusts her dress. "The lace itches at the top."

"I did my best."

"I know. I'm not complaining."

I grin, which does not make the make-up artist happy. "Yes, you are."

She laughs at me and Lillian strolls into the room. "Hey, Nemy, you think Brennan would go out with me?"

I pull my head away from the make-up artist's hand and turn around. "Seriously?"

Teagan giggles. "Watch out, Nems, she may have the hots for Clancy."

Lillian swats at her. "Shut up, I do not." Then she grins. "But his brother is damn sexy."

"They look identical!" Teagan swats her back. "You couldn't tell last night during Brennan's striptease?"

Lillian turns to me. "Is that what Clancy's body looks like?"

"Of course it is. Why do you think she was all hot and bothered and jumped up to get away from the man?" She leans toward me. "By the way, that was damn funny. Your man's got one hell of a sense of humor."

My eyes narrow on Teagan. "Bite your tongue. I did *not* get all hot and bothered."

She bites her tongue while sticking it out at me.

"You sure do like to do that a lot. Got a tongue fetish, Teags?"

"Maybe."

I let the make-up artist go back to work after rolling my eyes at Teagan.

"And yes, you did."

"So, what do you think?" Lillian interrupts before I can respond to Teagan.

"I don't know. Want me to ask him for you?"

"No!"

"Then why are you asking?" Teagan says.

"Yeah, I barely know the man. Except that he has three wonderful boys."

"Three . . . *boys*? Is he married? I didn't see a ring."

"No, he's not." I grin. "Want me to ask? He just asked me recently if I had any single friends."

Teagan elbows Lillian. "I think she just wants that body of his."

"Right, and you don't have the hots for Killian." I smirk at her sneer.

"Oh, never mind," Lillian says in a huff and walks out of the room.

"Wow, what's up with her?"

Teagan shrugs. "Who the hell knows? She's probably sexually frustrated."

I laugh. "Go check on Toni for me, would ya?"

She hops up and runs out of the room, which has the make-up artist happy because Teags isn't distracting me anymore.

The make-up artist finishes with me and mom returns with my veil. Teagan has to help me put the damn thing on and once everyone's finished—boys included from their suite—we get the go ahead to walk to the hall (it turned out to be cloudy this morning, so the wedding was moved inside—I am not happy about it, but I'm lucky I even got this place for the wedding).

We're standing outside the doors, my father on one side, Teagan on the other adjusting my dress, the girls behind me fixing the train, and Kennadi picking at her nails with a small knife she'd hid in her garter. I bite my fingernail.

"Stop that." Teagan slaps my arm. "You'll ruin your lipstick."

I stick my tongue out at her and lower my hand to my side as Kennadi laughs.

Papa's hand squeezes my other arm. "Are you all right, Anna?"

"Yes, Papa, I'm fine."

"It's not too late—"

"Don't you dare finish that sentence." The command startles me a little and I gasp. "Sorry, Papa."

He smiles and nods. "I believe you have found the right man, even if he *is* Irish."

That's it? That's all it took? He approves of Clancy. Wow, I'm flabbergasted.

I smile at my dad. "Thank you, Papa."

"If he hurts you, I *will* kill him," he adds.

Lovely.

The doors open as the music starts to play. One of my cousins enters the hall first, meets one of the groomsmen, and they walk down the aisle. I can't see anything past Teagan, she's so damn tall. This is probably a good thing.

Finally, the wedding march begins and my father and I stand in the open doorway. People stand, turn, gasp, but I don't see any of them past the first glimpse. All I can see is the man I'm about to marry standing at the head of them all, dressed in his tux/kilt combo with his beautiful long black hair flowing gracefully over his shoulders. My heart skips a beat and I catch my breath when he smiles. Oh yeah, he is so the right one. I didn't feel like this the last time. Not in the slightest.

Papa and I begin our walk down the aisle, and still, all I can see is Clancy, his smile growing wider as I approach. He lifts his hand to his face, and his fingers brush his cheek, wiping something away. Is he crying? I know I'm about to turn into a heaping sobbing mess.

Papa hands me over to him, and he takes my hand.

He leans over me. "I love you, almost-wife." His voice, the merest of whispers because someone's recording this shit.

I giggle at his words. "I love you too, almost-husband."

So, I guess I found my Prince Charming, even though he's been right under my nose for the last year and a half. And no, I still haven't punched him in the face. I don't think I need to now.

In the chest was sufficient.

About the Author

N.L. "Jinxie" Gervasio has been a creator and destroyer of worlds for several years, in both writing and editing. She has discovered she's quite good at the romance thing—writing it, that is. Jinxie works in multiple genres: contemporary romance, horror thriller, urban fantasy, paranormal romance, and fantasy. She welcomes you to her worlds.

Born on Friday the 13th, Jinxie's dad wanted to call her Jinx. Her mom said no. It took 34 years for her to discover the nickname, and she's grown quite attached to it. She lives in Tempe, Arizona with Umi (her mother), whom she cares for. Jinxie enjoys riding her beach cruiser "The Betty" around downtown Tempe, loves a good pub crawl, and has had the pleasure and the heartache of experiencing a love far greater than she could have ever imagined.

Find Jinxie online for updates to upcoming works:

Website: http://jinxiesworld.com
Twitter: http://twitter.com/Jinxie_G
Facebook: http://www.facebook.com/Jinxi3G
Email: jinxieg13@gmail.com

Nemy and Clancy each have their own blogs:

Foxy's Den: http://nemysfoxyden.wordpress.com
Clancy's Den: http://clancysden.wordpress.com

SPECIAL PREVIEW

ASSASSIN

Book two in the Kick-Ass Girls Club novels

by

NL Gervasio

Back to Black

"Stop moving, Teags," Alanna says and smacks me on the leg.

"What, I can't sneeze?" I reply. "Jesus, woman, that's just cold."

"Shut it." The whirring continues as a million very sharp needles prick my skin. Okay, maybe not a million, but that's what it feels like.

My mom died two months ago. She had cancer. So today, I'm in Alanna's shop getting a tattoo in her memory. For specificity, mom had breast cancer, so the tattoo will be a pink ribbon and it's going on the inside of my right forearm, near my wrist. She's added some Celtic knot work into the ribbon for me too. It's going to be awesome.

"Where the hell is Nemy?" I look out the window. "She's supposed to be here for this." When my mom died, Nemy and Clancy happened to be in California visiting her parents. She felt horrible for not being here for me, but they did cut the vacay short to come home. I love them to death for that.

"Cut her some slack," Alanna says. "The woman's nearly as a big as a house now."

"I am not," Nemy says from the doorway. Then she gets that look, the one I haven't seen on her face since she and Clancy hooked up. The insecure one. "Am I?"

"Good job, Lan, you gave a pregnant woman a complex," I say. "You're like so my new BFF for that."

"Fuck you," Alanna snaps, and that damn tattoo machine grinds into my skin. Rule number 43 when getting a tattoo is to not piss off the tattoo artist. They hold your pain in their hands and determine the amount of infliction. Alanna is very good at inflicting pain, and she doesn't need a tattoo machine to do it.

My face twists in agony. "Okay, okay, lighten up, Iron Fist. Fuck." I look up at Nemy as Alanna giggles. "Where's Toni?"

She sits down in the chair against the wall and fans her face. "Clancy's watching her. They're having a father/daughter day. Watching some fucking show that drives me batty." She blows out a breath. "Fuck, it's hot in here."

Alanna stops inflicting pain on me for two seconds to point a fan out to Nemy. "Just turn it toward you, chica."

Nemy repositions the fan and sighs. "Oh, that's much better."

"It's freezing outside and she's acting like it's summer," I say to Alanna, who laughs.

"You don't even know what freezing is," Nemy snaps. "Move to the east coast for a couple of winters, then come talk to me about freezing."

"Oh, somebody didn't take their mommy happy pill today," Alanna chides.

"Don't fuck with a pregnant woman, Alanna," Nemy threatens. There's the Nemy we know and love.

Alanna just laughs at her and continues with the tattoo. "So you never told us about California."

"What's there to tell? It was just a quick little getaway to visit my insane parents. That's all." Nemy picks at the hem of her skirt and this small action is what has me thinking. She's been awfully quiet about the trip. Usually when she goes somewhere, she tells us all about it, every minute detail—with exception to her honeymoon in Italy—but not this time.

After that whole fiasco with James and the detective questioning Clancy all night, I'm a little curious if she's not talking. Oh, and then there's the whole who-her-father-is thing. Yeah, that was a shocker. Who knew Nemy would turn out to be a goddamn mafia princess? Makes me wonder what really happened to James, that bastard. I'm not saying he didn't deserve whatever he got because he beat the hell out of Jada, but damn, and I don't think I really want to know the truth.

Speaking of Jada, she's doing all right. She's back to work now, since it's safe and all because that bastard boyfriend of hers is dead. Jada is like this cute little porcelain doll, and right now the girl is irretrievably broken, but I think Nemy has hopes that she'll get better. I say that's a long time coming.

How do I know? I live with the girl.

Other Books

Anthologies

Into the Darkness

R.C. Murphy

Be Ours Forever (self-published)
Enslaved

N.L. Gervasio

Nemesis
The Dracove
Gods & Vampyres

Raven McAllan

Impulse
Temptation

Leona J. Bushman

Mayhem in Mexico: Zombie Infestation

Coming Soon from Just Ink Press, LLC

A Griffin Scorned by Veronica R. Calisto

Dream Hunter by Maya Tyler

On the Edge by Joe O'Toole and Katie Cann

Dusk of Death by N.L. Gervasio

Nightmare's Dream by S.M. Blooding

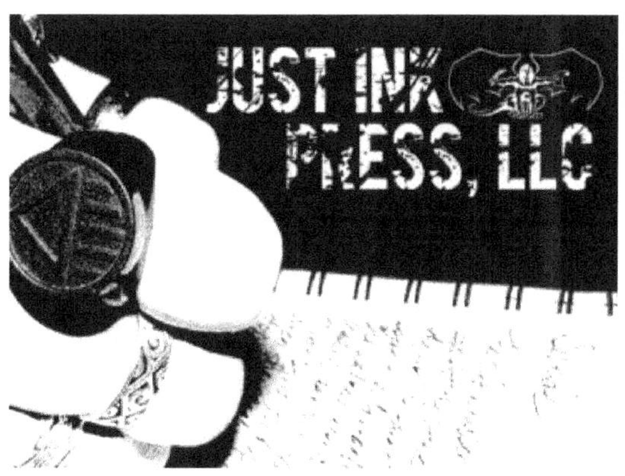

justinkpress.com

www.ingramcontent.com/pod-product-compliance
Lightning Source LLC
Chambersburg PA
CBHW071042250626
47159CB00002B/338

9780988272118